CACIQUE

A Novel of Florida's
Heroic Mission History

CACIQUE

A Novel of Florida's
Heroic Mission History

Bishop Robert J. Baker

with

Tony Sands

Saint Catherine of Siena Press
Indianapolis

Saint Catherine of Siena Press
4812 North Park Avenue
Indianapolis, IN 46205
888-232-1492
www.saintcatherineofsienapress.com
www.bishopbaker.com

To order additional copies of this book:
contact Theological Book Service at 888-544-8674

Printed in the United States of America.

ISBN-13: 978-0-9762284-4-8
ISBN-10: 0-9762284-4-0

Library of Congress Control Number: 2006920930

Portions of *Cacique: A Novel of Florida's Heroic Mission History* were previously published in serialized form as "Cacique" in *The Cathedral Times*, St. Augustine, FL; © 1995 Robert J. Baker, STD. Reprinted with the permission of the author.

Also by Robert J. Baker:

Welcome the Stranger: Contemporary Ministry in the Church of Florida
        Edited with Jane Quinn, Regional Seminary Press
        St. Vincent de Paul Regional Seminary, Boynton Beach, FL, 1983.

Historic Catholic Sites of St. Augustine
        Edited with Albina M. Davis and Margo C. Pope
        Published by Cathedral-Basilica Bell Tower Religious Shop,
        St. Augustine, FL, 1983, Second Edition, 1993.

When Did We See You, Lord?
        With Father Benedict J. Groeschel, CFR
        Published by Our Sunday Visitor, Inc., Huntington, IN, 2005.

Illustrations, maps, and front cover art by Christopher J. Pelicano
Back cover photograph by Joe Benton, Joe Benton Photography, Charleston, SC
Back cover design by Joseph Sadlier

Dedicated to
the memory of the missionaries of Florida's past,
especially the Franciscan friars
who served continuously for over a century

"We hold the time well spent
and the labors undertaken worth the while,
for we know that for one such soul alone, if it were necessary,
Christ our Lord would suffer His death passion again.

How much more then should be suffered for… so many converted
in these lands and for those whom we hope to convert."

Fray Francisco Pareja, OFM
missionary to Florida, late sixteenth century

Prologue

At mission Santa Fé, a letter delivered by courier from the Spanish civil and military headquarters in the mission San Agustín resulted in the hurried flight of the last vestige of residents. The document read:

From Don Francisco de Córcoles y Martínez
Governor of Florida for His Majesty the King—

To all military, religious, and civilian residents of the Mission of Santa Fé:

No longer can we bear responsibility for the lives of the inhabitants of your mission. You are to depart immediately for San Agustín. Your efforts to serve God and His Majesty the King have been laudable. Your mission and that of your predecessors, to bring the Gospel to this region, has been a noble one. Success, however, is in God's hands, not in ours. Return at once! Francisco de Córcoles y Martínez

Bearing the seal and signature of the Governor, Don Francisco de Córcoles y Martínez, and dated September 8, 1706, the Feast of the Nativity of Mary.

What once was a settlement of sizable proportions, Santa Fé de Toloca was now but a shell of human habitation. The raids of Carolina Governor James Moore with his parties of Indians hostile to the Spaniards had almost obliterated the Franciscan Friars' hundred-year-old outreach effort to the native Potano people of this region.

A cross still stood erect over a dilapidated Spanish-style chapel, now vacant of the reverential celebrations that were centered within its walls. A clapboard shutter banged rhythmically with the wind against the wall of the military barracks that once quartered a Spanish garrison. The bare structure was all that remained of a meeting hall that once housed the civic and social events of the mission, and was now quiet except for the sound of roaches and rats scurrying for leftover food.

The final phase of de-settlement had occurred, and the last day of occupation had seen a soldier and a friar make the final rounds of inspection as the remaining residents trailed off into the horizon. The soldier and the friar were symbols of the fortunes and failures of the mission from its earliest days. It was fitting that they were the last to go.

Mounted on his horse, an Indian *cacique*[1] watched it all silently from a distance. His bearing was dignified. Though his bronze skin showed the wear of his years, his pleasant features were now overshadowed by a somber spirit. No one was near enough to him anymore to see the tear in his eye or to understand the memories of his mind and heart. He preferred to bear his sorrow alone.

---

[1] "chieftain," pronounced "ca SEE kay"

Part One

The Beginning

TRIBAL GROUPS *of* CACIQUE

The Utina, Potano and Ocale were tribal groups within the Timucua Nation.

Map labels:

ATLANTIC OCEAN

St. Augustine

TIMUCUA NATION

UTINA

UTINA

UTINA

Santa Fé River

POTANO

OCALE

Suwannee River

APALACHEE NATION

GULF OF MEXICO

Apalachicola River

I
- 1608 -

The young friar could not contain his youthful enthusiasm as he bounded through the woodlands, overcrowded with palmettos and large live oak trees. His racing footfalls were muffled by the thick carpet of pine needles that had built up from years of being undisturbed. Wielding a sharp-edged machete, the priest cut his way through the tall grass, bushes, fledgling oaks, and pines.

Sweat streaked down the thick brows and high cheekbones of his angular but honest face. The heavy robes matted against his tough Spanish skin in that humid midday summer afternoon did not slow his pace or his zeal.

Fray Tomás was on a mission.

Since he was ten years old, Tomás always wanted to be a Franciscan friar like Fray Luís Mendoza, his uncle and godfather, back in Madrid. The padre had visited the boy's home often and had introduced him to the life and teachings of the thirteenth century founder of the Order, San Francisco de Assis. Tomás Sanchez wanted to be like the padre and the saint he had come to know—poor in spirit, zealous for winning souls, and fearless of the consequences.

Fearless to a fault, this trait was to be both a help and hindrance—a virtue and a vice—to Tomás all through his life. Danger did not act as a deterrent to him as it did to the ordinary human being. It seemed to entice him all the more to the quest before him. And such was the case that day, as Fray Tomás, the newly ordained, newly arrived missionary, set out from his Franciscan headquarters in San Agustín. With the veteran friar, Buenaventura, Tomás was to begin a new mission west of the city founded by Pedro Menéndez de Avilés.

Fray Buenaventura was to accompany Tomás, help him get the mission started, and then return to his own mission in San Agustín, called *Nombre de Dios*. Much to the contrary of his fellow friar, Fray Buenaventura preferred the settled and stable ways of his mission, established in 1565, to the one his *confrere,* Tomás, was now appointed to establish. Buenaventura was on this mission under orders from his superior, and the vow of obedience was the only factor that would have led him here into the backwoods. He did not pretend to be a hero nor did he want to pay the price for becoming one. He just wanted to survive the day and perhaps save a soul or two in the process, with no fanfare or praise expected.

Why he agreed to join this starry-eyed idealist, he would never know, other than that his superior's request was framed in the form of a command: "You *will*, Padre Buenaventura!" "I'll do my best, Tomás, but don't expect much from me," was Buenaventura's agreement, as he set out with the fast-paced friar bent on saving the world.

Two weeks at the most, Buenaventura figured. That would give Tomás time to find a suitable location, establish a connection with the military outpost in the area, and most importantly, make contact with the Potano tribe of the region. Tomás already knew the Potano dialect well enough to pass. His tutor in San Agustín the past month had been an Indian servant named Ocatu. Though he could understand the language well enough, Buenaventura was not nearly so fluent, but now he was the one doing most of the talking. "Slow down, slow down!!" Buenaventura constantly shouted ahead to Tomás throughout their day-and-a-half journey, "You're going to kill me and deny me the privilege of dying a martyr's death!" It had to be a shout because Buenaventura was usually a long distance behind.

Finally, there was a reprieve for Buenaventura. Tomás had stopped and he was able to sit on a stump, catch his breath, and fan his face with a palm frond.

Tomás had sighted the river! He saw Indian camps sporadically settled. He looked at his map and smiled.

"Buenaventura, this is our mission site! Look around you! Can't you see? History is in the making. We are on sacred ground!"

The only profound response Buenaventura could muster up to such a startling revelation was, "*Amigo*, just wait and see; wait and see!" Buenaventura had been a missionary too long to react in any other way.

They spent an hour clearing the site and making a natural barrier of fallen timber and branches to protect their camp from the elements. Then the two friars settled into their new home.

Dusk drifted into night, and the priests had a fire just beginning to blaze so that a simple broth containing vegetables and beef could be heated. Over the crackle of the fire, Tomás and Buenaventura heard a rustling sound and the scuffle of footsteps on the earth. It was the sound of another human being. An Indian woman emerged from a bank of trees not fifty paces away. As she crept into the clearing before them, the priests could see a terrified look on her face and an infant child in her arms. The men exchanged questioning glances.

"Maybe you should go greet her, Tomás," Buenaventura suggested in a low voice.

His words caught the woman's attention, and seeing the robed friars, she hurried in their direction after nervously glancing over her shoulder.

Her terrified expression did not change as she ran to the Spaniards. Tomás stepped forward to welcome her, when she suddenly interrupted him by thrusting the child into his arms. "Take him," she pleaded in broken Spanish. "He cannot be my child. His name is Kocha. I love him, but his father is not my husband. I must leave quickly." She kissed the child, then pressed Tomás' hands tightly with the anguish and pain of a mother who has failed in her greatest responsibility.

The woman was away before the young friar could react.

Buenaventura noted immediately the Spanish features of the child, and shook his head. He understood the woman's plight.

"But wait!" Tomás called after the Indian mother who had almost made it to the trees adjoining the clearing. Then a sharp whistling sound cut through the air and a wet "thump" brought her movement to a halt.

Neither Tomás nor Buenaventura saw anything except the Indian woman falling to the ground. Buenaventura ran to her and discovered an arrow imbedded deep in her body. As he turned her over, he saw blood spurting from where the arrowhead protruded from her chest. Her eyes were already fixed in a stare.

"Tomás," he cried out, "she's dead! *Vamos, pronto!*"

Tomás nodded and with the baby in his hands, he sprinted after his fellow friar. But before he moved any farther, he was startled by a shrill cry and by Buenaventura's horrified expression.

"Look out, Tomás!" the older man yelled.

Out of the corner of his eye, Tomás caught sight of an Indian warrior, wielding a tomahawk, charging at him from behind. With one motion of his body, Tomás tossed Buenaventura the infant and roll-blocked his attacker.

As the native swung his weapon at the priest's head, Tomás caught the Indian's wrist, then he swiveled himself under the native's arm and pulled forward while heaving with his feet. The warrior suddenly found himself thrown head over heels until—CRASH! He landed flat on his back, momentarily stunned. A seasoned fighter, the Indian quickly recovered, but not fast enough. Before the assailant could grab his weapon, Tomás tore the tomahawk from him with one hand and had the other on the Indian's throat, pressing hard.

"You can have your life if you let the child and us alone. Do you hear me?" Tomás yelled in the Potano language.

The Indian understood, but did not answer. Shocked, he stared into the priest's eyes. A friar who knew how to fight…and kill! Now, the warrior was the potential victim! Unthinkable! But Tomás lost patience with this delay. "Do you hear me?" he shouted again and his grip tightened.

Now the Indian knew it was thinkable. Unable to speak, the warrior nodded. Tomás released his grip gradually as the Indian did the same. The native leapt up and quickly fled for his life.

As Tomás watched him go, he knew he would never forget the look in the warrior's eyes—half fright, half amazement. And the Indian, glancing back, knew he would not forget the look in the priest's gaze—courage, strength, determination. He would never cross that padre again, he decided.

Tomás beamed proudly and dusted himself off. Instead of being shaken by the battle, he was exhilarated.

Buenaventura looked with amazement at his companion. "What…I…how did you do that?" he asked the young friar.

"Oh…well, um…before I became a priest, I worked for my father's store in Madrid," Tomás explained, breathing hard from the fight, "and he worried because I had to walk home from the riverside at night. As a favor, a mulatto merchant from Portugal, who was a friend of the family, taught me to fight."

"I should certainly say he did," Buenaventura commented.

Tomás nodded, "He called it *Capoeira*,[2] a way to fight without killing. I just didn't think I would be needing it after I became a priest."

"But—you act as is if what just happened was part of an average day's work," Buenaventura exclaimed.

Tomás gently took the infant child back from his elder partner and shrugged, "Maybe I should feel afraid—but I don't. I feel…I feel alive!" As soon as he uttered those words, guilt flashed across his face. He remembered that everyone had not survived the battle. His gaze drifted to the woman's body, and pity welled up within him. "I will go see what I can do for the mother."

---

[2] a martial art form still practiced throughout the world.

Buenaventura just shook his head. Maybe he had underestimated the prowess of this man after all.

Coming back to reality, both of them began to wonder what to do next. The darkness of the evening would have made plans to move anywhere impractical. Now, with the lateness of the hour and the infant suddenly thrust upon them, it was impossible.

Fray Tomás covered the body of the mother with palm fronds as best he could, and then said what prayers were appropriate. Meanwhile, Buenaventura quickly improvised a means to feed the hungry child a little broth. Looking at the baby, Buenaventura realized the complicated situation facing them. They had enough trouble surviving themselves. Now they had a nursing infant to keep alive. Once again, Buenaventura's regrets began to well up within him. He had bargained for many things, but not for this. And it wasn't even his idea to accompany Tomás in the first place! "Why me, Lord?" he asked himself over and over again.

Fortunately for the two of them, the child fell fast asleep in Tomás' arms and remained motionless throughout the night. Apparently, the excitement was all he could handle in one day.

The priests let the fire die down, but they took turns keeping watch, switching every few hours. Mostly, they prayed that nothing else would threaten their lives or their peace the first day of their mission.

"*Soli Deo gloria!* To God alone be praise!" was Tomás' final thought and prayer as the moon danced playfully behind the swaying pine branches overhead, and the frogs next to the rivulet croaked evening melody, slightly off-tune.

II

Land of sunshine, land of rains,
Land of hillsides, land of plains.
Silver springs that never cease,
To land bring life, to man bring peace.

The Potano people prized the land they held. It was their only real possession, one they regarded as sacred. For what it held in its bosom as treasures, it gave abundantly to them. In the summertime, its forests offered them food of flittering fowl, bounding deer, and the occasional roaming buffalo. Its streams were overrun with alligator for the brave and turtle meat for the timid. Its watery coffers also held an endless array of fresh-water fish: silvery trout, emerald bass, sapphire-streaked bluegill, and these were but a few. Its fields welcomed the seeds they planted, and the soil nourished them into stalks of amber maize, trees holding golden globes of citrons, and vines bearing brass pumpkins that would peer out from amid the beans, cucumbers, and gourds. Palm berries, acorns, and nuts grew wild in the area, and they also served to nourish the people. In harder times the tribe depended on these foods to keep them alive. Tobacco, too, was a favorite crop, growing in green and yellow rows. After harvest, it would be dried in bundles and then smoked in pipes or burned and brewed so that its fumes could be inhaled.

In the winter, fallen timber gathered from the forest served as firewood for cooking and for heat when freezing weather sometimes laid hold of the night. Stones were carefully selected to be hewn into utensils and working instruments, like hoes and hatchets, knives and arrowheads. Wood, shells, and bones were fashioned into tools and were sometimes crafted into jewelry. The Potano cooked in stone vessels and stored food in pottery made of the clay that was abundant in the area. They turned gourds, wood, and turtle shells into containers as well. The land also provided the Potano with material for their houses and council meeting-halls. Circular in shape, these buildings were constructed of palm-thatched walls and roofs. The villagers' beds were platforms made of poles or hewn logs and were set off the ground on small posts. Beneath them smudges were lit at night, warding off the ever-present menace of insects.

The Potano's homes, their happiness, and their means of survival all came from the land—the land and the abundant, perpetually flowing springs that fed the region's waterways. The Potano people had a treasure. They were fortunate to settle near the water that often came from deep beneath the earth and rose up in the form of a spring, a lake, or a river. The Indians called the area *la chua*, meaning the sinkhole, and all about were small bodies of water connecting to an underground source. These bodies of water made this area vital and precious and sacred to the people.

Encamped around each body of water and near the springs and rivers and rivulets were the thatched homes of the Potano People. Like sentinels these houses and their occupants stood guard over the region. Let no intruder enter who had thoughts of taking the land or the water away. It would be like taking away the breath of life.

It was in this area that Fray Tomás awoke on the second day of his mission. As dawn broke bright and brilliant in the eastern sky, Tomás crept off silently to survey the area while Buenaventura lay fast asleep next to the child. The older Franciscan had finally managed to drift off only a couple of hours before daylight, and his dreams were of the tranquility of *convento*[3] life back in San Agustín. Buenaventura was in the garden he had just planted near the bay-front, west of the mission chapel. The wheat and the kidney beans he had been growing there were beginning to look like they did back in Spain. They were taking well to the soil of the New World, but keeping them watered would be the major challenge in this wretchedly hot climate. He was going back and forth to get the water from the community well. Back and forth, he went as the leaves in the trees rattled in the warm wind. Back and forth...

Rattle, rattle...rattle, rattle. Buenaventura barely opened one eye. Something was shaking in his face. Rattle, rattle. Someone was staring in his face! A hideous sight, the eyes of a man looked at him from out of the mouth of what appeared to be a grizzly bear. The friar almost screamed, but then he realized what he was seeing: an Indian shaman. Fray Buenaventura had heard about them, he had read about them, but he had never seen one. He remained motionless so as not to give the stranger pretext for doing him or the baby harm. Buenaventura figured inaction was the best course of action and with squinting eyes, he continued to monitor the quick, fierce motions of this creature that seemed to resemble half-man, half-animal. Over him at one moment, now over the child, the shaman would rattle, rattle, rattle with the little apparatus in his hand, shaking here, shaking there, and occasionally emitting a primeval groan or grunt. Then, the native spoke a few words in the Potano dialect barely audible to Buenaventura. "Child, son of *holata* sister," were the only words the shaman uttered that the priest could decipher. The medicine man moved again over the child, then returned to Buenaventura. The Indian reached into the folds of his bearskin cloak. Buenaventura began to panic. Was the shaman reaching for a weapon or something else? Should he act or should he wait, and if he waited, would it be too late? Suddenly, the shaman froze, then scurried off into the woods that bordered the Potano village.

---

[3] a residence for members of a religious order; a convent.

Fray Tomás made his way back to the clearing just in time to glimpse the shaman's retreat. Buenaventura had immediately set about the task of tearing up camp, very intent on a rapid departure, when Tomás greeted him with the question, "Who was that? What did he want?"

Buenaventura pointed after the now vanished medicine man, "That, my friend, is your and my biggest obstacle to peace and contentment, and maybe even to life itself. If what I heard is true, that is probably the tribal shaman;` he is going off to tell someone, perhaps this cute little fellow's uncle, that you and I have a special child in our possession."

"This child? What is so special about him?" Tomás asked.

"If I heard the grizzly bear right, or whatever he pretends to be," replied Buenaventura, "our newborn friend here had a mother who was a sister of the cacique."

"The head of the tribe? Hmm…*está bién,* so his uncle is the chief," Tomás said, "His father was one of our illustrious countrymen, who was assigned to pave the way for our visit. Now it seems that he, God have mercy on him, has complicated everything for us and for this child as well. But I don't see how this threatens our lives."

"Then let me open your eyes," Buenaventura responded. "You haven't been here long enough to understand these people and their traditions. We are dealing with matriarchal bloodlines. It's the child of the woman in the chief's family that inherits the position; so a sister to the reigning cacique is parent of the next cacique. Little Kocha here could quite possibly be slated as the next cacique. You and I are looking at one precious papoose in little Kocha, and we best roll him up tight in his blanket, give him a farewell kiss, and head right back to San Agustín. Thanks to his birth, he will survive here, now that our friendly shaman has discovered him, but you and I won't."

"Aren't you overreacting, *mi amigo?*" Tomás asked.

"Overreacting?" challenged Buenaventura. "You remember Guale, don't you? I believe you may also remember the warning from Ocatu, to never step between a bear and her young." The veteran missionary pointed toward the village and the vanished shaman. "Well, you just saw the grizzly bear; this is the cub, which means you and I are standing in the middle. I'm sorry, Tomás; we tried hard, but our mission to this group of people is over. Give them a blessing and rest assured that someday, somebody will tell them what you had wanted to say and do what you had wanted to do. Some day, but not this one…Let's get moving!"

The older friar had almost made it to the edge of the clearing when he looked back and realized his young partner had not moved. "Tomás!" Buenaventura barked at him.

The youthful friar just shook his head, "No, Buenaventura, I'm not leaving."

Walking back Buenaventura demanded, "Didn't you just hear—"

"*Sí,* I heard what you said," Tomás said, interrupting. "But why did we come here—to be knocked over by the first wind to blow against us? What a shame that would be! I know one life has been lost already; may her soul rest in peace," Tomás indicated the woman's covered body, "but we can't abandon hope before we have even begun. We came here to start a mission for our founder San Francisco and for the Lord. And what is more, we have orders from our Superior in San Agustín!"

"Yes, but we don't have orders to be killed, Tomás," Buenaventura shouted back. "And that is what we are facing now! I know! After eight years in this wilderness, I know!"

Their gazes locked, each strengthened with unwavering conviction. One backed by idealism; the other, by wisdom—neither willing to give way. Finally, Tomás lowered his eyes. Buenaventura nodded and relief flooded his face.

Then Tomás said in a soft voice, "I will not force you to join me further, if that is how you feel, Buenaventura, but this is my reason for being here. And right or wrong, I'm staying!"

Buenaventura's mouth dropped open. He clenched it shut. He turned to go, and then turned back again. He shook a finger in Tomás' face. Then, slowly, he dropped it. In a strained voice, the senior Franciscan said, "Good-bye, Tomás. I shall pray for you. Please do so for me. May God go with you!" With that he placed the child in Tomás' arms. He swiftly turned in the direction of San Agustín, but not swiftly enough to hide from the young priest the tears of sadness and guilt welling up in his eyes.

III

Cross in hand
And bold of heart.
He took a stand,
He made a start

Fray Tomás waved to Buenaventura and watched as his heavyset comrade disappeared into the green refuge of trees. A rush of emotions, memories, and thoughts began to possess his soul and to disturb his peace of mind. Was he making the right decision? Was he acting recklessly? Was he acting on pride? He could not judge Buenaventura's departure nor attribute it to timidity. He had only hoped that Buenaventura would stay with him until he had laid the foundations for the mission. Buenaventura was experienced in the mission field. He was not.

Tomás knew the origin of Buenaventura's sentiments. The older priest had talked about his reservations incessantly on the journey all the way from San Agustín. He made his reasons clear to Tomás why caution was needed in starting any new mission.

Not many years before, Potano Indians killed the Spanish captain Andrada and thirty other soldiers. The Spanish responded with swift and brutal military force. Many of the Potano would still remember the bloody retaliation by the Spanish.

And then there was the Guale revolt, which Fray Buenaventura had mentioned during their argument. It happened far to the northeast, shortly after the Franciscans had arrived in La Florida. Fray Pedro de Corpa, stationed at Tolomato opposite Zapala Island, would not allow the Indian youth Don Juan, a Christian and heir to the caciquedom, to have more than one wife. Embarrassed and angered by the reprimand and affront, the young chief joined with Indians like him, who also engaged in polygamy, and instigated a revolt against the friars.

Decorated with feathers on their heads and war paint on their faces, the marauding tribesmen enlisted the support of other pagan Indians and broke in on the friar one morning while he was at prayer. They killed him with a stone hatchet called a *macana*. They placed his head at the end of a lance and mounted it as a gruesome warning sign at the landing place. The decapitated body they hid in the woods. The native war party proceeded to sack the house of another friar, Fray Miguel de Auñon, on the isle of Guale, killing him and a lay brother.

In the town of Tupiqui, the murder of Fray Blas Rodríguez was delayed two days until after he had offered Mass and was dispossessed of the few belongings he had. They crushed his skull and smashed his brains into pieces. Though the Indians threw this body to the birds, an old Christian man secretly took it away for burial in the woods.

Another missionary, Fray Avila was spared execution, but he was taken captive and enslaved. The Indians kept him naked in captivity, forcing him to carry wood on his shoulders, guard the huts of the villagers, and protect the cultivated maize fields from the birds. After a year and a half, the Spanish found and rescued him.

Thinking about his Franciscan brothers who had suffered and lost their lives on mission, Tomás concluded that Buenaventura was simply being realistic in turning away from this venture. He himself was being rash in taking on this challenge, and he knew it. The hazards other Franciscans had faced already had to portend what lay ahead.

Tomás was torn by his feelings. The savage ways of the Indians were all too real to him. Yet, he thought of the great faith and heroism of the martyrs of Guale. He remembered the many others as well who had already made inroads into the mission fields, like Fray Francisco Pareja, a veteran missioner and a skilled linguist, who helped the friars learn the language of the Timucuan tribes like the Potanos. Tomás recalled Fray Pareja's own words in the wake of the Guale revolt, which the young priest had committed to writing. Tomás mulled over these words now:

"Although this vineyard is a waste country full of woods and thickets difficult to cultivate and but little fruit is obtained after much labor, nevertheless the value of the harvest is great. We hold the time well spent and the labors undertaken worth the while for we know that for one such soul alone, if it were necessary, Christ our Lord would suffer his death passion again. How much more then should be suffered for the reduction of so many converted in these lands and for those whom we hope to convert ...."

Tomás had been in a position to request a safe accompaniment of Spanish soldiers to journey with him to this mission area. He had declined to do so, however, sharing the sentiment of other respected friars: "What Indian would not convert to Christianity when a gun was pointed at his face? When and where possible, enter the mission field only with another friar." Besides, a military garrison was already well established in the area, and he planned to let the soldiers know of his arrival after meeting with the Potanos. For a moment, Tomás considered going to the garrison first, now that the situation had changed and blood had been shed. Then, he dismissed this option as well. The shaman was probably alerting the tribe to Tomás' presence at this moment. If they came and found him missing, he would only look more suspicious when he returned later with soldiers behind him.

Still, Tomás was torn as to what he should do next. Should he wait for the Potanos to come, or go to them, or should he follow after Buenaventura while he still had time? The wrong choice could easily mean death. The missionary decided to turn to the one option that had never failed to guide him—he prayed. After reciting an Our Father and a Hail Mary, he became aware of a weight pressing against his side. Tomás reached into his robes

and pulled out the medals of Our Lady of Loreto that he had brought with him to give to the Indians. He ran them through his hands and looked at the image of the Madonna, Mary the Mother of God. Suddenly, he felt her presence blessing his mission to the Potano people. Catholics often asked the Holy Virgin to pray for them to her son, Jesus, just as a child might ask his mother to pray for him to God. When Tomás requested prayers from Mary, he had never known them to go unanswered, and now he felt something stirring within him.

A message from his heart kept coming to him, prodding its way into his brain: No, he could not turn back! He must do as planned!

With eyes cast down, Tomás offered a prayer for the mission ahead of him. He signed himself with the sign of the cross, and then, with the mission crucifix he had received on his departure from España, he made a large sweeping blessing over the Potano village and again over the little infant committed to his care.

The friar secured the child in a papoose-like carrier on his back, then grabbed his important belongings, and left behind what he could not carry. Tomás moved briskly into the wooded area that remained as the only barrier between himself and the Potano people.

IV

Two Potano tribesmen intercepted Fray Tomás as he entered the clearing. They were rather tall, by Spanish standards, with bronze skin stretched over their sturdy, muscular frames. Both wore only a deerskin leather breechcloth, but the bows in their hands and the arrows that hung by a strap at their sides marked them as warriors. Their hair was tied in a knot over their heads, a characteristic peculiar to the Timucuan tribes, including the Potano. Tomás eyed them cautiously. In their native tongue, the Indians communicated quickly with each other in a somewhat nervous fashion, and the friar did not catch a word of what they said. Then, the braves pointed to a fenced area that appeared to contain a number of Potano dwellings.

On his early morning reconnaissance expedition, Tomás had seen the enclosure and suspected that it housed the cacique. It appeared that this structure was erected for the protection of the cacique and the other leading tribesmen. There were many other dwellings outside the fortified area,

and the priest guessed that the entire village could probably take refuge inside the stockade when they were under attack.

One of the Indians led Tomás while the other followed. They did not offer assistance with the child or his baggage, nor did he request it. Passing a couple of Potano thatched dwellings, he saw the women for the first time. They wore their long hair unbound and were clad only in a skirt made of what appeared to be Spanish moss. Tomás averted his eyes out of modesty, but soon he was the one who felt everyone looking at him, as he quickly became the center of the villagers' attention. People began to follow the priest, and soon they began to press in on every side, until the two warriors motioned them away with their bows, even kicking two young boys who made their way too close. The friar's guards, or guides (Tomás was still unsure as to which duty the braves were serving), seemed proud to be his escort, as they led him to the entrance of the fortified area.

The high wooden fence wrapped around in a spiral fashion, with the outer fence overlapping the inner by about fifty feet, leaving an entrance-way. One tribesman stood guard in a circular hut at the beginning of the entrance. A second was stationed farther on at another guardhouse, next to the inner fence.

When Tomás had arrived at the inner guard post, a large, handsome man emerged, flanked by warriors on either side. Extensive tattoos were etched heavily on his chest, thighs, forearms, and wrists. He wore a crown banded by gold feathers on the outer edge with red and green in the center.

"Holata Toloca," one of Tomás' escorts said.

"Holata," Tomás recalled meant "cacique," chief of the tribe. He was face-to-face with the man who held his destiny in his hands. Would he say the right words, make the right impression, use the correct language to be understood? And where should he begin? Then the cross in his hand reminded him.

Tomás lifted his mission crucifix and began to say in the broken speech of the Potano dialect of the Timucuan nation, "This is my reason for coming to your village. I come to bring you the Lord Jesus, your Savior…and your God."

Dead silence. Everyone stared or looked at one another. Then, the cacique smiled and responded quickly in broken Spanish, "Then, why are you bringing me this child?"

He grabbed the baby from the carrier on Tomás' back, but immediately little Kocha emitted a loud shrill cry that could be heard from one end of the village to the other. Apparently, the infant had been taken too quickly from the soft, comfortable spot he had just gotten to know. The cacique tried unsuccessfully to hush the little one.

Suddenly, a grotesque-looking individual, smelling like a bear, parted the crowd. It was the shaman. Tomás noticed that the man was smaller in stature than most of the Potano men, but the grizzly head gave the shaman height and the animal skin cloak gave him size. He looked quite formidable as he approached the cacique.

In Potano, the shaman said, "Holata Toloca, of course the baby weeps. He has been with the Spanish all morning and maybe all night. Give him to me."

Toloca hesitated as the medicine man reached for the crying child. "Very well, Matala," the chief consented.

Then he moved to give up the infant, but before even getting to the shaman's hands, the baby screamed even louder. Even some of the braves winced. Matala, the shaman, looked around at everyone watching. Some children covered their ears, and a couple of villagers tried to hide smiles.

Tomás interjected in stilted Potano, "The baby happy with me."

Taken aback, both the cacique and shaman looked at him. Again, all eyes turned to Tomás.

The priest realized the boldness of his statement, and in what he hoped was a more humble tone ventured a suggestion, "Maybe the baby misses …the sack." He indicated his make-shift papoose.

The cacique nodded his head and quickly placed the baby back in Tomás' carrier. Almost immediately, Kocha's wailing subsided.

Toloca smiled and tried again in Spanish, "Baby happy with padre."

Matala gave the priest a cold glare.

But, Toloca continued, "Baby stay with padre."

Grabbing Tomás' one free hand, the cacique began to shake it profusely, giving Tomás the distinct impression that he would be quite welcome. Tomás breathed a sigh of relief and his scalp began to rest more comfortably around his skull. Tomás silently thanked little Kocha for helping pave the way for his reception by the cacique. He noted, however, that he had made no friend of the medicine man this day. The young Franciscan also realized that the cacique's Spanish was not going to help much in communication and hoped that the chieftain would return to his native tongue.

To his relief, the man did. "My name is Toloca. I am the cacique," the chief explained in the Potano language. "I am uncle to this child, and I thank you for saving his life. One day he will lead my people, and that he owes to you…because you freed him from death."

Tomás sensed his exploits of the night before had been reported back, but how? As if reading the priests questioning look, Holata Toloca gestured to his guards. Two disappeared and returned with the man who killed the woman and attacked the priests last night. His hands and legs were bound. The guards tossed the captive into their midst, and the man rolled to the ground at the friar's feet.

"As we speak, my tribesmen retrieve the body of Kocha's mother," the cacique stated. "This man will die for what he did to my sister. He will die for trying to kill Kocha, and he will die for what he tried to do to you, Padre." The chieftain held up three fingers, making sure the prisoner could see. "Do you hear me? Three times you will suffer death! Take him!" the cacique ordered the two guards.

Tomás saw the terror in his attacker's eyes. Though memory of the man's evil deeds flashed vividly in Tomás' mind, concern for the man's fate got the better of the priest. The strong urge to intervene overcame the young man.

"Please, Holata Toloca, no!" Tomás began to fumble for thoughts and for words to express them. "I know he did bad…wrong, but please, do not take his…his living." The priest struggled with the new language. A man's life depended on his words. Tomás' lessons with the Potano tutor back at St. Agustín were a haze in his mind. But the young friar knew he had to speak. "In return for the…the help I have done you in saving the child. I …I ask you a…help as well…. Not to kill this man. To save his life."

The cacique was truly perplexed by the padre's reaction. Even the captive Indian looked intently at Tomás, who was pleading for mercy with his eyes.

"You want me to spare this man?" the chief asked.

"Yes, Holata Toloca! I will help you take care of Kocha…. I will help Kocha learn…many, many good lessons. Please, spare this man…and he can help me." Now that Tomás knew the cacique was listening, the language came easier. His lessons came back to him. "Let him be my…helper, so I can learn the ways of your people from him. I will be able to help your sister's son. I want to be his teacher, but I need to have someone to help me."

It was an interesting trade-off. Tomás was gambling for a life. He would help train and educate Kocha; the Indian at his feet would help train and educate him.

The cacique's gaze bore the venom of disgust for the wretch on the ground, but he saw the earnestness in young priest's eyes. He pronounced judgment on the criminal. "You will serve the padre. He is your master. But hear me, if you harm him or my nephew in any way, you will wish that you had died today." With a wave of a hand, Holata Toloca signaled the guards to take the man away. To Tomás he turned and motioned for the Franciscan to come into his thatched home. All the others knew they were not to follow.

Once inside, Tomás was offered an herbal drink he was already familiar with, called *cacina*.[4] It was like tea. He nodded approvingly after sipping a little of the drink from the gourd container.

Fray Tomás gave his name and thanked the cacique for his hospitality. He presented him with his mission cross, a medal of Our Lady of Loreto, and an onyx ring. The cacique was especially fond of the ring, but was obviously intrigued with the other gifts as well. In Spanish, he identified the cross, *la cruz*, and the medal, *Nuestra Señora*.

Tomás was delighted. How had he come to learn about these sacred objects?

The answer was simple. The cacique was a Christian. Once he had come to know the ways of the Spanish were important for him to learn, he had gone to San Agustín on his own and sought to be baptized. Tomás suspected that Holata Toloca's motivations were probably pragmatic, but he was willing to give the man the benefit of the doubt.

Given the presence of the Spanish militia a few leagues to the west, a few leagues north, and those troops sporadically placed in hamlets and villages all the way east to San Agustín, the friar could imagine someone finding an advantage in conversion. This was the reason the Franciscans preferred keeping the military presence at a distance from any of their endeavors. Conversion was a matter of persuasion and faith, not of compulsion and force.

So the cacique was baptized! That was good news! At least a door was open.

---

[4] a type of tea, also known as "black drink," used in a purification ceremony held before a battle or important tribal events.

What about the other people of the village? Were there any others who had been received into the Church? No, Toloca alone had become Christian and had chosen the same name as the friar—Tomás.

"Great!" Tomás exclaimed. "You and I will celebrate our saint's day together."

"Saint? What is a saint?" the cacique asked.

Fray Tomás tried to hide his surprise. Obviously, the cacique's instruction in the faith had been rapid and weak. "I will teach you about saints, and many more beliefs of our holy faith, if you would like," Tomás responded. "That is my reason for coming to you."

"I know," Toloca said. "You are here because I sent for you. I asked for a padre for my village. I went to visit your padre cacique and asked him to send to my people a padre like the Potano people to the south have."

The statements came as a surprise to Tomás. Why hadn't he been told? He was glad for the welcome, but would have appreciated being told in advance. Surely Buenaventura would have as well.

Holata Toloca spoke again, interrupting the padre's thoughts, "My people are a good people. They have lived here many years, and this land they love like their own child. They suffer much from their Apalachee enemy, to protect their land. Many of my people have died. My people are proud people. They are brave people. They will die for what is theirs. If you help my people know about your Great Spirit, they will die for your Great Spirit."

"But be warned, Padre, on the path you wish to lead my people; there is a mountain in your way – you have met the mountain this day, Matala, the medicine man of our village. He is like you, a priest. He brings belief to my people for many, many years. He is not happy that you have come to the Potano people. He is not happy that the Spanish people come to take away the Potano land, Potano life, Potano beliefs. He tells my people over and over about the Spanish slaughter of the Potano people. He will not let them forget, ever. His powers are great. My people fear him. They listen to him, sometimes more than to me. He will never be your friend."

Tomás knew the cacique was speaking the truth.

"But I welcome you," Toloca said. "Come, I will show you where you will stay tonight. Kocha will stay with you, Padre. You seem to be the only one he is happy with. He never cries when he is with you. You will be his teacher, his guide, and his friend. I place the future cacique in your care. And I think I will not take him from you for a long, long time."

V

Despite the excitement of the past day, Tomás slept soundly through the night in the private dwelling given to him by the cacique. The child, too, back in familiar surroundings, and feeling safe with the padre, rested peacefully in a tiny bed with soft matting, only an eyeshot away from Fray Tomás. Early in the evening, an Indian woman, nursing her own new-born child, had lulled the infant to sleep and kept vigil periodically throughout the night.

Shortly after sunrise, Toloca, the cacique, appeared at the entrance of Tomás' new home. The chieftain was accompanied by the nursing woman who carried a basket. It contained berries, nuts, and a food mixture made from corn, which the Indians called maize. Toloca gently touched the friar on the shoulder but got no response.

"Padre, it is I, Toloca," the Indian said, and his words broke the priest's slumber. "I am sorry to awaken you, but I wanted to present you to my council this morning. From these brave men, I seek advice in leading my people. You must seek their advice, too, as you bring the Great Spirit of the Spanish nation to my tribe. But first you must eat what I have had prepared for you."

Taking the cue from Toloca, the woman served Tomás from the basket. Eyeing the unfamiliar food, the priest offered a prayer for protection as well as thanks and praise and then treated himself to a taste of Potano cooking. The maize concoction was actually quite good! He just might enjoy a little of the culture and cuisine of this people after all. Time would tell.

Soon, Tomás and the cacique were making their way to the center of the village. Like the rest of the dwellings, the council meeting hall was constructed of palm branches, but it was larger than the other structures, and as Tomás walked inside, he noticed it had another unique feature. A little removed from the inner wall of the building, a bench had been constructed that completely encircled the room. The leaders of the tribe—about fifteen in all—were already seated, awaiting the arrival of Tomás and the cacique. Though most of the men looked to be around Toloca's age, the councilors ranged in years. A handful had gray hair, while a couple of the men were notably younger. Since most had not seen a brown-robed friar before, they eyed Tomás intently.

The cacique sat at what was a slightly elevated portion of the bench, and he motioned for the friar to sit next to him. Holata Toloca handed Tomás a gourd containing the *cacina* drink he had the day before, and it was then passed to all the council members. From among their midst, the shaman stood, and with outstretched arms, invoked a blessing on the chief and the assembly. The sight of the shaman made Tomás tense, but his mind turned to the thought that prayer was not foreign to these people even if it meant something different from his own prayer. He liked what he saw.

Toloca then stood and addressed his council, "Today, I welcome a new member of our Potano tribe. His skin is not as ours, nor are his looks or his clothes. But his spirit is one with us. And he comes to help us to know about the Great Spirit. He comes to teach us the ways of the Great Spirit. He will ask the Great Spirit to bless our people, our land, our fields, our springs, and our rivers."

He motioned to Tomás to stand, as he himself sat down. Tomás got the impression it was his turn to speak, and he began to fumble for the right words. He had mentally rehearsed opening remarks to the Potano people many times before setting out on his mission. In fact, he had been quite proud of the speech he had memorized in Potano for an occasion such as this, but now his mind was blank, the words gone. For a moment, the priest closed his eyes and bowed his head.

Then, this part of a Psalm from the Bible came to him, *"You, O Lord, shall open my lips, and my tongue shall announce Your praise. Come to my aid, O God. O Lord, make haste to help me."* Tomás said mentally, "Holy Spirit, tell me what to say."

The friar opened his eyes and mouth and his words came out in the form of a prayer. "Great Spirit, help me to know this people You have sent me to serve, who honor me by making me one of their own. I want to be their friend, to promote the goodness of their ways, the wisdom of their sacred values and customs, the beauty of their way of life. I come not to mock them or to condemn them, but to love them. I pray to You to help me to find You, Great Spirit, here among this good people, in this good and beautiful land. For You are here, and I want to make You better known and better loved by all Your Potano people. Help me, Great Spirit!"

The council joined the cacique in saluting Tomás, raising their hands twice to the height of their heads and intoned, "Ha, he, ye, ha, ha." This was a special verbal recognition that they reserved for the cacique, but extended now to Fray Tomás. The cacique nodded, smiled, and then motioned for his councilors to speak in response to the words of the priest.

They were not reticent, and one by one, the leaders began to challenge Tomás to explain the meaning of his presence among them.

Why was he wearing brown robes in the hot sun? Would he not be better dressed as they were, with few clothes?

They had taken note immediately of the style of hair peculiar to a tonsured cleric of the Catholic Church, with a large round spot in the middle of the head, completely shaven. This feature of Tomás' appearance especially intrigued them. If they shared in his beliefs, would he want them to cut their hair in a similar fashion?

They had heard from other Potano villagers that friars had forced their people to live with one wife. That would be very hard. Some of the people had three wives, and they would not want to have only one.

The friars also spoke of peace that could make their people weak in the defense against the Apalachees to the west of them. They would die quickly if they were not brave warriors. Would the padre make them give up their weapons and become the slaves of the Apalachees?

Why were the Spanish taking from them their land, grazing cattle on their fields, and subjecting them to labor for the great Spanish cacique instead of their own cacique? Many of their people had died at the hands of his people. How could they trust the Spanish not to take all that they held dear? The pale skins had taken so much already.

One by one, Tomás addressed the issues raised by the council. No, he did not prefer to dress in the manner of the Potano people, though he respected their clothing – he smiled, as he spoke—what little clothing there was! His reference to the scanty breechcloth they wore, they found to be amusing, also.

Nor did he expect them to wear their hair the exact opposite of what it was. Theirs was full and bound at the top. His head was shaved at the top. Actually, he preferred their hairstyle to his own and would suggest something like theirs to his superiors.

A counselor said, "The Spanish are more stiff-necked than the alligator. Do you think they will change?"

"No," Tomás responded in a forlorn tone.

That remark received a hearty laugh.

Moving along to the next topic, the priest said that, yes, he would ask them to live with only one wife, for the same reason they would not want to be one husband among many others to a single woman. While some nodded in grudging assent, others looked less than convinced. But Fray Tomás moved along with his responses.

In teaching the lesson of peace, the friars were not telling the people to avoid arming themselves for defense against an invading enemy, just to not become the invading enemy of another people themselves. The priests wished for them, and all people, to stop responding to evil with evil, but instead to respond with good. As Tomás said this he saw many skeptical glances and some councilors shaking their heads. He realized that it would take them a long time to understand what he was trying to tell them.

Their last concern Tomás found to be the most difficult one. He had long before imagined himself in the place of the Potano people, being dispossessed of land and deprived of culture. In reality they were being exploited on many fronts, Tomás admitted.

But the friars, he argued, were also Spanish. They were trying to represent the noble ideals of the Spanish people. They and many of the military people, as well, were here not to take from the Potano, but to give to them, not to rob or pillage or replace their own culture with a foreign one, but to make their people better, happier, and closer to their Great Spirit. He himself had come to help them to know this Great Spirit, to love and to serve the Great Spirit and be happy forever with this Great Spirit in the life beyond this one. He was not here to take away from them anything that was good, but to give them more than they already had.

Tomás' final words were interrupted by a shrill cry. All heads turned to see Matala, the shaman, writhing grotesquely on the floor of the council hall. His limbs bent and contorted at unnatural, seemingly impossible angles. Unintelligible words spewed forth in an ugly torrent from his mouth, and a frightful expression twisted his face as he spoke, as if he was in an animated conversation with someone no one else could see. Tomás had heard stories of people being possessed by demons or evil spirits, and though the priest had never seen it happen, Tomás thought he might be witnessing such a possession now, as Matala entered a trance-like state.

Suddenly, the shaman became calm and remained motionless for a short time. The council members watched, captivated. Then Matala emerged from the strange trance that had enveloped him. He rose and stalked over to the friar, moving to within inches of the priest's face.

"You have not come to free the Potano people," the shaman hissed as he pointed at Tomás. "You have come to enslave us. Your flattering words do not deceive us." And turning to the council members, he continued to rant. "The brown-robed friars are like all the Spanish people. They have come to take from us our land and our way of life. But the brown robes are even worse than the others, because they come to take from us our sacred beliefs."

Tomás looked around and saw a number of the council members nodding, and many others with looks of agreement on their faces as they listened to what Matala was saying. Tomás recalled the words spoken by Buenaventura, and later by the cacique, that indeed the shaman posed a very serious threat to all Tomás hoped to accomplish in this village.

Then, Toloca came to his defense, "Matala, you insult my guest."

"And his presence insults me, Holata Toloca," Matala shot back. "I am the medicine man of this tribe, and for many seasons, I have brought the blessings of the spirits to our people. Now you bring this—outsider—to replace me. Do you seek to weaken our people?"

Toloca rose at this accusation, "Do you question my authority or my loyalty, Matala? Beware your words, shaman!"

"And you beware of your ways, Cacique!" Matala responded. "When you learned the Spanish tongue, we commended you for being wise, like the owl, to know the language of the invaders. When you went to go visit their great dwelling, we understood, thinking you crafty like the fox, who learns the lair of his prey. When you said you wished to bring a brown robe here, we kept silent. Some questioned you, but others thought you cunning, like the bear tricking strong hunters. You would strike fear in the Appalachees by making them think you had made a treaty with the Spanish, and you would keep the Spanish at bay by holding in your palm one of their own. But then the great spirits whispered something that gave fear to my heart, and now hearing your words today, I must know if it is true. Have you, Holata Toloca, been baptized—a *Christian?*" Matala spat the last word.

"It is true," replied Toloca, "but I have not kept this a secret from anyone."

However, one could see a look of surprise on the face of more than one council member. Tomás struggled to keep up with this ferociously fast conversation, and while he did not understand everything, he could feel the tension simmering in every person in the room.

"So the spirits are right," said Matala. "Then tell me Holata Toloca, have you done this to complete your deception of our enemy, the Spanish, or have you been corrupted by their ways?"

"Neither," the cacique countered. "Any wise man can see that the

Spanish are a mighty people, mightier perhaps, than any tribe in our land. They must have a great spirit to guide them to make them so strong, and I would know more of this spirit and have this spirit bless us."

"Then you may well be poisoned by this brown-robed snake," Matala shouted as he pointed at Tomás.

This accusation Tomás understood, and the insult burned him like a brand. He leapt up from his seat. "You are the snake!" he yelled in Potano, glaring at the medicine man whose own gaze did not falter. The swelter-ing heat of the day paled in comparison to the burning intensity of the locked stares between these two men. They were as mountain rams poised to clash heads, and any onlooker could see a major confrontation brewing deep within them, as if their very souls were in mortal spiritual combat.

Tomás continued as best he could, "I am a man of God…I come with the Great Spirit of God. Holata Toloca has become a—a real…a true son of the Great Spirit, and true sons of the Great Spirit will—will…crush the head of the snake."

Matala's eyes flashed, but his tone became mocking, "Brave words, friar, and where are your soldiers to prove them?"

Now, immediately, Tomás thought, I must confront this man and all that he stands for, or I will ever be held hostage by his evil ways. Tomás gave voice to the inner anguish of his soul by placing a challenge to the shaman.

"You and I must face one another in…in a fight of our beliefs and the—the spirits we hold to be sacred," Tomás stated as best he could over his boiling emotions. "If your great spirit and your beliefs stand…stronger than my Great Spirit and my beliefs, I will be forced to say your ways are better than mine. But if my teachings and beliefs are stronger over yours, then you will become the servant of the Great Spirit I preach and the ways of this Great Spirit."

The shaman looked surprised and stared at him shrewdly. "How do you propose to show that your medicine is stronger than mine?" he asked. "The challenge you choose could be a trick."

"My Great Spirit is the spirit of all things," Tomás replied. "You may choose."

Matala hesitated for a moment, as a wolf eyes the bait in a snare. Was this a trick, the shaman wondered? Was the priest bluffing or being over-ly arrogant? The medicine man found such confidence to be surprising, but he could not back down from such a challenge. The shaman stepped bold-ly up to Tomás and presented the contest. Each of them would build separate piles of wood, mounted high up to the heavens, and through their own private incantations, ask that a fire be ignited by their respective spirits. They would use no flint or torch to create a spark. Their prayers and the power of the spirits that guided each of them would be the only force to set the fire ablaze. Whoever's woodpile was the first to be consumed by the fire of the spirit, that man's beliefs would prevail over the Potano people.

"Yes," Tomás responded quickly, even as he wondered in his heart how he had ever allowed his boldness of faith to proceed this far. It was clearly a win or lose situation, and Tomás found himself against a very strong opponent whom he had even allowed to formulate the rules of the contest If he did not face Matala now, the shaman would be confronting him every step of the way. He had to meet the opposition immediately and challenge the medicine man directly, or he would forever be haunted in the shadow of the shaman.

The day was set for the contest. It was to be tomorrow, at sunset.

Tomás thanked the council members and the cacique for hearing his message. Once more he directed his gaze to the frightful figure of the shaman, whose rigid scowl reflected his contempt for the friar. Tomás then returned to his temporary home to prepare for the next day's contest.

VI

It had now been two days since Buenaventura had left, and Fray Tomás was all alone. He had never felt so alone.

Though the rest of the tribe had gone to sleep, the young priest was wide-awake as he knelt by his bed. He had decided to make this a night of prayer. He knew that even if he had wanted to, he could not have slept. This restlessness did not surprise Tomás, but what did was the fact that his prayer that night seemed to be more an experience of the absence of God, rather than of God's presence.

His knees ached from weariness, and the rest of his body complained as well from a lack of rest. It also yearned for nourishment, because Tomás had chosen to follow the penitential practice of fasting, depriving himself of even bread and water, so that he could be more open to the things of the Spirit. But the longer he prayed, the more the Spirit seemed to depart from him.

He felt like Christ on the cross: abandoned by all, crying out to His Father, "My God, my God, why have You abandoned me?"

Every time Tomás tried to concentrate, he found his thoughts shattered instead by the image of the shaman deep in his demonic trance, writhing on the floor of the council meeting hall. The friar could forget neither the sheer hatred on the medicine man's face, nor the enraged epithets that flew like wasps from his mouth. All through his prayer, Tomás felt the wrath of Matala growing heavier on his mind, crushing his heart, and tearing at his spirit.

Never had he felt so alone.

As the new day dawned, Tomás felt empty and disturbed. The duel was taking place in an area east of the Potano village, and on his way there, a sense of foreboding entered the priest's heart. As hard as he tried, Tomás simply could not shake the notion he had lost the presence of God. The shaman had begun building his tower on a hilly area near his own dwelling. Tomás started his edifice a slight distance away. Despite his growing doubt, the young priest hacked away at every piece of fallen timber that he could find. Tomás decided he would not build just a mound but a mountain of wood. Therefore, it's burning would prove God's power—that is, if God responded. Partially from pride, partially from a growing feeling of desperation, the friar threw himself frantically into the effort, and his woodpile grew and grew.

Matala was meticulous in his efforts to build a carefully structured edifice of wood, and he had great help in his efforts from the craftsmen among the villagers. The structure of the shaman was more like a tower than a woodpile, for he wanted to be sure his god would be pleased with his effort.

Tomás was not so painstaking and careful in building his monument. His only objective was to see his edifice crumble. He knew the beauty of the structure would lay not in its survival but in its destruction. He flung the branches in a disorderly fashion, one upon the other, until they finally reached a remarkable height that astonished even the shaman.

The Potano people watched in amazement. Their fear of the shaman did not lead them to lend Tomás any more assistance than the time afforded by the curiosity of their gaze.

The cacique moved carefully between the two combatants, keeping an objective aloofness from each, lest he go down with the vanquished party himself. At sunset he signaled the start of the contest. "May the Great Spirit make evident His power and strength today," he proclaimed. "May He show to us the instrument He has chosen in our village to make His presence known. May we come to know who speaks for the Great Spirit: the padre or the shaman. My friends, proceed!"

And so the contest began.

The two men moved to the woodpiles in unison and placed at the top of each of them a special token of their faith. For the shaman, it was a deer he was sacrificing to his god. For the priest, it was a cross that symbolized the faith he came to proclaim and the sacrifice of Christ on Calvary that was depicted by that cross.

The sun had reached the rim of the earth, slowly passing into the horizon for a rest from its daily vigil. With the light of the day fading, the

shaman and the priest began their prayers to seek their respective god's blessing and ratification of their priestly service to the Potano people.

Matala began his ritual with a dance, slowly stalking around the tower of wood, while chanting incantations as he raised and lowered his voice.

The people of the village struck pieces of wood to accompany the invocations of their medicine man.

Tomás, instead, simply clasped his hands, dropped to his knees, and began his silent oration, principally beckoning God to come and show these people a sign of His majesty and power. The priest prayed with intensity for the Lord to demonstrate His might. Yet, for all of his fervor, Tomás felt he was speaking into the void. Soon, doubts ran like madmen though his mind, tearing with wild hands at the walls of his self-confidence.

As the chaos increased in Tomás' mind, so did the intensity increase in Matala's dance. He spun and pranced around his tower. Ducking toward it, then darting away, the shaman called to his spirits. He sang to them, pleaded with them, and yelled for them, all to the ever rising, resounding beat played out by his faithful followers pounding upon their wooden instruments.

As the medicine man's dance built to a crescendo, the priest's concentration shattered into a myriad of tormenting questions. Where was God? Did he not have enough faith? Was there something wrong with his prayers? Why was God not responding? Would God really let him lose? Had he somehow made a mistake?

A single thought came to him, cutting through the questions: "You shall not put the Lord your God to the test." These words were from the Bible spoken by Jesus, when he was tempted by the devil.

Suddenly, a horrible feeling struck Tomás deep in his heart. God would not be commanded in this way. Something dark inside Tomás told him that he had failed. He was not going to win this contest. Under the weight of that realization, the friar slowly slumped forward, until his forehead touched the ground. If he hoped to see the woodpile consumed, the friar thought he would probably have to ignite it himself.

A commotion erupted among the villagers that drew the friar's attention away from his quandary and made him look up. A spark, then a flame, then a puff of smoke rose, not from the priest's woodpile, but from that of Matala. Indeed, it was now more than just a flame; it was a full-blown fire that was jumping out in all directions and rapidly consuming the lower levels of the shaman's tower of wood.

The tribe gasped and pointed. Some villagers even applauded. Tomás could only stare. Then he pushed himself off of his knees, made the sign of the cross on himself, and then moved in the direction of the shaman. He would concede defeat—not, however, to acknowledge the victory of the shaman or his beliefs, but the Franciscan would acknowledge his own unworthiness in even considering such a ridiculous venture that put his God rashly to the test.

Before Tomás reached Matala, he found himself apprehended by two Potano warriors, the ones who had escorted him into the village. The shaman proudly signaled to his followers and they laughed and jeered at the Franciscan. Holata Toloca looked away. Tomás could not even respond. He began to feel that he deserved every cruel comment.

Matala shouted above the din, "The spirits of our people have been challenged. And they have responded. This Spaniard promised to show us the true way to the Great Spirit. I told you he was full of lies and trickery. This is the truth!" the medicine man gestured to his burning tower. "You see our spirits have spoken," and then he indicated the padre's woodpile, "while his mockery of a god hangs silent on his tree."

These words roused Tomás. "Do not insult the Lord!"

"Quiet, Brown Robe! You have tainted this village long enough. Bring him to the Rock," the medicine man said.

The warriors holding Tomás hauled him to the edge of the clearing, followed by all the witnesses of the event, including the shaman himself. There stood a large, low stone with a flat top, like a table. It was stained black with traces of red. Seeing those ancient bloodstains, Tomás realized that here he was going to be killed.

Thunderclouds moved over the site of the contest and began to signal the start of rainfall. No one had sensed the threat of a storm before, but it was suddenly upon them. Within minutes heavy drops forcefully pelted down on everyone and everything in sight. The shaman tried to retain control of the crowd, but the onlookers were swiftly becoming drenched. The tribe stood on the verge of running back to the village for shelter.

Holata Toloca spoke, "Perhaps the Great Spirit has been angered today. Go back to your homes; we will finish this matter when the Spirit's wrath has lessened."

Matala shot a look at the cacique, but he knew he could not hold the villagers. He nodded, and indicated the padre, "We will deal with this snake soon enough."

Thunder cracked in the distance as if sounding a signal, and the people rushed back to the village for shelter.

Realizing that his life has been spared, Tomás sagged from relief in the arms of his captors. They tightened their grip on him and hauled him back to the village, reminding him that this reprieve was temporary. Then, the priest felt the urge to turn to look back at the mountain of wood, his own standing tall, and the shaman's partially burned. He saw the rain had extinguished the fire that had been encompassing Matala's woodpile. The deer at the top of the medicine man's construction remained unscathed.

Toloca followed the friar's gaze and made the same observation. "Matala, look," he said pointing the medicine man in the direction of the woodpiles. "Neither sacrifice has been consumed."

The shaman snorted, "It is of no matter. That can't save your pet priest now." He saw his chieftain's pained expression. In a softer voice, Matala said, "I'm sorry, but you should never have brought him here." With that, he ducked into his dwelling, which was close to the clearing.

The cacique gave Tomás a lingering sorrowful glance and then ran swiftly to his own *buhio*.[5] Tomás was not taken to his temporary home next to the cacique. Instead, he was locked in a small hut made of wood. Unlike the other homes constructed of palm fronds, its walls were much too strong for any man to break out of and escape.

But the Franciscan was not thinking about fleeing. Though fear of death slunk like a panther through the darkness in his heart, it was but a shadow in the face of the greater terror that consumed him: the loss of his Lord. It was one thing to die, but to die without God was more terrible than he could possibly fathom. It was that fear and the overwhelming feeling of failure that flooded the priest's thoughts. In the prison hut, he fell to knees once again. Exhaustion and starvation drove him to the ground, but he focused past them to embark on one last search for what he had lost. "My God, my God, why have You abandoned me?" he cried out once again.

Now, he knew what the desert was like, where the Chosen People had wandered forty years, and the desert where Jesus fasted forty days and forty nights. This desert, Tomás found, had become the landscape of his soul. And the priest discovered that, in this interior wasteland, nothing could hide. Every thought, every motive, and every desire lay exposed to the harsh light of self-examination.

Again came the thoughts that had haunted him from the moment he ventured into the village. Had he acted rashly? Had he recklessly sought martyrdom for false reasons? Had he been seeking honor for himself?

---

[5] a hut or dwelling

Had he acted out of pride? As he anguished over these questions in prayer, Tomás discovered more than a little pride lurking behind his motives.

He found himself face-to-face with his exaggerated sense of his own greatness and power. It was a false idea that, through his own strength and power, he was invincible. This part of his personality strutted about crowing, "No one and nothing could stop Tomás. No one ever has and no one ever will."

Then came the second overpowering insight into his motives—a deep hatred for anyone or anything that stood in his way. Matala was his enemy, not because of the shaman's opposing beliefs, but because he was an obstacle to the friar's success. Tomás hated Matala, not the man's evil teachings and moral practices, but the man himself. He hated the shaman pure and simple, because the medicine man could ruin his plans.

"My God, my God, why have You abandoned me?" Tomás uttered, but the words sounded hollow now, as he came to the profound realization about his own great arrogance and deep hypocrisy. He was not here because of the Faith and the desire to spread it.

He was here because of pride....

Tomás realized he was not here not to serve the Lord, but to serve himself. His zeal had been misplaced. His enthusiasm was ill-conceived. His motivations were based on hypocrisy. The only god Tomás had worshiped was Tomás. He cried out in desperation, "My God, my God, why have I abandoned You?"

Tomás began to weep, as he never had done before.

Tomás now realized his desire for a showdown had been vain and foolish from the start, as was most of what he had done since embarking on this mission. Tomás had to face the truth that for as much as he had suggested the duel to show God's glory to the shaman and the tribe, he had also wanted it to prove his own holiness and righteousness. Deep inside, the friar had desired the contest to demonstrate that he was the better, more religious man. This motive directly opposed his vows and his duty. A priest's position was to serve God and God's people, not to have God serve him. Tomás was God's to command, and not the one to be commanding God. His failure lay in his pride. With this new insight, Tomás knew now what he needed to do: beg God for forgiveness for the selfishness and sinfulness of his life.

And he prayed. He implored Jesus to remove from him all his self-serving ambitions, and instead of consuming the pile of wood, to consume the false ego of Tomás' life.

The young priest felt the sting of regret as he wished that he had come to this realization before what would probably be the end of his life, and a new fear gripped him. If the shaman had him killed tomorrow, he would go to face his last judgment by God that very same day. And what would he have to show for his life—an oversized ego which he had overcome just before his final end? Would his last minute repentance save him from hell, and if it did, how long would he have to suffer in purgatory to atone for his pride? Tomás now felt that not only was his life in danger but also the state of his immortal soul.

So he prayed anew, "God, my God. Please...please, spare me. Do not let me come to You empty-handed. Save me, I beg You. I beg You. I beg You. Save me so that my work may bear You some fruit and do some good. I offer You, my Lord, a new sacrifice: my life, for Your glory, and not for my own." In his despair, the young friar's thoughts wandered to Christ, and the image came to mind of Jesus praying in the garden before He was arrested and crucified. Fray Tomás knew then that his prayer was not finished. There was more he had to say, but the fear he had of these words sucked the moisture from his mouth, leaving his throat feeling like it was full of sand. He managed to choke out, "But Thy will, not my will, be done."

Upon making this act of faith, it was as if a weight lifted from his chest. It gave him the courage to say this one final petition, "Lord, though I am unworthy to ask anything of You, and I am the lowliest of the low, I beg You this: do not let my failure stop Your Holy Faith from coming to this people. May the message of Your Son come to this village...even if it must be over my death."

A bolt of lightning struck so close to the village that the hut shook with the boom of the thunder. Though partially deafened by the sound and almost blinded by the flash, Tomás' fear was fading. Instead came the beginning of peace, and though the storm still raged outside, the storm in his heart slowly began to subside. Just as the lightning would sporadically illuminate the darkness outside, the desperation in his soul was gradually being filtered with intermittent rays of light. Tomás began to feel the hollowness, emptiness, loneliness, and discouragement of the night and day lift off his spirit like fog rising from a field. The contempt that he experienced for his own pride and hatred was now being replaced with compassion and understanding. He could begin to distinguish between the human person and the evil that lurks within everyone, even himself. He could begin to hate the sin and still love the sinner, even when that sinner was himself, as long as the sin was identified, acknowledged, and rejected from his heart.

He even began to see the shaman in a new and different light. Matala was no longer the enemy to be conquered and destroyed, but a brother and friend, in need of his compassion, support and prayer. Anger, hatred, contempt, suspicion, and fear were being transformed by love. That love gave him strength and courage. When he thought of what dawn would bring, fear still stirred in his heart, but it was tempered by the knowledge that God had returned to him. In fact, God had never left him, but finally, he, Tomás, had returned to God.

The thunderstorm had abated by morning, and when the warrior guards unlocked the door of the prison, they found Tomás still on his knees. Because of the continuous prayers and fasting, the priest needed help to stand. But the friar accompanied the warriors willingly as they led him to Matala. They brought him in front of the shaman's *buhio* where most of the tribe had already gathered. A few stragglers were still running over to see the end of this confrontation. Holata Toloca had already arrived, but he did not look at the padre other than to acknowledge that the priest had been brought.

The guards forced Tomás to his knees, and fear suddenly gripped the friar. A cold sweat broke out on his body, and wild fright threatened to take him over completely. He silently cried out, "Lord Jesus, have mercy on me. I trust in You." He repeated the litany again and again, which pushed the terror away just enough to allow him to keep from panic.

They waited for Matala to appear…and moments passed.

The crowd began to fidget, people looked at each other, but the medicine man did not emerge.

The cacique broke the silence. "Matala, come out!" he shouted. "Let us finish what you and the Franciscan have started."

Silence was the only response. The cacique gestured to one of his braves and the man entered the medicine man's dwelling. An instant later, a sharp gasp could be heard from within, and the warrior came running out.

"The shaman is dead!" the warrior proclaimed in shock.

The crowd erupted in chaos, and everyone talked at once. Questions swarmed from every mouth. Disbelief and wonder took hold of every member of the tribe. Toloca rushed into the dwelling followed by his bodyguards. They returned within moments, the body of Matala carried out by two braves. The ashen color and stiff limbs bore grim testimony to the first warrior's words. There were no signs of violence, but beyond any doubt, the medicine man was dead.

Then came the accusations, flying like arrows. Some aimed at Tomás, others at the warrior whose life the priest had saved, and others were whispered against the cacique.

A shout cut through the cacophony. It came from the clearing where the duel had been held. As the tribe wandered over to investigate the new commotion, silence once again fell over the people.

In the field one could see the two sacrifices, or rather what was left of them. The shaman's tower of wood had blown over in the wind. The carcass of the deer lay untouched on the ground.

But the padre's edifice was gone. Obliterated. Only a few smoldering ashes were left in the middle of a huge scorch mark in the earth.

Then Tomás remembered the night before; the lightning bolt that had struck right next to the village. Without thought, the priest stood and walked on stiff, unsteady legs to the remnants of his woodpile. His guards did not stop him. There in the middle of the ashes he found the remainder of his crucifix. The wooden cross was gone, but the iron sculpture of the crucified Christ lay amid the embers. He gingerly lifted the metal figure. It was blackened but mostly untouched. He stared at it for a moment in amazement, a sense of wonder flooding his being.

When he turned back to the crowd, he was shocked again, to find most of the tribe facing him, down on their knees.

VII

For Fray Tomás the first four months in the Potano village were like living in a new and exciting, but very strange world. He was making a real effort to immerse himself in the culture and lifestyle of the people. But he knew that adaptation to the ways of the Potano would take years—probably as long as it would take them to become accustomed to the presence of a Spanish priest in their midst.

Tomás knew that the faith had been translated into many cultures over the centuries in many different ways. Some of the variations that Church leaders had sanctioned in earlier centuries had given the faith a distinctly regional or national character.

In the century that preceded the padre's own, the Church had faced the greatest division in its history and was still reeling from the movements set in motion by the Augustinian monk, Martin Luther. The people of Tomás' own country, España, had almost uniformly rejected the reforms of Luther, Calvin, and Zwingli and opted instead for the reforms of Ignacio de Loyola, Teresa de Avila, and the Council of Trent.

The faith Tomás brought to the New World reflected that perspective. It was a faith carefully defined and cautiously presented that left little room for adaptation, other than simple translation. What he brought in the way of faith was what he had learned from his religious family upbringing and his seminary training in Madrid, which was modeled after the spirit of San Francisco de Assis. And the way of San Francisco was no small reform itself four centuries earlier. It continued to be a challenge to people like Tomás. Living the Franciscan ideals of poverty, simplicity, and peace, he was called to see all his possessions as coming from God, who had first ownership over everything and everyone. A Franciscan did not really "own" anything. God did. The friars just used money, clothing, and the like "for the glory of God." Tomás found this outlook to be a very freeing one. He tried to live by it as best he could, and he wanted to help others to be freed of the weight of their material baggage and their empty, but alluring attachments.

The Franciscan found the Potano lifestyle quite a shock. While the friar had believed and preached this ideal of simplicity for a number of years, he had now found an entire nation that lived it. This made the Potano intensely appealing to him. Though the Indian people lacked the conveniences of the Spanish, they managed to survive. He hoped these Native Americans wouldn't be too attracted by some of the material blessings España would bring to them.

Though Fray Tomás had come to preach to this tribe, he found that they had much to teach him. Most importantly, he was learning from these people how one could live from the land and the rivers. Plants he had never known, he discovered, were edible and nourishing. Certain herbs had medicinal qualities and others could be used for flavoring. Daily hunting and fishing expeditions with the Potano helped him develop new skills, and he found the Indians more than happy to teach him. Ruefully, he realized he gave them entertainment in return, because they were constantly amused with his fumbling efforts to learn.

His best teacher and constant companion was the very man who had earlier tired to kill him, the husband of Kocha's mother. Since Tomás had trouble pronouncing his Indian name "Tofucunatchu," he one day just called him "Tofu," and Tofucunatchu gave one of his rare laughs. The padre asked him if he could call the warrior by this nickname instead; and with a smile, the tribesman accepted.

The two became inseparable, because both now shared the feelings of being foreigners to the Potano tribe, seeking total acceptance. Tomás knew he could never really become one of them, nor could they, or should they, become Spanish. It would be wrong to ask more of them. It would be wrong for them to ask him to totally leave behind the life and culture of España. Tomás was more welcomed by the tribe because of the outcome of the contest with the shaman, but that was just the opening of the door. For Tofucunatchu, however, the door was permanently shut because of his cruel murder of the sister of the cacique. Only the padre called him a friend.

In the time Tomás was in the village, summer had turned to fall, and fall was rapidly becoming winter, with occasional cold nights and days that called for special provisions. Tomás offered his extra robes to help the Indians defend themselves against the colder climate, but they preferred their own blankets or furs.

Little Kocha remained in the care of Fray Tomás, and the priest cared for him tenderly, to the satisfaction of the cacique. However, the friar had one special concern that he deliberately postponed, until a strategic opportunity could present itself. The cacique provided that opportunity for him when, on one of his regular visits, Toloca expressed admiration for the padre's careful protection of Kocha.

Tomás reacted quickly. "Holata Toloca, I am honored by your kind words and appreciation, but I really have not fulfilled my responsibilities to your nephew. As a Christian, you know I have failed to bring Kocha the greatest gift I have to give him: his Lord and Savior. I must baptize this child a Christian soon or suffer the loss of my own soul. I have only waited this long because Kocha is someone special to these people, and they would have resented any hasty intrusion into their way of life. Now is the time, at last."

"I understand, Padre," the cacique responded, "and you are wise, for one so young. It is good that you waited, for my people do not know Jesus. But I ask you, until they do, what will this action mean to them? You must teach them the story of Jesus well, before they will know what the water of Baptism brings."

"You are right," Tomás agreed, "and thank you for your advice." The friar pondered for a moment and then it came to him. "I have the perfect way and the perfect time, but you must help me," he insisted.

"Very well," the cacique said cautiously, "and what do you have in mind?"

"You will see very soon," Tomás replied.

The great Christian feast of Christmas was but a few weeks away, and Tomás began to lay the foundations for a Christmas Baptism of the future cacique. He decided to reenact the Christmas story for the Potano people in a dramatic way, using live figures. A presentation of the Christmas story would be his way of introducing the faith into the village and paving the way for the child's Baptism. He began by translating the account of Christ's birth in Luke's Gospel into the Potano tongue. He did the same with familiar Christmas hymns and songs. He then sought a couple of craftsmen to construct a small building resembling a shelter for animals that would be the setting for the Christmas story.

Finding people to audition for roles was easy. Even the cacique wanted a part in the play. Tomás found that the Indian people loved opportunities for celebration in song and dance and dramatic presentations. There was tremendous excitement in the village surrounding the stable that was erected with a star overhead.

For several hours each day, Tomás rehearsed his Potano chorus. The songs sounded well in the Potano language. The singers liked the melodies, even though they contrasted starkly with their own music.

Tomás persisted in his efforts to make this a unique event. He contacted the captain of the military regiment in the area and asked him to supply soldiers to act in the play and to sing in the chorus. He extended an invitation to the Spanish governor from San Agustín to come to witness the event and received a favorable reply.

Tomás wanted with all his heart to leave an indelible memory of this occasion on the minds and hearts of the people. He felt, however, one unique added feature would crown this achievement as a special

Christmas present to the Potano people. To obtain this present, he would have to leave the village for a few days. With the baby placed properly in the care of a mother nursing her own infant, and the cacique duly informed, Tomás departed from the Potano village in the company of Tofu.

A week passed by and only Tofu returned, looking forlorn. When the cacique asked the location of the friar, the outcast said that Tomás had left him with a message to say that all was well and that the priest was in God's hands. Tofu himself, however, didn't look convinced. The cacique accepted the answer, but when Tomás was still missing after a second week, he demanded to know the padre's location. Tofu hesitated, but then agreed to go get him. Two days later, he returned accompanied by Tomás. The Franciscan moved slowly and looked exhausted, but he wore a steady smile. Tofu looked incredibly relieved. However, they were not willing to share at this time the goal of their efforts.

"You will know on the eve of Christmas day," Tomás told the cacique, "on the evening of our celebration, the night before the child's Baptism."

When Christmas Eve arrived, the village was astir with people rehearsing lines and donning costumes. Young and old felt the desire to contribute something to Padre Tomás' spectacle. What it was all about they didn't quite know, but they were enjoying the small part each had to play in the drama unfolding in the village.

Guests began to arrive from outside the village, including the captain of the local Spanish regiment and the governor himself. Tomás proudly welcomed them all. At the appropriate time, they were formally led to their seats. Everyone was resting comfortably, when suddenly a great commotion arose, with shouts of alarm echoing from sentry to sentry at the outskirts of the area.

A lookout rushed to the stage and brought the news: a contingent of enemy Apalachee warriors, accompanied by their cacique, was approaching from the West. Panic washed like a wave through the Potano village. Holata Toloca bellowed commandingly and gained the attention of the crowd. He immediately began to order his tribe's defense, calling some warriors to lead the women and children to safety while others were summoned to join the cacique to face the attackers. The Spanish soldiers looked to their captain to see if they should prepare to join the battle.

When Tomás discovered the cause of alarm, he immediately raised his hands and shouted over the shrill sounds all around him. "Have no fear, have no fear!" he cried out. "The cacique of the Apalachee nation is here not to do battle with the Potano people or the Spanish military. He is here to witness the Christmas pageant of this village. I have invited him."

Toloca looked at him in shock, bordering on anger. "Fray Tomás, what have you done? These people are my enemy! They cannot enter this village!"

Tomás replied, "You asked me to come to your village to bring the message of Christ. That message is peace. Today, I wanted to bring peace to your people and to your enemies, the Apalachee. Everyone please stay seated. We will be back shortly." With that, he and Tofucunatchu proceeded directly to the edge of the village, to greet the cacique of the Apalachee nation.

Before the priest was halfway to his destination, he was overtaken by Holata Toloca and the rest of the chief's handpicked braves, all armed for battle. The Potano cacique paused long enough to say, "I don't know what agreements you made, Padre, but you do not know these people. They are traitorous murderers. If one of them enters this village without my permission I will kill him myself." Then, the war party rushed off to meet the intruders.

"Wait!" Tomás shouted, but the warriors did not stop. With great effort, he and Tofu ran after Toloca.

The Potano village had been built in an area surrounded mostly by water, which came from the river and the sinkholes. The major route into the village was over a land bridge at a point where the river went underground. The tribe's sentries were posted, so if all went as planned, word of danger could be relayed to the village in time for the defenders to reach the land bridge just before any invader. That way an attacker would either have to face the Potano warriors on a relatively narrow strip of land or try to ford the river, in which case the splashing would alert the Potano to the location of the intruder.

Even though the defenders had quickly removed their costumes and extricated themselves from the pageant, doing so had slowed the braves' response, and Holata Toloca desperately hoped the delay had not cost his people this precious advantage. But when he and his men reached the land bridge, the cacique did not see the Apalachee. For a moment, relief flooded his chest only to vanish a moment later, as he looked past the clearing around the land bridge to the woods just beyond. He could see the shadows of men, many of them, lurking there amidst the trees.

Toloca approached the Potano lookout at the land bridge. The sentry looked relieved to see his chieftain and the reinforcement. Toloca asked him, "Is that them?"

"Yes, my cacique," the sentry replied. "They arrived here first, and they could have overrun me. But they stopped out of bow range and have simply been waiting."

"Then we must be cautious," Holata Toloca counseled. "With the Apalachee, it is difficult to know what kind of trap they may be setting."

On the far side of the clearing, the Apalachee warriors waited restlessly, looking expectantly at their cacique, Ybitachucu. He was a timber wolf in the form of a man—gray and white hair, wise eyes, lean, and proud. Despite his age, he looked both dangerous and inspiring. But the confidence of his braves was shaken when they saw the appearance of the Potano warriors.

"Look," shouted a young Apalachee, "I said it was a trap!"

"Great chieftain," said a veteran warrior, "we must either flee or attack now before they are ready."

But Ybitachucu was unmoved.

Back among the Potano, tension rose like a viper preparing to strike.

One of Toloca's warriors spotted Ybitachucu. "See there, the white and gray hair? That is the Apalachee cacique. Holata Toloca, let us attack swiftly, and if we strike well, we can kill the chief of our enemy."

Toloca replied, "But we must know what they are doing, first. It is like they are waiting for something."

"They are waiting for me," said a voice, out of breath. It belonged to Fray Tomás. Without hesitating the priest walked into the clearing heading directly for the Apalachee. At first, the Potano made an attempt to stop him, but no one was willing to run after him into the open and expose himself to enemy arrows. The friar stopped halfway into the clearing, so he could be seen and heard by both groups. First, looking back to the Potano, he said in a loud voice, "Several moons ago, your medicine man and I struggled so that you would know which of us to follow to the Great Spirit—his way or mine. The Great Spirit, the Lord God, prevailed through me. Tonight we celebrate the time when the Great Spirit sent His son, Jesus, to become a man, like us, so that He would be a brother to us. That way, if God, who created us all, could be our brother, then we could be brothers with all people—even our enemies. Holata Toloca, I present to you your brother—Ybitachucu." The priest gestured to the Apalachee chieftain.

"Cacique! The priest is bait," the young Apalachee warned. "Do not take it!"

Ybitachucu gestured abruptly for silence, and he leveled a commanding eye on all of his warriors. "You do nothing unless I give the word." He then moved to meet the friar in the clearing.

Every Potano tensed. For years they had fought and feuded with the Apalachee, and now many were seeing the leader of their great foe for the first time.

A seasoned warrior, Utachu, said, "Cacique, the priest has delivered this wolf into our hands. One arrow and we can be rid of him."

Fray Tomás called out, "Holata Toloca, *por favor*, come. I beg you."

One could see the indecision tearing at the cacique's heart, and yet he said, "Do not attack unless I say." Then, he too went out to the middle of the clearing.

For a moment the braves were stunned, but as many watched with baited breath, Utachu went to talk to the sentry.

"I believe the cacique is being tricked," he said in low voice, "or perhaps he is under a spell. Go to where you will have the best shot, and do what we know must be done."

No one else noticed as the sentry quietly moved away from the group.

On the Apalachee side of the clearing, the veteran warrior held quiet counsel with the young warrior.

"Choose your best vantage point," the older brave said, "and I will choose mine. If anything happens to the cacique, I will put an arrow through their chieftain and you shoot the priest."

The young Apalachee nodded, and they went to take up their positions.

In the middle of the clearing as the two caciques faced each other, Fray Tomás continued speaking so all could hear. "As God put His son into the hands of men, I too put myself into your hands. Holata Ybitachucu, I will sit by your side at the Christmas play. If the Potano harm any of your men at that time, my life is yours. Holata Toloca, pick your most trusted warrior to sit on my other side. If the Apalachee break their promise of peace, then my life is given up to you."

Back at the Potano's side of the clearing, the sentry had found a place that was out of sight of his fellow warriors, but gave him a clear view of Ybitachucu. Before Padre Tomás had even finished his speech, the sentry fitted an arrow in his bow and took aim. Suddenly, a forearm clamped like an iron vice around his throat and a strong hand grabbed his wrist holding the arrow, preventing him from taking the shot. It was Tofucunatchu. He had seen the sentry sneak away and had grown suspicious. Now, he held the would-be assassin helpless.

"What are you doing?" the friar's friend demanded. "You are betraying your cacique and you may cost both him and the priest their lives!"

Just then Tofu felt the sharp tip of a knife press into his ear. Out of the corner of his eye, he could see Utachu holding the blade against his head.

"Let him go, outcast," Utachu said. "You are the last one to talk of betrayal. This is for the good of our people."

Tofu did as commanded.

"Kill the wolf, now!" Utachu said to the sentry. And the lookout pulled back his bow to as ordered.

At the Apalachee side, the veteran and the young brave found clear positions near each other.

"My arrow cannot miss," said the veteran. "Do you have your shot?"

"He will not escape me," the other brave assured him.

They readied their bows.

In the middle of the clearing, Fray Tomás continued, "Jesus, the Son of the Great Spirit, gave up His body to death, so that men might have peace. I must be willing to do the same. I believe that Ybitachucu trusts what I say, but if you do not Holata Toloca, that you may believe, let me show you proof." And with that, friar removed the top of his robes.

Silence fell like a stone on all.

The friar's chest was a mass of scars, so new they glistened red. It looked as if he had been slashed time after time after time, and then each gaping wound had been melted back together. The mystery of the padre's slowness and fatigue was solved. The only mystery that remained was how he survived such abuse. The braves of both tribes were no strangers to warfare and most had seen many battles. But not one could keep from gaping at the friar's wounds.

The sentry lowered his bow, aghast. Utachu's knife dropped to his side, forgotten. Even Tofu could only stare.

The only person who did not seem surprised was Ybitachucu. Instead of gaping, he embraced the padre, and said, "I accept your offer, but you may sit where you like. I have faith in you." Then, he turned to his warriors. "Come!" He ordered, and they obeyed. Turning to the Potano cacique, Ybitachucu said, "Holata Toloca, as Fray Tomás put his life in my hands, I now put the lives of me and my men in yours—unarmed."

Sounds of shock and disagreement came from the Apalachee braves.

"I said leave your weapons!" Ybitachucu insisted. Then he pointed to the veteran and the young brave. "You and you will stay here to watch over our belongings until we return. That is, if you agree, Holata Toloca."

Toloca was finally able to close his mouth. It had been hanging open for quite some time. Soon after, he found his voice. "I...I agree. With a man like Fray Tomás to speak for you, I could do no less," Toloca responded. "As long as you are in my village, you will come to no harm."

The Apalachee warriors did as they were told, and they were escorted to the pageant with Toloca and the priest leading them.

The crowd had grown worried and restless during their absence, and the captain of the Spanish regiment approached the friar as he returned.

"You had us quite concerned, Padre Tomás. We were just about to come after you. *¿Está bién?* (Is everything all right?)" the commander asked.

Fray Tomás just smiled and nodded. The rest of the assembly remained motionless, as they watched an event unfold before their eyes that amazed everyone in the village. The cacique of the Apalachee nation was personally seated by Tomás. He sat next to the Spanish governor and the captain of the military regiment. This was to be Fray Tomás' Christmas present to the Potano people.

The Potano warriors, who had stayed to guard the village, laid down their weapons and the villagers, who had hidden in panic, returned. Tomás rose and called the cast of Indians and Spanish military to come forward to take their positions. The actors who had left came back, and the cast resumed their costumes and their places.

All were dressed in the clothing proper to Palestinian people in the time of Jesus, with the Potano cacique acting as Joseph, the wife of the captain as Mary; and Kocha, as the baby Jesus. Potano villagers were dressed as shepherds; Spanish military personnel were dressed as the three Kings, with their large retinues. Cattle and sheep were even brought in to complement the scene.

The play began.

VIII

Clad in his best Potano finery, a young Indian who had just graduated to being a warrior acted as the narrator:

"In those days Caesar Augustus published a decree ordering a census of the whole world. This first census took place while Quirinius was governor of Syria. Everyone went to register, each to his own town. And so Joseph went from the town of Nazareth in Galilee to Judea, to David's town of Bethlehem—because he was of the house and lineage of David —to register with Mary, his espoused wife, who was with child.

"While they were there the days of her confinement were completed. She gave birth to her first-born son and wrapped him in swaddling clothes and laid him in a manger, because there was no room for them in the place where travelers lodged...."

All the while the narrative continued, one could hear a pin drop, so rapt was everyone's attention in the dramatic presentation and at the diverse array of guests in the audience who were present for this event.

The story continued with "Joseph" and "Mary" finding nowhere to stay, the holy couple taking shelter in the stable, the birth of Jesus and the coming of the shepherds and the wise men. At the end of the description of Jesus' birth, given by the Indian warrior all by memory, the crowd cheered loudly in praise of the performance. Then they waited for the next part of the program.

Tomás raised his hands, and the choir of Indians formed. With Tomás as director, a beautiful Spanish Christmas melody, sung in the dialect of the Potano people, glided to the ears of all assembled. One song after another followed, bringing a sense of joy and peace to the hearts of all who were present.

At the end of the drama, Tomás turned and thanked everyone who had come and told them that the little infant in the crib represented Jesus the Son of the Great Spirit who had become one with all the world. The Great Spirit, the Lord God, did this by sending His son, Jesus, to become a little child like all of them. This was the great mystery of the Christian faith that he had come to preach to the Potano people.

"Although we are people of different lands and nations," the priest explained, "the Great Spirit is with us here tonight, and He is among us whenever we come together, in His name, as brothers and sisters and friends. The Great Spirit has brought us here so that we will know why He sent His only son, Jesus, into this world as a little child like Kocha. Jesus came to bring peace to all peoples.

"The Great Spirit is present in the life of Jesus in a unique and special way," Tomás said. "The child, Jesus, is the Great Spirit, and He will touch the life of Kocha tomorrow, on Christmas day, when Kocha will receive the water of Baptism." Tomás insisted, "We can not become the Great Spirit. However, Kocha and anyone who so desires will become like Jesus by Baptism. This special blessing will help Kocha, and anyone who receives Baptism, to bring the gifts of peace and happiness to the people of our land, which the infant Jesus first brought to our world. And it will bring those baptized to life everlasting."

"Let us thank the Great Spirit for bringing us together tonight. May He bless us in many ways in all the days to come." Tomás did not know how his message registered with his listeners, but at least they were attentive. He thought that they still might be shocked at the interesting group of people he had assembled for the Christmas pageant. But he hoped what he said would have an effect.

Then, the cacique of the Apalachee nation drew near with a smile on his face. When the cacique of the Potano people, still dressed as Joseph, came next to him also, Tomás knew he had accomplished something.

The Apalachee leader chuckled and said, "Holata Toloca, I prefer to see you dressed in this way, with a robe and shepherd's staff, than to see you in war paint with a bow and arrow."

The Potano cacique smiled, and the smile was contagious to all the people around them. A brief discourse ensued between the two chiefs, which was not overheard by the rest of the crowd. The cacique of the Apalachee then signaled to his warriors, and with profuse signs of gratitude and affection, they thanked Toloca and the friar who had invited them to his Christmas celebration. Immediately afterward, they left, and Tomás escorted them to the edge of the village.

"Fray Tomás," the Potano leader called to the priest when he returned. When Tomás came over to him, he said, "I thank you for what you did here this evening. When I first heard you had brought the Apalachee upon us, I was about to deliver you into the arms of the Great Spirit forever. But, I realize now that you are a wise teacher, who will bring much good to my people. I just never know how you will surprise me next.... But I have a surprise for you, as well."

At that point, there emerged from the back of the audience a familiar face. It was Fray Buenaventura, the *confrere* of Tomás who had abandoned him early in the mission. Now, he came with an abashed look and out-stretched arms.

"Tomás, *mi hermano in Cristo,* (my brother in Christ) I come to seek your forgiveness and offer you again my assistance, if you will consider taking me back. You can't imagine how tortured my soul has been since I abandoned you. Please forgive me. I—I have decided to leave my mission, Nombre de Dios in San Agustín, to accept the challenge of serving here permanently with you. That is…if you will take me back."

Tomás said nothing, but simply opened his arms to receive his companion and friend. He blinked hard to keep back the tears in his eyes, and there was much joy in his heart and great hope for their future labors together.

Christmas Eve became a night of peace and reconciliation for all who set foot in the Potano village.

The celebration of the Baptism of Kocha flowed naturally from the events of the evening before. The cacique was to be the Godfather. The wife of the captain of the military garrison was invited to be the Godmother. Fray Tomás, assisted by Fray Buenaventura, prepared to celebrate the Baptism.

Before the sacrament began, the Spanish governor, accompanied by the head of the local garrison, Captain Mérida, pulled the young priest aside.

"A moment, *por favor,* Fray Tomás," the politician said.

The young priest nodded.

"I would like to say a few words before the ceremony, to mark this historic occasion."

"By all means, Your Excellency," Tomás replied.

"Oh, and I would like to congratulate you on doing an excellent job here, my young friend," the governor continued. "I'll admit that you had everyone nervous yesterday when that other group of savages showed up from Apalachee.

Captain Mérida added, "I saw the look on our Potano cacique's face when they arrived, and I thought that if the Apalachees didn't scalp you, he would."

The friar blushed and said, "Perhaps my plan was a bit rash, but it did work."

"Yes, it certainly did," the captain interjected. "In fact, I was thinking of asking the governor to put a garrison here, but after seeing what happened yesterday, and with this baptism today, I believe that can wait. You have done a great service to the king by saving him much in material and supplies."

"Not to mention pay for more soldiers," the governor added.

"A garrison? Here?" Tomás said, taken aback. "I was hoping not to have a garrison here unless it was absolutely necessary. But, I appreciate your words, though all thanks should go to God."

"Yes, of course, of course," the governor interrupted. "But thanks and honor should also be given to our king, who had the foresight to go forth into the New World. The land of this village is rich, and it will do much to provide supplies and labor to expand the territory and the glory of Mother Spain."

"But this isn't just about more land for España," Tomás countered. "This is also about converting souls for the greater glory of God."

"Ah, but the greater glory of España is the greater Glory of God," the governor replied. "Is not España God's country and King Ferdinand the servant of God? That is why the pope declared him Defender of the Faith. But I don't need to argue these semantics with you, Fray Tomás. We are of the same ilk."

The captain clapped Fray Tomás on the shoulder, "Exactly. You and I are alike, Padre—men in the battlefield. We know how this game works. Not like some cloistered monks or noblemen in the courts, waxing philosophical about God miraculously converting nations of brutes as soon as a man in a habit holding a Bible sets foot on the shore."

"They are not brutes, Captain," Tomás interrupted. "I have lived among them and—"

"Then look at them!" Captain Mérida exclaimed, while still trying to keep his voice low. "They fight with stone arrows; they run around practically naked in this wilderness. They respect the Spanish sword, not a Bible they cannot read. I mean no offense, Padre. You friars are necessary. It is not as if the bishops are going to come out to the frontier to preach to these heathens. I mean to say, where would the Gospel be without men, like you, forsaking home and country to come here? But, where would you be without the military to carve the way? Remember Guale? That is where you would be."

"Gentlemen, gentlemen. We all had a hand in this. It is simply necessary that everyone, savages included, understands the importance of this day," the governor lectured while smoothing the ruffles on his dress jacket. "And time to take some recognition where recognition is due."

Before Tomás had a chance to say anything more, Captain Mérida and the governor strode out in front of the altar.

Fray Buenaventura whispered in a panic, "Did I hear correctly?" As Fray Tomás nodded, he said, "This will cause an uproar and scandal. Or at the very least, it will completely rob the sacred meaning of this event!"

Fray Tomás knew Buenaventura's words were true. The young priest said, "And they're treating it as if it was their victory and not God's and ours."

The governor addressed the crowd. "My fellow countrymen, my good friars, natives of La Florida. Today the Potano people take a significant step toward becoming one with España, the greatest nation on earth. And today we have taken a step closer to increasing Spain, and making certain her glory never fades."

"Just as God's glory never fades," Fray Tomás suddenly spoke as he quickly and graciously moved to the font that was set up for the Baptism. "Thank you so much for your kind words, Your Excellency." As the governor looked on with his mouth open, and indignation and rage building in his face, Fray Tomás proceeded to take the baby in his hands and raise him up in a great gesture of profound gratitude and praise. "To the Great Spirit, God the Almighty," the friar intoned, "I now offer this child, the future cacique of the Potano people. May You receive him, Great Father and Lord of All, into Your hands and bring Him to Your heart so he may find there true peace and joy and happiness. May he receive from You, in the Sacrament of Baptism, all that he needs. Through this sacrament may he gain the grace to know You, to love You, and to serve You as a great leader of his people and a loyal devoted servant of You, his Lord and his God. Into your hands I now commend his spirit."

With these words, Tomás continued with the age-old ritual of Baptism that brought to Kocha, whose baptismal name was also to be 'Tomás,' a new life in union with the Great Spirit. "Tomás, I baptize you in the name of the Father, and of the Son, and of the Holy Spirit," Fray Tomás stated slowly, as he poured the baptismal water on the child's forehead.

Many Potano people followed the event with great attention, feeling that what was good for the future cacique must be good for them, as well. All would mark Christmas Eve and Christmas day as the time when the Christian way of life entered this Potano village. Only a few noticed the glares and angry silence given to the priests by the governor and Captain Mérida as these two men left the village with their retinues.

IX

Since his arrival in the Potano village, Fray Tomás had experienced the great hatred and animosity of the Potano for the neighboring Apalachee nation to the west. This hatred had erupted many times, often culminating in treacherous raids by both parties into enemy territory, leading to great loss of life. The taking of scalps as booty of war, as well as the dismemberment of body parts, reflected the depravity and hostility that existed between the two nations.

Tomás' overture to invite the seventy-year-old cacique of the Ivitachuco tribe of the Apalachees to his Christmas pageant was an event unheard of in the history of relations between the Timucuans and Apalachees and the cause of much conversation, as well as consternation. Tomás decided he could not, and should not, let his Christmas peace venture rest as an isolated event in history. He had opened a door. Now he must tear down the wall that surrounded it.

Tomás' rationale was simple. Peace will work, if given a chance, because people prefer peace to war.

Shortly after the new year began, he ventured to the dwelling of the Potano cacique, Toloca, with a request. "Holata Toloca, you and the cacique of Ivitachuco have met for the first time outside of battle, and your meeting seemed to be for the two of you a very happy occasion. I would hope to see the prospect of some future meeting with the leader of Apalachee. Indeed, I would not be reluctant to act again as an emissary for you and your people, if you would find the use of my services helpful."

"Fray Tomás," Toloca interjected with a wry smile, "when has there ever been reluctance on your part to take on any difficult venture since your arrival here in my village? Why should you be afraid of another one?" The priest blushed and the chieftain chuckled at his own joke. "In seriousness, I was wondering when you would approach me about this. It has been on my mind too, since talking with the great cacique of Ivitachuco.

"And I am happy to share with you what he said to me privately after your Christmas celebration," Toloca confided. "He told me that during the seventy years of his life, he had known the people of Timucua only as enemies. In the remaining years of his life, he would like to know some of them as friends. I share the cacique's feelings, Padre. I would like to know some of the Apalachee people as friends. And I think you are the person who can help me to become friends with them.

"Before enlisting your services, though, there is something I must know. How did you convince Ybitachucu to come to our village? And your scars …you are a priest, but those are the scars of a warrior. Among my people, a warrior's story is his own, but I must admit, curiosity burns within me. As leader of my people I wish to know."

The padre considered for a moment, "Do you remember the night Kuteli passed out of this world?" When the chief nodded, he continued, "That is when it began."

✳

A man lay dying on a low straw bed. Two arrows stuck out of his body. He tried to breathe. It was a struggle, and his face contorted in pain with the effort. It was a homely face, broad and round, but welcoming despite the agony that twisted it. It was a Potano face that belonged to Kuteli, a member of the cacique's council. He was in his forties and had the massive body of a born fighter. But the fighter had fallen. His wounds seeped blood as red as the embers in the flickering fire.

As Fray Tomás looked on, the healer of the village, a woman named Nyalatchu, examined the body with a trained eye. Her baby daughter, not quite a year old, stood nearby, watching with wide eyes. It struck Fray Tomás again, how in this wilderness Life and Death stood so often side-by-side.

Holota Toloca was also present, and he talked to two other Potano tribesmen who related what had happened. Kuteli and these braves had been hunting to the west. They had been tracking a marsh boar, which had made so much noise they had not heard the other hunting party also tracking the animal. Kuteli and his men came upon the boar at the same time as three Apalachee. The boar was immediately forgotten, and the fight began. Without hesitation, Kuteli charged and was hit by two arrows, but he still killed the nearest enemy with his *macana*. The second Apalachee was struck down by arrows from the other Potano braves, and the third fled after he missed with his bow shot. The Potano would have pursued but decided against it. They did not say that Kuteli's wounds kept them from following. That would have been an insult, and Kuteli was much respect-ed by the tribe. His companions proudly stated that, despite his blood loss, the elder tribesman walked by himself to within a mile of the village. At that time, he collapsed and the other two carried him to his home, but they did not mention that aloud either.

The healer stood up with an air of finality. Kuteli twisted to look into her face. He saw no hope in her eyes. His head sank back down again. The healer touched his cheek in a gesture of comfort, then washed the blood off her hands, and picked up her child to leave.

As she passed the cacique, she nodded her head in respect and said, in a low voice, "There is nothing I can do. If I pull out the arrows, he will only die faster."

Toloca clenched his jaw trying not to show grief. He nodded. Then the healer signaled Kuteli's wives to follow her so she could tell them and the family who waited just outside the *buhio*. Toloca approached the fallen war-rior, and they clasped forearms. Toloca praised him for his bravery and spoke of their friendship. Through his pain Kuteli joked, that it took two arrow wounds to make Toloca say nice things about him. Toloca laughed and then choked on the sorrow that immediately followed the laughter. He would not say good-bye. To do so was strictly taboo, because it was believed that doing so would seal the dying man's fate even more surely than the healer's words. The chieftain told Kuteli that Fray Tomás greatly wished to speak with him. Kuteli looked over to the young priest, and after a moment, nodded.

As Fray Tomás knelt by the wounded man's side, Kuteli coughed and drops of blood flecked his lips. As the fit passed, he asked, "What do you want of me, Brown Robe?"

Fray Tomás responded, "I want to baptize you and have you accept Jesus Christ, the Son of the Great Spirit, as your Savior. If you do this, He will bring you to Paradise."

"Paradise?" Kuteli forced out the word. "Where is that? Is it across the great waters with the cacique of España?"

"No, it is in heaven," the priest replied.

"I do not know this 'Paradise,' " the Potano warrior stated, "and I do not know your Jesus."

Fray Tomás continued determined, "He is the Cacique of caciques, the Prince of Peace."

"I do not see peace here," Kuteli said. "We have Nicoguadco and

Ivitachuco, God of War and Son of Thunder. They are the gods I know. I respect you, Fray Tomás, and your magic is strong, but your ways and your savior are strangers to me. I am a Potano and that is the way I will always be. Now, I must rest."

"But the Potano ways and the Christian ways can be one," Fray Tomás protested. "I offer you everlasting life."

Kuteli coughed violently, interrupting the priest. Fray Tomás heard sounds behind him, and he turned to see that the family was making its way into the dwelling. Some looked indignant and others were murmuring angrily that the priest was making the wounded man talk too much. The Franciscan did not want to cause the man suffering, but he believed with all his heart in the words of Christ, that Baptism held the key to life everlasting, that a man must be born of "fire and the Spirit" to enter the kingdom of heaven. This man's soul hung in the balance, and the priest felt he had to try to bring him into the family of God now, because the Indian's time was short.

When the coughing stopped, more blood trickled from Kuteli's mouth. He stared far off as if looking for something. Then he shook his head. His voice was thick with fluid when he spoke. "No, Pale Skin, I cannot see it. Go. Let me rest."

The Franciscan's heart fell, and he wanted to say more, but he felt a hand on his shoulder. It was the cacique, he looked into the priest's eyes and shook his head. Reluctantly, Fray Tomás came away. As he left the *buhio*, he could not help but feel he had lost this battle, and all he could do was shake his head. That and pray. And Fray Tomás did pray.

In his room, he knelt down once again, and begged God for help. This time he did not plea for his life but for the life of Kutleli: that the Lord might somehow spare the warrior and open his heart to Jesus and to salvation. He prayed that way late into the night, interrupted only when Kocha whimpered and cried. The priest picked up the child and rocked him, but the friar was still in deep thought. When the infant settled, Fray Tomás went back on his knees and that was the way Tofu found him in the morning.

The Indian came to check on his friend, and when he saw the Franciscan kneeling, he was concerned. "Padre, are you well?" he asked.

Fray Tomás could only answer with a question, "Is Kuteli...?" He let the sentence dangle, unsure of the proper custom to use in what he was asking.

"He is dead, Padre." Tofu responded.

Fray Tomás sagged back, and Tofu moved to his side worried, but the priest slowly rose, on his stiff legs.

"Why were you kneeling?" The outcast asked, after Fray Tomás had steadied himself.

"To talk to the Great Spirit," the priest responded.

Tofu thought a moment and then said, "Why do you have to kneel?"

Fray Tomás shook his head and then said, "You don't, but God is the Lord and Maker of everything, all people, all animals, all the lands and waters. He knows all things both past and future. I am just a man. I kneel because I am His servant. I want to be humble before Him, when I come asking His help."

"Did He answer?" Tofu queried. "I did not hear a voice."

"I believe He did answer. But He spoke to my heart not to my ears, so He did not need words," Fray Tomás explained.

"I don't understand, Padre," Tofu admitted.

"I don't understand it myself, friend; yet I feel it to be true," Fray Tomás said. He wandered over to Kocha's small bed and stared down at the child fondly. He ruffled the sleeping infant's hair. Tofu followed him, waiting. Tomás looked at him. "I feel I now know what I must do. Were you not a mighty warrior?"

Tofu was taken aback. He had not expected this question. When he replied both pain and pride had crept into his voice. "Before you came, I was a *nicoguadca*."

"Is that not the highest rank of warrior?" The padre went on to ask.

"Yes. There was once a time when the name Tofucunatchu was much feared by our enemies," he replied. His voice became distant.

"Does that include the Apalachee? Did you ever raid their great village to the west?"

Brought back to the present by the question, the former brave nodded.

"I need you to take me there," the priest stated.

Shock slapped across Tofu's face. He could not have looked more surprised than if the priest had asked him to go to the moon. "Why?" Tofu was not one to mince his words.

"Because I must go to the chief of Appalachee and give him an invitation. I will welcome him to come to our Christmas Pageant and to visit the village of the Potano as a friend in an offer of peace," Tomás explained.

"Padre, what you say cannot be done. The Apalachee are cruel and without mercy. They will kill us on sight, or capture us and sacrifice us as soon as they return to their village. You will die before you are able to say your words. You must have heard the Great Spirit wrong," Tofu concluded.

Tomás shook his head. "I do not think so. In a short time, we will celebrate the birth of Jesus, the Prince of Peace, the Son of the Great Spirit —and that will mean nothing to this village. I don't blame them, because Jesus will be like a story told to children, pleasant but something that no one really believes. That is unless someone makes Jesus real. He came to bring peace to the world. He loved us so much that He was willing to die to give us that peace and life everlasting. The founder of my order, San Francisco, used to pray, 'Lord, make me an instrument of Your peace.' How can I call myself his follower, or a follower of Jesus, unless I spread that peace?" The priest inhaled slowly trying to come to terms with the decision he was about to make, "At least I must try. Otherwise, your people will never understand and never see. Like Kuteli."

"But this is certain death," Tofu stated.

"Perhaps not," replied the priest. "Long ago, in the time of my father's father, a group of explorers from España went into Apalachee territory. At first they fought with the Apalachee, but eventually, a treaty was made that lasted a number of years. When these explorers continued their journey, contact was lost; but the Apalachee may still respect this treaty. I could try to bring soldiers with me, but that might seem like an invasion. It would probably require permission from the governor, and my superior, and maybe even the Great Cacique of España. That could take months, and who knows how many more lives will be lost in that time."

Tofu added, "Even if the Spanish again made a treaty with the Apalachee, that does not concern the Potano. We would probably still be at war."

"Yes, and the Spanish governor might not see that it was his duty to get involved in a tribal war," Fray Tomás added to the Indian's observation. "It may be the greatest risk for us, but I believe the quickest way to stop the killing is for me to speak with the Apalachee chief myself. I need you to take me as close to the village as you think it is safe for you to go, and then I will continue alone."

"And if I will not take you?" the tribesman asked.

The padre thought a moment. "I would understand…but then I would go to San Agustín, find those old explorers' maps, and try to find the way myself."

"And what if Holata Toloca will not let you go?" Tofu asked trying to find anything to dissuade the friar.

"I am not asking him," Fray Tomás stated. "When my people give gifts, the giver surprises the person he gives it to. I have been trying to think of a gift to give to your village to honor the birth of the Lord, as He gave us the gift of Himself. This will be my gift to your people."

"Is there no way I can stop you?" the brave finally asked.

At that question, the priest smiled, "No."

Tofu let out a deep sigh. "I will take you," he conceded. "But I have one demand. Teach me your way of fighting."

Fray Tomás was taken aback, and he gave a short laugh. "I am trying to establish peace and you want me to show you how to hit people?"

Tofu shook his head. "I would like to help you with this peace, Padre. But I am not ready to give up the ways of a warrior. When I sought to kill you, though, you stopped me and we both lived. If my enemy tried to plant a *macana* in my head, do you know how I would stop him?"

When Fray Tomás indicated he did not, Tofu continued, "I would drive my knife into his heart. That would stop him, but he would not live."

Fray Tomás gave a wry grin. "Do you know what a 'lawyer' is, Tofu?"

The brave shook his head, no.

"Well, you would make a good one," the priest said. "I agree to your demand."

Rays of sunlight rained like gold through the canopy of palmetto fronds and branches of live oak. It provided enough illumination for Tofu to lead Fray Tomás along a creek that cut through a narrow ravine. They halted just before the ravine opened up to a wide valley. In the far distance, smoke from many fires could be seen, and a single large hut seemed to rise above the lush vegetation around it.

"There," Tofu pointed, "is the great Apalachee village, Ivituchuco. Here, we must part. Any farther and we may be seen by sentries. If they find us together, it will doom your mission and mean my death, and probably yours, as well. Follow the water, Padre, and you should be there before sundown."

"Thank you, my friend," said Fray Tomás. "Please meet me back here three days from now. Hopefully, it will not take that long. But if four days have passed, and I have still not come, then return to Potano." The priest took a deep breath. "I will probably be dead."

Tofu nodded grimly, and they clasped forearms. Then came a distinct crack as a twig or tree branch snapped nearby. Instantly, the Potano brave was alert. Tomás started to ask him what was the matter, but Tofu gestured for him to be silent. Then came a birdcall, and Tofu's eyes went wide. He leaned toward the priest and whispered, "That was not a bird! Run!"

The two men sprinted back into the ravine, but Fray Tomás stumbled on a branch. Then they heard the sound of many feet running in their direction. Tofu rushed back to the friar to help him up, but Fray Tomás whispered, "No. This is why I came, to be found; but you must go." Tofu hesitated and the priest hissed, "Go!"

The outcast nodded and dashed off. Moments later, Apalachee warriors burst into the ravine, their bows at the ready. Thin tattoos were etched across their faces, and feathers were tied into their braided hair. They were paler than the Potanos, and maybe a few fingers shorter, but they were broader and more thickly built.

Fray Tomás raised his hands to show that they were empty. The braves immediately surrounded him, their arrow heads inches from him. If they even slipped, he would be skewered instantly. The lead sentry yelled something at him in Apalachee. Tomás did not understand and looked at him confused. The leader grunted in anger, lowered his bow, grabbed his knife, and went for the friar's throat.

Fray Tomás quickly rattled off the only Apalachee he knew. He had learned it specifically for this journey. "Greetings. I come in peace. My name is Padre Tomás Sanchez of España. I come to speak with your cacique words of peace and words of treaty."

The leader hesitated. His knife inches from the priest's neck. He glared at the priest suspiciously. He made a demand again in his language, but all Tomás could do was shrug and shake his head. One of the warriors spoke to the leader, who nodded, then said, "Tsst-tsst" to two of the braves. The braves moved cautiously but quickly down the ravine in the direction Tofu disappeared. They were on the hunt.

The leader then spoke grimly to the padre, and pressed his blade into the soft part of the priest's throat. Tomás could not understand the words, but the threat was obvious; whatever happened on that hunt, his life hung in the balance. He silently prayed with all his might for himself and Tofucunatchu.

For his part, Tofu ran as fast as he could while still trying to remain as silent as possible. The floor of the ravine was rocky, and there was a chance the sentries had not seen him. If he could make it far enough away undetected, the Apalachees might not know he even existed, and he and the priest might survive this deadly encounter.

He came to a fork in the ravine. One way was narrow, the other wider. He and the priest had originally come through the narrow path, but if he went back that way, there would be nowhere to hide from his pursuers, and he could be easily caught. He decided to take the wider, untried path. If luck were on his side, his pursuers would take the wrong fork. But luck seemed indifferent today, because Tofu's trained ears could hear the sentries' voices; they had paused at the intersection, carefully weighing which way to go.

Then luck seemed to turn against the Potano. As he tried to quietly climb over a fallen tree, some rotted bark gave way, spilling him to the ground. To make matters worse, he knew those who hunted him must have heard the cracking bark. Just as he suspected, the hushed voices went silent, and he knew they were coming his way. Then, when he stood up, his foot kicked some small pebbles. They bounced forward then suddenly disappeared into the sandy ground before him with a soft "plop." Quicksand! A pit of it lay right before him. When Tofu looked more carefully, he could see that the far end of the fallen tree lay half submerged in it. The Potano tribesman could see where on the far left of the ravine there was what looked like solid ground, but the problem with quicksand was that where there was one pit, there were often more. The wise thing to do would be to grab a tree branch and slowly pick his way along, testing the ground at every step. But there was no time for that solution. He could hear his pursuers just moments behind him. His choices were either to try to climb the sides of the ravine, and almost certainly be spotted, or he could sprint on ahead and just hope the earth didn't swallow him. The Apalachee were almost on top of him. He had to decide now.

The two Apalachees leapt over the fallen tree, and noticed the crumbled bark where Tofu had slipped. But there was no one in sight. They looked warily around the area. One brave motioned to the other to be careful of the quicksand. The second sentry nodded. They had patrolled this way before, and they knew of the dangers.

The first warrior relaxed and said disgustedly, "I think we chase shadows."

"No," replied the second. "I heard someone. And look at that broken tree bark. Someone has been this way."

The first warrior gave a deep sigh, "Humph! Do you think he fell into the quicksand?"

The second shook his head, "We would still see him struggling."

"Then he must have moved on. Hurry!" the first sentry said.

The two man-hunters skirted the pitfall and rushed off in haste.

A moment after they had gone, what looked like a clump of dirt shook as it clung to a branch of the fallen tree that stuck into the quicksand. The clump was a hand. Then a second hand shot forth from the quicksand and grabbed higher on the branch. With a heave, Tofu hauled himself out of the morass. He gasped for air and then struggled to quiet his breathing so as not to give himself away. Tofu crouched by the fallen tree for a moment, as he listened for the sentries. Then he heard them moving deeper into the ravine, and silently, he slipped away in the opposite direction.

X

Fray Tomás had been waiting for what seemed to be an eternity, not knowing if the next moment might be his last. The lead sentry had grown tired of holding his knife to the priest's throat, and had forced the padre to kneel while they kept their bows and arrows in hand. Then, they bound his wrists with coarse rope braided out of palm fronds. If he tried to run, he would be a porcupine before he even made it to his feet. He sensed they were waiting for some word from the other sentries, but he could not tell for what. He had even lost track of what decade of the Rosary he was on, he had been praying it so much. He found himself getting lost in the Sorrowful Mysteries, which were all reflections on the death of Christ. He was somewhere before the decade of Christ carrying the Cross, as the sun hovered just above the horizon.

"…Deliver us from evil. Amen." As the priest finished yet another Our Father, the two other sentries returned empty-handed. The leader asked them a question. The two braves shook their heads. Fray Tomás could not understand their Apalachee, but he knew that they had not found Tofu. He breathed a sigh of relief. The leader shot him a sharp look, and the padre covered the sigh with an exclamation to God and started another prayer. The leader turned his attention back to his hunters.

"There is no one else," the first hunter reported.

"But we heard two men talking," the leader countered.

The second hunter shook his head, "We heard this man talking. We thought it was to someone else, maybe he was just talking to himself."

"This fool has been muttering to himself the entire time you were gone," interjected the sentry who had stayed with the leader.

"Maybe he was casting a spell," said the first hunter. "I heard brown robe Spanish do that."

"The shaman says they are crazy," said the second hunter.

The sentries had initially thought that they heard two men moving through the forest. That was why the leader sent the two sentries to see whether the friar was alone, or perhaps part of a scouting party, or maybe even a war party. But one could never tell with these Palefaces. They often made so much noise in the brush that one or two could sound like a war party. It was amazing that they managed to catch anything while hunting. Also, stories said that the Spanish wearing brown robes often talked to themselves. Some said they were praying to the Great Spirit, other said they talked to invisible allies, and other said that the brown robes were insane.

"But you are certain he was alone, that there was no one else?" the leader pressed.

The hunting sentries were not certain, but they had not found anyone. To admit that there was the possibility of another man, and that he had escaped, would be a shame to their reputations as both trackers and guardians of the village.

"We are certain," the first hunter said.

The leader nodded, then glared at Fray Tomás. The priest simply repeated the little Apalachee speech he had learned. The leader grunted derisively then started barking out orders. Two of the men vanished back into to the woods to their posts. Another hauled Tomás to his feet and soon the priest found himself being led, the leader in front of him, and another guard behind him, just like his Potano escorts so many months ago. This time, however, they ran. They cut away from the creek and soon hit a wide road. It was overgrown and unkempt but still much easier to move through than the sumac. On this route, they made good time. Before sunset, they had reached the great Apalachee village of Ivitachuco.

Fray Tomás caught only glimpses of the village, because his hands were tied and his captors moved swiftly. After stumbling badly once, the priest realized that, if he didn't keep his eyes on his feet, he would quickly find himself tripping head-over-heels. He could only look up occasionally, but when he did, he saw more *buhios*, more people, and more sentries than he could count. Many more. The village had to be at least one-and-a-half times the size of the Potano village and twice as well guarded. The more startling difference between the two villages, however, was the huge mound in the center of the compound. It loomed like a massive manmade hill rising out of the earth. Fray Tomás glimpsed a lone building residing on the top.

But before Tomás had time to ponder this edifice, his guards threw him to the ground. One pressed a spear to the back of his neck. Fear rose in the friar. He tried not to show it, but it threatened to choke him.

All that the priest could see was a pair of feet that strode up to him. They were old and yellowed but strong. Then the blade of the spear on the back of his neck was moved to under his chin forcing him to look up at the one standing over him. It was the Apalachee cacique, Ybitachucu, wrinkled and gray, yet lean and commanding. Faded tattoos lined his face, streaked down from his chin and spilled across his body. He regarded the priest with cold, imperious eyes.

The shaman, a rock-like man of hard, knotted muscle, accompanied Ybitachucu. However, one of the medicine man's arms was withered and deformed. He wore buffalo horns on his head, a necklace of animal fangs around his neck, and black stripes of paint across his face. He glared with open hostility at the Franciscan.

A crowd started to gather at this spectacle.

The sentry leader did the cacique homage, then gave his report. The cacique nodded and the sentry prodded the padre with his spear. Once more, Fray Tomás gave his memorized message. He actually had a longer message that he wanted to say to the cacique. It was written on a piece of paper tucked inside his robes. Since the Apalachee had no written language, he had sounded the words out on the paper. But he could not reach the note now, and he was at a loss for what to do. He tried talking to them in Spanish, to ask them to untie his hands so he could get that note. But his Spanish words met with impassive stares. He tried to reach in his robes with tied hands, but the sentry pushed in his spear tip just enough to break the friar's skin—and stop his struggling. Fray Tomás' heart fell. He had held out on the hope that the Apalachee would respect him as a Spaniard, maybe even know some of the language from the years the explorers had lived among these people. But if these Indians knew any Spanish, they didn't show it. The dirt on his face showed how much they respected him. He had the sudden feeling that his life would be stripped from him as quickly as his hopes.

The shaman spoke, "I have told you before, Cacique, all Spanish are dangerous, especially the Franciscans. He is a trick sent by the Potano to destroy us. Let me sacrifice him, now, for the good of the village."

"For the good of the village, Nytuchko? Or for your own good?" asked Ybitachucu. "I do not much trust the Spanish and the Potano not at all. But I have heard in the wind that a brown robe came to the Potano and his magic swallowed the shaman. Now they have no shaman, but a Franciscan. Maybe this is the same brown robe. Maybe he has come to swallow you."

The shaman gave a startled look at the chieftain, and his face betrayed that the cacique's barb had struck close to the heart. But Nytuchko quickly recovered and replied indignantly, "I do not fear him, and I will show you that he is a liar. Give him to me. Let me take him to Ivitachuco's *buhio*, and I will make him speak the truth!"

"Very well," Ybitachucu consented. "For I would know the truth of this man."

A moment later, Fray Tomás was being hauled up the great mound to the dwelling at the top. Sweat, cold and thick, pooled under his arms and ran down his body. He had the distinct impression he was being marched to his death. It was that same heavy dread he had felt when he had been brought to Matala's *buhio* to be executed. The urge to run gripped him. He slowed his pace, the spear tip poked into his back; rough hands tried to shove him forward. Still the thought came that he could fight his way past the guard and at least make a run for it.

But then Fray Tomás remembered his blackened crucifix, the twisted figure of Jesus, and the words from the Bible, "Jesus went to His death, like a lamb led to the slaughter." Lambs did not resist when they were brought to be killed; out of love, neither did Jesus. Because of His sacrifice, men still sung His praises sixteen hundred years later. As if lifting huge weights, Fray Tomás put one foot in front of the other and once again moved forward into the hut on the mound.

Once inside, the priest saw that, even though it might once have been a residence, it was now empty except for a number of macabre relics he could only assume were for religious purposes. There were skeletons of animals, human skulls, ceremonial weapons and headdresses, and what he thought at first was a tapestry hanging from floor to ceiling. He then realized these were scalps mounted side by side on the wall. In the center was a crude crossbeam standing alone. The priest did not understand its purpose, until he saw the bindings on the top. The shaman strode up to the priest and drew a knife. It had a stone blade and a bone handle. He brought it within inches of the priest's face.

"I come in peace.... " Fray Tomás protested.

Ignoring the friar's attempts to communicate, the shaman moved past Fray Tomás and thrust the blade in a clay pot full of burning coals. The medicine man gestured to the guard who swiftly struck the Franciscan in the back of the knees with his spear. Fray Tomás' legs buckled and he toppled to the ground. Suddenly, he felt his world twist upside-down as his ankles were lashed to the crossbeam, his head hanging a foot off the floor. The leather bindings bit into his flesh as they held his weight, and his blood rushed into his brain, making his ears pound. Then the guards stripped the robes off of his body, and left him dangling like the day's fresh kill.

"Leave him in my hands, Holata Ybitachucu," the shaman said. "I will have the truth out of him soon enough." He pulled the knife from the coals and smoke licked off of the blade.

Ybitachucu nodded, then added, "His answers are important to me. Question him. If he dies, so be it. But if I find that you have killed him deliberately, you will answer to me." He held the shaman in his gaze so there could be no uncertainty. Then he strode away, but before he reached the bottom of the hill, he could hear the priest's screams.

The evening drew on and in his *buhio,* the cacique stood pondering, lost in thought as his eyes watched the flickering fire. Then the door guard called from outside, breaking his reverie, "The Ursolina, to see you." *Ursolina* meant "favorite child," in this case his daughter. Though Ybitachucu was old and had three wives, she was the only child he had left. She entered and did him homage. He stopped her and embraced her.

Ybitachucu gave her one of his rare smiles. "It is good to see you, Little Bird," he said, using her nickname. "What brings you to me now, my child? I have much on my mind."

"So do I, Father," she replied, "but tell me your cares. What do you think of the Spaniard?"

"I think he is on his own. He may have come with a few others, but I do not think he leads a war party. He does not bring soldiers, and he does not speak of treaty with the Spanish, but of peace with the Potano. I do not think he comes with the blessing of the great Spanish cacique. Perhaps he is a lone madman…or a prophet. Wisdom would probably say that we should kill him quietly and if other Spanish ask of him, deny he was ever here. That is what I was thinking wisdom would say."

"I hear your thoughts, Father, but I too was thinking," The woman replied. "I was thinking of my brothers—your sons. How they were many and all of them warriors…. I loved them all and with you, I have buried them all. My oldest son is now of age to become a warrior. Death swiftly takes those we love by disease, by famine, by wild beast. This brown robe speaks of peace with the Potano. Do we need to help Death along by continuing a war we do not even need to fight?" She let the question hang for a moment then said, "I miss my brothers, Papa, and I love my son."

Ybitachucu said nothing for a time, then nodded. He said nothing more and did not look at her. The Ursolina recognized this mood, and she quietly departed, leaving him to his thoughts. When she had gone, the cacique began searching through a pile of items stacked against the wall of his dwelling. Finally, he pulled forth a long parcel wrapped in bearskin.

In the *buhio* on the mound, Fray Tomás heard someone scream followed by pain wracked moans. Slowly, the priest realized that he was the one making those sounds. Between the blood rushing to his head, the blood flowing from his wounds, and the searing pain from the torture, Fray Tomás hovered in and out of consciousness. The shaman barked a question at him; the medicine man's assistant, who spoke Potano, translated. Fray Tomás didn't really hear the question, and his reply came out in Spanish. It was part prayer, the rest babble, begging Jesus and Mary to save him. It didn't matter, for even when the interrogation had started and Tomás understood the questions and answered in Potano, the result was always the same: the slice of the knife. Each cut was shallow and long, meant to inflict minimum damage; but maximum pain. The Franciscan's body involuntarily writhed like a fish on a hook from each searing gash. He could no longer tell how long he had been tortured. It seemed like an eternity. Blood and sweat, his own, dripped into his eyes; when he could see, everything was tinted red. This was hell, he thought, or at least the closest one could get to it on earth. Then, Fray Tomás heard a third voice. There was the sound of an argument. The priest could not be certain what was happening; all he knew was that for a moment the torture had stopped.

Ybitachucu looked at the medicine man and then he examined the Franciscan. The missionary looked like freshly-skinned game ready for the butchering. The chieftain knew the cuts looked worse than they were, but these wounds, though shallow, could still be lethal. He could tell by the rise and the fall of the man's chest that the friar wasn't dead, but if the shaman continued his "questioning," the captive soon would be. Ybitachucu held back his anger. He did not want this stranger dead—yet.

The cacique turned to the medicine man, "And so?"

The shaman snorted, "These Spanish are weak. Every time I cut him, he cried out—like a woman."

"So where is the war party?" Ybitachucu asked.

The shaman was caught off guard by the question. "He didn't say," the medicine man replied.

"Well then, the scouting party? The Spanish troops?" Ybitachucu continued. The shaman hesitated, "He didn't talk about those either," he finally admitted.

"I have listened to this man's screams through the night. You said he is weak. He must have told you everything you asked. He probably even told you things you wanted to hear, whether they were true or not, just to stop your cutting," the chieftain said, his irritation sharpening his words until they came out as knives. "Tell me you learned something of use. Tell me he said something of value. Tell me you are not wasting my time!"

The burly shaman shrank beneath this interrogation. "I—he came with a guide, but now he is alone.... He came in peace with an invitation.... "

"Those are the same words he spoke when he came into the village," Ybitachucu interrupted.

"He babbles mostly in the twisted talk of the Spanish," the shaman hedged. "It is difficult to understand him."

"I didn't ask for excuses, I asked for the truth," the cacique said, cutting him off again. "So he hasn't changed his story?"

"No, but just give me some more time," the shaman replied, and reached for the stone blade he had put back in the burning coals.

Ybitachucu knocked the clay pot to the ground with a sweep of his arm. The coals and knife spilled across the dirt floor and the shaman was left grasping at air. "Go," the cacique commanded.

Stung by this dismissal, the shaman turned on the cacique with the anger of injured pride coiling within him. But the cacique of the Apalachee gave no inch. His face was stone and his eyes were burning embers. "Go," he commanded once again, "I will finish this."

The shaman's anger broke beneath that gaze, and he could not hold it with his own. Instead, he drew himself up haughtily. "Be careful who you insult, Cacique; such words could earn you the wrong kind of enemies," he said and then swept out of the *buhio*. He barked a command to his assistant and the man obediently followed.

They were gone, and there was silence as Ybitachucu watched them go.

Water splashed on Fray Tomás' face, and he coughed and sputtered as it ran into his nose. It also rinsed enough of the blood out of his eyes to allow him to see. There appeared only one figure before him, Ybitachucu. The cacique unwrapped the animal skins from an object he held in his hands. And what Tomás saw cut through the pain, the fear, even the blood pounding in his ears.

It was a sword. An old Spanish sword.

"Why you here?" Ybitachucu asked. And he asked it in Spanish!

Fray Tomás' mouth hung open, which was quite a feat considering he was hanging upside-down. He could only stare.

The Apalachee chieftain unsheathed the sword and put the blade to the padre's throat. It was still sharp. "This end now, priest. Why you here?" the cacique questioned. But Fray Tomás could only laugh, harsh and hysterical, ending in a choked sob. The cacique was taken aback.

"Habla Español?" the friar finally managed to say.

"Sí," the Indian replied. "Many, many years ago Spanish come from over great waters. Apalachee fight Spanish. Many, many Apalachee die. Make treaty with Spanish. From that day every cacique learn Español. Spanish leave. Still we learn the talk. Spanish do not return. I am the last to learn. Now Spanish return.... Are you with a war party?"

"No," Fray Tomás replied.

"Are you here to make new treaty with Apalachee?" Ybitachucu pressed to know.

"I can help with a new treaty," the priest said, "but I come to invite you to the village of Holata Toloca to celebrate the day we remember the birth of the son of the Great Spirit."

"Nicaguadco, son of Thunder?" Ybitachucu asked thinking that Fray Tomás might be referring to their native god of war.

The priest's body began to tremble. "N-n-no, Jesus Christ," Fray Tomás corrected. "He is the greatest of all caciques, greater even than the cacique of España. I wish you to celebrate His birthday with Potano, together."

"To lead us into a trap." Ybitachucu stated.

Now the Franciscan's body was beginning to noticeably shake. He felt feverish and freezing at the same time, while hanging upside-down was bringing waves of nausea over him. "Jesus speaks of peace. I am His messenger."

The old warrior pushed the blade farther. "Why should I believe you?"

Then a dam broke inside the priest. The pain and wounded pride, the fear and frustration, the righteousness and rage flooded forth giving him clarity and strength. "I don't know!" Tomás snapped. "I don't know! You have me hanging here! You keep cutting me! How am I supposed to prove it to you? But I say this, as God is my witness, no matter how many times you cut me or how long you torture me, I have told you the truth. Apalachee kill Potano. Potano kill Apalachee. There is no peace. And it does not have to be this way!"

The sword blade withdrew, but only slightly. The chieftain did not know what to make of this bizarre prisoner. He had captives scream and cry and beg for mercy. Most braves would struggle to remain silent, refusing to give the torturers the satisfaction of hearing their pain. But the cacique had never had a prisoner yell at him. His heart told him that the priest was telling the truth, but his head was telling him to end this foolishness. "And you will change this, Franciscan?" Ybitachucu asked, unconvinced. He readied the sword. He had always been a practical man.

His outburst over, Fray Tomás felt completely drained. Blood loss and trauma were inducing the friar's body to go into shock, but he fought to say, "Not me—us, together. Peace will work if you try."

At these words, Ybitachucu's sword arm hesitated, but only for an instant. Then he struck. Fray Tomás never saw the blade complete its arc. He passed out and knew no more.

Darkness swallowed the priest. Thick and pulsating, it surrounded him. Was this death, he wondered? Then a cool hand touched his face. Suddenly his eyes opened and he stared into the gaze of the Ursolina. Tension eased from her face and she smiled. The priest felt himself smile in turn. That movement hurt, but it showed that he was still alive.

He realized that he was lying on a low bed common to the Indians of this region. A blanket of sewn rabbit skins covered him, and beneath it he could feel that his torso had been wrapped with a pungent-smelling poultice. Then, as his head cleared and consciousness returned more fully, agony came with it. Despite the blanket and the warmth of the day, he was chilled with fever. In addition, his entire body burned, throbbed, itched, and ached. A sharp pain came from his head. Seeing his discomfort, the woman said something in Apalachee and gestured with her hands. Fray Tomás could not understand her, but he became aware that something was wrapped around his head. Instinctively, he reached up to touch it, and then immediately wished he hadn't as the movement of his body and the touch to his temple brought forth pain so intense he almost passed out again. Then he realized what the Ursolina was saying, "Don't move and don't touch. Just rest."

Seeing that he had reached for the bandage on his head, the cacique's daughter tried to explain. In broken Potano, she said, "My father…cut you," and she gestured to his ankles. Tomás understood, the chieftain's sword stroke had cut his leg bonds. She continued, "And you…" she put one hand on top of the other and smacked them sharply together, showing how his head got introduced to the floor.

The friar smiled at that. Again smiling hurt, but the woman could tell he understood and smiled back. An announcement came from the door and the Ursolina stood. A moment later Ybitachucu entered. He exchanged words with his daughter, and then he turned his attention to the Fray Tomás.

"You live," he said in Spanish.

"*Sí,*" Fray Tomás mustered the strength to say.

"*Bueno,*" Ybitachucu continued. "You sleep three days. Many think you might die. Many hope so."

"Why?" the priest managed to ask.

The chieftain answered, "You die, nothing changes. People afraid to change. But there are many others who pray that you live."

"And if I live?" the priest persisted, though at the end of his frail endurance.

Ybitachucu thought for a moment, then said, "You know why the Potano and Apalachee fight?"

Fray Tomás shook his head, it made him wince, but he could not find the energy to talk.

"I not know either," the cacique replied. "No one does. One day it start. No one remember why. And it never end." Ybitachucu looked the friar in the eye, "If you live," he said, "it is a sign. I will take my braves, and we go to the Potano Christmas—in peace."

And Fray Tomás did live. When he emerged, the villagers saw him, scars and all, still standing. They hailed him as a bringer of strong medicine and a true messenger of the Great Spirit. Scouts were sent to meet with Tofu, and the priest's friend was taken to see that the padre was alive and being cared for, but Tomás could not make the journey back to the Potano village. That is why Tofu at first returned to Holata Toloca alone. He waited for the friar's recovery. Fortunately, when Toloca sent him to retrieve Fray Tomás, the priest had regained just enough strength to accompany the outcast back to the village. Although not fully recovered, Fray Tomás did not want to be away any longer than absolutely necessary, so he wouldn't worry the Potano cacique or arouse suspicion. He knew that if the Potano had heard that the Apalachee had tortured him, it might lead them to war instead of preventing one. His speedy return also guaranteed that the Apalachee guests would be a surprise gift to the Potano.

XI

At the story's conclusion, Holata Toloca snorted, "And quite a surprise they were!"

The friar smiled sheepishly, "Forgive me, Cacique. I know now I should have given you more warning."

"Yes, you should have," the chieftain admonished. "This story, Padre, turns inside of me. I am happy at its ending, but I am angry hearing what happened to you."

"And that is why," the friar replied, "I wanted to keep it a secret. I thought you might have ordered me not to go."

"You are right. I would have," confirmed Toloca. "You could have been killed."

"But then what you are doing today would not be happening," Tomás countered.

The cacique gave an exasperated sigh, "I know, Fray Tomás. You are a hard man to argue with. So we will argue no more. Instead, I want to suggest two men who I think might best help us at the moment. In one of my warriors' last forays into Apalachee country, we captured two men of the Ayubale tribe. They are a people located close to Ivitachuco. These men could carry an invitation from us to the cacique of Ivitachuco and the neighboring tribes of the Apalachees.

Toloca continued, "You would not have to leave again so soon. My nephew cannot afford"—here the cacique winked at the friar—"to miss his padre's very capable care, since you are the only father the child shall ever know." Toloca's words were meant as a compliment and sign of his deep trust in the friar.

Fray Tomás took the words as they were meant, secretly releasing a sigh of relief that his bold maneuver with the Apalachee had not destroyed the faith the cacique of the Potano had put in him. "Thank you, Holata Toloca," Tomás responded, "for your words of appreciation. I do my best in caring for little Kocha. I am also truly happy to hear of your deep desire for peace with the Apalachee people.... I humbly ask, do not forget me when the day comes for the two nations to meet," Tomás insisted.

"Padre," the cacique quipped, "there can be no meeting without you. I will be accompanied by all of my warriors and by my fellow caciques of Timucua and their warriors. Even still, I will not be so bold as to venture into Apalachee territory for a meeting without you leading the way. Let us prepare now for our meeting," the chieftain continued. "I will release the two hostages with a message for the cacique of Ivitachuco. We will await his response to our invitation for a meeting between the peoples of Apalachee and Timucua."

The two Apalachee warriors carried the offer to the cacique of Ivitachuco with a suggestion for a time and place for the gathering. Since the Apalachee cacique had visited Timucuan territory before, it seemed best that the meeting would be on Apalachee ground this time, in the village of Ivitachuco. The cacique of Ivitachuco held the same opinion, and he in turn extended the invitation to all the caciques of the Apalachee nation. Unanimously, they agreed to the proposed meeting.

Two messengers were sent back to the Potano cacique with a ratification of the proposal. They also carried a special invitation to one "Fray Tomás" to come as a special guest of the Apalachee nation.

Fray Tomás beamed with pride when Toloca told him he was to be not only his companion and representative at the meeting, but apparently the friend and representative of the Apalachee people as well.

Neighboring caciques of Timucuan tribes gathered with a hundred and fifty of their braves to accompany Tomás and Toloca on their trip to Ivitachuco. This journey was Toloca's first one to that village that was not a raid or a war party.

When the Timucuans were within three leagues of the village, they began to experience a special sense of welcome upon discovering a wide, clean road awaiting them. Fray Tomás recognized the avenue leading to the town from the time of his captivity, but it seemed the villagers had apparently cleaned it of debris to let the travelers know that they were welcome guests.

Once in the village, a crowd of over three thousand Indians waiting in the central plaza of Ivitachuco greeted the Timucuans.

Immediately, they were led to tables filled with food consisting of cakes made of maize. The Indians, fond of novelties, were excited over the unique visit of foreigners who had been their enemies, but they were especially intrigued by the visit of the Spanish friar.

The cacique, Ybitachucu, came forward from his dwelling to greet the Potano chieftain Toloca, and then the friar, whom he warmly embraced. Toloca introduced him to the other caciques accompanying him, and Ybitachucu in turn led Tomás, Toloca, and all of the visiting caciques to greet the heads of the tribes of the Apalachee nation. One by one, he introduced them: Tafunsaca, Pastrana, Paslali, Hinacchuba, Savacola, Ynac, Pansac, Usunaca.

As cacique of Ivitachuco, Ybitachucu, was the most important cacique of the Apalachee nation, and he raised his voice over the crowd and began to speak:

"When did I merit that so happy a day should dawn upon me, that I should see peace in my enemies and behold them eating in my plaza and home, in the spirit of friendship. Today, we can have a meal together as brothers and friends, a meal that will be a sign of our comradeship with the people of Timucua. Now we can hope for a time of peace in the villages of Apalachee and Timucua."

"My friend, Fray Tomás, is the one who has brought us together through his faith and his drama about the child who is Son of the Great Spirit." Ybitachucu continued. "I welcome this pilgrim of peace to my village! May the good he has brought already to the people of the Timucuan nation bring great blessing to us also, the people of Apalachee." Ybitachucu and Tomás once again embraced each other. Then the cacique of Ivitachuco embraced Toloca and each of the caciques of Timucua.

It was a sacred moment. Many people of both nations wept when they saw what was happening.

Tomás could not contain his emotions either, for he saw the hopes of many people, as well as his own hopes, realized that day. Now he knew his mission to the Potano people was not just of his own doing or of his own wide-eyed idealistic imaginings. It was the will of the Good God, who had brought him to this strange foreign land for a purpose. This was truly a work that San Francisco de Assis had set in motion.

Toloca saw the tears on the friar's cheeks, and the cacique's heart was moved with compassion for his friend.

"It is not good that my people see their padre crying," he said, "though, I fear, I cannot but do the same myself. The tears that flow from my people's eyes today reflect the joy of our hearts, hearts that yearned for peace but always thought peace was forever foreign to us, as the sun is a foreigner to the moon. Today the impossible has happened."

Ybitachucu and Toloca each led warriors of their own tribes in versions of their own peace dance, and all present shouted and clapped to accompany the singing of words that said: "Peace has come to our land this day. May it never end."

The caciques of the Apalachee and Timucuan nations delegated Ybitachucu and Toloca to go to the city of San Agustín. Then, in the presence of the governor of San Agustín, who represents the great cacique of the Spanish people, they would make a pact that would enable the people of Apalachee and Timucua to be friends with each other forever. The people of the Apalachee nation would also, at that time, join the people of Timucua in an alliance with the people of España. This was an added success even greater than Tomás had dared imagine.

He had hoped that the Apalachee might respect the ancient treaty they had with Spain, and that the Potano might one day sign a treaty with Spain of their own. But to have the Apalachee renew their treaty at the same time the Potano made theirs would be a momentous event. It would be written in their histories. To think he had been God's instrument in this endeavor. He, a simple merchant's son! How proud his father and mother, and especially his godfather, would be! Fray Tomás recalled the quote from the Bible, "He has raised up the lowly," and the priest gave thanks to God.

Great rejoicing continued on into the night and through the next day. It did not end until long after the friar, caciques, and warriors had returned to the villages of Timucua, because now, the peace blossomed and grew in the people's hearts.

One incident, however, did mar the beauty of this event. After the Timucuan Indians left the Apalachee village and the great band of warriors divided, going their separate ways, Holata Toloca's contingent encountered a brigade of Spanish soldiers laden with supplies bound for the local garrison. At the head of the brigade rode Captain Mérida. He requested the Indians to help his men with the portage. The Spanish military commonly impressed the Florida natives into service, carrying supplies, ammunition, and goods to the different garrisons. The Potanos balked. Captain Mérida insisted. Fray Tomás tried for a compromise—perhaps the Potano would do the work for pay? Captain Mérida brushed aside the suggestion, reminding the friar that the Indians were expected to help without question and without recompense, because, in this way, the natives would compensate the Spanish for the protection their garrisons provided. But many Indians did not agree with this arrangement. The Potano were among these Indians. Captain Mérida ordered his men not to allow the Potano to pass until they provided some men as porters. A fight seemed imminent.

Then Holata Toloca spoke, "On the day I have made peace with one enemy, I will not create another. There will be no bloodshed this day." He selected a dozen braves to assist the soldiers. Fray Tomás volunteered himself, and Toloca assented, knowing this would ease his warriors' bitterness against the foreigners.

Some of the Spanish, however, protested using a priest in such a way.

Captain Mérida silenced the dissenters, saying, "If he wishes to be one of them, then let him treated like one of them." To Tomás he said, "Think you're above the governor and me, Padre? See where you are now."

The captain spoke in Spanish, but Toloca heard and understood him. This increased his respect for the padre, though it intensified his disdain for the captain. Later, when Toloca had misgivings about proceeding in regard to the treaty with the Apalachee and the Spanish because of this incident, his respect for Tomás won out. He agreed when the priest pleaded that he continue with the signing.

And so, he found himself standing in the strange stone and wood *buhio* of the Spanish cacique of San Agustín. Toloca wore his ceremonial best: deerskin breaches, bright paint on his face and bare chest, and the crown of feathers adorning his head. Ybitachucu stood next to him dressed in similar finery. Across an elegant mahogany desk, the Spanish governor stood as he read the newly written treaty. He wore his most expensive velvet dress coat with a ruffled shirt that had lace at the wrists. Holata Toloca thought the man looked ridiculous, like a stuffed bird. The governor thought the caciques looked barbaric. But the leaders kept their personal opinions to themselves. The three nations declared peace with each other, forever. Toloca, Ybitachucu, and the Spanish governor made their mark upon the paper for the Great Cacique of España. Everyone smiled. Even Captain Mérida and Fray Tomás, who were present as witnesses, smiled. Still smiling, Toloca clasped forearms with Ybitachucu and the governor, in turn, as a sign of friendship. Fray Tomás beamed from ear to ear. But just after Toloca left, Fray Tomás' smile began to fade.

Out of curiosity, the priest had been glancing over the introduction to the treaty. The peace agreement had been read aloud and repeated by translators, but the governor had skipped the introduction, dismissing it as a formality. When Fray Tomás reviewed the document, he read it in its entirety and felt a pang of disappointment at what he saw. "Excuse me, Your Excellency," said the Franciscan

"Yes, my good friar?" said the governor. "I trust you are pleased with this day's events. Our Lord Jesus being the King of Peace and all."

"Oh, yes—of course...this is wonderful.... Thanks be to God," Fray Tomás replied. "But I was reading the introduction to the treaty, and...well, it says that as a result of a good will visit you made, accompanied by Captain Mérida to the Potano village, you orchestrated this treaty."

"And?" said the governor, prompting Tomás to get to the point.

"Well, it doesn't mention the Franciscans really at all," stated the friar.

"Oh that," replied the governor. "That's just politics, my dear priest. Besides, God knows who the credit goes to, doesn't He?"

"That is true," conceded the missionary, but he continued a little indignantly, "But with all the work Fray Buenaventura and I did for this—"

"Really, Fray Tomás!" exclaimed the governor in exasperation. "Tsk, tsk! Weren't you the one telling me that all glory should go to God, or some such thing? You seem overly concerned about recognition, if that is what you truly believe."

"It's not that," Fray Tomás tried to defend himself. "I just—"

"Padre, isn't pride a serious sin?" interrupted Captain Mérida.

The comment ambushed Tomás into astonished silence. In disbelief, he looked from one man to the next. Then, understanding crept through the shock. "This is about the baptism, isn't it?" he said.

Their silence confirmed it. This was not about his quest for approbation, but theirs.

Tomás shook his head and kept shaking it. "Incredible," was all he could say. Surprise, anger, and hurt all welled up inside him, but bowing stiffly to each of the men, he left so they would not see any of these emotions break free.

Part Two

The Harvest

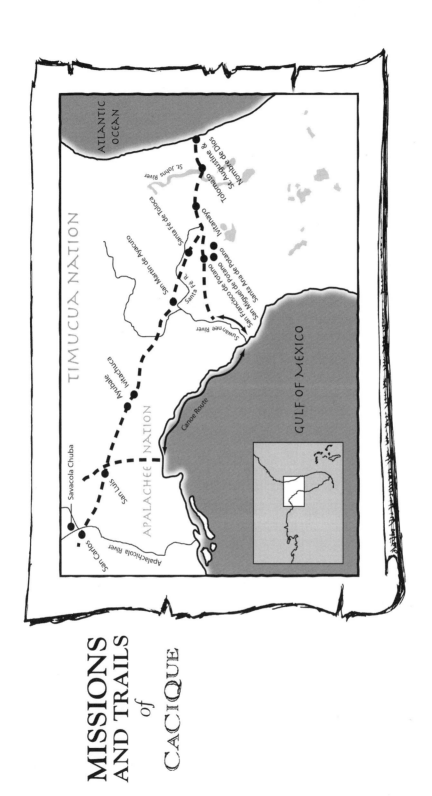

MISSIONS
AND TRAILS
of
CACIQUE

XII

- 1612 -

The sweltering summer heat slowly surrendered to the cool kisses of the soothing autumn winds. The harvest season had finally arrived. For Fray Tomás, it had come none too soon. After much persistent and painstaking labor, he now beamed proudly over the crops he had helped produce. During the past four years, the villagers had instructed him well in the Indian ways of farming, and they, in turn, learned from him the Spanish. The friar discovered that both had gained much from the interchange of information.

With their primitive agricultural instruments and rugged ways, the Potano accomplished much, to the amazement of the padre. With crude axes, they struggled to clear densely forested woodland, overgrown with saw palmettos, evergreen shrubs, cacti, and sunflowers. With fish bones, pointed sticks, and clamshells, they attacked the soil, winning fertile ground from the wilderness. Many villagers preferred their own primitive hoes made of sharp stone to the metal implements offered to them by the friar. But many others succumbed to the easier ways presented by the Spanish priest, and now results were beginning to show for their strenuous effort. Their work made each row sown a triumph and each planted field a victory. Finally, the hardened soil had been vanquished. It had given way to the careful nurturing they had provided.

During the month of January, the villagers had burned the grass and weeds from the land to prepare it for cultivation. In April the planting had begun, with the men opening the trenches and the women following behind, sowing the grain. The wheat crop had been planted in October and harvested already in the month of June, with a *fanega* [6] of seed yielding seventy *fanegas* of grain.

In this month, bean plants, pumpkins, peas, plums, and wheat in abundance were in view as far as the eye could see. Even the cucumbers Tomás had introduced to the Potano diet were doing well. But the corn was the true treasure: field after field of it, crowned with tassels flying like flags that called to the planters to reap now the fruit of the harvest. Shortly, the maize would be harvested and taken to the buildings erected for storage. Part of

---

[6] one to two bushels.

the corn crop would be cracked or ground with wood or stone mortars and made into corn cakes. The rest would be saved for roasting, or simply dried for future use.

With hoe in hand and the bottom of his friar's frock tucked up around his waist for easy maneuvering, Tomás wiped sweat from his sun-baked brow and breathed a sigh of relief. Together, he and his Indian comrades had labored to produce the best crops ever seen by the Potano people.

The friar looked in the direction of the sun standing directly overhead and knew it was time for noonday prayer. He called out for little Kocha in the language of the Potanos, which was the only language he ever used in speaking with the young cacique-to-be. "Kocha, it is time for prayer and a break from our labors. You know what to do!"

It was Kocha's special privilege to ring the bell that hung from a makeshift tower near the mission church. He came running from the field and began to tug on the rope that hung from the crossbeam. The crisp copper clang called to the people to come in from their fields to praise the God of the harvest.

In they came to the small Spanish-style church constructed of wood, with a palm-thatched roof. Already Padre Tomás had taught the village converts the value of prayer at certain times of the day. In the mornings, they celebrated Mass. At midday and at sunset, he prayed the psalms with them and gave a brief instruction in the faith.

Today Fray Tomás introduced the praying of the psalms with a few words.

"I have found much joy in working the fields with you, my friends. It has been like a contest with the elements, but you have taught me that if you befriend the earth, it will befriend you. And so I have.

"You have taught me to use creatures always as they should be used, the earth and sea, the sky and the air, the rivers, and the springs. And so I have.

"I only add this message to the one you have given me. Give praise and glory to the Creator for all that you find beautiful and wonderful in creation, and the Creator will bless you also, for you are the greatest of all His creation."

Together the friar and the Indians recited Psalm 96:

"Sing to the Lord a new song. Sing to the Lord, all you lands. Sing to the Lord; bless His name; announce His salvation, day after day. Tell His glory among the nations, among all peoples, His wondrous deeds.

"For great is the Lord and highly to be praised; awesome is He, beyond all gods. For all the gods of the nations are things of naught, but the Lord made the heavens...."

The Potanos loved the psalms. They could easily identify with the spirit of the Jewish people who, like themselves, were coming to believe in a God not identified with earth and sea and sky, but a God who was totally of the Spirit and totally other than all of His creation. That message did not come easy to them. They had, up to now, always identified God closely with the created universe to which their Great Spirit was wedded like soul to body. Like the Jews coming out of Israel, the Indians were coming to terms with a new relationship with their Creator.

After reading the psalm together with them, Tomás began to reflect on its meaning. The psalm was once again a starting point for his instruction in the faith, as were the rest of the Jewish Scriptures. Before Tomás could bring his people to understand the message of the New Testament, he painstakingly had to walk them through the message of the Old Testament revelation.

Questions abounded from his little congregation about the God of Psalm 96.

"Why cannot the god of the sun and the god of the harvest be worshiped like the God of the Jewish people?" was one of the questions.

Tomás' answer was that the God of the Jewish people was the God of the sun and the God of the harvest. "He is the only God, but He is not to be identified with any of His creatures. He is spirit, the Great Spirit, behind all and above all.

"All creation is the work of His hand. All creation gives glory to His name. But no part of creation could be said to be the Great Spirit Himself. He has existed for all time, before the world and the universe came to be."

Tomás knew that his words would not be understood quickly, but insights into his teaching did come back in the words of his hearers. One Indian spoke up in response to his words to say he no longer was afraid of thunder and lightning. They were not a superior power of the spirit. Only the God of Padre Tomás held that kind of power. Tomás had freed him of a fear he and many others had since they were little children.

The friar saw this as an occasion to remind the people that the God of the Jewish nation wanted all people to know that He was a God of love. And in Jesus, the Messiah, He showed His great love best of all by becoming one of them, by living for them, and by dying for them.

At the conclusion of his words, he signaled to the little choir made up of children and adults, of which Kocha was a proud member. They sang a beautiful hymn composed by one of their members, to thank the Lord for blessing them with so great a crop and so successful a harvest.

Tomás then ushered them all out of the door to an area that resembled an open-air pavilion. It was to be a meeting hall, but the walls were not yet completed. At this sight, Tomás had a table set with a wide variety of foods on it, prepared by his band of helpers. It was the noonday meal.

Already the friar had assembled a retinue of faithful and devoted workers, men and women, boys and girls. Among them were about twenty children, in ages from three to twelve. They comprised an orphanage that had gradually emerged under Tomás' direction and care, made up of children like Kocha, whose parents had died from natural causes or as a result of conflict.

Fray Tomás, assisted by Fray Buenaventura, conducted a school for them that became so popular that children from Potano villages throughout the area were brought to their mission for instruction. The native students were taught the same lessons Spanish children of comparable age were taught, but in the language of the Potano. And, with the approval of their parents, they were also instructed in the Christian faith and prepared for Baptism.

Already, Tomás had baptized two hundred and eighty-five Potano children and adults.

Unfortunately, this number did not represent the majority of the Potano. Although more villagers came to accept the Franciscans' message as the days went by, a Traditionalist contingent began to form. These natives directly opposed adopting any of the European ways. Though most of this group respected (or feared) the friars and the Spanish settlers, they viewed the foreigners with a certain amount of mistrust and they didn't believe that the lifestyles of the two cultures could be integrated, so they politely refused to adopt or engage in anything distinctly "Spanish." A minority that arose within this group believed that the Spanish sought to destroy the Potano way of life and replace it with their own, in order to control the native people. They disapproved of their more open-minded brethren, and they would occasionally accuse some of their fellow tribesmen of being "traitors" to their nation, because they accepted the Spanish beliefs and ways.

Fray Tomás felt if he could really speak to these antagonistic Potano, he could convince them of the error of their accusations. But he did not have the time or manpower to reach everyone. In fact, his only regret was that he did not have enough help in his work. How many more people, he thought, would find a home in the Christian community if only there were sufficient laborers in the mission field!

How right were Christ's words: "The harvest is good, but laborers are scarce." And Fray Tomás prayed that the Lord, the Harvest Master, would send more laborers to gather in the fields of souls. The priest's special hopes lay in the child Kocha. This one person could reach the Potano people better even than the friar himself. As a Potano and a future cacique, Kocha could single-handedly guide the tribe and transform the village in a truly Christian way. But that hope rested on Tomás bringing home to the boy the ways of Christian life. This was the Franciscan's special goal. If he succeeded here, he felt, all else would fall into place.

"Kocha," the padre called out, "It's your turn to lead the prayer."

Little Kocha came next to the friar, closed his eyes, and began to pray from the heart as only a child could. "Thank You, Great Spirit," he said slowly and deliberately, "for blessing all the Potano people. Thank You for blessing me. Thank You for blessing Fray Tomás and helping him to be happy here with my people. He is one of us, and we know You love him very much, as we love him. Please, Great Spirit, never take him away from us. Help him to be Your good friend, so that he can teach us how to be Your friend, too. Through Jesus, the Mess—the Mess—"

"The Messiah," Fray Tomás finished for him.

Kocha continued, "Your Son and the Holy Great Spirit. We pray in His name. Amen."

The child opened his eyes and looked up to the friar with his face silently asking for the padre's approval.

The friar simply placed his arm around the child, hugged him warmly, and then thanked him for sharing so very well with all these people his strong faith in the Great Spirit.

"Now everybody," Tomás shouted aloud, "fill your bowls and eat to your hearts' content, because we've got a lot more work in the fields, and I'm afraid it's a long way to sundown!"

XIII

Fray Tomás sat on an oak stump with the drawing of the future of the mission in his hands. It depicted the meeting hall that Potano villagers were helping erect for him, along with the friar's *convento* residence and a home for children. Tomás acted as architect. Tofucunatchu was the construction supervisor. And Kocha was the hod carrier, lugging daub mortar and water to the craftsmen plastering the inner and outer walls.

Soon after Tomás had decided on the site for his mission, the little church had been completed to the pride and satisfaction of everyone. Tomás wanted the entire mission near the enclosed area where the cacique and his leading tribesmen dwelt, but far enough away so that Tomás could properly call the area his own. Toloca, the cacique, told him to choose a spot not already claimed by any of the Potano people, and the priest selected an area about an eighth of a league southeast of the compound of the cacique.

Up until his third year in the village, Tomás continued to live, and even celebrate Mass, in a thatched hut near the cacique's dwelling. His sensitivity to the care of Kocha and the other orphaned children suggested that he move slowly and win the confidence of the people before venturing to erect his own buildings. But it was the orphan children themselves that helped him gain the trust of the villagers. Despite their ferocity and cruelty toward their enemies, the Potano loved their children, to the point of almost spoiling them. For Fray Tomás, the older orphans reminded him of his younger brother and sister back home. The younger ones became for him the children he would never have. Once a young council member just a little older than the priest asked him, "Why do you not have a family, Brown Robe? Some say that you do not have a wife because you are not really a man."

Fray Tomás responded, "I am very much a man, and I am already married—to the Church, the bride of Christ."

"I'm not sure I understand. What I am asking is, do you ever want a woman?" the councilman asked.

"Sometimes I do, very much. But I have promised the Great Spirit that I would belong to Him alone," Fray Tomás said. "And look at how many children He gave me!" The priest indicated the orphans, and the councilman had to laugh.

When the villagers saw the genuine love that both Tomás and Buenaventura had for the orphans, the respect they had for the priests grew, and even the Potano who had not been converted accepted them a little more in the community.

When the number of orphans and converts neared three hundred, and the bountiful harvest provided the Franciscans with enough food to pay for labor, the time was ripe for the priests to begin. They found many willing workers, and now, the building venture had been underway for about a year.

"Padre!" Kocha cried out. "I'm tired! When will we have our new home finished? I would be just as happy sleeping under the stars. If the Great Spirit wanted me to have a roof over my head, He would have made one; but I do not think we can make a better one that His own—the sky, the moon, and the stars. They would make a better roof for me to look at when I go to bed."

"Kocha," the padre quipped, "I would agree with you completely, until the first rain clouds blocked our view of the moon and the stars at night and dropped a few hundred buckets of water on us. Or until the noon-day sun scorched our faces as dark as the marsh boar. Think of that when you start getting tired, and you won't feel so tired anymore."

Kocha scratched his head, then nodded in agreement. Grudgingly picking up his shoulder harness with the skins containing water, he resumed the task at hand. Kocha was on the job only because the Padre was. He wanted to show the priest he could be a good worker like the big people. Tomás knew this, and he let it continue, because he felt it would not hurt in preparing the boy for his future role as cacique.

At the end of the day, Tomás had been calling everyone together to thank them for their work and to note the progress they had made. He also gave them a *fanega* of wheat or corn and some vegetables for each two days of labor. He only regretted that he could not pay them more, but the people never complained. They seemed happy just making the friar happy.

The Spanish garrison stationed near the Mission of San Francisco de Potano to the south had offered Tomás assistance, but he preferred to have the Indians do all the work on these buildings. He did consult the military on occasion for suggestions on ways to cut corners on architectural techniques, but once again his sensitivity to the Indian people prevented him from bringing in military personnel for the labor. His father had always taught him that what you are given for free, you may be grateful to receive or you may not. But what you make yourself, you cherish as your own. Fray Tomás wanted the Potano to feel that this was their mission as much as it was his.

Spanish tools, iron nails, and spikes were utilized in construction. They had helped greatly with erecting the rafters for the church, and now they were of much use with the other buildings as well. The priest's plans called for the church to be at the northeast end of the mission compound, and a meeting-hall to the west of the church. He would place the *convento*—with a separate *cocina* for preparing the meals—to the southwest, and the children's residence further west of the *convento*.

They erected around the entire area a large, high fence made of evenly cut, sharply pointed pinewood. They arranged it to allow plenty of extra space for additional dwellings on the south side. Tomás was hoping some of the recently converted Potano people would follow Tofucunatchu's example and take up residence in the mission.

Tofu continued to be Tomás' most reliable supporter and guide. He took the padre's advice and erected his own palm-thatched dwelling close to the *convento* residence of Tomás and Buenaventura so as to be available for any emergency. In addition to supervising the construction work, Tofu was also in charge of organizing the mission's maintenance crew and overseeing the orphaned children as they were trained in the trades and skills of Indian life.

He was ever a silent, somber man, who went about doing his work, at times, almost frenetically, and with total dedication. He would never forget how Tomás had interceded with the cacique in order to spare his life. Although stripped of his dignity by the cacique and fellow warriors for his murderous act, Tofu found his dignity again through the work he was doing for Fray Tomás.

Noticing the usual relentless pace of Tofu's work, which set the outcast noticeably apart from the other Potano laborers, Tomás moved in his direction and placed a hand on his shoulder. "Slow down, *mi amigo*. If you keep at this pace, I fear you will die before our buildings are completed."

"Padre, I see the pictures on your map, and I see very little on the land. When I see all that you have drawn standing tall on this soil, then I will rest."

"Yes, Tofu," Buenaventura interjected, as he moved within earshot of the conversation. "But remember, the padre is going to need your help not just now, but long after the buildings are standing. Your feet have many more paths to tread before your journey's end, which we pray will not be soon."

"Fray Buenaventura speaks wisely, Tofu," Tomás added. "Slow down and enjoy your work, hard though that might be for you! The people of a magnificent city in a far-off land beyond España have a saying, 'Rome was not built in a day.' Neither will our little mission, or our efforts for your people, be built in a day. What we are doing will take many, many years, Tofu. What is more, my friend, the success of what we do here does not lie in our hands. It lies in the hands of the Great Spirit, for whom we build this mission. To Jesus and His Mother Mary, we dedicate all that we do. We devote our labors to them and to the holy faith we bring to your people. For the cause of this faith, you and I and Buenaventura are here."

Little Kocha came out of nowhere and offered his own commentary on the discussion. "I hope our mission will be here forever and ever," he said.

Tomás quickly added, "I hope the wonderful buildings Tofu is making for us can weather many storms and many struggles. But most of all, I hope that the holy faith we bring will be here long after Fray Buenaventura and I and all of our people have gone to be with the Great Spirit. That is my hope and prayer."

By now, Tofu was beginning to understand what Tomás and Buenaventura were saying. His buildings were important, but not as important as the work for souls that would be going on inside of them.

"Fray Tomás and Fray Buenaventura, I will slow down because I want to help you not only in making these houses, but also to join you in what you will be doing in these buildings. I will help you to teach my people more about the holy faith."

Tofu drew a breath, then a perplexed look crossed his face. He raised a question. "What are the words the Spanish people use for our Potano words 'holy faith'?"

"*Santa Fé,*" Buenaventura answered. "Why do you ask?"

Tofu responded by asking the friar to draw those words on the ground, as they would look in Spanish.

He noted them carefully and took special care that none of the children or other workers did anything to disturb those marks in the earth.

He would often be seen looking intently at them.

Five days later, the workers completed the fence. As Fray Tomás entered the newly erected mission gate, he saw two Spanish words spelled out in pine branches over the entrance: "S-A-N-T-A F-E."

Tomás knew that he had the answer to a long-standing concern he had since arriving in the Potano village. He now had a name for his mission.

XIV

The giggles and happy screams of children at play washed across the grounds of Mission Santa Fé de Toloca as as the afternoon sun bathed the buildings in heat. Kocha sat cross-legged in a bit of shade, as he pored over a book in his lap.

"Is the book speaking to you?" asked a soft voice coming from over his shoulder.

He turned to see a girl, Tuola, the healer's daughter, gazing down at him. She lived with her mother in the village but she came to the Franciscans' school. Though only a little older than Kocha, she stood with a natural poise as she appraised him with the gray, gentle eyes she inherited from her mother. She was asking him if he was reading. The Potano did not have a written language; therefore they had no word for "reading." They said instead that a book would "say" something.

Kocha nodded in reply to the girl's question and said, "It's a book Fray Tomás gave me."

Another boy shouted at Tuola from a distance away, "Tuola, come and play with us!"

Tuola glanced at the caller, then turned her attention back to Kocha. "What does it say?" she asked.

"Well, it's exciting. It tells of the great heroes of the Holy Faith. They're called saints," Kocha said, but that was as far as he got with his explanation.

"Tuola, didn't you hear me?" said Ycho, the boy who called her earlier. He talked loudly even though he now stood only a few feet away. Tall for his age, Ycho reigned as the cacique of the mission playground. He did not attend the school run by Fray Tomás and Fray Buenaventura, because his father sided with the Potano who saw the Spanish as a threat and viewed the Franciscans with suspicion. However, because of the orphanage, every child in the tribe knew you could always find ready playmates at the mission. The friars encouraged their orphans to play with the other children, knowing that if they could not break down the mistrust of the older generation, they could at least make some headway with the younger.

Ycho came to play daily, and he talked with the authority of one used to commanding respect. Two smaller kids followed Ycho the way vultures trail lions. "I said, 'Come play with us,'" he repeated.

"I'm talking with He-who-will-be-cacique," Tuola replied to Ycho. Then she pointedly turned her back on the bigger boy and focused her attention on Kocha.

Ycho scowled at this dismissal. He craned his head to look around the girl at Kocha. More out of obligation than out of honor, he hastily gave the sign of respect touching his hand to his heart then his lips. This was the traditional greeting his father had taught him. "He-who-will-be-cacique," he said in greeting.

Kocha cringed at the title and nodded in acknowledgment. Then he tried to hunch down in the book as if he could hide himself in the pages. To the orphans and most of the children, he was just Kocha, another ten-year-old boy. But then someone would remind him of his position. He did not particularly mind his tribal rank, but the title singled him out and made him feel…different. He thought it marked him as an outsider just as his features did. Kocha bore the unmistakable traits of both his Spanish and Potano heritages. He had the straight hair and bronze skin of the Native Americans, but the dark eyes, heavy brows, and wide cheekbones of the Spanish. Also he had inherited his father's height, making him broad but short for his age, about as tall as most Potano girls. Ycho towered over him, which emphasized the difference.

The taller boy saw the text in Kocha's hand. "Are you speaking with a book?" he asked.

"Yes, it's—" Kocha did not get a chance to finish his sentence.

Ycho took the book out of the smaller boy's hands.

Kocha gasped, "What are you doing?"

"True Potano don't speak with books," Ycho declared. "That's what my father says."

"Well, Fray Tomás said the Great Cacique of España can speak with books, and so can Jesus the son of the Great Spirit," Kocha countered.

"But they aren't Potano, are they?" Ycho said. "Are they?" he asked more forcefully.

"No," Kocha said quietly.

"Are you?" he demanded.

"Yes, " he answered. "Please give me back the book."

"Why? You just said you were Potano," Ycho continued.

"He doesn't look like a Potano," said the boy by Ycho's right hand.

"His face isn't right," said the child on his left.

Tuola stepped in between Kocha and Ycho's gang, "Leave him alone. I like his face."

Ycho sneered, "You have a girl talking for you, Kocha?"

"N—no," Kocha replied, stepping past Tuola. He gave her a glare, trying to prove to the other boys that he did not need her to fight his battles. He hoped the glare would also hide how scared he felt as he came face to chest with Ycho. "I can speak for myself. Now, give me back the book...p—please." He hated how pathetic he sounded with that 'please.'

Ycho snorted, and shook his head with scorn. "You want it so much?" he replied. "Here." He tossed the manuscript to Kocha and turned away, saying over his shoulder "Maybe, you're not Potano. Maybe that's why my father calls you a half-breed."

This cut Kocha to the core. He might be the future cacique, but he was also a boy, and he could not help but shout, "Yeah, well, your father is going to hell."

Ycho spun around. He did not know really what that meant, but he knew an insult when he heard one. He charged Kocha. The smaller boy tried to backpedal out of the way, but Ycho slammed into him before he could escape. The two boys tumbled to the ground in a tangle of fists, arms, and legs. The book fell face down into the dust.

Angry words and hostile barbs could be heard throughout the mission area. Scuffling sounds punctuated these insults as the two young boys wrestled on the ground, striking one another hard with their fists on the face, forearms, and chest, wherever a free hand could penetrate. From the eyes and nose of both boys, blood ran freely, dropping on blades of grass and in the dirt beneath them. It was clearly meant to be a fight to the finish.

There was a crowd of onlookers, other boys and girls who watched passively, until adults began to converge on the scene. Then the children sheepishly crept away to watch the outcome of the fray from the sidelines.

The first adults on the scene were Tofu and Fray Tomás, with Fray Buenaventura, as usual, bringing up the rear.

"Tofu, you grab Ycho. I'll take Kocha!" the friar yelled to his *confrere*. Tomás could barely handle Kocha, who kept swinging at his opponent. Tofu took one on the chin from the taller boy, but had him subdued very quickly and pinned to the ground beneath his own substantial weight.

"Now what do you want me to do with him, Padre?" Tofu asked.

"Just hold him for right now. What's going on here, Kocha?" the padre asked.

The boy's bruised and bloody face was now tear-streaked as well, as he tried to get out a few words, but couldn't. It was obvious this usually placid boy had been hurt more inwardly than outwardly.

He broke loose from the grip of Tomás and ran hastily to the orphan house, twenty *varas*[7] away. Tomás did not attempt to pursue him.

"Why were you fighting, Ycho? You could have killed each other," Tomás questioned the young combatant, whose face seemed almost submerged into the ground by the weight of Tofu.

"Padre," said the muffled voice from below Tofu. "He didn't like what I had to say, but Padre, it's the truth. Kocha is a half-breed! He is not like the rest of us. He is not fully Indian like us. He and I are the same age, but I am much taller. I just told him what all the other Potano boys and girls are saying about him, and…and then, he insulted my father. So, I…I grabbed him to make him take it back. Then, he began to kick me, then strike me, and…and I did not fight half as hard as I could have, because I did not want to harm the one who is to become the future cacique. But Padre, we do not like the fact that our future leader resembles the Spanish people. He should be Potano, and only Potano. That is what the learned Potano tell us. They say they will never accept him as their leader."

Tofu scowled at the boy then began to push his face further into the ground until Tomás pulled him back.

Tofu said, "I would love to plant you upside down into the soil, Ycho, but I would be afraid you might hurt the good earth. Besides, the soil might just spit you back out again!"

"Let him go, Tofu, we have some healing to do, and I'm afraid it is not going to take place in a short time," said the friar.

Tofu looked at his prey with disgust, then let him loose; the boy scur-

---

[7] a *vara* is close in length to a yard, approximately 32.9 inches.

ried through the mission gate and ran for his home in the Potano village beyond the mission walls.

Back inside the house constructed for the orphan children, Tomás, Tofu, and Buenaventura found Kocha weeping with his legs hugged to his chest, as he sat on the side of his bed. Tomás felt so helpless, knowing what must be going through the young boy's mind at this time. The young friar simply gazed at Buenaventura, then Tofu, and shook his head. A moment of truth had arrived, and they all knew it was time they could avoid it no longer.

"They are right, aren't they, Padre?" Kocha said though his tears. "I am a half-breed. Look at me; look at my hands, my face, my arms. How can I be Potano when I look like the Spanish? Padre, you tell me that I am special. I will do great things for my people. But my people do not want me."

Tomás laid a hand on the small heaving shoulders and said, "*Mi hijo* [8]..."

"But I'm not your son," the boy cried, not in anger but in pain. "I don't even know who I am. I...I...I know who my mother is. I know where her body lies. I visit her grave often and pray for her. But what about the rest of me? What about that? I don't even know my father. You have never told me about him. I...I must see him. I want to know why I am like the Spanish people. When I see him, maybe I'll understand."

Tomás tried to swallow his own pain caused by the boy's words. Then he looked in the direction of Tofu and stared intently at him for a short time. The Indian nodded. The priest's eyes returned to the boy.

"Tofu will take you to him, Kocha, back in San Agustín. As you walk on this journey, you will also talk, and together, you will find your father. I pray that then your questions will be answered."

"With Tofu? You're not coming with me?" the boy asked looking up. In truth, the boy was not sure he wanted the friar with him when he met his real father, but Tofu? Like most of the orphans at the mission, Kocha found the strong, silent outcast intimidating, and although he bore no anger in his heart for Tofu, the dead body of his mother lay between them like a valley.

Fray Tomás shook his head in response to the boy's question. "Tofu must go for many reasons, and I am needed here. But remember my love will go with you."

Instinctively, Tofu knew what the Padre was saying, and he nodded in

---

[8] "My son"

agreement. Tofu would indeed be the right agent in this healing process. Buenaventura came with a cloth and a bowl filled with water and began to wipe the blood and tears from Kocha's face. He knew, as did the others, that it would be much easier to heal the cuts and scrapes on the boy's skin than the inner wounds of his spirit.

The next day, Tofu and Kocha set out on foot. During their search for the boy's father, Tofu said he would give him more lessons about the Potano way of life. The outcast was sincere in his effort to help Kocha become thoroughly skilled in his people's methods of survival.

XV

These lessons were only part of the reason why Tomás wanted Tofu to lead this quest. The padre learned long before that Tofu knew the identity of Kocha's father. Tofu had told Tomás that no two people leave the same footprint. Each person presses on the ground in a different way, with a different force and at a different angle.

One fateful day, years before, Tofu discovered the footprints of a stranger leading to his home where he lived with his wife, Kocha's mother. This stranger wore boots. No Potano used such shoes. He saw the interloper's footprints at the door of their dwelling. When he questioned his wife about this visitor, she denied any knowledge of a stranger. He loved her, so he believed her, but he wanted to solve the mystery of these footprints. He ventured to find similar footprints to the ones by his dwelling and he succeeded. He followed them, and they led him to the young Spanish captain. Suspicion began to grow in his heart. But he said nothing, and when his wife became pregnant, his joy at this news swept his worry away. Then Kocha was born. Looking at the baby with its Spanish features not only brought back all of Tofu's suspicions, but confirmed them. This betrayal wracked his heart like a lightning strike to the soul. It ignited within him white-hot rage.

Not long after Kocha's birth, this fury led Tofu to take the life of the boy's mother. Only his newfound faith and friendship with the padre had prevented him from killing again. Tomás had spared his life. He spared the life of Kocha's father, the man who had become his enemy. Now he and Kocha went to seek this man.

Tofu and Kocha followed a pathway already cleared and often used. It was known as the Mission Trail, and it connected all the existing Franciscan missions to the mission headquarters in San Agustín. In that town lay their destination.

Sadness and silence hung heavy on Kocha as they plodded off together with provisions and shelter for sleeping overnight. Then, as the miles wore away, the questions from the ten-year-old boy's heart gradually came to his lips. "Tofu," he asked, "what was my mother like?"

Tofu thought a moment. "Beautiful," Tofu answered, "beautiful, and loving, and wild. She had a temper—worse than a badger." The Indian man smiled as he thought of his wife.

"Did you love my mother?" Kocha asked.

"Yes," Tofu replied.

"Did you hate my father?" the boy continued.

"Yes," Tofu said.

"Why did you kill my mother and not my father?" Kocha questioned.

The man's step hesitated for a second in his surprise at the directness of this question. Then Tofu and Kocha began walking on their long journey into the past. The outcast said, "Kocha, I took the life of your mother because a Spanish man took your mother from me. Your mother came to love this man more than me, and I was her husband! How sad my heart felt when I learned that! It ached, like yours does today. I hated this man and all that he stood for. I hated all the Spanish people. They had done this to me! They had robbed me of the one person I truly loved!

"After your birth, I knew that I was not your father. You did not have Potano eyes or hair. Then the rest of the tribe knew, too. It destroyed my pride. I fled the village and became insane with hatred and jealousy.

"When I left, your mother went to your Spanish father, but he was too proud to take your mother into his home. She went back to the village. She had nowhere else to go. Your mother was the sister of the cacique. You were to be the future cacique. She begged the cacique for help and he gave it."

"Then I also returned. Your uncle asked me to forget my anger, but I could not. My hatred and grief gave me no rest. The only way I thought I could free myself was to take your life and that of your mother and father. I believed I could release my hatred only through death...I was wrong."

He fell silent, then squinted at the fading sun. "Come, now it is time to get ready for the night."

Before sunset Tofu and Kocha found a place to camp for the evening. They started a fire, spread their deerskin on the ground, and began eating the food that had been prepared for them. As they shared their meal, Kocha asked, "What happened then?"

Tofu explained the arrival of Tomás and Buenaventura and the rescue of baby Kocha by the padre. Then, thanks to Padre Tomás, his own life had been spared the otherwise inevitable penalty of death for killing the sister of the cacique.

"What the padre had taught me, Kocha, was a new lesson. One I had never heard before. It was the lesson of this Jesus of the Christian people, 'Do not do to others, as they do to you.' It was forgiveness. It took me a long time to understand why Fray Tomás did not kill me when I tried to kill him. But I learned. I did not seek to kill your father."

"You forgave him," Kocha said.

Tofu nodded. Then he stared into the fire for long time. When he spoke again, his voice was low and hoarse. "Maybe some day you can forgive me for what I did to your mother," he said.

Now it was Kocha's turn to look into the fire. He nodded. "I wish you hadn't done that," he said. Then for more reasons than he could name, Kocha felt emotion well up inside him and tears threaten his face. He hated to cry. "I am going to bed now," he said, and wrapped himself in his animal skins.

The older Indian sat by the fire for a while longer before eventually giving into sleep.

On arriving in the city of San Agustín, which was enclosed by a palisade of wood, Tofu proceeded immediately to the headquarters of the Franciscans located within the walls. He had indicated to the guard that he had come as an emissary of Fray Tomás Sanchez. At the friary headquarters, he requested the assistance of one of the padres, to whom he whispered a special request. Would he please accompany the young boy and himself to visit the dwelling place of the boy's Spanish father? The friar looked at the child and readily agreed.

The Franciscan knew where to go and led the way. Through the village they walked until they reached the edge of the town near the mission church. The area sat enclosed by a wall made of coquina stone. "We have reached your destination," the priest said.

"But this is a cemetery!" Kocha exclaimed.

"The padre is right, Kocha," Tofu replied, and proceeded to a gravesite that had been carefully attended. It was the grave of a captain and man of noble heritage: a Spanish *hidalgo*.

The name on the grave was Don Miguel Espinoza, and the dates on the stone marker were 1582-1608.

The Franciscan friar gave a brief account of the captain's life.

"Your father died when a disease called by the Spanish 'smallpox,' swept through the town of San Agustín. He was a respected leader in the Spanish military who was assigned for a short time as the leader of the Spanish garrison at the mission of San Francisco de Potano. He came from the city of Barcelona, in Europe. He died as a young man.... May the Lord forgive him his sins. May he rest in peace."

With eyes closed, Kocha tried to repeat the last words of the friar, as he knew Fray Tomás would want him to do, but he could not. He did not feel at peace! "Tofu, he is dead! You didn't tell me my father was dead. You and...and Fray Tomás said I would get the answers I wanted. How can I get those answers now?" the boy demanded.

The Franciscan looked taken aback by Kocha's outburst, but Tofu met the boy's gaze steadily.

"Padre, would you pardon us a moment?" Tofu asked the friar. The young priest nodded and left them alone. Tofu then turned to the boy and said "Kocha, you did get answers. You heard who he was, how he lived, and how he died. What other answers did you want him to give you?"

Kocha opened his mouth and then blinked. He realized that he didn't know what he wanted to ask his father. He thought that somehow something would happen when he saw the man, or that his questions would come once they started talking. He had hoped that this meeting would put to rest the doubts and fears that most troubled his heart. Now, he thought, that dream would remain just that, a dream. Miserable, he said to Tofu, "I don't know. It's just...I feel so alone. Tofu, I know I have you and Fray Tomás and Fray Buenaventura. You have given me all that I have in life, and I thank God in my prayers for you all. But now the most important thing is that I am one with my people. And I can never be that. I am different. I am..." and here Kocha uttered the words he had heard from Ycho, and not from him alone, "I am a half-breed. How can I ever be the leader my uncle and the padres want me to be? Who am I? Why didn't my father want me? Where do I fit in?"

"Kocha," Tofu grabbed the boy by the arm, "look at me. Yes, in your veins flows the blood of a Spaniard. A Spanish man is your father, just as a Potano woman is your mother. You were also born to be the next cacique. These things have already been decided for you. But the rest is up to you. Listen to me. I have learned that what makes a man is not the blood that flows though his veins but the heart that beats in his chest and the brain in his head, and how he uses them.

"It is true. The Spanish people, in coming to our land, have deprived us of many things. They have taken from me my wife. They have taken from you your very Potano heritage and appearance. They have brought us insult and injury from our own Potano people. But in Fray Tomás, they have brought us the great faith. And you and I are better people because of it. I would die for Fray Tomás and the faith he brings. And Kocha, I know you would die as well."

Kocha nodded in agreement, though part of him worried about the fact that just recently he had been almost too afraid to get in a fight, much less die for something. But he knew he would do anything for Fray Tomás, and he wanted to do good for the Great Spirit.

"Kocha," Tofu continued, "you cannot change what had happened to you, just as I cannot, but you can do as I have done, and as Fray Tomás did for me long before." He paused, waiting to see if the boy understood what he was saying.

"I can forgive," Kocha said.

Tofu nodded and said, "Forgive your father for what he did to you and your mother. Forgive Ycho and the other children for insulting you. Forgive…" he almost said 'me' but he didn't have the courage to ask again. Instead Tofu said, "Move on. Listen to me. I have learned. If you could move on, that is a big step to becoming a good man. If you are a good man, you will make a great cacique."

"What if they don't accept me?" Kocha asked.

"They will accept you!" Tofu declared. "Before my fall from the good graces of your uncle, I was known as the best warrior among the Potano. And, Kocha, I will teach you to be as well. You may be small like the Spanish, but you will be tall in the ways of defending yourself. I promise you!

"Besides you already belong, because you have people that love you. Your uncle loves you. So do Fray Tomás and Fray Buenaventura…and so do I," Tofu said; though the last words came out with a struggle. At first he could not meet Kocha's gaze, though he knew the boy was looking at him. Tofu had faced death many times, but it took more courage to meet the child's eyes than any battle or war party he had faced. He feared to see rejection in Kocha's gaze. When he finally looked, he saw the boy staring at him piercingly.

Suddenly, Kocha hugged Tofu. "I love you, too," he said, "and I forgive you." For a moment the embrace continued, then the child broke it and knelt by his father's grave. "May the Lord forgive you," he said. "May you rest in peace." He crossed himself, then said over his shoulder to Tofu, "Fray Tomás must be worried about us. Don't you think we had better head back to our village?"

"Go ahead," Tofu responded, not looking at the boy, "I'll be with you in a moment." Tofu rubbed his eyes furiously. He hated to cry.

Later, the future cacique and his guide and friend bid the friar who helped them a fond farewell and turned in a westerly direction toward the only place the two could call home—the Mission Santa Fé.

XVI

- 1624 -

In a small clearing by the bank of the river, a fish flopped, slowly gasping its last breath as it lay amidst a blanket of fallen leaves and branches. The glittering scales sent a beacon to any predator that here lay a meal waiting to be eaten. But no animal interrupted this seeming suicide and only the sound of the wiggling body against the leaves broke the silence.

Then a voice, young and male, came from the bushes. "He's not coming," it said in a whisper.

"He's coming," responded another whispered voice, but this one sounded older.

Another moment of silence passed. "It better be soon or some alligator or bear is going to come as they did last time and eat that fish," the young low voice said again.

"Patience is the strength of both the warrior and the hunter," reminded the older voice.

"Patience?" responded the younger voice. "The ceremony is less than a week away! Am I supposed to show up empty- …"

"Shhh!" hissed the older voice. "Look!"

A black dot appeared in the blue sky, and swiftly it grew in size. One could see wings and the sun glinting off golden feathers. Then suddenly the wings folded and the shape plummeted out of the sky at incredible speed. In a second, the eagle swooped upon the fish, but just as its great talons sunk into its prey, a voice from the bush cried, "Now!"

A rope, carefully hidden by cleverly strewn debris, pulled taut. With the rope as the drawstring, a net leapt from beneath the fallen leaves and branches concealing it and swallowed the eagle. With the fish still in its claws, the eagle screamed and struggled, but it was caught.

From out of the bushes came Kocha, but a Kocha changed by time. The days of childhood and childhood disappointments were cast aside, because Kocha, the boy, had begun to grow into a man. Neither still a boy nor yet a man, Kocha wandered in the time of transition between the two. In appearance, the man began to absorb the boy. His face was rugged, ruddy, and pleasant-looking, with eyes that were wide, welcoming, and happy. His disposition was generally friendly and pleasant, though he could be, on occasion, somewhat moody. Bigotry about his heritage had left emotional wounds sometimes rubbed raw by the intense feelings that afflict every growing teenager. Though not tall in stature, he always stood erect and was physically very strong. His presence commanded respect.

Tofu carefully secured the net and lifted the bird. The eagle was magnificent. A robust and confident Kocha crossed his arms and surveyed his catch.

One week later, Kocha crossed his arms again in satisfaction, but this time for a different reason. To the Potano, transition times in life had special meaning, and the tribe celebrated them with elaborate rituals and festivities. Today was a special day for Kocha and all the Potano villagers, because today the future cacique would become a Potano warrior.

With hair braided up in the fashion of an adult Potano, Kocha boldly began to chant a striking Potano melody held dear by all the people of the village. Drums beat steadily to accompany him, and following the chant, the slow, rhythmic shuffling of feet could be heard as the young warriors of the tribe, with their arms decorated like eagle wings, danced to the chant. They mimicked the flight of an eagle as they circled around a triangular structure surmounted by an eagle's nest. Ornaments made of snail shells decorated the bands on their arms and legs and hung from pins in their ears. Their bodies were painted with red ochre, and their heads were full of multicolored feathers.

The song of Kocha rested favorably upon the ears of all the Potano villagers, including Padre Tomás, who stood flanked by Padre Buenaventura and Tofu. The younger Franciscan beamed proudly from among the spectators.

Kocha sang strong and clear, his gaze directed to the farthest point of sight imaginable, beyond any physical object in view.

> *Soar, soar like the eagle / Mighty lord of earth and sky.*
> *Climb high above the highest cloud / Where none can ever die.*
>
> *Spread wide your wings of glory. / Envelop all below.*
> *Rising o'er the tallest oaks / To regions few will know.*
>
> *You'll see with vision clear and bright. / You'll hear the furthest sound.*
> *You'll overpower the strongest prey. / All creatures you'll confound.*
>
> *In courage none will be your match. / In wisdom none your peer.*
> *With speed so swift and flight so sure, / No foes you'll hold in fear.*
>
> *Such grace of movement to behold! / Such beauty you display!*
> *So great a spirit you possess! / All honor you this day!*

The dancers swooped high and low and began to quicken their steps, moving rapidly around the wooden structure. Kocha continued:

> *When you return to earth again, / Encourage us to fly.*
> *And take us with you from this land / To heights beyond the sky.*
>
> *And we shall...*
> *Soar, soar like the eagle, / Mighty lord of earth and sky.*
> *With him climb o'er the highest cloud / Where we shall never die.*

The drummers increased their beating to a rapid cadence then stopped abruptly to signal the end of the song. The dancers shook their feathered arms and released a loud war cry in unison. The crowd of onlookers began to shout and clap, until their voices grew hoarse from the strain.

Then, the cacique, Toloca, appeared wearing feathers in his headpiece and his arm and leg bands bedecked with shell ornaments. He moved toward Kocha, and gradually lifting his hands, he called for silence. The crowd quickly heeded him, and they began to look for places to sit on the ground.

Toloca then described to the villagers the tasks Kocha had completed on his road to manhood. These accomplishments earned him the right to assume this day his status as a *tascaia*, a warrior of his tribe. Normally, the taking of one scalp was one of the requirements to become a warrior, but such was not asked of Kocha because the Potano were not presently at war with any nation.

In place of the procuring of a scalp, Kocha had to prove himself by capturing, without injury, an animal most loved and respected by the Potano: an eagle. That he had done successfully. He must then, in turn, set the eagle free, so he would never be held in bondage under the dominion of the spirit of any eagle.

To further increase his rank as a warrior, however, Kocha would need to take scalps. Toloca went on to explain the significance of taking scalps. From ancient tradition, this act demonstrated to the Potano people one's ability as a fighter, and it was necessary for a brave to do so, if he wished to advance in warrior status. By exhibiting the scalp and dancing ceremonially with it, the brave provided proof of his right to advancement. To ascend to the rank of *noroco*, Koch must bring the scalps of three of the enemy. More would be required of him to rise to the rank of a *hita tascaia;* and to become a *nicoguadca*, he would need to have killed seven enemy *tascaias* and three *hitas tascaias*.

Fray Tomás turned to Buenaventura with a look bordering on disbelief. The idealist priest took mental note of the conflict this perspective presented with the mores he hoped to instill in these people. Buenaventura merely shrugged his shoulders. He was never surprised by any of the primitive ideas he confronted among these people. He gave a slight shake of his head and his eyes seemed to say to Tomás, "What do you think you'll ever do to change such ideas? Very little, I'm afraid!"

At this point, Toloca presented to Kocha a carefully chiseled stone breast-plate, symbolic of the young man's warrior status. The future cacique hung it around his neck.

"I now present our newest Potano *tascaia*," Toloca proclaimed. "May our people be protected from their enemies because of his skills and his courage!"

Kocha quickly signaled to one of his friends, who brought him a wooden cage. It held the large eagle he had captured.

"Go free, my friend," Kocha beckoned. "May my spirit climb with you to the highest of heights, so I may be with the Great Spirit in all I do!" He lifted the wooden peg from the door of the cage. The stately eagle proudly pushed free of its prison and then bounded quickly into the air.

All watched the eagle soar high beyond the confines of the village, beyond the confines of the Potano territory, beyond the confines of the very earth itself. Rays of sunlight reflected back to the earth from its shiny brown and white feathers, and a cry rang forth from its golden beak. The cheers of the Potano answered that cry and the beat of the drummers accompanied the swift departure of the eagle from the village.

"Now, let us proceed with the game!" Toloca proclaimed.

The young warriors took the special wooden structure that had been at the center of the eagle dance and mounted it onto the top of a pole that stood in the middle of a large open field. This wooden figure was the focus of the semi-religious, semi-recreational activity that literally consumed the energies of the young and old among the Potano. It was the ball game.

Referred to by the Spanish as *juego de pelota,* this game was played by teams from rival villages. The object was for a team to score eleven points by propelling a small buckskin ball, a little larger than a musket ball, into the post. Only the foot could be used when shooting the ball at the post, and a player scored one point each time the ball struck the shaft. If the ball lodged in the eagle's nest at the top, two points were awarded.

Today, the team of Toloca's village consisted of none other than Kocha and his selected group of about forty teammates. They would do battle with another team of comparable size from a neighboring Potano village. The players dressed in deerskin loincloths, and their bodies were elaborately painted with distinctive colors to set them off from their rival team.

The players all huddled closely together in a bronze-skinned mass of tense anticipation. Holota Toloca held the ball for all to see, and the players eagerly watched for the slightest movement of the village leader. When the cacique tossed the ball, the game would begin.

Toloca threw the ball high into the air, as the crowd cheered loudly in the hopes that one of their team members would be the first to retrieve it. It dropped into the middle of the combatants, all of whom had their arms stretched high to catch it. Instantly, they began to pile up on the skillful but unfortunate player whose hands had grasped the ball. Though a point would result only when the ball hit the post propelled there by someone's foot, the combatants could use their hands as well as their feet to move the ball around the field.

For the next five minutes, no one saw anything but a mound of human bodies, one pouncing upon the other in an attempt to steal away the ball. There appeared to be no rules as players continuously punched, gouged, and elbowed each other. They squeezed throats, kicked stomachs, and twisted arms. Within moments, blood began to flow.

Once again, Tomás looked hard in the direction of Fray Buenaventura and began to shake his head. Though he had heard about the game, and occasionally watched it from a distance, Fray Tomás saw it close up for the first time, and he was amazed at its violence. The contest turned these boys into wild animals. The teams fought this game with a seriousness that could easily involve the loss of life! He thought to himself that one form of internecine conflict had been avoided, only to be replaced by another one that was equally reprehensible. But Fray Tomás could not think of any way to stop this match now.

Since no one had succeeded in wresting the ball from the catcher, one by one the bodies peeled away from the heap of humans crushing one another. Then, Fray Tomás saw Kocha, bleeding and breathless, lying at the bottom of the pile, with the ball clasped tightly to his chest. The players backed away to allow the new *tascaia* the opportunity to throw the ball to one of his teammates.

Kocha tossed the ball to a teammate, who passed it to another; and with great accuracy, they moved the ball toward the post. As the ball sailed through the air, a rival player hit the receiver with a forearm to the throat and intercepted the ball. One of Kocha's men tackled the rival, but not before the interceptor threw the ball up high. Another teammate leapt and caught it, only to have an opposing player knock his legs out from under him. The catcher landed on his knee with an audible crack. The onlookers collectively winced. Fighting past the pain, the player hurriedly tossed the ball in Kocha's direction, before more opponents pounced on top of him. The ball bounced on the ground, and a rival reached for it. Kocha dashed in and tapped it with his left foot, knocking it just out from under the boy's hand. Then the newly made *tascaia* shifted his weight and kicked the ball with his right foot. It shot through the air and hit the post with a crack. He scored the first point!

Tofu smiled with pride. He had trained Kocha for years in every aspect of Potano life, including the ways of a warrior and, especially, in the ball game. After the fight with Ycho, Fray Tomás had even consented to teach the boy *Capoeira*. Today, Kocha proved he had mastered his lessons, Tofu noted, and in fact, it took every fiber of reserve in his body to restrain himself from jumping into the game with his trainee.

Tomás gave no evidence of any emotion at all over what he saw. The whole event repulsed him, but he knew Kocha and tribe would be watching not just the game but also his reaction. So far, three players had sustained serious injuries, broken hands and ribs. After seeing the fourth participant removed from the field, unconscious, with a broken knee and bloody face, the friar dropped his pretense. On occasion, he muttered almost involuntarily, "This is the ball post of the devil!" while staring intently at the structure that was the center of the players' attention.

Out on the field, the competition raged fiercely. One team scored a point; then so would the other. The host team held the lead for a while, then lost it to the visitors. Then they gained it back again.

If one were to judge by the blood, sweat, tears, and even skill that went into the match, it was indeed a well-fought game. The spectators became so engrossed by the activity, they seemed to teeter on the edge of bursting onto the field themselves. The intensity increased even more when the visiting team once more took the lead and then scored their tenth point. Kocha's team lagged just behind them with nine. Even Tomás felt himself drawn in by the tension, and he watched like a hawk every move of his adopted son.

As the ball flew toward a rival, Kocha blocked the opponent's hand and grabbed the ball out of the air. The opposing player moved to attack him and get back the ball, but Kocha shifted his block into a tight grip on the player's arm. Suddenly, with a twist, he tossed the rival into another opponent who had darted in to tackle Kocha. The two rival team players went down in a tangle, leaving Kocha free for a second. He dropped the ball to the ground, took careful aim, and to the amazement of all, he landed the ball securely into the eagle's nest at the top of the pole! He kicked the only two-point goal of the game. His team's score jumped from nine to eleven immediately giving them the victory!

Kocha beamed as his teammates slapped him on the back and pounded his shoulders and head as a sign of approval and praise. Tofu helped them lift him onto their shoulders and carry him to the ball post, where he removed the eagle's nest and carried it to Toloca. Inside the eagle's nest lay nestled a stuffed eagle, some small spiral shells, and now the ball that Kocha had so deftly kicked into it.

As the cacique of the hosting village, Toloca placed garlands of flowers around the necks of all the members of Kocha's team. "You have made our village proud today! You have given honor to all of us! In your victory, we have found victory! Long live Kocha!" cried Toloca.

"Long live Kocha!" cried all the people of the village.

When the uproarious shouting had subsided and the people of both villages had returned to their dwellings, Kocha began to look around for the one person whose approval meant the most to him in the world to him. "Where is Padre Tomás?" Kocha asked of Tofu. "I have to share this with him! Without the two of you, this never would have happened."

Tofu and Kocha scoured the village in search of the Franciscan, with no success. Finally, at sunset, they came upon Fray Tomás, alone and in prayer in a densely wooded area.

"Where have you been? We won! Our team was victorious today!" Kocha shouted elatedly. He was very surprised to find his spiritual father looking sad and disappointed, his face shrouded in gloom.

"Kocha," the padre began, "today was a day you and I and Tofu, and even Buenaventura, had been looking forward to for a long, long time. I know this day begins a new time in your life, and I am very happy for you. You have worked so hard and achieved so much. You have faced every obstacle and become a true Potano warrior.

"You know I have wanted very much for you to succeed as the new cacique of your people. I only now realize the price you must pay for this success, and I ask myself, was it all worth the effort?" The priest held up a hand at Kocha's shocked expression. "Please, Kocha," Fray Tomás continued, "do not misunderstand me. I am proud of you, and I love you dearly. I only wonder, now, how a Potano cacique can be at once a good leader and a good Christian. I was hoping that you could be both. I just do not want for you to succeed so well as a chieftain that you stop being a follower of Christ. Because then I will have failed in my responsibility to you!"

"Padre Tomás," Kocha responded, "all I can say is that I hope to be true to my Potano family and my Christian family as well. I, too, do not know how this is possible, but I will try. That is why I have you as my spiritual father and friend. I will always stay close to you to test the strength of my faith. You know that!

"When you assigned Tofu to me as my teacher, you and I did not know that he was a *nicoguadca* and the best warrior of our village, and I would say the best instructor, too. I will try to use the skills he has given me wisely and in a Christian way. But to do that, I need you to teach me, Padre. I want the Spirit you possess to be fully in my life. All my people admire and love you, for the Great Spirit is so much evident in you. That, Padre Tomás, is the victory you have won for me and my people. May your victory be mine also one day. Then I shall truly be happy. But I know I have much, much more to learn from you in the lessons of life."

Kocha wrapped his arms around his spiritual mentor and friend, and then he led him and his other mentor, Tofu, back to their home at the Mission Santa Fé.

XVII
- 1627 -

It was not uncommon to have torrential rainfalls in La Florida in the early months of the fall. Spawned by lingering hurricanes, the north-central part of the peninsula would occasionally experience flood conditions at this time of the year. Such was the situation once again as no fewer than three hurricanes passed north of San Agustín and unleashed their violent forces on the mainland to the north. One totally destroyed the *convento* and mission church of San José de Zapala.

Since rain forests and wetlands of that area served as a reservoir providing water to the underground rivers and springs many miles to the south, the springs and sink holes surrounding the Mission Sante Fe were at flooding stage. The adjoining river, referred to affectionately as the "Rio Santa Fé," was climbing high on the riverbanks, threatening the Indian village and the Franciscan's buildings.

The structures of the mission compound consisted of wood or daub and mortar. The rains fell steadily upon them and the winds beat heavily against them, yet they held. Their endurance came in no small part from the diligence of the friars and mission workers. Tomás and Buenaventura daily canvassed the mission with Tofu, checking on the conditions of the buildings and their inhabitants. They reassured the young orphans of the mission school that they would be safe. Tomás assigned Tofu to stand guard at the children's residence through the nighttime, and he and Buenaventura took turns keeping vigil from the *convento;* such was their concern for the well-being of their charges.

About midnight on the twentieth day of the autumn rains, there came a loud pounding at the door of the *convento* and a grief-stricken cry for help in the Spanish tongue. *"¡Ayúdame, ayúdame! Help me!"* were the words spoken, barely audible over the thrashing sounds of wind and rain. The midnight visitor identified himself as José Navarro, a sergeant from the garrison stationed at the Mission of San Francisco de Potano. As Tomás hurriedly pulled the soldier into safety from the torrential rain, José Navarro explained that he had been with the lieutenant, Esteban Moreno, who commanded the garrison of that mission. The officers and a small band of soldiers were bringing food and supplies in boats to beleaguered Spanish farmers north of the Santa Fé Mission. Just a short time ago, en route to their destination, the boat in which he and the lieutenant were riding capsized.

José Navarro had made it safely to shore, but Lieutenant Moreno, having sustained severe injuries, could not swim and was marooned on a marshy wooded area in the middle of the river a few leagues to the north. The other soldiers were already far ahead of them and had not noticed their mishap. Could anyone in the mission or Indian village help him bring the lieutenant to the shore?

Without hesitation Tomás looked toward Buenaventura, and requested that he retrieve Tofu at once from the children's residence. The younger Franciscan then took off his friar's garb, and after rolling up his woolen Spanish trousers, he darted out of the *convento* into the pouring rain. Barefoot and barechested, he headed for the house now inhabited by Kocha, in the nearby Indian village.

Arriving at the young man's *buhio,* Fray Tomás cried, "Kocha, we must help Lieutenant Moreno. He is in danger in the river north of here." Kocha caught the urgency in the friar's summons and roused himself from sleep. He showed not the least reluctance to join in any rescue attempt. After all, his own Spanish father had once headed the garrison Lieutenant Moreno now commanded; besides, he had himself grown fond of the young officer. Kocha had worked closely with Lieutenant Moreno on many projects, not only for the benefit of the Spanish people, but also in an effort to understand better his own heritage through this man, and he deliberately fostered that relationship.

Within minutes, Tofu, Tomás, Kocha, and José assembled at the river's edge where the tribe had moored two canoes made of hewn cypress and measuring about four and half *varas* in length. They were just about ready to board the small crafts when Kocha halted the expedition momentarily and ran back to enlist the support of his uncle, the cacique. Kocha felt, without hesitation, that the prowess of the aged, yet agile leader could only help in the effort before them.

When Kocha and Toloca arrived, Tofu paddled off, leading the way with the sergeant and Fray Tomás in his boat. The cacique and his heir in their boat brought up the rear. The darkness and rain prevented them from seeing each other clearly, and often, the lead canoe would completely vanish from view. Only the occasional warning shout from first boat enabled the rescuers to forge ahead in unison on their mission.

Battling the strong current, the paddlers struggled upstream. As they came near the site where José believed their boat had capsized, the rescuers repeatedly called out Lieutenant Moreno's name.

Lack of visibility, caused by the darkness, complicated their search. Also, the dense rainfall and the strong winds further frustrated their task. But there were other things out this night that made this mission not just difficult but deadly. Alligators infested these waters, and their scaly bodies could often be seen sliding through the water alongside the canoes. The Indians were adept at handling these predators. The Potano used large, sharp-pointed arrows attached to long poles. If an animal attacked, they would thrust the point through the opened jaws of the reptile and into the back of its throat, quickly ending its life. But in their alarm, the crew had acted hastily, and the only weapons that they brought with them were their canoe paddles. Now, the rescuers' only recourse was to slap at anything that moved in the water too close to their boats. Hopefully, this would frighten the intruders away.

Despite the slapping oars, the cagey animals continued to drift menacingly behind the boats. Their eye sockets peeked above the water's edge, enabling them to maintain a better sight of the boat than the canoeists could of the predators.

When the men finally found the marooned lieutenant, they saw that he clung to a high oak stump that leaned against the fallen trunk of another tree. It was the highest point of this island that was quickly disappearing. The floodwaters had nearly submerged his small island and the rescuers saw the man frantically fending off a horde of threatening alligators. Curious by nature, the animals had gathered here in such great number that one could walk on the backs of them all the way to the terrified soldier. Tofu moved his craft cautiously through the barricade of horny-backed bodies. He noted their size and some of them measured much larger than his own boat.

Tofu turned in his seat and tried using his hands to call for slowness and silence. Not seeing Tofu or his hand motions, Kocha and Toloca sped quickly up from behind, disturbing the calm, but more inauspiciously, ramming the boat commandeered by Tofu. Within an instant, the whole rescue attempt turned to chaos as the horde of alligators moved rapidly, causing Kocha's craft to suddenly overturn.

Kocha quickly heaved himself back onto the overturned canoe, and from there into the canoe of Tofu, Tomás, and José Navarro. Toloca did not fare so well, and because of the dark water and lashing rain, he did not know in which direction to swim. He drifted away from both canoes.

Tomás cried out for him. "Where are you, Toloca? We will get you.... Where are you?" We will come to you.... "

A faint, sputtering sound could be heard: "Get the lieutenant first! I will distract the animals. Get the lieutenant!" Toloca then began to kick and splash, to divert the alligators in his direction away from the island. Predators of opportunity, the alligators turned from the prey that hung out of reach and went for the victim in the water. Now Toloca had become the main target of the strong, swift, hungry vultures of the river.

"No!" Kocha cried. "Stop, or you will be killed! You don't need to do this! Call to us so we will know where you are!"

Then the remaining canoe abutted Estaban Moreno's perch. They pulled him aboard and shot rapidly to the area where they heard the sounds of heavy splashing in the water.

In the water, Toloca fought for his life. One large alligator swam straight toward him. The cacique struck at the animal and it twisted aside, but it whipped him with its tail as it passed. Then pointed jaws slammed on his leg like a bear trap, as another reptile bit him and then pulled him beneath the water. He struck at the creature's eyes and snout, its few areas of weakness. The grip of the teeth began to lessen; the chieftain almost broke free when a third animal attacked from the side and its reptilian teeth gouged into his chest.

On the river's surface, Tofu and Kocha pounded with the two remaining canoe paddles. They struck at all the animals in sight, but to no avail. The alligators continued to swarm and fight back.... They had a victim! They would not release him now. The alligator that had Toloca tightly in its grasp swam quickly downstream, and the others followed closely behind. Tofu sensed what was happening. An alligator ritual had begun and all wanted part of the feast.

"We must get to him before it is too late!" Fray Tomás cried.

Tofu paddled hard, while trying to maintain a steady, balanced craft that was weighted down by the heavy load of passengers. As a *nicoguadca,* he knew when the odds were in his favor and when they were not. Right now he felt as helpless as on the day he learned that Kocha's mother no longer loved him. And his feelings proved tragically true. Search as they might, the rescuers could not find Toloca. The cacique and the alligators had disappeared into the dark waters of the night.

Only three days later, when the rains ceased and the river began to subside, did any sign of Toloca appear. It was very uncanny. Immediately in front of the Potano village, on a formerly submerged tree limb, hung the medal given to Toloca by Tomás when the priest first entered the village. It was the medal of Our Lady of Loreto.

One of the Indian warriors brought it to Fray Tomás, and the priest, in turn, took it to the house of Kocha, who had been in mourning since the night Toloca disappeared.

"You must stop blaming yourself, Kocha," the friar softly counseled the young man, as he entered the dwelling, "Life continues. You must continue with it or it will leave you behind."

Kocha remained silent for a while, as if his spirit were still back in the boat with Toloca. "If only I had left my uncle alone that night.... If only I had not called him, this never would have happened," he said, choking on his words.

Tomás noticed the weariness in Kocha's eyes—clearly the young man had not slept in the past three days—but even more, the padre sensed weariness in the young man's spirit as if he bore a heavy burden. Fray Tomás could sense the crushing guilt.

"No mas, Kocha, what is done is done," Tomás admonished gently. "Here, take this," Tomás beckoned. "It is a gift from me, and it is a gift from your uncle. I want you to have it, and I know he wants you to have it, too."

Instantly, Kocha recognized the medal as belonging to Toloca because of the special chain on which it hung. Toloca had always worn it proudly. "Fray Tomás," Kocha began, "I do not know if I grieve more for the past or for the future. I look at my friends and the other young braves like me, and I can't be like them anymore. I will never be the same again."

The reality of the cacique's death had settled upon Kocha's mind and heart, with all its manifold consequences—especially those affecting him. He had always known he would succeed his uncle one day, but he never imagined that day would come so soon or in such a tragic manner.

Tomás put into words what Kocha had been pondering deeply. "Kocha, you feel as any young man of nineteen would feel today.... Your youth is being taken from you, your freedom, your ability to come and go as you wish, your privacy, your right to follow the commands of another. Now you must lead. Now you are the leader. Now you are the cacique!"

Then Tomás added words that struck his adopted son like the weight of a tall oak crashing down on his young shoulders. "I can no longer be your teacher. This is the last time I will come to you without invitation."

"What? Padre, why? What did I do?" Kocha asked in a panic.

The priest waved him to silence, "It is nothing you have done, and it is not something we could avoid forever. You are the chieftain, now. Your people must see you as the leader, Kocha. If we continue as before, some in the tribe might think that I am trying to rule through you. I will be here if you need me, Kocha. You know that. But I won't interfere. I hope to remain always your friend, but I will never offer you advice from now on unless you seek it from me."

"Then ready yourself to be called often," Kocha replied bleakly. "Padre, I don't know if I can do this. I feel this responsibility, and it is so heavy. It presses on me. I...I feel it crushing me." His voice dropped to a near whisper, "What if I fail?"

"Kocha," the friar began, gazing squarely into the eyes of the young man, "you can do anything you set out to do. You can do anything," the padre reiterated, "if only you believe. Nothing is impossible unless you believe it is impossible. You believe in the Great Spirit, and you believe that the Great Spirit is working through you. I know you do.

"This village is yours; this world, vast as it is, is yours. The universe is yours. And yes, the life that comes after this one is yours too, Kocha, if only you believe. I have tried to teach you this many times before, and the Great Spirit will teach you more each day as you listen to Him. Have faith in God, trust in Him and in yourself. You will make a great cacique."

For a while Kocha said nothing. He had a far-off look, and in his eyes lurked fear, guilt, and dismay. But then he closed his eyes and straightened. He returned Fray Tomás' gaze and nodded.

Tomás placed the chain with the medal of Our Lady of Loreto around Kocha's neck and blessed him. Kocha grasped the medal, then kissed it. To the two of them, the little medal and this blessing spoke much more than all the other symbolic rituals and ceremonies in the days ahead that would accompany Kocha's rise to power when he took his position of authority over his people.

The priest said, "Holata Kocha—Tomás by Baptism—let me be the first to recognize you and promise my obedience to you, the new cacique of your people."

A faint smile began to break from around Kocha's lips, and a hopeful look appeared in his eyes for the first time.

Tofu and Buenaventura were there to greet Kocha and the whole tribe of well-wishers cheered as Fray Tomás led him forth from his dwelling to assume his great role as the Cacique of the Potano people of the village and Mission of Sante Fé.

XVIII

The new cacique wasted no time in calling together his council of leading tribesmen. They met in the large meeting hall that had been the sight of Fray Tomás' formal welcome to the village almost twenty years before. Kocha had soon made it clear to all the villagers that he, as cacique, would now go by his Christian name, "Tomás," rather than by his Indian name. That announcement immediately raised concern among a certain faction of tribesmen, particularly among the young warriors. They feared that he planned to abandon the age-old traditions of the Potano people.

Fray Tomás deliberately kept himself at a distance from the new cacique

after his private meeting following Toloca's tragic death. The friar's paternal concern for the young cacique made him anxious for the chieftain's well-being and many times led him close to seeking the cacique out alone to offer him encouragement and support, but his own better judgment kept his solicitude in check. Any overt rapport between the two at this juncture could easily spell disaster for the young cacique and undermine his credibility as a leader of his people. The youthful brave did, however, have a number of private, late night meetings with Tofu and these lasted several hours.

Cacique Tomás, decorated with an eagle feather in his hair and tattooed extensively on his arms and chest in the manner of a chieftain, entered the meeting hall. He strode in, confident and self-assured, welcomed by his council members with the cheers that should greet a man of authority. His eyes quickly scanned the room and noted carefully the facial expressions of every single tribal leader present. He detected repressed hostility in the looks of many.

"I am very honored by the presence of each of my leading tribesmen," Cacique Tomás began, "honored because I know what each of you have done to make our people respected far past the boundaries of our village." He was sincere in commending this group of men—they were brave beyond words, and most had distinguished themselves by more than just taking many scalps of the enemy. They bore the scars from numerous combats on their arms and faces, and these marks gave mute testimony to their courage.

The young cacique continued, "I look forward to striving with each of you to make our people even greater and your reputation among all tribes and nations will then grow even more. Let us give special honor today to the man who led us bravely for so many years, the great cacique, Toloca. As a chieftain, he gave all that he had—his life and his death—for you, for me, and for other people he did not even know. May the Great Spirit now give his spirit rest in the land beyond the sun. May his spirit rise to the heights of happiness and peace in his new eternal home with the Great Spirit."

Ecstatic cheers greeted his words. This indicated with simple eloquence how deeply Toloca was loved and how much he was missed. Ruefully, Cacique Tomás thought no one would miss him more than himself. The young chieftain allowed the loud acclamations to continue for this man whose body was never recovered. This fact made the tragedy an even greater one for all the people of the village.

Fray Tomás had celebrated a Mass for Toloca, and nearly every person in the tribe attended. Even people from outside the village came. These visiting mourners included Ybitachucu, the cacique of the Apalachees who had made peace through Toloca with the Timucuan nation. Cacique Tomás knew, after seeing that multitude of sad faces, that it would be impossible to for him to replace Toloca, but it was his duty to continue what the former had left undone. He must now lead in his own way the best he could.

As the cheers died away, Cacique Tomás signaled his braves to bring in Toloca's wife and younger sister to the meeting hall. The two women entered into the assembly and were welcomed with great respect. The new cacique embraced each of them. They were dear to him as family, and both had been like mothers to him after his own mother's death. Then he handed to the wife of Toloca the symbols of Toloca's leadership—his warrior clothing, his weapons, his gifts that Toloca had received from the Apalachee cacique and the other caciques friendly to the Potano tribe.

The parting words of Toloca's wife to the young leader touched him deeply and gave him a source of great encouragement. "Toloca's spirit is with the Great Cacique now, but his spirit is also with you and always will be. Fear no enemy, however strong, because Toloca will always be your friend and guide."

Once again the cheering commenced, and it continued long after the two grieving women departed from the assembly hall.

The next matter before the new cacique and his tribal council was the appointing of one of his leading tribesmen as his *inija*, his second-in-command. Preferably a *nicoguadca,* this member of the council would command the tribe in the absence of the cacique and oversee the defense of the village and its people. The man Tomás had chosen, however, was not in this gathering; in fact, for a long time, this man had been banished from all tribal functions and activities. Cacique Tomás had selected as his *inija* none other than his mentor and friend, Tofucunatchu. The young chieftain had Tofu summoned and brought immediately to the meeting hall. Cacique Tomás formally reinstated him as a Potano tribesman, and then as the highest leader of the village after the cacique himself.

"Tofu, everyone respects you for your bravery and skill, and no one honors you more than myself. Whatever you have done in the past to diminish your honor, I now erase for all time. No one in this village may judge you again for your past crimes, and no one in this village has more right or authority to take this action than I do. You are not only a distinguished Potano warrior and *nicoguadca.* You are now also *inija* of our Potano people. In the past, you have helped me to know the ways of my people; may you long continue to be my trusted advisor and friend."

The choice of Tofu was a good one and acceptable to all in the room. Many in the tribe still remembered his past prowess. For those who would still despise him as a murderer, if Cacique Tomás could forgive him, they could do no less. Those gathered loudly applauded Tofu, and he was visibly overcome by this amazing change of events. He had considered himself dead in the eyes of the people of his village for many years. Now, he had not only come back to life, but he returned to a place of unexpected honor. He moved through the assembly to personally greet every tribal leader in the room. The cacique noted that he had picked a good diplomat for his chief assistant. Cacique Tomás allowed Tofu to complete his cordial canvassing of the assembled warrior-leaders and then placed him on the seat at his right.

With his *inija* now installed in office, the cacique moved to the center of the room. In a gentle but commanding voice, he addressed the crowd, directing his eyes at each one of the council members. "In assuming my role today as your leader, I do not hesitate to challenge all my tribal councilors to set a special example for the people of our village, because all people look to you and me to understand the direction we are to go as a people. We must show by example how we as a people are to arrive at our destinies. They will only learn if you and I help them to do so by the way we live together and work together.

"First of all, I want you to know that I will maintain the great traditions of the Potano that are truly important to us as a people. We are Potano. We are not Spanish."

A glimmer of delight shone in the eyes of all, for the cacique had spoken wisely. Their traditions were sacred to them. Many felt that the continued presence of the Spanish in their land increasingly threatened those traditions. Toloca, as cacique, had always trod cautiously here, never pushing the tribe to alter its ways beyond a safe and secure limit, but even the changes he had brought to bear on the tribe had been resented by many.

Apparently the new cacique would tread cautiously as well.

"I repeat," the cacique continued, with eyes piercing his audience, "we are Potano! We are not Spanish! Yes, the blood of a Spanish soldier flows in my veins.... But that was not by my own choice or by the choice of my people. You and I, have to live with the choices of other people who have wronged us and have made our lives difficult beyond words.

"I will always have to bear the marks of the sins of the Spanish people that they have committed against my people, because those wrongs are written"—here he began to point to all the members of his body—"on my face, on my hands, on my arms, and in the blood that flows into my heart. But, my friends, my heart and my spirit will always remain the heart and the spirit of a Potano!"

Once again the shouts of approval rang through the assembly hall. Tofu got to his feet and joined with his voice in support of the young leader. His yells could be heard over the cries of all the others, for today all the wrongs that had torn his life asunder were vindicated by the wise actions of the new cacique.

"I now ask that you listen further to my words," The chieftain continued. "Being Potano, and being one who is true to his people, means also to be wise with the wisdom of the Great Spirit. Only by making His wisdom our own, will we gain His blessing on the Potano way of life. I pray that I will be guided by that wisdom in what I ask of you today."

Cacique Tomás paused and deliberated. Then, he proceeded with his address to an audience that carefully attended to his every word.

"The days of rewarding our warriors with higher honors for the taking of enemy scalps are now at an end. We do no honor to our warriors or to our people by encouraging such behavior. All enemy scalps are to be burned this day, and all who take enemy scalps in the future are to lose rank among their people. In place of this, honor will be given to those who bring back to our village alive any enemy who becomes a captive of the Potano people."

Before anyone could react to these words, the cacique spoke further. "We will begin immediately, under the direction of Tofucunatchu, the training of all our villagers, warriors and women and children alike—all who dwell here—in the manners of defensive combat without weapons." Here the cacique was intending to develop among his people the defensive skills that Fray Tomás had taught both him and Tofu.

"Also," he quickly added, "our ball game will change as well. No longer will it be played without penalties for those who do harm to other players on the field.... And we will give no honor in this game to any false deities." The cacique referred to the tradition that the game represented a mythic reenactment of a contest between two native gods: Ochuna Nicoguadca and Ytonanslac. "From this day on, the game will be played for the greater glory of the Great Spirit, Jesus Christ, alone."

Instantly, murmuring reactions rumbled, heard form every direction of the meeting hall. The rumble spoke the voice of widespread resentment. The subdued anger of one young warrior erupted, and he jumped immediately to his feet in rage.

"No!" he shouted. "Never! You will be leading our people to ruin by such foolishness. You will make our people weak! The ball game must stand as it always has, as a training ground for combat and a spiritual preparation for war against the hated enemy! And we will never accept a change to our rules of war. If the enemy is to take our scalps as a prize for victory, we will be wrong not to take his. We will kill our enemies and dismember them completely or they will never fear us, nor will the Spanish! No, we will never accept your ways."

The speaker was a young warrior respected by all the other young braves. He had risen rapidly in the ranks and become a *nicoguadca*. The cacique remembered him as the boy he had fought years before for calling him a "half-breed." It was Ycho.

Ycho's boldness did not stop with those remarks. He blundered ahead arrogantly and called for Holata Tomás to immediately step aside as cacique and allow someone more capable to lead the Potano people.

He turned to his fellow councilors, "We cannot follow a man as weak as this one who is Spanish on the inside as well as the outside. Let us hear nothing of this nonsense about his heart being Potano. His heart is like the rest of his body. He is Spanish to the core. We reject your attempt to corrupt our Potano way of life, Holata Kocha!" (The name was purposefully placed and heavily emphasized). "Let us have Ynaja as our leader! We know what blood he has in his heart and to what people he is true!"

Ynaja was Cacique Tomás' blood cousin, the son of his aunt who was Toloca's younger sister. She had just visited the assembly with Toloca's wife. Ynaja was next in line of succession after Tomás.

The challenge to Holata Tomás' authority had been made, and the cacique could not continue in his role with such opposition before him. The cacique accepted Ycho's direct challenge to his leadership and turned it back on his new adversary.

"You are bold in words, Ycho. How bold are you in strength? You question my ability to lead. You say I will make our people weak. Why don't you see how weak I am? Test my strength and prove the truth of your words. We have not done so in many years. Then we will see who is fit to lead our people."

Ycho gave a war whoop and grabbed his weapons, a spear and a knife. He rushed to the center of the meeting hall and brandished them in front of the cacique.

But Cacique Tomás shook his head. "No, Ycho. We will fight with no other weapons than the ones the Great Spirit has given us."

Though Cacique Tomás had grown much in height and weight as he reached adulthood, Ycho still rose well above his opponent. Adolescence had transformed the tall and gangly boy into a towering, lean killer. Ycho looked at his weapons, then tossed them to the ground. Without hesitation, he launched at the cacique. With his long reach, he clasped his hands tightly around the chieftain's neck.

In a fluid, practiced motion, Holata Tomás put his hands together as if he was praying, then he thrust them up like a wedge between Ycho's arms. With the pressure of his arms pushing up and out, the cacique popped Ycho's hands off his throat.

Ycho lost his grip, but rushed forward, throwing his weight against Tomás. The move surprised the smaller man and he fell back, but he kept his grip on his adversary and both went down, locked in mortal combat. Ycho buffeted Tomás' face until the blood began to flow. Then as his next blow came, the cacique rocked with the motion, causing the two of them to roll over. For a second, Tomás was on top, and he used his momentum to push himself free from his attacker. He sprung to his feet with Ycho scrambling after him. Holata Tomás swung his leg in a savage arc, and as Ycho began to stand up, Tomás' foot slammed into his temple. Ycho's head whipped sideways, but he recovered and lunged again for his prey. Dazed by the last blow, Ycho's attack was sloppy. Tomás sidestepped his opponent's thrust, but he grabbed the warrior's arm and yanked forward. At the same time, he kicked hard. Cacique Tomás basically pulled Ycho into his foot, doubling the force of his strike. When his foot connected with Ycho's chest, he knocked the wind from the taller man's lungs. As his opponent doubled over, Tomás shifted his grip on the warrior's arm and pulled it behind the man's back, locking it into position. He had Ycho in a submission hold. The challenger couldn't turn around and he couldn't escape. Every time he tried, Cacique Tomás twisted Ycho's arm a little more until the taller brave felt like it was going to snap.

"Yield, Ycho," Cacique Tomás demanded. "You've lost. We can both walk away from this alive."

Ycho sagged as if in defeat, and Tomás relaxed his grip a little. Then, Ycho suddenly dropped to his knees and reached out with his free hand for the knife he previously dropped to the floor. Ycho stabbed backward with it blindly. He managed to plunge it into the cacique's right arm and leg before Cacique Tomás could tighten his pressure on the submission hold. As Tomás twisted the captive arm, the torque drove Ycho's face to the floor. The cacique then quickly caught the knife wielding hand and wrested the weapon from his assassin's grip. But blood ran freely from the two gash marks on his body.

"Kill Ycho!" came a cry from one of the warriors, "or he will kill you!"

For a second, rage twisted the cacique's face and he savagely twisted Ycho's arms. The brave cried out involuntarily. Holata Tomás knew with just a little more pressure, he could snap the bigger warrior's arm like a dry branch. That would teach Ycho a lesson. He could also grab the fallen knife and slit this killer's throat before the man had a chance to defend himself. By tribal law, the council expected him to do no less. Then he would be rid of this opponent forever. He twisted his enemy's arm again. Ycho whimpered—like a baby.

Slowly, Tomás, formerly Kocha, shook his head and blinked the sweat from his eyes. "I could kill this man…but I won't. Let him live out all the days the Great Spirit gives him. But, it will be in exile from his people. Do you hear me, Ycho?" he jerked the man, eliciting another sharp cry. "I banish you forever from the territory of the Potano people! Give me something to bind him with, Tofu," the cacique called out. The new *inija* helped the cacique tie Ycho's hands and feet together behind him. The challenger's face still pressed against the ground.

"Take him!" he commanded.

Tofu and two other braves from the cacique's personal bodyguard lifted Ycho and hauled him from the meeting hall like a captured wild animal. He twisted and fought but could not escape.

"You will regret today, Kocha," Ycho yelled. "You have not seen the last of me. You will try to destroy our people but some day I will stop you. I swear!"

With blood flowing from his head, his arm and leg, the cacique stood, facing the throng of warrior leaders. "If there are any others among you who wish to test my strength, speak now. Challenge me now. Take your opportunity, while I do not have the full use of one arm and leg!"

No one spoke or came forward.

"If not, then let us proceed." The cacique stiffly resumed his seat.

One elder protested, "You are wounded, Cacique. Let us call for the healer, and we will resume again tomorrow after your wounds have been bound."

Holata Tomás again scanned the faces around him and though many still looked unfriendly all of them contained something new: respect. He looked back to the elder and nodded. "Thank you, I will take your wisdom, but I will say this. We are proud because we are Potano. And we will defend ourselves against any enemy who wishes to take away from us what is rightly and truly ours. But we will do so in the right way, at the right time, as the Great Spirit leads us to do. I have nothing more to say to you today."

A wounded but strong and confident cacique dismissed his tribal leaders and proceeded, limping somewhat, in the direction of his dwelling escorted by his *inija,* Tofucunatchu.

Word traveled ahead of the new cacique and his contest with Ycho spread throughout the village. As he came close upon his home, he spied Fray Tomás in the distance. The priest had heard all about the events in the council meeting hall. The friar deliberately feigned that some children had caught his attention, though he could not help noticing the injured young man. Worry lines creased Fray Tomás' face, but he tried to pretend that his concern was focused on the Indian child in front of him who was showing the priest her scraped elbow.

"Aren't you concerned that your cacique's blood is flowing outside of his body rather than inside, where it belongs?" the cacique quipped to the friar.

The priest blessed his "patient's" scrape and sent the little girl on her way. Then looking this and way and that, he turned to his limping friend. "Do you think it wise to talk to me openly, Cacique?"

Flashing his ready, warm smile, Kocha replied "You need not fear anymore being seen in public speaking with me. It is clear to my people that I am more than ready to fight my own battles. Tofu taught me long ago that I would not be respected for my title as much as for my skills as cacique. And both of you taught me some important skills that I just used moments ago, Fray Tomás. I am sure that your reputation was greatly increased today, as well."

The priest couldn't help smiling in turn, but he also let out a little groan of protest. "May I ask you a favor, Holata Tomás…that you not report to my superiors who it was who taught you how to fight that way. Such skills were not part of my official training as a friar!"

"I think I can safely leave out that detail if any of your brown-robed brothers come asking. However, my silence has a price. I want my people to know how to defend themselves without killing, and I may need you as a tutor for many more people in the village."

The friar sighed deeply and said, "If you insist, I will help you as best

I can, especially if it stops the scalping, but I would prefer to leave the teaching of such skills as these to Tofu and yourself, Holata Tomás. You have learned them far better than I."

Fray Tomás moved to help his wounded friend walk. Then after a few moments he said, "But, you have to watch the hands of your opponent more closely! How could you let him bring a knife to your skin? That was simply careless!"

"Padre, I practiced late into the night with Tofu," the young cacique responded.

"So that's what you two were doing," the priest said shaking his head. "Maybe I will have to take up teaching again to keep both of your skills sharp!"

"The Great Spirit works in strange ways, Padre," the cacique replied, with a mild grin on his face. "Ycho and the other warriors would have done much better if they, too, had allowed you to be their tutor.... I have only one regret today, and that is that my people will suffer much because these braves were not, like me, disciples of Fray Tomás!"

XIX
1634

Cacique Tomás emerged proudly from his *buhío*, raising high in his hands a special treasure he wished to display to all in the village, to all in the world, in fact. "My son! So small, but so good-looking, like his father," the cacique jested with the interested spectators, who came toward him from all directions. "I shall call him 'Felipe-Toloca'—'Felipe,' because he is born on the feast day of San Felipe...'Toloca,' in memory of his great uncle."

The crowd pressed in to see and touch this newest and most distinguished member of the Potano tribe. The Indian people were ever in awe of the mystery of new life. It was for them the greatest gift of the Great Spirit.

Mónica, the Potano wife of the cacique, remained within their *buhío*. She was weakened by childbirth, but relieved by her delivery and joyous over the healthy condition of her first-born child. The baby was born in the eleventh month of their marriage, three years after the cacique had begun his leadership of the Potano people.

It was a new era for the tribe. Through they kept many of the same traditions, the village embarked on numerous new courses set by the cacique. Generally, the young leader had won the confidence and support of his people as he continued to introduce Christianity to the village in a direct, yet kindly way. Holata Tomás personally felt that the way of the Great Spirit was the way of Christianity. The cacique continued to hold faithfully to the Christian teachings, as he understood them, and subsequently, spared no effort in translating the Christian way of life into the Potano culture.

Fray Tomás found himself amazed at the young cacique's courage and steadfastness in putting his faith into practice in a meaningful way. As an alternative to the more violent forms of Indian combat, the chieftain introduced training in martial arts, particularly in defensive skills. This became very popular with young Potano children, such that every boy and girl was becoming a master at self-defense. Fray Tomás could not walk through the village without some child asking for advice on a particular arm or leg movement. "See Tofu, see Tofu!" he would always say, smiling and shaking his head in disbelief.

In addition, the ball game had changed. Though it still demanded a level of skill and endurance that challenged the best of athletes, the tribe now played with a modicum of civility; few serious injuries resulted. Matches no longer resulted in a half dozen maiming and crippling injuries.

The leading warriors no longer proudly displayed scalps. Even the *nicoguadcas* refrained from the practice. Scalp-taking simply wasn't acceptable anymore.

Opposition still existed and discontent reared its head sometimes vehemently time and again among different factions of the people. The most impassioned dissent came from among the eldest generation, who in their old age, generally feared and thus disliked any change, and it also came from the braves around the cacique's age. These young men held similar beliefs to those of Ycho, though they did not openly support him since his banishment. Lack of enemies and the changes Cacique Tomás made to the rules of warfare prevented many of them from advancing in warrior status, and many felt robbed of the honor dearly desired as braves. However, peace held throughout the Timucuan nation; this made the warriors' voices ineffective whenever they called for change.

Despite the occasional resistance, the new cacique's agenda had won the day. The vast majority of tribesmen respected him for taking a bold position, defending it, and holding to it. They knew his beliefs came from deep conviction, and the cacique supported his decisions by action. This formed the foundation of Cacique Tomás' success as a leader. He did not say something he did not believe, and what he said he acted upon.

The Potano people had never been more united or happier as a tribe, and they attributed this spirit of unity to their new leader. This day they rejoiced as much as their cacique for the birth of the child, Felipe-Toloca. That name went through the village like a fire in dry brush. Very soon all in the village surrounded the cacique and his newborn infant. Like brothers and sisters of a proud family welcoming their newest kin, all huddled close to see the babe.

The cacique noticed the arrival of Tofu accompanied by Fray Tomás and Fray Buenaventura. The trio beamed proudly. Tofu carried a small wooden structure, and the friars held bundles under their arms.

Tofu had become a master carpenter during his days working on the mission. Now, he placed on the ground a small cradle he had fashioned for the new baby. Padre Tomás placed a soft straw mattress and a quilted coverlet in the cradle to make the child comfortable, and Buenaventura placed inside a soft pillow for the baby's head.

Gently, the new father lowered his son into his gift bed, and kneeling, Cacique Tomás began rocking the baby to and fro, while softly singing to his boy an old Potano song. Fray Tomás found it difficult to determine what captivated the child's attention more, his father's singing or the rocking motion of the cradle, but through it all the infant's eyes stayed riveted on the man who looked lovingly at him. The chieftain continued to sing him sweet songs about the birds that soared in the sky and the friendly animals that guarded the land of the Potano people. If ever harmony existed in the world, a piece of it lived here in the beaming glances exchanged between a doting father and an admiring son.

With the child back in his mother's arms, the cacique invited Tofu and the two friars to accompany him in a canoe ride on the Rio Santa Fé. Holata Tomás suggested the excursion for no other reason than to have his friends share the joy of the day with him. This pleasure had been denied all of them since the young man had assumed the position of cacique.

They could not have picked a better time for an afternoon boat ride, for no month of the year was as delightful as the month of May. New spring growth had given a fresh scent to the air as blossoms crept out from bushes, and plants and berries of all kinds dangled carelessly from vines that clutched them protectively. Sable palms, scattered throughout the area, seemed to stand ever so erect, with their dagger-like leaves thrusting into the sky, while the majestic live oaks, with branches protruding in every direction, seemed to stand straighter, wearing leaves even greener, despite the weight of their years.

Little emerald lizards darted playfully from palm leaf to palm branch and changed in chameleon-like fashion to the color of the plant's surface to conceal their presence from any threatening intruders. Fish flashed silvery in the sun as they leapt from the water to catch the tender young insects newly hatched in the springtime sun. As the four men began to slide their canoe into the river, they spied a large moccasin snake, almost five feet in length and nearly as thick as a man's arm, lazily sunning itself on a bed of warm rocks. Their movement had disturbed its languid state, and it slid surreptitiously into the river.

Fray Tomás gazed at the lush vegetation about him while paddling the canoe along the river, and he thought how fittingly his Spanish forebears named this florid jungle–"La Florida." How happy he was to be here with three of his best friends!

The river wound to the west and south and then suddenly disappeared. The cacique and Tofu each grabbed an end of the canoe and lifted it over their heads. The two friars went beneath it in the middle. With the four spreading the burden, they easily carried the craft through an already heavily worn pathway to the spot where the river resumed its flow several leagues to the south and west. The Rio Santa Fé had for that short distance become an underground river, forcing overland passage by foot.

But when the river resumed, it gave life to a veritable wonderland of scenery that always captivated Fray Tomás every time he traversed it. Moss dangled from the majestic oaks, making them look mysterious by giving them the appearance of towering figures wearing blue-green robes or having gray-green hair. Numerous springs adjoined the river, supplying it with clear, fresh water in abundance. Never had the friars seen an area like this in their Spanish homeland, with so many natural springs. The water was so clear one could see the bottom of the stream and so pure one could actually drink from the spring at its source. Traveling on this part of the river always renewed Fray Tomás' soul. This day's journey was like a spiritual retreat.

At a certain point on the river, Fray Tomás suggested they divert their travel off the Rio Santa Fé down a tributary called the Ichetuknee. This would allow them to visit the small mission of San Martín. The Spanish established new missions with careful planning and consideration, or at least, with as much planning as they could employ when dealing with new territory, strange native cultures, and a minimal number of missionaries. Despite these obstacles, the system flourished and proved to be an effective method of exploring and colonizing foreign lands. This mission lay under Fray Tomás' general supervision, but it had a resident priest, Fray Alonso Gomez. Fray Alonso was the only friar there and often requested visits from his *confreres* at the Santa Fé mission. Perhaps, Fray Tomás suggested, a brief visit would be encouraging to the good padre and not take the sojourners too far off their path.

As the four travelers approached the mission area, they were quickly spotted by Fray Alonso and welcomed heartily. "Where have you been, *mi hermanos?*" he wasted no time in asking. "Have you forgotten us missionaries alone in the woods, without the consolation of familiar faces and a familiar language?" Fray Alonso greeted them with great joy. His mission served the Utina tribe. Also belonging to the Timucuan nation, the Utina lived in harmony with the Potano, though the two occasionally got into disputes over bordering territories. The Utina chieftain came to receive the visitors as well, and the friars listened attentively while Holata Tomás proceeded to converse with his fellow cacique. The two leaders were already well-known to each other. After some exchanging of news and polite conversation about health, hunting and harvests, the friars and the Indians went their separate ways for a while, to share their own concerns among themselves.

In the small *convento*, Fray Alonso bade Fray Tomás and Buenaventura sit, and he served them a bite of food. "I'm sorry it's not more," he apologized, "but I have to survive off the meager rations the soldiers bring me here. It's not much, but the native food," he shuddered, "doesn't agree with me." Fray Buenaventura commented immediately about their friend's haggard and worn appearance. They soon discovered that in the few years Fray Alonso had been at Mission San Martín, he had already lost thirty pounds.

The three Franciscans began to discuss the mission, but shortly, Fray Alonso broke into tears as he recounted his efforts of the past three years with the Utina tribe. The padre's success with converts to the faith had been minimal. The shaman of the tribe constantly discredited his efforts. The few converts he had were reverting to their old moral habits and pagan practices, and the cacique of the area had provided him with very little assistance.

"I believe the presence of a few Spanish faces would help me immensely. Languages were never easy for me, and this dialect is so foreign to my tongue. At the end of the day, I am simply exhausted from translating into the Utina dialect from my Spanish brain," Fray Alonso complained. Tomás and Buenaventura tried to console him and promised to see what could be done to help.

Later, the visitors said their fond farewells. Then, reunited and back in their river craft, the travelers retraced their way to their own village.

"The cacique is not pleased with the presence of Fray Alonso," Cacique Tomás began, as they paddled back along the river well beyond the San Martín mission. "The padre constantly criticizes the people for their ways. He dislikes their food. He shuns their company. I wonder whether the good friar is fitted for this work he has undertaken.

Buenaventura had been a seminary friend of Alonso and suggested to them that he was indeed a dedicated and holy man, but probably suffered from the same problem that most of the friars faced. These missionaries had a great difficulty in communicating with the Indian people and a terrible longing for some kind of social relationship with people from a culture familiar to them.

Fray Tomás was sympathetic to Buenaventura's assessment of the situation. "Perhaps the captain of the Spanish garrison in the mission of San Francisco de Potano would be able to send a couple of men to be with the friar," Fray Tomás commented. "Unfortunately, we have no friars we can send him at present. But we must take care that a military presence will support the work of Fray Alonso there, and not undermine it. I will see what arrangements we can make to help him in the best way possible."

During the remainder of the trip, the friars reflected together on their days at the Santa Fé mission and thanked God for the many blessings that had come their way.

Tofu, usually the silent observer, ventured forth his own commentary. "The grace of the Great Spirit has been with us in our mission, but also people must listen to the voice of the Great Spirit for His presence to be with us. Listen, for I have heard. I believe our mission has been sent two very special padres, perhaps unique among all the others.

"Amen to that!" was the quick response of Cacique Tomás.

Fray Tomás blushed and Fray Buenaventura seemed to find something very interesting to stare at in the water.

"I will not embarrass my two friends by saying any more," Tofu concluded.

Their paddles dipped in unison and the craft sped swiftly north and eastward, arriving at the home port of the village just before the sun began to drop behind the trees on the western edge of the Santa Fé Mission. There to greet the travelers was little Felipe-Toloca nestled in his mother's arms. The cacique warmly greeted his wife and quickly freed her of her precious possession. He took the boy in his hands, gazing at him in great delight. "Only the Great Spirit knows what a gift He has given to me today! This is the happiest day of my life!"

It was a happy day for the friars too, and all who dwelt in the village and mission of Santa Fé.

XX

1645

The summers and winters were passing quickly, thought Fray Buenaventura, too quickly. As the afternoon sun swung toward evening, the aged missionary sat reminiscing in front of the friars' *convento* on a chair fashioned just for him by Tofu. Sunrises blurred into sunsets, and together, they melted into months and years—too quickly for anyone to absorb, least of all himself. At seventy-eight, Buenaventura's mind held a strange mirage of memories: overly ambitious dreams, hopes unrealized, and projects uncompleted. Yet it also contained a thousand friendly faces of people loved and loving, of brother friars who overlooked his many foibles and shortcomings, as he overlooked theirs. He remembered bonding with these men into a true Christian community.

He also recalled memories of Potano Indians actually becoming like mothers and fathers, sisters and brothers to him. In his wildest imaginings, he could never have expected anything so wonderful to happen to him in his missionary work. In the space of over forty years, he, Buenaventura, the realist, had seen the impossible come true. People he had regarded as savages were now more Christian than he—not all of them, certainly, nor even most of them, but many of them. Fray Tomás, he had to admit, had done it!

Love begets love. Love responds to love, he thought. It's all in the Gospel. It's all there. He had just never really believed it, until he saw it happen before his very own eyes. And he, Buenaventura, by the grace of God, was far more than a passive observer in this impossible transformation. He, too, had played an active part in what had happened, even if he had become involved somewhat begrudgingly at the outset. The order to follow Fray Tomás, which had seemed more like a punishment than a mission, had led him to a work that spoke to his heart.

In particular, the orphaned children Fray Tomás had entrusted to his care had captivated him, and to his surprise, he captivated them. He was their instructor, their mentor, and their friend. He filled these roles principally by sharing with them whatever knowledge he had of music, math, science, and the Spanish language. Beneath a brusque veneer, he had a patient heart and would repeat a simple fact or lesson a thousand times over, if necessary. Anything less in a teacher of mission children would simply not do, the friar came to realize.

He used examples and told stories to illustrate a point—like the time he told them how the world had been thought to be flat; but really, it wasn't. The courageous Italian explorer and sea captain Cristoforo Columbo had taken a ship from one country, España, Buenaventura's homeland, and arrived on an island not too far from the land of the Potano. The explorer managed to accomplish this great feat without dropping off the edge of the earth to some bottomless pit as many people, even wise men, claimed he would. For the earth is round, you see, not flat, the friar explained.

The Indian children were fascinated with the stories Buenaventura told them, including the histories about his fellow countrymen venturing toward the Potano land. This tale of brave men sailing big ships from some far-off land entranced the children, and they loved to hear about España with its huge dwellings and large temples to the Great Spirit. Buenaventura would show them pictures in books that helped them realize that, beyond their village, there was a whole other world very different from their own.

"Can we visit your home someday, Fray Buenaventura?" they would ask, and he would tell them, "Of course; I myself will take you to visit my home village, where I went to school."

One little child said, "No, you never went to school. School's just for children."

Fray Buenaventura laughed, "Ah, but back then I was a child and very much like you in school...seldom attentive to my teacher and always wanting to be outside playing with my friends." The other boys and girls laughed, and the friar continued, "Yes, I hope to take you there someday."

He had seriously hoped to do that, though now, he found himself moving about only with great effort. When hiking with the children, he would be forced to find a resting place more often than ever before, in order to catch a quick breath. And how his legs ached and pained him always! The thought of making the great voyage back to España grew more remote with each passing month.

The orphaned children absorbed much of his time before, during, and after school hours. He always enjoyed spending time with them, even if he was tired from the day. When he wasn't with them, he was with the children of the cacique. The chieftain's family had grown. In addition to Felipe-Toloca, the wiry teen-ager blossoming into manhood, Cacique Tomás now had Agustina-María, Fernando, Sebastián, Eduardo, Jaime, and little Catalina. Fray Buenaventura had been informally adopted as kind of an uncle, and he became a regular visitor in the dwelling of the cacique. When the aged friar came by for visits, the children's spirits immediately lifted, no matter what difficulty they were facing.

Always with children, Buenaventura became a big child himself. That is why the young loved him so much. Under his direction, the mission school thrived, and the family of Cacique Tomás welcomed him as one of their own.

On this quiet Saturday afternoon, as Buenaventura's mind relished the memories of many happy days so quickly gone by, his thoughts returned rapidly to the present when he noticed the cacique's children strolling together in his direction. Catalina, the youngest, led the way and Felipe-Toloca brought up the rear. The boy carried something in his hands that the old Franciscan could not quite make out in the distance.

Catalina approached Buenaventura, all smiles, making sure the friar could not see what her oldest brother had in his hands. "We have a present for you!" She exclaimed.

"From all of you?" Buenaventura asked.

The little girl nodded. "From all of us, but you must close your eyes first before we will give it to you," Catalina explained. The other children giggled as she scampered behind the priest and placed her hands over his eyes. The friar willingly obliged his favorite little friend in her wishes. When she tugged on the cord of his friar's habit, he knew it was time to look.

Felipe-Toloca uncovered the object in his hands: a cage holding two small white doves with patches of black feathers on their wings. As light suddenly entered their little home, the birds began entertaining their new master with a pleasant chirping melody.

"See, they like you, Fray Buenaventura." Catalina told him. "We heard you were not feeling well and wanted to bring you something special to cheer you. My brother caught these two doves just a few days ago."

"Tofu made this cage for you," Felipe-Toloca commented, as he spied Tofu coming their way. The Indian craftsman beamed with pride at this recognition of his work.

"Thank you, Tofu! Thank you, my dear children! How thoughtful of you." The friar beamed with pleasure at this special gift. These simple signs of affection he always treasured.

"My father told us we could keep nothing in captivity unless we had two of the same kind of animal," Felipe-Toloca explained. "Animals are like people; they get very lonely if they are by themselves."

"The Great Spirit made all of creation to help us know His love for us, to show us that we are not alone," Buenaventura said. "Every creature is a sign of the Great Spirit's love for us. A very holy man, San Francisco, who formed my religious family, taught us to honor the Great Spirit in all of His Creation—the birds of the sky, the fish of the sea—they all speak of the Great Father's love.

"There is a special story told about San Francisco," the friar continued, "and a boy who lived in a town called 'Siena' in a land called 'Italia.' The boy was a lot like Felipe-Toloca here. He managed to catch a lot of doves in a trap he had made, and one day he decided to carry them off to the market to sell them. Well, San Francisco happened to see him, and he had pity on the poor little doves. So, he persuaded the boy to give him the beautiful birds to prevent them from falling into the cruel hands of people who would kill them. The boy was so inspired by the holy man that he actually gave him all the doves. San Francisco spoke gently to the little doves.

'My simple innocent Sister Doves, why did you let yourselves to be caught?' he said, ' I want to rescue you from death and make nests for you where you can lay your eggs and fulfill your Creator's commandment to multiply.'

"And the doves settled in those nests and laid their eggs and reared their little ones among the friars, and they increased in number. They became tame and very friendly with San Francisco and his fellow friars and only left when Francisco gave them permission with his blessings.

"And what is more, the saint told the boy who gave him the doves that he would one day become a friar in the Franciscan Order and serve Our Lord Jesus Christ well. That actually happened exactly as the saint foretold. The boy became a Franciscan friar and led a very praiseworthy life until he died. San Francisco not only looked after the little birds and cared for them, but he helped obtain the joys of eternal life for the young boy who gave those doves to him."

"Which brings me back to this gift you gave me. San Francisco would be proud of you, as I am, for giving me such a precious gift, and this saint would tell us these little doves need our love, too. They need to know we care about them. I will always treat them with care, and I will think of you and thank God for you as my dear and precious friends."

The children always enjoyed hearing Fray Buenaventura's stories about San Francisco more than any of the other stories he told, and today's story especially pleased them.

"Why do we kill animals, Fray Buenaventura?" Fernando asked. "If they are special to the Great Spirit, we should not kill them and eat them. We should save them!"

"I, too, would like to protect all animals, as San Francisco did those doves," the friar assured Fernando, "but I am certain that he would tell you that the spirits of the animals are not like ours. Theirs were made to live only for a time, to be our friends, our helpers, and, yes, on occasion they are meant to keep us alive as food," the friar went on, suspecting that the lesson would be hard for the little ones to understand.

Indeed it was. Eduardo reacted instantly. "I could never eat Juan and Juanita!" he said, referring to the two little doves.

"Oh, are those their names? Well, you had better not," the friar retorted, "or Catalina and I would get after you mighty quick, right Catalina?"

"Right, Fray Buenaventura! Those are not food-birds. They're friend-birds!" the child explained with authority.

"Now you best be on your way," the friar said. "Let the birds sing their beautiful song to me so I can get some midday rest. And thank you for this special gift that I will treasure always."

The children went one-by-one to the friar to wish him a good day. They each gave him a farewell hug before going off to their games and afternoon chores.

The last one in line was Felipe-Toloca.

"When I was telling this story, young man," the friar began, "I was thinking of you as the boy who brought me the doves. I believe the Great Spirit has a special invitation for you, too, Felipe-Toloca. Listen carefully to His words to you, and pray often over what you hear. Will you do that for me?" the friar asked.

"You know I will do anything for you, Fray Buenaventura. Though I do not quite understand what you are asking me to do," the boy replied.

"Then do this. Tell your father what I have said. He is very wise. He will help you understand my words to you. God bless you, my son," the friar said, making the sign of the cross with his hand over the boy. "Now go with the rest of your brothers and sisters, and have a happy day!"

How blessed I am, Buenaventura thought. In the midst of the wilderness, in this strange land, there was the universal language that crossed all cultures and bloodlines, all nations and all peoples. It was the universal language of love, and it was spoken not in words. It was spoken with the heart.

The birds continued chirping out a love song to their new master and friend, as he fell fast asleep. He drifted off while thanking the Lord for the many blessings he had received while on mission in his new homeland of La Florida.

After a few hours of play, Catalina wandered back to check on the two little doves the children had left with the friar. When she arrived, she was immediately surprised to hear no chirping sounds coming from the cage.

"Fray Buenaventura! Fray Buenaventura!" she called out in alarm. "Why are your little birds not singing? They look so sad. Don't they like their new home? They have always sung such beautiful songs to me before."

When she could get no response from the friar, whom she shook repeatedly, she ran quickly to her father, the cacique, to ask him why the birds were not singing anymore. "Fray Buenaventura was not able to tell me. He sleeps so soundly."

The cacique instantly understood the situation that his youngest daughter described to him. He knew what she failed to comprehend. The little birds had stopped singing their happy melody because they were saddened by the sudden departure of the happy spirit of their new master. And Holata Tomás felt even more keenly the loss of this man, this mentor, this friend that he had come to know and love so well.

XXI

I am worried about Catalina," Mónica told her husband, the cacique. "It is now almost a week since she has spoken to anyone. The death of Fray Buenaventura has shaken her spirit and locked it tightly within her. How will it ever be set free?"

Cacique Tomás shook his head. "You know I have tried many times to lead her out of the darkness that has settled over her like a cloud ever since our good friend died. But I, too, have not succeeded. This is the first person she has ever known whose spirit has left this world. We have not done well in preparing her for such an event, I am afraid."

"What could we have done, Tomás?" Mónica asked. "Death is a foreigner to one so young as Catalina. In her few short years, she has only known life, and I think death has robbed her life of its happiness."

Cacique Tomás nodded saying, "Even the two doves no longer bring joy to her spirit. It is almost as if they respond to her sadness. They do not chirp or sing. And she stares intently at them all day long, waiting for them to speak with her. Everywhere she goes, that cage moves with her." The cacique paused, thinking. "That may be what she needs. Someone to speak to her."

"But we have tried talking to her many times," Mónica said.

"Perhaps we need someone to whose words she will listen,' her husband replied. "Felipe-Toloca," he called out to his son, "please come here for a moment. Your mother and I wish to speak with you."

The cacique regarded his oldest son as a young man whose wisdom far exceeded his years. Although the cacique spent long hours training and guiding the youth, he found, on occasion, the boy teaching him, so from time-to-time the chieftain sought his son's advice, as well. When his eldest arrived, Tomás marveled at how the boy's broad forehead and bright eyes gave hint of the remarkable intelligence he actually possessed for one so young.

The cacique began, "You have seen your little sister experiencing great grief over the death of our dear friend, Fray Buenaventura. What can we do that we have not already done to lift her spirits? Could you offer your mother and me some advice?"

Felipe was honored that his father had come to him in a matter so grave.

"Father, you know I would be happy to help you in any way I can with Catalina. I too have been worried about her. I have felt closest to her, of all my brothers and sisters.... I would be happy to talk with her, if you feel that may have some effect."

"She admires you as her big brother," Mónica noted, "and she has always wanted to please you. Perhaps you can succeed in doing for her what we have failed to do, bringing her back to life again."

The cacique grasped his wife's hand tightly, and looked at his boy. "Go to her with our blessing," he added, then pulled his son close to the two of them.

After receiving the warm embraces of his father and mother, the venturesome young man went off in the direction of his sister's latest hideaway. It lay near the river's edge, away from the usual playing sites of the boys and girls of the village. Felipe-Toloca saw that, once again, Catalina was ensconced with the caged doves, watching carefully their every movement.

"Hello, Catalina," the eldest brother said in a friendly, though hesitant manner, searching his sister's face carefully in an attempt to determine how she was feeling. "I…I came by to see how you are doing. You know your brothers and sisters and friends miss having you join them in their games. And I miss seeing you, too. I have told you many times how special you are to me and how much I depend on you to help me with all the animals I have as pets."

In silence, Catalina continued to direct her gaze at the two caged doves. Her eyes riveted upon them so intently she seemed to be staring right through them, even beyond them, into some other world, inaccessible to everyone else. She appeared to not even notice the presence of her brother, so strongly was she focusing on whatever was troubling her.

"Catalina, the spirit of Fray Buenaventura is now with the Great Spirit; his spirit is happy. His spirit has been freed from the prison of his body, but that same happy spirit is still with you and me, just as before. Only now, he is with us in so many other ways, ways that are real, but in ways that you and I can see only with the heart, not with the eyes. Catalina, do you hear me? Do you understand what I am saying to you?" The boy began to realize that he was making no progress with his sister.

Then he caught on an idea—there might be a way he could demonstrate to her what he was trying to say. "Catalina, do you remember the story Fray Buenaventura told us about the doves that were going to be sold…and San Francisco rescued them by getting the boy who had captured them to give them to him? And then remember what San Francisco did for them because he cared so much for them…Catalina, he set them free!

"Well, I am going to ask a special favor of you, and I know this is not something that is going to be easy for you to do. But if you do this for me, you will understand what I am telling you about the spirit of Fray Buenaventura. Catalina, I must ask you to let the two doves you and I gave to Fray Buenaventura go free. His spirit is free, but theirs is not. His spirit is happy, but theirs is not…. "

"No!" came Catalina's reply swift, loud, and clear. One word, the first word from her lips in a long time, a word that at least indicated she was listening to her brother and aware of what he was saying. She was afraid of letting go of Fray Buenaventura's friends…her friends.

"Catalina, you are holding these two doves as prisoners, and they want to be free," Felipe-Toloca explained. "If you let them go free, they will be happy. And Catalina, what is more…you will be happy, too."

Catalina said nothing more, but just looked directly into the eyes of her brother, then back to the birds, then again to Felipe-Toloca. Then she began to cry, first in a whimper, then with great tears that flowed down from eyes that were weary with lack of rest. Floodgates of emotion opened up from within the little girl and poured forth in great torrents. The tears quickly drenched her clothing.

Her brother grasped her tightly to himself and cradled her in his arms. "The little doves will be fine, Catalina. You have taken good care of them, because they were Fray Buenaventura's special friends. He will always be grateful to you that you protected them. Before I caught them, they were able to get food for themselves, but once in a cage they depend on you to feed them and keep them alive. Now, if you let them go they will be able to take care of themselves once again. Just set them free now Catalina, so they can be happy."

Catalina's tight grasp around her brother's neck loosened slowly then gave way entirely as she moved from him to the cage that Tofu had so carefully constructed. She lifted the peg that held the door in place. Then, after easing open the portal, she stepped back to her brother's side and watched the two doves make their way out. They fluttered off into the sky. Their flapping wings sounded like applause accompanying their newfound freedom.

Both birds circled the area repeatedly, as Catalina continued to eye them. She signaled a somber good-bye with a wave of her hand. Then she said, "I hope Fray Buenaventura knows I took good care of his doves for him.

Juan and Juanita were so special to me. They helped me remember him."

Then, with second thoughts, she turned to Felipe-Toloca. "Why did you want me to let them go? Now I have no way to think of him! Now I have lost both Fray Buenaventura and his dear friends."

Her brother answered, "Catalina, they were sad, and the reason they were sad was because you were sad. They were not singing anymore because you were not singing to them. Surely they would have died soon, and perhaps you would have, too, if you had not given them their freedom. Remember Fray Buenaventura's words about the little doves rescued by San Francisco, how San Francisco wondered why the little birds allowed themselves to be caught and caged up.... Well, I think it was wrong for me to put our doves in a cage, too. Birds have wings to fly. That is when they are most happy, when they are in the sky. That is when they give the greatest praise to God.

"So in letting your two friends go free, you let them do what they do best. You let them fly…Catalina, I know they are happy now. And you should be happy, too, because you have made them happy."

"Look, my brother," Catalina shouted, "there they are! There's Juan and Juanita! You are right. They are having fun, chasing after each other. I have never seen them so happy. I am glad I did what you told me. I am glad I let them go free."

No sooner had Catalina spoken those words then she heard the fluttering sounds of the two doves again, this time circling closely, over the heads of her brother and herself. Suddenly, the sound was much louder, right next to her ear, as one of the doves, Juanita, came to rest on her shoulder. Almost immediately the other descended onto the shoulder of Felipe-Toloca.

"See, they remember us!" Catalina cried out. "They are still our friends. Hi Juanita! Hi Juan! I love you. You have come back to visit me, have you? Well, this time I won't put you in a cage. This time you are free to come and go as you please."

Just then the cacique and Mónica came by to see how their son and daughter were doing, and Catalina greeted them with a little dove propped on the edge of one of her fingers.

"See, our friends are free now, but they came back to see us. I am so happy," she squealed.

"Maybe," Felipe-Toloca added, "maybe Juanita came to deliver to you a special message…from Fray Buenaventura. I mean, Juanita was the gift you gave to him. Maybe he has sent her back to tell you that he is still with you, that he went away, but his spirit didn't leave you. I think Juanita came back to give you that message."

"I think you may be right, Felipe-Toloca. Little Juanita helps me think of Fray Buenaventura and helps me feel like he is still with me. I am so happy that she came back to tell me that. But if that is the message from Fray Buenaventura to me what is the message that little Juan has brought to you? He must have some special message for you, too, as Juanita did for me. I wonder what that message could be?"

"You're right, Catalina," her father interjected. "I think you are very right. Why did Juan come to rest on his shoulder, just as Juanita did on yours? You are right, I believe. Your brother needs to think about that for a little while. Because the little dove on his shoulder seems quite comfortable there and may not take off flying again until this young man has figured out what message is coming from our friend Fray Buenaventura. I think, Felipe-Toloca, that you may have to do just a little praying before you can tell us what the friar's message to you may be.

XXII

Felipe-Toloca had taken his father's advice. Though many days had passed, the boy once again sat thinking in front of the little grotto he had hewn out of a high oak stump. Inside, he had hung a small wooden crucifix in the niche. The little figure of the crucified Christ was a personal gift to him from Fray Buenaventura.

When Felipe-Toloca's brothers and sisters could not find him anywhere else, they would know to look for him in his "thinking place." That is where he would go to make sense out of the world around him. Sometimes he would take his book of prayers, sometimes his Bible, sometimes just himself. Always he would come away knowing himself a little better, and always he found peace in this place.

Many times, as he pondered one question or another, his thoughts would move in the direction of prayer. And so, also, today…as he pondered over what his father and sister had said to him several days before. Yes, maybe Fray Buenaventura had sent a message to him as well.

"I wish I knew what they were trying to tell me, Lord. I wish I knew…" For almost a week those words were the only prayer he seemed to be able to utter. This day his thoughts trailed back to his last meeting with Fray Buenaventura. The parting words of the friar lingered with the youth and he remembered how the priest had associated him with the boy in the story he told.

Surely the friar was not suggesting that he could be like Fray Tomás and Fray Buenaventura one day. That he could become a friar—a priest! He was a Potano. He had not seen anyone but the Spanish wear the brown robes of the friars. No one but the Spanish acted as missionaries to the Potano, and no one but the Spanish preached the Gospel message to his people. It was unthinkable that he could step into the shoes of his departed friar-friend, Buenaventura…. It was utterly unthinkable….

"Where is Felipe-Toloca?" Mónica asked her children as she placed the evening meal before them and the cacique.

"Oh, he is probably down at his 'thinking place' again. He is there all the time these days," Catalina said, ever perceptive of anything dealing with her oldest brother and dearest friend. "I can go bring him back," she offered. "I am a very fast runner, and I could be back before Jaime finishes his cornmeal."

"Let her go; then I can eat her meal and mine both," Jaime quipped in turn.

"Thank you both for your suggestions," the cacique interjected, "but I will go myself to remind him of both the food that is waiting for him, and his family as well. Though it is very unlike Felipe-Toloca, he must have forgotten the hour. Sometimes when we get overly concerned about something important, we forget about everything else. Go ahead with your prayer and your meal, I will be back shortly." With that the father went off to retrieve his son.

Felipe-Toloca began to realize he was quite overdue for dinner about the time the cacique began to near the site of his "thinking place." Ever adept at sensing the approach of another human long before the person arrived, Felipe-Toloca had the keen sensitivity of a Potano hunter. He knew that an adult was coming his way even before he spied his father.

"Please forgive me," he said when the cacique came in sight. "I know I must be late for dinner, but I got lost in my thoughts again. I have been doing that a lot lately. You would be right to correct me for delaying your dinner, father," he said in apology, as his father was drawing near.

"I am not here to reprimand you, son," the cacique answered, with an encouraging smile. "I know what matter weighs heavily on your mind. Remember, I helped to put the matter before you. And I am here to tell you not to let your heart be heavy. The Great Spirit, when He speaks, does not make the heart feel a burden, but rather His peace."

"Father, can a Potano become a padre?" the boy asked. "Could I become a friar like Fray Tomás and Fray Buenaventura?"

"I would be the proudest father in the village if you could, my son," Cacique Tomás responded. "And I certainly would hope that you could do so, if that is your desire and the will of the Great Spirit."

"And how will I know if that is the will of the Great Spirit?" the boy pressed him further.

"Well, I believe there are certain questions you should ask first. Do you want to be like the two friars one day? Do you want to serve your people as a padre? Do you want to bring the Great Spirit to them and the Gospel message of Jesus? Do you want to help them know the peace He brings to people's hearts, as to your own? Do you want to free them from the evils that lurk in their hearts and their homes? And can you be kind and understanding, strong and courageous, as the two friars who have been with us?

"I believe you can, Felipe-Toloca! I have long believed you could. But

I cannot answer these questions for you. Only you can answer these questions for yourself. But let us leave all this thinking for now and feed your body. That will allow your mind to have the strength to think more on these questions in the future. Let us be on our way before your mother sends the braves to come search for us."

※

"What do you think, Fray Tomás?" the cacique asked the friar. "Felipe-Toloca wants to know whether a Potano can become a friar. Is that possible?"

"Well, why not! If the Potano you have in mind happens to be the very one who put the question to you," Tomás quickly responded, "then I could not be more pleased."

"Nor I," the chieftain added, with fatherly pride evident in the tone of this voice. "It will never be Felipe-Toloca's privilege to become the cacique of his people, but I would consider it an even greater honor for him to become like you, Fray Tomás. Had not my destiny in life been to lead my people, I would surely have followed your path, but obviously, such was not the will of the Great Spirit. Instead, He has blessed me with a wonderful wife and loyal and devoted children."

"And with the people of your village, who are also your devoted family," the friar added.

"And with the great Potano people of my village, as you say," concurred Holata Tomás. "I thank the Great Spirit for every one of them!"

The two came to see that indeed Felipe-Toloca was serious about becoming a friar. Now, Fray Tomás and the cacique faced the task of paving the way for a Potano Indian to begin the demanding spiritual and intellectual formation program of a Franciscan. Within a few days, Tomás traveled to San Agustín to consult with the Friar Custodian at the Franciscan Headquarters. The custodian must give approval before any candidate could be accepted for admission to the training program of the friars.

The custodian, Fray Miguel Morales, was a balding man in his late sixties, who had large, dark brown friendly eyes, and a welcoming, handsome face that revealed distinctly Mediterranean features. A veteran of missionary labors, Fray Miguel held the respect of all the friars. Tomás had always felt at ease during his occasional encounters with this man.

"It is good to see you, Tomás," Fray Miguel said as Tomás entered the room. "Come, sit down; let us discuss what brings you to San Agustín. I hope you have good news of your work at the Mission Santa Fé."

"Yes, I believe I do, Fray Miguel, though my news is not the usual kind you may hear. It has to do with one of the Potano of our mission, the oldest son of our cacique. The young man has a special request he wishes to make of us. He wishes, Fray Miguel...to become a friar. He feels drawn to the way of life of San Francisco.... I have come to ask you how we might go about helping him realize his dream. He is a very intelligent and devout Christian, and I believe he would make a good member of our order."

There was a pause, as the custodian's face took on a startled look that turned reflective. Tomás saw the man's bright cheery eyes turn somber. "Fray Tomás...the young man you speak of is a native.... As you say, this is very unusual.... " Once again the custodian sought to make sense out of the situation as he thought deeply on the matter. Fray Miguel was a pragmatist. He admired people like Tomás for their courage, zeal, enthusiasm, and sincerity. But idealists, whose sites were always set on the stars, had a way of living in a world other than the real one. The custodian felt this was just such a case. It was simply too much to expect any Indian to step into the shoes of a Franciscan at this point in time. It would be unfair to the young man in question. It would be unfair to the Franciscan community. Fray Miguel spoke to Tomás in carefully chosen words, knowing Tomás was not going to like what he had to say.

"Tomás," he began again, with his head slightly titled downward and his eyes squinting upward to Tomás, "I have to tell you honestly what I believe. Though your proposal is truly an admirable one, and I wish it could be a reality, I sincerely believe no native could master all the requirements for becoming a friar, let alone to become a priest. To live the demands of such a life of prayer and spirituality, and even morality for that matter, required of a friar, is beyond what you or I could expect of any members of the Timucuan nation and that includes your Potanos. You know that, Tomás!"

"Many could not, Fray Miguel, but this one could!" Tomás boldly commented, very disturbed and shaken by his custodian's reaction. "Father Custodian, I would not have the courage to tell the cacique or his son that there is no place for a Potano in the Franciscan community, especially when the candidate in question is one of the finest Christians I know. Could the young man try the way of San Francisco? Could he just try?" Tomás pushed the issue resolutely.

"We have no provisions for training candidates to the priesthood from among the natives," the provincial answered, "and I would not assume authority for judging the qualifications of such a candidate." He felt this argument would put the nail in the coffin on this proposal and close out any further objections.

"Father Custodian, this is important to me. You don't understand." Tomás was overstepping his bounds now, and he realized it once those words slipped out, but he felt it best to proceed anyway. It was for him a crucial matter. "The cacique is not like other caciques. And his son is different too, from other Potanos. Please reconsider, Fray Miguel! Please reconsider!"

The custodian stood and put his hand out to Tomás, "My answer is final, Tomás. No Potano is called to be a friar."

Tomás' thoughts went quickly to his departed friend, Buenaventura, who, he knew, greatly respected Felipe-Toloca. "Buenaventura, please do something!" he said in silent asked the friar he believed was already in heaven. "Pray God to tell Fray Miguel it's all right." Then the words came to him. "Father Custodian, would you please take the time to meet the young man.... His name is Felipe-Toloca…and his father also, the cacique. I only make this one request of you. Please, just do me this one favor."

Shaking his head, the provincial finally relented, beaten down by his persistent confrere. "Tomás, I will agree to meet them; but I assure you, it will not make any difference. So do not put any hope in their minds that anything will happen.... I know I will not change my mind."

"Thank you, Fray Miguel! Thank you! I knew you would give them a chance. God bless you, Fray Miguel. God bless you," Tomás reiterated as he kissed the priest's hand and moved quickly out the door and out of the residence. He immediately began a hasty trek back to Santa Fé.

The persistence of Fray Tomás bore good fruit. During the meeting with the custodian, Felipe-Toloca struck the friar as alert, intelligent, and devout. The longer the young man was in his presence, the more Fray Miguel showed evidence of a change of heart. But repeatedly he came back to the simple fact that he had not the staff capable of preparing Felipe-Toloca to become a friar and priest. The cacique's son would need much more training and preparation than for the typical Spanish candidate for priesthood.

He would need to enter a preliminary course of classes that would involve languages and philosophy and, then if qualified, "and only if qualified," the custodian emphasized, could he begin to study for the priesthood. Would the young man be willing to do all that?

Felipe-Toloca did not know what the word "philosophy" meant. Fray Miguel had used the Spanish word for it in conversation. He looked inquisitively at Fray Tomás for an explanation.

"Don't worry, Felipe-Toloca. You will manage.... You will manage," Fray Tomás promised. "We will see to that."

The cacique, who had accompanied his son and Fray Tomás, sat mystified by all the conversation, but was ever confident that Fray Tomás would work out whatever problems lay in the future. He simply said, "My son will do whatever the friars ask of him. Whatever is necessary for him to become a good padre, he will do."

"Very well, then. I am amazed to hear myself saying this, but…we have a candidate.... However this is only on the condition that he goes through the necessary studies…" Fray Miguel announced. He became silent and stared intently at Felipe-Toloca, then the cacique, then Tomás,"…in España!" He noted their surprised expression, but he continued, "As I said, we do not have the staff to train him here, but I am sure some Franciscan seminary in España will help us. Passage on a ship to España can be arranged, Fray Tomás. I will take the matter up with the governor and inform you of the date of departure of the next ship for the motherland." Fray Miguel was skeptical about his decision and the reversal of his earlier opinion, but he would leave the ultimate decision on Felipe-Toloca's qualifications to some seminary rector in the mother country.

Fray Tomás and his friends were greatly shaken by the thought of sending someone so young and inexperienced to a strange, foreign land. Nonetheless, they thanked Fray Miguel for helping them in their request. After taking leave of the provincial, they departed quickly from the city of San Agustín.

"Why must you leave us, my brother?" Catalina sobbed, as she joined all her family and many of the Potano villagers at the dock to see Felipe-Toloca off on his journey to España.

"Why can't they bring all those learned men here to teach you, instead of taking you away from your family and friends, and especially from me? You know how much I will miss you. You know how much I love you."

Not half as much as I will miss him, thought the cacique. He tore his gaze away from his eldest son and turned to his wife's attractive hazel eyes that now appeared almost as weary as her heart. He and Mónica did their best to hide their feelings, lest they discourage Felipe-Toloca's resolve.

Catalina was not so controlled. She hugged her brother to herself and cried aloud once again.

Her brother stroked her hair, and tried to calm her. "Catalina, I love you too," Felipe-Toloca responded, "and all my family and friends. But I must go. If the Great Spirit is calling me as Fray Buenaventura said, I—I must follow that call. Please pray for me. And write to me often. I will do the same."

Though tearful, Catalina tried to be strong for her brother. "And remember, Felipe-Toloca," she said, "you have to be like our two doves. We will let you go, but don't forget to come back, as they did! Promise me, say 'I promise.' "

"Yes, I promise to come back one day to serve my people as Fray Tomás and Fray Buenaventura have done," he said then embraced his parents, brothers and sisters, and all the Potano tribesmen who came to see him off. Finally, he said farewell to his friend Fray Tomás, who did his best to hide how much he hated to see the courageous youth depart.

Felipe-Toloca moved from the dock to the platform leading to the ship; and once on board, he waved repeatedly to everyone, as the ship rocked to and fro with the waves. If he felt as lonely as they did, he did not let them know.

His family and friends stayed at the side of the sea until only a dot could be seen on the horizon, a small speck barely visible to the eye. No one wanted to leave until they were certain that they were no longer visible to this brave son of the tribe. All the Potano watching the departure felt they were giving up something very special of their own to their Spanish conquistadors. Parts of themselves went off on the sea that day. Would that part of their lives ever be with them again?

Fray Tomás did not force their departure. They left gradually, realizing the boy had truly gone. The friar kept close by the side of the cacique and his wife. "I only hope I have done the right thing," he said softly so as not to be overheard by the children.

"Do not worry, Fray Tomás!" the cacique said. "The Great Spirit will guide him, but as you know, it is just so very hard to say 'goodbye' to someone you love so much."

Part Three

The Drought

XXIII
- 1647 -

Fray Tomás wiped his brow and pushed back the few strands of gray-ing hair that remained on his head. He looked at the mission farm field that he and his faithful Potano had planted, hoed, and carefully tended the past thirty years. His brow furrowed at what he saw. Much of the crop would be lost this year. What plants would survive would bear little on their hapless stalks. Never had the friar seen anything so depressing. The prob-lem—no rain for the better part of the growing season. The soil lay hard-ened, dried, and cracked from the tremendous heat of La Florida's over-bearing sun. All the hard work and effort of so many would yield so little. It simply did not seem fair.

The poor Potano, Tomás thought. How would they make it through the year?

Grace, however, flowed favorably upon the priest's own village. Even though the Rio Santa Fé had shrunk to little more than a trickle, as the deep aquifer that fed it was fast drying up, the sinkholes—*la chuas,* as the Potano called them—drew on an underground source closer to the surface, which miraculously still provided water. Tomás took advantage of this great resource by establishing a bucket brigade to pass pails of water from the sinkhole areas to his mission fields. Others in the tribe saw his method working effectively and began to imitate him.

The people of other Potano villages were not faring as well since they did not have large numbers of sinkholes located near their farm fields. Corn and wheat stalks, bean and pumpkin plants sprawled like skeletal remains, bearing no sign of life in most fields of the neighboring villages. Fray Tomás faced the obvious. He and his cacique friend would have to work hard together this year to prevent wholesale starvation among the Potano population.

The date at the top of the letter read 18 March 1647. The correspon-dence came from little Catalina, who had been writing regularly with the help of her older brother Fernando. He would actually be the one to put pen to parchment for Catalina's letters. She would tell him what she wanted to say and he and he would help her with bigger words and better ways of expressing her ideas. These letters always went to the same person, Felipe-Toloca who had now settled in Salamanca, Spain, where he had been at his studies already over a year in preparation for becoming a Franciscan friar. This message read:

Dear Brother,

It is a long time since I have written to you, and I ask you to forgive me. Since you have left us, much has changed in our Potano village. We used to labor hard with the ground and it would give us back great plenty. But now this is not so. It does not give back to us as we have given to it. Food for our people is no longer in great supply. We are more fortunate than many of our Potano neighbors, who are facing starvation from want of food, but we ourselves often go hungry to bed at night.

Our father and Fray Tomás have been trying hard to help our people keep the fields alive so they will produce more food for us, but their efforts have not succeeded. I worry about both of them. People say the Great Spirit no longer smiles on our people.

What is worse is the illness that has struck our village. We are daily losing young and old to a sickness called by the Spanish viruelas.[9] *It has taken the life of my dear friend Chuguta Francisca and now threatens the life of your brother Sebastián.*

I am sorry to have to tell you this, and it makes me so sad to think about it that I can barely write it. I wish the good God would not take him. The only thought that makes me happy, and it is a sad happiness, is that our dear Fray Buenaventura should not be lonely. There are many people laid to rest next to him in the special site Fray Tomás has blessed near the mission church for the burial of our Christian Potano. There are now many crosses to mark their resting places.

Fray Tomás calls us to prayer each evening in our little church, for he says that only prayer will stop the many dangers that threaten us. You must pray for all of our friends who are going to the Great Spirit, and also for dear Sebastián, who, I fear will be the next to leave us.

And there is one more thing that our father has spoken about to us, but only in a very hushed manner. And it makes me afraid. He tells us some of the Apalachee nation to the west have risen up against the Spanish people. The Apalachee say the Spanish have brought to our people diseases and hardship. They say the Spanish have taken the hunting grounds from us and placed their cattle in our land to graze and destroy the home of all our animals. They have placed Spanish burdens on native backs. They say the Spanish bring nothing but misery.

---

[9] smallpox

Father agrees with those that say the Spanish people take from us many things that do not belong to them, and that the sickness we now face was not with us before the Spanish came. Also, Father tells Fray Tomás often that the Spanish should not make the Potano people slaves, which they do when they force our men and boys to carry their supplies to and from San Agustín.

Even worse, Felipe-Toloca, now the Spanish demand that we bring some of our food from the village and mission to their soldiers in the military garrison at San Agustín. Fray Tomás has tried to explain to the Spanish leaders that we have none to give at this time, but they insist ours is the only area in the region with any harvest. Some of our food must go to them, they tell us. And so, what little we have becomes less.

Father agrees that the Spanish have harmed us much, but he says that the Spanish have also brought us one special gift that we must never forget—our faith. We should show our gratitude to them for this greatest of gifts, for in that gift lies our happiness. So Father says the Apalachee were wrong to break the treaty and raise their spears and bows against the Spanish. Father says that the rebellion in Apalachee is the evil work of the warrior Ycho, whom our father banished from our village many years ago. Ycho went to live with the Apalachee, and now lights a fire in their hearts against the Spanish.

Father would never turn his back on the people who brought us Jesus, the Son of the Great Spirit. Father would never betray Fray Tomás and the memory of our dear friend Fray Buenaventura. Nor would I, Felipe-Toloca. Nor would you, I know. They are just as much a part of our family as you and I.

Father speaks of you often and misses you very much. He has made markings on the medal that he wears of Our Lady of Loreto, the one once worn by our great uncle Toloca. He has carved on it four letters – "F.T.H.M." which stand for the Spanish words "Felipe-Toloca, Hijo Mio" – "Felipe-Toloca, My Son." In this way, he carries your memory always next to his heart, and he prays for you daily, as do all of us, my brother.

We miss you greatly, we remember you dearly. And we will love you always!

Your devoted sister,
Catalina

After three months, came Felipe-Toloca's letter in reply to his sister.

21 June 1647

Dearest Catalina:

Your letters to me get better—and longer—each time, and I treasure each one and look forward eagerly to their coming.

Being so far from home and from my people is so very hard for me—you could never imagine how hard! With all my great hopes, I did not ever think how lonely I would be in this strange place. Only for the love of Christ have I ventured to come here, and only with my hopes centered on Him and on returning to labor for Him with my people one day, can I continue here.

My disappointment is great at the slowness of my learning, Catalina. Fray Miguel, the Friar Custodian in San Agustín, was correct about the difficulty in becoming a friar. The languages I must conquer make my progress so difficult. I learn only half as quickly as my Spanish classmates. In fact, I was told just yesterday that I can expect at least ten more years of study before I could return to serve my people as a priest. With all that they ask of me in my preparations, I fear I shall be dead before that time.

I truly miss the great freedoms of the tribe. I want to roam the Potano forests and fields, to breathe the fresh air of the Potano land, to fish, to hunt, to work the farmlands, and to walk the mission fields with Fray Tomás. I miss my family, my friends, my people. But most of all, I miss you, Catalina. So please continue to write to me and to share the news of our village.

Your last letter brought me great distress when I heard of the many hardships of our people and of the death of your dear friend Chuguta Francisca. And how it pains me to hear that Sebastián has contracted the illness that took the lives of so many others! How I wish I could be with him now! Please tell him that, and tell him I pray for him always.

I will bring your letter to the Friar who raises funds for our missions in La Florida so he can tell the Spanish people your plight. And I will speak of your situation to everyone I know here.

Pray, too, for me in my loneliness here. What I endure, I endure as a penance for all of you, as I ask the Lord each day to bless you and give you strength. To be alone here, with none of my people around me, brings me to tears sometimes, Catalina. I share that with you only, please.

The others in my house have yet to accept me, as my habits and customs are so strange to them and their ways are strange to me. They eat with things that look like tiny spears with three points. They call them 'forks,' and I have learned to use one as well, though it took me many tries. Here people wear shoes all the time, inside and outside and even on the grass! It is very odd.

One day recently, I overheard another student in conversation refer to me as an "Indian half-breed." Please do not tell Fray Tomás, but I suddenly found myself wrestling that person to the floor. I grabbed him tightly around the neck and demanded he take back his words.

Once I realized what I was doing, I quickly let him go and apologized to him. Then he quickly felt the top of his head. I asked him if he was hurt and he said he wanted to see whether his scalp was still safely in place. I began to laugh, and he did, too. I hope he and I can become friends, but as you can imagine, I was severely reprimanded by my superior when he learned of this incident.

Please pray for me, Catalina, that I can control my fears and loneliness so that nothing like this will happen again. I want so much to be a good friar like Fray Tomás and Fray Buenaventura. My spirit is with you and with all of my family. You are all in my prayers I say each day.

May the Great Spirit bless you in these difficult times and protect you from all harm.

Your brother,
Felipe-Toloca

XXIV
- 1650 -

Fray Tomás made his way swiftly to San Agustín to direct an immediate appeal to the Governor Robenedo. The Franciscan had just received word that a military garrison was to be stationed at the Mission Santa Fé. He wanted to put a stop to that order.

He harbored no grudges against the military. In fact, he had great respect for most of the Spanish militia he knew. They were dedicated, God-fearing men, who put their lives in jeopardy daily to protect people like himself. However, while the moral lives of most in the military were commendable, there were plenty of examples of those who did not represent Christianity's highest aims to warrant the friar's alarm. The friar thought of people like the father of Cacique Tomás, a Spanish captain, who had not used good judgment in his personal relationship with the cacique's mother. Other soldiers lived even more dissolute lives and more than a few acted harshly in their dealings with the natives.

These kinds of abuses had become worse in the recent months with the uprisings by the native population in Apalachee and the growing threat of uprisings by the Timucuan tribes. These events had set the Spanish leadership on edge. The governor and the military did not want to lose the territory they had gained for the Spanish crown

Fray Tomás could understand his compatriots concern, and he understood the measures the governor sought to take; however, the missionary shared a common concern with his fellow friars. Experience had proven that evangelization of the native people could best be accomplished with the military personnel and their families slightly removed from the mission settlements. The Franciscans knew that the Gospel message of peace and love had much less effect when swords and muskets arrived along with it. Tomás felt his own great success at his mission came largely from the fact that he was free to conduct his work unimpeded by outside forces, controls, and problems. He felt the presence of a military garrison could set his work back thirty years

After a modest wait, the friar was shown into the governor's quarters by a youthful-looking Spanish secretary, who had greeted him cordially when he arrived.

"Welcome, Padre! What can I do for you?" the governor asked, as the friar entered his spacious office. Governor Robenedo was a man in his forties who had a noble bearing to go with his noble heritage, but Tomás noted the age that responsibility had woven into his features.

Informed by the secretary that the Spanish leader of La Florida had many meetings that day, Tomás went directly to the issue that had brought him there. "Thank you for agreeing to see me on such short notice, Your Excellency. I realize the boldness of my coming directly to you, bypassing my own superior; but I was so distressed when I heard of your decision to place a garrison at the Mission Santa Fé that I had to speak to you myself. Governor Robenedo, putting a garrison there would be a grave mistake, not only for the Spanish government, but for the Potano people.

"Our Potano village has never presented any reason for the Spanish government to fear an uprising. Cacique Tomás has always cooperated with us in all the legitimate aims of our people. The faith is thriving. The people are very supportive of our mission. And despite the current drought, perhaps because of it, they are closer to me and to the Church than ever. They are looking to us desperately for help."

"Well, then," the governor observed, "they should welcome the help a garrison would provide them."

"No, Your Excellency. You see, when the people see the military, they think of past conquests. They think of the land that has been taken from them by the Spanish people. They think of their women being abused. Now they see fewer animals in their forests and fewer fish in their streams. A lieutenant of yours in one garrison to the northwest has set up his own ranch, with cattle grazing on native land. I will mention no names. There are other similar examples. What does this do to our missionary efforts? It undermines them. When Pedro Menéndez de Avilés came to San Agustín with Father Francisco López de Mendoza Grajales in 1565, he was given by the king a religious as well as a military mission. Governor Robenedo, it is the missionary purpose that the military serves and not the mission serving the military."

"I believe, good friar," the governor retorted, "that noble ideals must not be confused with harsh reality. Yes, the Spanish goals include missionary endeavors, but we are here to serve not only the Lord but also the king. The Crown has many reasons for being in the New World, not the least of which, of course, is the religious concern of which you speak. But we also have to keep our militia alive, our people fed, and the Spanish outreach here in San Agustín functioning properly so that we can protect the boundaries of Spanish territory in the New World. That is no small challenge, Padre. I do not think your vision of the Spanish presence fully encompasses the scope of our endeavor."

"Your Excellency, I am not a politician. I am a priest," Fray Tomás responded. "I do not know all the concerns that confront you in the course of a day, but I truly sympathize with them. I only place before you the one concern that is most important—the religious missionary purpose for our being here. If we forget that, all else is lost. If we are consumed with obtaining gold, or land, or people under our dominion, we have very shallow reasons for placing our flag in La Florida. But if we are here to win souls for Christ, then our other objectives should be at the services of that one goal.

"Earlier, I mentioned to you the missionary mandate of King Philip to your predecessor, the first governor of La Florida, Pedro Menéndez de Avilés. I brought with me today part of the *cedula*[10] of the king that clear-

---

[10] an official document.

ly indicates Spanish objectives in the New World. You must be familiar with them."

The governor took the paper from Tomás, nodded his head, indicating familiarity with the text as he read it aloud softly.

As we have in mind the good of the salvation of those Indian souls, we have decided to give the order to send religious persons to instruct the said Indians, and those people who are Christians and our subjects so that they may live among and talk to the natives so that by association and conversation with them they might be taught our Holy Catholic faith and be led to good practices and to perfect behavior.

Tomás handed the governor another paper, and said, "A few days after landing in San Agustín, Menéndez wrote back to the king these words."

Again, though somewhat reluctantly, the governor read, this time inaudibly.

As for myself, Your Majesty may be assured that, if I had a million ducats more or less, I would spend it all upon this undertaking, because it is of such great service to God, Our Lord, for the increase of our Holy Catholic faith and for the service of Your Majesty.

I have offered to Our Lord all that He may give me in this world, all that I may acquire and possess, in order to plant the Gospel in this land for the enlightenment of the natives, and in like manner, I pledge myself to your majesty.

Governor Robenedo slid back in his chair, indicating his wish that this meeting begin to seek a speedy conclusion. Fray Tomás caught the insinuation, but continued to present his case.

"If I can have just a few more minutes of your time, I promise to end very shortly.... May I just read briefly from a letter of His Holiness, Pope Pius V to Governor Menéndez, in 1569?"

Tomás took the governor's silence to mean permission, and he proceeded to read.

You understand, we know, well, that those Indians should be ruled and governed with good judgment and prudence, that those who are still weak in the Faith may be encouraged and fortified, and that idolaters may be converted and receive the faith of Christ, that the converts, who know the benefits of divine mercy may praise God, and that those who are still unbelievers, guided by the example of those who have been rescued from their blindness, may follow them and be brought to the knowledge of the truth. But there is nothing more important for the conversion of these idolatrous Indians . . ."

Tomás began to emphasize strongly these words of the pope,

". . .than to make every effort to keep them from being scandalized by the vices and bad habits of those who go to those lands from Europe. This is the keystone of the arch of this Holy undertaking and in it is contained the very essence of your pious aim.

Tomás had made his point, but not without making the governor very irritated. He began to look intently, almost angrily at Fray Tomás.

"This is all well and good, Padre." The governor stood and drew a deep breath and in so doing made his figure appear more commanding and forceful. "I planned to place a garrison at your doorstep, Fray Tomás, not only to protect you from what I, and others, regard as a serious threat to your health and well-being, the uprising of warrior Indians hostile to the Spanish, but also…" Here the governor hesitated, carefully choosing his words. "…also because of my concern with the conduct of our Franciscan Friars in their 'missionary' endeavors.

"We have received reports that some of your friars have been using the natives, or shall I say 'exploiting' the natives, for personal gain. I am not accusing you personally of such activities, but in conducting their 'religious' activities, some friars have set up their own trading relations with the natives and have side-tracked the ones our own office has established. Some of the natives have accused your friars of 'overworking' them and giving them little recompense."

"Precisely the charges," Tomás retorted, "that our people have been bringing up against the Spanish authorities. We hear complaints often, and I have seen them well substantiated, that your own military personnel have forcibly conscripted our people, and even our caciques, into leaving their families for weeks at a time to carry supplies to and from San Agustín.

"I am sorry, Your Excellency, the shoe deserves to be put on the other foot. It is not *our* friars who are guilty of such acts, or if so—very rarely. It is the people working under our Spanish customs officials and military. I do not agree with the charges you are now leveling against the friars, though I have heard them wrongfully expressed before."

"*Our* people? *Our* caciques?" the governor responded. "Do you hear what you are saying, Fray Tomás? Perhaps, good Padre, your days in the

Spanish missions of La Florida have clouded your vision of reality. You seem to have…lost your Spanish pride, your Spanish heritage, and taken on some ill-defined outlook akin to the people you are living with. The heat of the Florida sun seems to have gotten to you…. If you feel the way you do, you can no longer be of service to España or to the Church. For your own sake, I will immediately suggest to your superior here at Franciscan headquarters some change of venue more healthful for you, to relieve you of these unnecessary concerns that are plaguing you."

Tomás sat dumbfounded by the governor's reaction. He could not believe what he heard. His trust in the position of governor and in the person holding España's highest office in La Florida had been something almost sacred. That trust crumbled at what he heard.

The priest finally managed to speak. "Do you mean to say that I am being rewarded for telling you the truth by having to give up something to which I have devoted myself for over forty years? My fidelity to my God and to my King, Your Excellency, has never wavered. I have managed successfully, all these years, to serve the noble ideals that I have believed to be España's objectives in the New World."

The governor shrugged, unmoved. "You had best gather up your belongings now, Fray Tomás. If there is anything I cannot tolerate in one of the Crown's subjects, it is insolence. I am sure your Friar Superior can find a replacement for you shortly, someone who understands the objectives of our government in a better way. I will see to it that he does."

"Thank you for taking the time to see me, Your Excellency," Tomás quickly responded, as he rose to his feet. "I am sorry we do not agree on España's objectives in La Florida."

With those words and a slight bow in the governor's direction, Tomás left downcast in spirit. He trudged wearily back home, his thoughts drifting over his four decades of service to the Potano people—the good times, the bad, the successes, and the failures. Now it was all about to come quickly to an end.

"Why did I tell this man the truth?" Tomás kept asking himself over and over again. "It was just too much for him to bear."

But farther down in the depths of his being, where feelings have their greatest resonance and the impact of life strikes most poignantly there lurked a profound feeling of guilt. Tomás blamed himself for whatever went wrong in that meeting. He should have gone directly to his Franciscan superior and let him address the concern. No, he had to do it himself! He should not have been so bold and prideful to think he, Fray Tomás, had the power to change politics. And now, what a mess he had made of things!

Not only had he failed in his goal, to prevent the establishing of a garrison at the mission, he had ended his days as a missionary as well. Now he would have to leave the one place he felt most at home and the one people who meant so much to him. The Potano of the mission were like his own family.

"May God forgive me my pride!" Tomás prayed, as he fell to his knees, midway on his journey. "May God forgive me," he said; and then, with the grief of great regret bringing tears to his eyes, he held his emotions in check no longer. Finally, he fell fast asleep on the backpack that contained his blanket and supplies.

When he returned to the mission, the priest crept silently to the *convento*. Tomás did not have the heart to tell anyone at the mission, not even the cacique, what had happened. Instead, he went into his room, sat at his table, and began writing to his Franciscan superior. The Friar Custodian would shortly hear the report of the governor, which would almost certainly contain the official's request that Fray Tomás' stay be terminated at the Mission Santa Fé. Fray Tomás only wanted Fray Miguel to hear his explanation of what had transpired at the meeting and why. He also wanted to give his sincere apology for bypassing his superior and going straight to the governor.

Knowing of the friar's important visit to San Agustín and curious of the outcome, Cacique Tomás soon came to see the priest. As a lifelong friend of Fray Tomás, the cacique could sense the situation before words were spoken, and he remained silent for a while in the priest's presence. When the Franciscan looked up, the grief-stricken look on his face confirmed the cacique's worse fears.

"You are leaving us, aren't you, Fray Tomás?" the cacique asked. "The governor was not only displeased with your words, but he also was not pleased with you."

Fray Tomás tried to speak but found he could not. Instead, after a few moments, he simply nodded.

The chieftain sighed deeply, not taking his eyes off his friend and mentor. "This is indeed a sad day. But I only ask; why now, of all times, when we need you most, do they consider this action against you, their most worthy servant? Why do they take from you now the great respect that should be yours after all you have done for them and for us? Why now, Fray

Tomás, when our Potano people are starving, and you alone give them hope? Why?"

"I do not know," Tomás replied, slowly shaking his head. "I do not know."

"Fray Tomás," he went on, "even if your body should happen to leave us, your spirit will always be here. The Spanish can never take from us the great gift they have given us in you. Always, you shall be with us. Always, you shall be in this village. This land will hold your presence and your memory until the end of time. By your life and by your faith, you have made sacred this land and this people. So do not fear. They can never take you away from us."

The cacique placed his large Potano arms about the priest and said nothing more.

In San Agustín, Fray Miguel had no reason to reject Fray Tomás' plea. The priest's work at the Mission Santa Fé had been nothing less than exemplary. In fact, the man's missionary techniques were being imitated and implemented elsewhere. Fray Miguel had no reason not to support his *confrere,* especially since the governor could not be more wrong about him and about the friars.

Oh yes, maybe a few intrepid, mercantilist friars had overstepped their bounds and started enterprises that were not according to their missionary calling. Perhaps, yes, some had begun employing the natives in ways that were contrary to their Christian vocation. And yes, some may have physically abused the natives when they acted too slowly or sluggishly or irresponsibly. Yes, he would have to rectify these abuses and chastise those who had committed them.

But not Fray Tomás! This poor brother must not be held responsible for the failures of others!

As to the military garrison, Fray Miguel would support Fray Tomás' request that it not be placed at the Mission Santa Fé—to the point that if the governor insisted on it, he would appeal to the Crown. It would not be the first time he had written to the Crown to protest a government action, nor, he wryly thought, would it be the last.

Rather than go through regular channels, Fray Miguel sent a Christianized Indian as a courier with word of his decision to Fray Tomás. This he did after having personally communicated his reaction to the governor. Then, Fray Miguel, Fray Tomás, and the cacique all sat back and waited for the governor's response.

The amazing outcome was that nothing happened. Life went on as usual. The military garrison never came. The only change appeared in the form of an occasional Spanish soldier who rode through the area to inspect and report on conditions at the village and mission.

Fray Tomás remained at his post, both in body and in spirit, and threw himself back into his work with the usual vigor. He prayed gratefully that Divine Providence had intervened and allowed him to continue in the work he had begun so many years before.

XXV
- 1656 -

The Dance of War had not been celebrated by the Timucuan nation since shortly after the treaty between the people of Timucua and Apalachee, but gradually the chants familiar to the older tribesmen were heard once more. In the villages of the Potano, Utina, and other western tribes of Timucua, drums once again beat out the call for bloodshed. How quickly the younger men of the tribes gave evidence of their knowledge

of the ancient ceremonial rituals in preparation for battle. They eagerly participated in the War Dance, abstinence from food and sex, and the black drink ceremony. With each passing month, the Dance of War spread, and everywhere the reason was the same.

The increasingly oppressive demands by the Spanish were driving the aboriginal people, including the Potano, to the edge of rebellion. Just as Fray Tomás and the Potano cacique feared, the intrusion of the Spanish livestock on the natives' lands and the levies of food for the garrisons which taxed villages already stricken by drought, all added fuel to a smoldering fire of discontent. In addition, the colonial forces conscripted the natives to bear food and materials to San Agustín from the western Spanish territories. This menial labor proved too demeaning for the people, especially when the Spanish demands forced the caciques to engage in servile labor. This gave insult to all the tribes. In the minds of the natives, Spanish gifts lay forgotten in the shadow of Spanish oppression. At any moment, the smoldering fire of discontent could burst into a blaze of insurrection.

The prospect of war engaged the conversation of every inhabitant of the village and mission of Santa Fé. Cacique Tomás had banned the Dance of War. The young men of warrior age viewed this decree as a denial of their rightful privileges and as an act of cowardice. They would quietly slip into neighboring villages that did practice the rituals, and there they also received training in the skills of deadly combat, not just the defensive fighting methods Cacique Tomás permitted. Many young braves were secretly progressing up the ranks of warrior status, from that of *tascaia* to *noroco,* to *hita tascaia,* and finally, to *nicoguadca.*

Late one evening, a very alarmed Tofu and Fray Tomás approached the dwelling of the cacique. They roused him from sleep, trying not to disturb the other members of his family still living in his *buhio.* They succeeded in getting him outside, where Tofu reported in whispered words that Ycho had returned to the area.

"He was seen today with fifteen of our young men. They were no more than seven leagues north of our village," the *inija* informed the cacique. "It is well known that he has conscripted many of the men of our village to join him in his intrigue. Young and old have gone out to join him. I knew this man would bring dishonor to our people one day. That day has now arrived!"

The cacique shook his head. He could not help but agree with Tofu's assessment of the situation. "What is worse, my dear friends, is that all of my brother caciques of the western tribes of Timucua are one with Ycho in his efforts to drive the Spanish from our lands."

Then the cacique looked about him cautiously before continuing in a softer tone of voice. He did not want to be overheard by his family or anyone else. "These leaders have told me that if I do not join them, there will be…consequences." He then lowered his eyes, and rubbed them with his hands.

Fray Tomás saw at that moment what the darkness had been hiding, the worry, frustration, and disappointment on the cacique's face. He almost had the look of—a defeated man. This disquieted the priest and rent his heart. He had feared his friend might be suffering this strain.

"Don't despair, Holata Tomás; there is still hope," the friar said, placing his hand on the shoulder of the cacique as a sign of sympathy and support. "But time is against us. Tofu and I came to you tonight because we feel something must be done quickly. We must act now if we want to offset the situation."

"What do you suggest, Fray Tomás?" the cacique asked. "I could never betray my people to the Spanish. Nor can I join in rebellion against my father's people and the many good Spanish people I care about, like you, Fray Tomás. What choice do I have in such a situation?"

Tofu spoke first. "I must take you and your family into hiding. You cannot be part of what will happen between the Timucuan and the Spanish people. We all know what is coming, and it comes very soon. You must avoid the conflict. That is our only hope."

The friar nodded in agreement. "He is right. You must leave with your family. If you remain here, you will be forced to join either the Spanish or the rebel caciques. Either way you cannot win."

"But if I leave, Fray Tomás, I could never return to lead my people," the cacique said to his friar mentor. "Yes, my family can hide and I trust their lives to you, Tofu; but I cannot leave my village and my tribe. My destiny is to be their cacique. My duty is to remain here.

"Fray Tomás, our only hope to save our people may be with you. Many years ago, you were able to persuade the people of Timucua and Apalachee to come together in peace. Perhaps now you can bring the Spanish and the Timucuan nations together. Could you not try one last time to bring the Spanish to change their ways in dealing with my people? Then, perhaps Ycho and others like him would be forced to come to a treaty of peace."

Fray Tomás began to shake his head, remembering his last encounter with Governor Robenedo.

The cacique persisted. "There is not much that I ever ask of you, Padre, but I know of no other way to peace. Would you not go to present our plea in San Agustín and seek redress for the wrongs against our people?"

Finally, the friar relented. "Yes, I will go to San Agustín for you," the padre replied, "but only if you do as Tofu asks and depart with your family. He is right. You are no longer safe here."

"You have taught me many things, Fray Tomás," the cacique interjected forthrightly. "One lesson is that I must be faithful to my people. I cannot lead them by leaving them. A cacique never abandons his people."

"Perhaps I have taught you too well," the priest half-joked, then fell silent. "How I wish life were otherwise than it is right now.... Tomorrow early, I will leave for San Agustín and attempt to do my best with the governor, difficult as that will be. That may be our only hope in trying to stop the slaughter of many."

"And tomorrow evening," Tofu spoke in an agitated way, "your entire family, with all the spouses and children of your older sons and daughters must leave the village with me."

The cacique nodded, then said, "But, as I have told you, I must remain here with my people."

A light cough from inside the cacique's dwelling interrupted their conversation. They also heard the sound of shuffling feet, and the men fell silent. The cacique peered quickly inside, looking to see who had awakened, but he found all the family resting soundly. Even so, the three friends decided to conclude their secret council for the present and to proceed with action in the morning.

Catalina, lying motionless, closed her eyes against the oncoming tears as her mind digested the conversation she had just overheard. She tried to ignore her fear and pray herself to sleep, but she did not succeed.

She felt around in the dark until she found her quill and a piece of paper stashed away in a little wooden box. Then she began to scribble a letter. She swiftly, almost frantically, wrote words that were invisible because of the darkness, but very clear in her mind's eye. She carefully crafted her message to Felipe-Toloca.

It did not matter that he would have trouble reading her scribbled scrawl, or that she had no idea how she would get this letter to him. What did matter was that he know that their father, and in fact, the entire family, found themselves in a desperate situation because of their loyalty to Fray Tomás and the Spanish. She pleaded with her brother to pray and pray hard, that the Potano people would understand why their father could not join in a rebellion against the Spanish. Would Felipe-Toloca ask the Great Cacique of Spain to intervene quickly on their behalf?

"Why are you stirring so late, Catalina?" said a whisper from the darkness.

She gave a little start, but then recognized her father's voice. He had crept quietly to her side.

"I had feared someone might be a silent partner to our conversation," Cacique Tomás continued. "What did you hear, Little One?"

"Everything, Father," she replied. "I could not help doing so. When Tofu called to you, I woke up, too. I knew something terrible had brought him and Fray Tomás here for them to come so late at night." She rushed ahead with the words weighing on her heart. "Father, can I stay behind with you? And all the family, too? If you have to stay in the village, then mother and all of the rest of us, we won't want to go. We would all want to be right here with you."

"Do not worry, my precious one, all will be fine. We will be separated from one another only for a very short time," her father consoled her. "Please keep our conversation to yourself, and let me explain to your mother and all our family my reasons for sending you away for a while. You will be safe and all will be well, Catalina. Do not worry."

She hugged him desperately. "I love you, Father. You are the greatest father anyone could have. I want to make sure I never, ever lose you. I want you to know I am afraid for you, but not as I used to be when I was afraid of everything. Fray Buenaventura and Felipe-Toloca taught me to look far past the present moment and today's dangers. They said to look to the future and I'm trying. But I must admit, I am afraid."

"I am afraid, too, Little One," Cacique Tomás replied, "for my family, for my people, but not for myself. Catalina, I have no fear of Ycho, of the other caciques, or of the anger of some of the Potano people against me. I hold on to what is important. And what is important is what I believe, for what I believe is what I am. Nothing can shake my faith because it is so firmly rooted, and nothing can change my way of living it. Nothing!"

Catalina wanted to protest further. But she saw the resolve in her father's face. She knew she could not change his mind, and in a way, she did not want to. She took courage and comfort from his determination.

She loved him for it. She said, "Father, I was writing to my brother in España to ask him for his prayers for us. When I am not able to sleep at night, I often begin to write. Writing always helps make my eyelids heavy. But this letter is one that will never be delivered, since we will be leaving our village in haste tomorrow."

The chieftain gave a wry smile. "You are wise, youngest. We do need your brother's prayers now more than ever. Finish tonight what you are writing, Catalina," her father said, "and I will give your letter to Fray Tomás early in the morning. He will be leaving tomorrow for San Agustín. I am sure he will be able to deliver it to a ship sailing for España.

"Tell Felipe-Toloca we love him and miss him greatly, and await the day when he will be a priest for us, which is fast approaching. And yes, please tell him I still wear proudly the medal to Our Lady that bears his initials. May the good Lord bring our greetings and our love quickly to the shores of España and to the home of our dear son and brother."

"I will write to him what you said," Catalina promised.

Then her father quietly moved across the floor of the dwelling to his own resting place.

Catalina got very little sleep that night, as she searched and prayed for the right words for this special letter to her brother. The quill was still in her hand when her father found her fast asleep early the next morning. He carefully removed it from her, and he saw her letter, just completed. She awoke and insisted on helping him deliver it to Fray Tomás. Together they went to see the Franciscan. Even though the sun had not yet risen, the priest had finished preparing for his journey. In his final words before departure, he told the cacique and Catalina how he regretted that he did not have the convenience of a horse. It was usually a three-day trek on foot to San Agustín. As it was, he would try to reduce the journey by walking all day and night.

"I assure you, Catalina," Fray Tomás said, "I will bring your letter immediately to the first ship sailing for España, as soon as I arrive in San Agustín."

The priest warmly embraced the sleepy young lady and bid a fond farewell to her father, then he hurried on his way to San Agustín. Thanks to the friar, Felipe-Toloca would soon learn of the distressful condition of his family and friends back home in La Florida.

8 April 1656

Dearest Brother,

How many times I have begun this letter to you! I have lost count already. A dozen maybe. I hesitate to write to you about something that will cause you distress. But just moments ago I learned of something terrible about to happen in our village, and I feel I must convey this news to you immediately.

People from our village and all the western villages of Timucua are getting ready to go to war with the people of España. The Dance of War has been celebrated in all the villages of the area but our own. Father has forbidden this ritual to take place here and his doing so has taken away his popularity with more than a few people of our village, especially the young braves. They feel it is time for the Spanish people to change their ways and stop forcing our men, and even our caciques, to carry supplies for them for weeks and months. It keeps them away from their homes and families. Many feel anger against the Spanish who let their cattle graze on our lands where we hunt and grow our food. The young warriors say they want to avenge these wrongs. Now we have learned that the evil Ycho has returned to encourage the hostilities of our warriors against the Spanish.

Most of the people here are in sympathy with Father's position to maintain peace with the Spanish, because they still have great love for Fray Tomás. Then I overheard something that brought fear to my heart. Our father said in conversation with Fray Tomás and Tofu late this evening that other caciques of the region will take action against him if he refuses to join with them in rebellion.

You know, as I do, that Father will never do this, and so I fear for him. He has decided to let Tofu take all our family into hiding, except himself. He believes he must remain here in the village to lead our people. Fray Tomás and Tofu worry that if he remains, he will be forced to side with either the Spanish or the other caciques and will be branded either a traitor to his people or a rebel against España.

Father's solution is to send Fray Tomás to San Agustín to appeal in this final hour to the Spanish leaders to change their harsh ways of dealing with our people. Father is hopeful that Fray Tomás, who brought the miracle of peace to our people and the Apalachees, will work a wonder once again, this time between our people and the Spanish. I pray Father is right in his decision; but quite honestly, I see little hope for Fray Tomás, because he does not find a ready ear in the person of Governor Robenedo, whom he has confronted in the past. I fear the Spanish will be deaf to his plea.

Felipe-Toloca, I turn to you, dear brother. Please do what you can for us. In you, I can always confide my hopes and my fears, even though you are miles from me. Can you please appeal to the Great Cacique of the Spanish nation to change the minds of his people who lead the Spanish in La Florida?

If he will make them mend their ways, then perhaps a terrible tragedy will be prevented. Please try to act quickly for your people. Father fears that something may happen very soon.

I am writing my letter in the darkness of night without being able to see the letters I am putting down. I cannot light a candle or I would disturb the others in our buhio. *I hope you will be able to read this somehow.*

I send our father's greeting to you. He found me writing to you and asked that I remind you of his great love for you and to tell you how much he awaits the day of your becoming a priest. So do I. He wants you to know he still wears the medal of Cacique Toloca that honors the Virgin Mary and which bears the first letters of the words 'Felipe-Toloca, Hijo Mio' – 'F.T.H.M.' He is so devoted to you and, like all of us, he misses you so very, very much.

Pray for father, that all his people, young and old, will understand the wisdom of his ways and his reasons for trying to promote peace with the Spanish. Pray for us, your family, in our great distress, and for all the people of our village and mission.

We truly love you and pray daily to the Great Spirit for you.

Your devoted sister,
Catalina

XXVI

"Padre, crouch low and stay quiet. I hear the movement of footsteps on the earth ahead," said Mateo, the Indian guide, to Fray Tomás. As he whispered the command, Mateo grabbed the friar and pulled him down out of sight. As a trusted co-worker who had assisted the missionary for many years as a catechist and sacristan, Mateo had been asked by the cacique to accompany the priest to San Agustín.

It was in the darkness of the early hours of morning on the first day of their journey when they sighted the outlines of other human beings on the mission road. A bright, nearly full moon filtered light through the slightly swaying branches, casting shadows on the ground. The friar and his companion were now carefully concealed behind a curtain of moss hanging from a live oak. They could just barely make out the figures of at least ten men bearing weapons in their hands. One passed close by the hiding place and Fray Tomás could see the man was a young brave. He had war paint on his body.

"They are Potano," Mateo said, after the Indians had passed, "and they are up to no good."

"Then we must hurry," Fray Tomás replied, though his body protested. "Rest is now a luxury we cannot afford. The rebellion is gathering support before our very eyes."

"Yes, but when we get to San Agustín, what will we accomplish, Fray Tomás? Cacique Robenedo has done nothing but add kindling to the fire of rebellion. Our mission, I think is…" He didn't finish the thought but just shook his head grimly.

"We have to try, Mateo," the priest responded with resolve, though the stone of despair in his stomach grew to the size of a rock. Mateo had spoken what the Franciscan had secretly felt from the start of this journey. But despair is from the devil, he thought. And this mission was the only thing he could do for his friends. Better to do this than do nothing. Aloud, he said, "It is our only hope!"

For safety reasons, they avoided the Mission Trail that connected Santa Fé to San Agustín. Nevertheless, they used it as a guide as they traveled through the day and on into the next night. Giving themselves few rest stops, they finally trudged wearily into a dimly lit San Agustín and headed immediately for the Franciscan *convento*, where they spent the remainder of the night.

Sleep came swiftly upon Mateo, but the friar did not fare so well. A great anxiety overwhelmed him as he pondered the fate of those he loved, and his consciousness seemed to slip from dreams to reality and back again. His mind, heart, and soul were still back at the mission.

At one point of his drifting and dreaming, he suddenly heard a voice, clear, distinct and identifiable. It called his name. He immediately bolted up from his cot, and saw a bright figure in the dark. It was none other than Cacique Tomás. The padre wiped his eyes and rubbed his arms to assure himself that he was not imagining what he saw. He looked again. Indeed the figure remained, and the man in the vision extended a hand in his direction. Fray Tomás responded by reaching out to him in turn, but just as the two hands were about to touch, the luminous figure disappeared.

It must have been an illusion or a dream, the friar thought. Certainly, I am so distraught I am now beginning to hallucinate!

Physical and mental weariness finally overcame the friar's distress, and exhausted, he fell asleep.

"Fray Tomás, Fray Tomás!" The words penetrated the barrier between the world of dreams and the world of reality. Tomás woke to the sound of Mateo's voice and sleep fell from him as Mateo gently shook him by the shoulder.

"Padre, it is morning! We must get on with our mission before it is too late. If you believe the governor is our only hope, then we must go to him immediately!"

Tomás squinted into the bright light of the *Florida* morning as the sun's rays narrowed the pupils of his eyes. It was a new day, and indeed, the mission loomed before him. Then, recollection of the night before and the stress of the events of the past days crashed upon him and forced his body back onto the bed. He wanted to slip back into blissful oblivion. He wanted to sleep for days.

But the cacique, the cacique's family, and the whole mission depended on him. Every moment could mean the difference between salvation and disaster. Then, gathering strength from within, the priest thrust his aged body forward and inched his legs over the edge. He forced his feet into his sandals but then stayed motionless. His entire body felt petrified in the face of the task at hand.

"Lord, help me!" the friar prayed. "Help my friends. I am in distress as never before. All I hold dear is at stake—the life of my friends, the success of my mission, the longstanding work of my brother friars for the past sixty-five years. You, who never fail those who entrust their lives to your care, help me now, as never before. Into your hands, O Lord, I entrust my soul."

With that, he was off with Mateo to visit the provincial, Fray Esteban Hernandez, who headed what was now the newly established Franciscan Province of Santa Elena. Fray Esteban had agreed the night before to accompany Fray Tomás on his visit to the governor's house, which was just a short distance from the *convento*.

Mateo tugged at the friar's sleeve as they exited the *convento*. "Remember the letter of Catalina to Felipe-Toloca. Sometime you must deliver it into the hands of a person sailing to España."

"You are in luck," Fray Estaban commented, overhearing Mateo's words. "There is a ship leaving this very morning with supplies for the homeland. You had best deliver your letter immediately, as the ship—*Felicidad*—will be leaving soon."

The three took a roundabout walk to the governor's house by way of the bay front so that Tomás could deliver his letter. They arrived just moments before the ship's departure, and the captain assured Tomás, much to the priest's relief, that the letter would arrive safely in España. The man personally promised that he would ultimately send it to Salamanca, where Felipe-Toloca resided.

When the Franciscan party arrived at the Governor's Office, they found the house in a state of general alarm. Two guards, posted at the front door, prohibited entrance to the building. They volunteered no other information than the order that the Government House was closed, and no official business would be conducted. Only military personnel would be permitted to enter. As the priests' group deliberated their next option, many officers passed in and out of the building. Fray Tomás' frustration got the better of him.

"I have an important message for the governor from the Santa Fé Mission," Tomás half shouted, half explained to one of the guards. "This is an emergency!" With that, Tomás simply strode passed the guards and into the building, leaving everyone dumbfounded. He knew where the governor's office was, and with a distraught guard hard on his heels, he moved quickly down the hall.

"Padre, I am sorry, but you are not permitted in here."

"I must talk to the governor. It is a matter of life and death," Tomás shouted back.

"What seems to be the problem, officer?" a deep, forceful voice sounded, as the office door opened.

The guard saluted. "Your Excellency, this friar bolted through our post. He says he has an important message for you."

"So, what is it, Padre? As you can see, I am very busy," Governor Robenedo commented brusquely. Then he recognized Fray Tomás. "You!" he said, his eyes narrowing. He spun on his heel and began walking in the other direction.

Suddenly, he reversed himself, and facing the friar, began to berate Fray Tomás.

"It's that meddlesome priest, returned. So, you have come to complain now that your mission has been overrun by rebels, as I told you it would be.... Had you not interfered, a military garrison would have prevented this disaster from happening!"

"What disaster?" the friar asked.

The governor looked at Fray Tomás and saw the genuine surprise on the priest's face. Then he glanced at Mateo and Fray Esteban who had entered behind the guard, and he noted the similar puzzlement in their expressions. "Are you the only ones in San Agustín who do not know what happened at the western missions of Timucua in the past two days?

"The cacique of San Martín has enlisted the other caciques to join in an attack on all persons and properties of the Spanish people. We know of the death of several Spanish military personnel already.... And how did you escape with your life, Padre?"

Tomás was silent for a moment, with the sober realization that he had arrived too late. The well-being of his friends was in jeopardy.

"And what of the Mission Santa Fé?" Tomás asked, ignoring the governor's query. "Have you heard anything about Cacique Tomás? He would never have been partner to such an intrigue. In fact, he sent me here, precisely...precisely to try to seek your help to avert such a tragedy. Have you any information about Cacique Tomás and his family?"

"Yes, Padre, I am afraid I do. There are refugees from the Mission Santa Fé now at the Mission Nombre De Dios. They brought news this morning just moments ago that...the cacique and his family were taken hostage and...executed by the rebel group.... They did, as you said, oppose the rebellion, and for that they died. The rebels have installed another cacique, and he has had the people of Santa Fé join in rebellion against the Crown. I do not know his name."

"Ynaja," Fray Tomás said, but he felt like he spoke in a dream. His voice sounded distant, toneless. "He is the cousin of Cacique Tomás and next in line as chieftain. He and Ycho, the rebel leader, they hated the Spanish."

"Whatever their names are," said the governor, "they will pay for their actions. And so will you, Padre." Robenedo continued speaking despite the friar's shocked expression. "All this would never have happened if you had not meddled in the affairs of state. Church people have no knowledge of the real world, and they should stay as far way from government affairs as possible. Their proper place is inside the sanctuary.

"You, Padre," the governor said, pointing his finger directly at Tomás, "you, and other ignorant friars like you, are responsible for this terrible situation. And when I have finally caught all those conniving caciques and the other treacherous rebels working with them in this plot, you will stand trial with them!"

Someone cleared his voice, catching the governor's attention. The sound came from Fray Esteban who moved to stand protectively beside Fray Tomás. "You seem to have forgotten, Your Excellency," remarked Fray Esteban to the politician, "that the Church alone has its special mechanism for evaluating the deeds and misdeeds of its clergy. And it alone can render the kind of judgment you have misappropriated to yourself. Such determinations are mine to make about my friars, Your Excellency, and I will not cede that authority to any civil official, yourself included."

"Will your friars resurrect the lives of their fellow Spaniards, whose deaths were brought about by their folly?" Robenedo retorted. "Will your friars restore peace or order to this mess they have created?" He glared at them in silence for a moment, pretending to wait for a reply. "No, I thought not. That you will leave to me and the military."

He waved them away derisively, "Go. Leave, so I can stop the hostile forces, including those within this very room, who are trying to destroy La Florida!"

With that, the governor rudely turned from the friars and stalked away. The guards briskly ushered the two friars and Mateo out the front entrance of the Government House.

The Franciscans had not gone far from the house when Fray Tomás swayed, stumbled and nearly fell. After the governor told him of Santa Fé's tragedy, the friar had barely heard the rest of the conversation. Shock and disbelief had shrouded him like a fog, numbing his mind and heart. Now, the impact of the news struck him like a blow.

"They are dead, Mateo! Fray Esteban, they are dead!" Tomás gasped. He couldn't breathe and he could barely stand.

Both Mateo and the Friar Provincial placed an arm around the aged priest to keep him from falling. Silence stretched between them as they each emotionally confronted the tragic tidings. They grappled with the grief in their individual ways.

Finally, Fray Esteban spoke. He answered Fray Tomás with denial, "We don't know that! Not for certain. We don't know yet if the governor is right. After all, you just left the mission, and all was well, was it not?"

"All was not well," Tomás quietly responded. "We came here to tell the governor that he had a rebellion on his hands, and...and I had hoped we would avert it.... We were too late. We tried...but it was too little, too late!"

Tomás put his head in his hands and broke away from them. "Please, let me be alone for a while."

The others would not oblige him. They felt he needed their support, just as they needed his. They stayed close to him.

Fray Tomás turned to Mateo, and looking squarely at his companion of the past couple days, he said, "You were right. This whole idea was madness. You knew, and I guess I did, too, deep in my heart, that the governor would never listen to us. Even if we had arrived months ago, his ears would have been deaf. We have failed, and all the Spanish people have failed miserably in the one important work we came here to do.

"We have failed to bring the Gospel message to the native people. All we have brought them is sorrow, pain, disease, confusion, and hatred of us. Hatred often inspired by our own miserable actions. We are now about to lose everything, all that we came to bring. And the governor, in his urge to crush the rebellion, will overreact and make these people even more hostile to us than they already are, all in the name of God and country! We have failed miserably!"

Sadness flooded into Mateo's heart at what he heard the friar say. He had long served the padre and held him in high esteem. Never had the Franciscan spoken so despondently of the mission work or the Spanish people. The Potano replied, "Fray Tomás, your pain is my own. I feel I can hardly bear it. To think that my people have turned against your people and their own tribe, is a horror I did not think possible. And now my own path lies in darkness because I have come with you. I am a Christian devoted to God and devoted to you, Fray Tomás. Am I now an outcast? What has happened to my wife and children? I do not know."

For a moment the man fell silent lost in the thoughts and worries that whirled in his head. Then he spoke again, "But I do know one thing. Never have I heard you speak before in despair. You have always brought hope to my people. Why do you speak this way now? You have told us many times that in this life we can only try. We can only strive. Only in the next world will we come to our goal. You have tried, Fray Tomás. The Great Spirit knows you have tried. I have seen your work and the fruits of that labor. What more could you have done?"

Fray Tomás stood in silence for a while, looking at his companion and reading the conviction in the native's eyes. Inside, he struggled. Part of him wanted to grab this lifeline of hope and consolation. The rest of him wanted to give in to anger and despair.

The Friar Provincial intervened, "Mateo has spoken well, Tomás. I pray we can take to heart at this most difficult time the Gospel message he has just preached so eloquently. Come," Fray Esteban said, putting a hand on his confrere's shoulder. " I wish to give you time to rest and grieve in peace, but there is much work to be done."

Slowly, Fray Tomás nodded and allowed himself to be led away by his superior. Swiftly and silently, the tears began to fall. And he let them. He could not stop the grief, but he would not let the grief stop him.

At the Mission Nombre de Dios, Fray Tomás and Mateo found the Potanos who had borne the message to the governor from the Mission Santa Fé. They must have arrived just before him and Mateo. The padre felt some comfort in the knowledge that some members of the tribe had remained loyal to their cacique.

When Fray Tomás arrived, the refugees quickly spotted him, and his friends, a group of six adults, came running to greet him. One of them was the wife of Mateo, a woman named María. Mateo saw her face marred by sadness and fatigue, but she lit up as he swept her up in his arms. Then, all embraced the friar and many burst into tears. They sadly recounted to him and Mateo the tragic events that had transpired at the mission.

María told most of the story, though others periodically interjected their version of the events. With great emotion, they described the tragedy they had witnessed.

"The very evening of the day you left the mission, Fray Tomás," María began, "word spread that Ycho was on his way into the village. It was late, and our sentries caused such an alarm throughout the village that many women and children fled. The intruders wore war paint, and they brought with them captives, Tofu and all the members of the family of our cacique. Next to Ycho stood the cousin of the cacique, Ynaja.

" 'Brave Cacique Kocha,' Ycho called out in a loud voice. 'Come forth from your dwelling! I want to return to you some people who have deserted your village. I believe you know them.'

"As the cacique came forward, Ycho showed him his family and Tofu. All were tied and bound. The cacique immediately ran forward to free them, but Ycho's warriors grabbed him and wrestled him to the ground. The ever-loyal Tofu, aged as he was, tried to wrestle loose from his bonds and help his cacique. But they grabbed him and beat him and he was subdued.

"After Ycho had the cacique in his power, he told Holata Tomás he would free him and his family…if they joined him in his rebellion!

"Cacique Tomás yelled back that he would never join Ycho in any cause.

"Ycho pled with him, trying to get him to change his mind. 'Do you want to see your family die, Kocha? Do you want to die yourself?' he asked.

"Our cacique answered him very clearly. 'I cannot live,' he said, 'and betray my people and my beliefs, Ycho!' Cacique Tomás would not bend.

"Then Ycho spoke again. 'The cacique of San Martín and the other villages of this area are in alliance against the Spanish people, who have oppressed us for too long. We are tired of their tyranny. We want to rid our land of them once and for all. You alone among our caciques have not allied with our cause. You betray your people if you do not join us, Kocha.

"Once again the cacique held firm. 'Betray my people?' he said, 'I have not broken the treaty with the Spanish as the other caciques have done, Ycho. I will not break my word, and I will not abandon my faith. Neither will my family.'

"At that Catalina spoke out boldly. 'We are with you, Father,' she cried out. 'All of us stand by you and Fray Tomás, because we know the Great Spirit is with us now and will never leave us!'

"Ycho simply shook his head, almost as if he was sad, but when he spoke again, it was with finality. 'If your family shares your traitorous ideas, Kocha,' he said 'then they must share your fate. Your views are a mockery and an affront to all Potanos. Your cousin and rightful heir, Ynaja, does not suffer your delusions. Because you will not renounce your corrupt ways, we choose him to lead our people. I am sorry, Kocha, that we have come to such an end.'

"Then Ycho motioned for the family to be taken away. At first, the cacique struggled to go after them, but his captors held him tight. Shortly thereafter we heard from a distance loud blows mingled with even louder cries that quickly fell silent."

"I recognized that sound, Padre," said another survivor, an old warrior. "It was the sound of a *macana* against their skulls."

María continued. "From what we could hear, we believe that, one-by-one the cacique's family and Tofu were…subjected to a cruel death."

"Though he had struggled at first, when the screaming began, the cacique changed. He became still and calm. Instead of bowing like a broken tree, he straightened and remained erect, maintaining the proud and dignified bearing he always possessed as our leader. He stared at the braves holding him. They were Potano. There was something about Holata

Tomás, something commanding, and the braves let go of him. The cacique did not run, but remained standing proud, his arms across his chest, his face without expression, as the horrible sounds continued. I think I saw a single tear fall from his eye, but I could not be sure.

"But at that moment I noticed," María continued, "Holata Tomás was carefully scanning the crowd as if to see who among us were with him and who against.

"When his eyes rested on me, they stopped. He had no doubt of my loyalty and that of my family. He knew we could never betray our cacique.... I saw him drop a piece of paper while he was looking at me. He must have pulled it out of his tunic when he crossed his arms. After it fell, he hid it in the dust with his feet. Ycho did not see this action, because his executioners had just returned. Several had blood on their hands and their weapons. The cacique's family was nowhere to be seen. Not one. Shortly thereafter, Ycho led our cacique out of the village by himself.

"All remained quiet for the next hour. Ycho's warriors stayed behind, surrounding our village and enlisting people to join them. They threatened to kill us if we did not cooperate.

"Then Ycho returned. I saw blood on his hands and chest, and I knew then, our dear, beloved cacique was no longer with us and never would be again.

"Ycho departed, leaving Ynaja and some of the rebel Potano in the village; but I was still able to find the spot where Cacique Tomás had dropped the piece of paper and stomped it into the ground. The paper had a message written on it. It was directed to you, Fray Tomás. When I read it, I knew you would want to have it.

"All who could, fled here to San Agustín. Our children and other family members are on their way to Nombre De Dios at this moment and should be arriving very soon. I came sooner because I showed this letter to some of your friends, who urged me to hurry with them ahead of the rest so we could tell you of this tragedy and to give you this letter from your son, Cacique Tomás."

Fray Tomás embraced María and the others once again, and then, began to read aloud the note written to him from Cacique Tomás. It had been written the day of his death and was dated 19 September 1656.

—To Be Given to Fray Tomás Sanchez, If Ill Health or Disaster Should Bring Me Death Before the Great Spirit Has Called Fray Tomás to the Eternal Kingdom—

To My Dear Friend and Spiritual Father, Fray Tomás,

I know that I shall be called one day to take my place with all the caciques of my people, with my uncle, Toloca, with my mother and father, and all my family and friends in the eternal kingdom of happiness and peace.

I have come to know that the reason we are to live and the reason we are to die one day is to be happy forever with the Great Spirit. Many people leave this world slowly, as they linger with a long illness. Others are taken abruptly from this world.

I do not know which the Great Spirit has planned for me. But I do not want to be taken from here suddenly without being able to thank the one person who has given to me and my people so much. That person is you, Fray Tomás. Should I die before you, Fray Tomás, I simply want you to know I am and always will be your devoted son in the holy faith.

Many years ago the Great Spirit sent you to rescue me, a little child, from death of the body. Then He allowed you to rescue me from death of the spirit and bring me to life in His Spirit.

As you know, I have anguished much through the years over my identity as a Potano with a Spanish father, and as a Christian living in a Potano village. I am happy to say that after all these years with you I have come to realize that it is possible for me to be a good Potano and a good Christian. That lesson did not come to me quickly or easily.

You have also understood that even though my father was Spanish, I and my people can never become Spanish. That means more to me than you know. You have been kind and patient with me, as I came to see myself in this light. You never shielded me from knowing well the ways of my Potano people. For this I shall always be thankful. You gave me Tofu, my great teacher and guide, to teach me the ways of my people. In doing so, he was able to repay the great debt of taking from me the mother I never knew.

Fray Tomás, how grateful I am to you, and will remain so for all eternity. You are the father I never had. You are the father of my faith. You have been the spiritual father and protector of my wife and children, and I pray you will continue to be so forever.

I have always wanted to share these thoughts with you in person, but you know how hard it is to speak to someone you love the words that are closest to one's heart. Maybe, someday, somehow, I will have the courage and freedom to speak them to you in words and not in writing. For this, I truly pray.

But if not, if instead they come to you in the way they are now, brought to you as my last testament of affection and gratitude, please regard them as no less sincere than if I spoke them to you myself.

The Great Spirit brought you into my life from a far-off country and people. Through the Great Spirit, you have become one with me and my people. When I dwell in the land of the Great Spirit, I shall still be with you, always. Please pray for me, as I will for you, without stopping. Pray that, with all our loved ones, we will be united with Jesus forever in happiness and peace.

Your devoted son,
Tomás,
Cacique of the Village and Mission of Santa Fé

Fray Tomás lowered his eyes and folded the letter slowly and gently. He slid it up the sleeve of his friar's habit for safekeeping. He knew he would read it again and again. Then the missionary headed in the direction of the nearby chapel, where he spent the rest of the day and night in prayer. Mateo and the other refugees from the Mission Santa Fé never left his side.

XXVII

Governor Robenedo was swift in quelling the insurrection and harsh in dealing out retribution. Within a very short time, he had identified all the hostile caciques of the rebellious villages. He bent all the might of the militia to capturing these leaders and soon he had them in his grasp. He executed them one-by-one, hanging them in their villages as spectacle to the rest of the tribe, warning them of what they would face if they continued the uprising.

For a short time, the cacique of San Martín remained elusive. Then a regiment discovered him upon a road leading from his *buhio*. He was caught, returned to his village and quickly executed.

Only one of the principal instigators of the rebellion remained at large —Ycho. Ycho had installed the cousin of Cacique Tomás, Ynaja, as the puppet-cacique of the Potano; Ynaja had been found and executed. Ycho, however, had slipped away and could not be found.

Despite this one loose end, the insurrection was over in a very short time. No one could accuse the governor of being cowardly or ineffective in the face of a rebellion. Some, however, did use the words "excessive," "harsh," and "cruel" in describing his actions.

"If you show these people any weakness," Robenedo replied to such accusations, "they will forever be a problem. It is best to act quickly and thoroughly when dealing with savages." And he did, mercilessly.

The Friar Provincial of the Franciscan Province of Santa Elena also acted quickly, calling together his friars from all the mission areas. He wanted to make certain they were safe, and he needed to assess the overall situation. To his great relief, Fray Esteban discovered that no friar had been killed or injured. He called an assembly at the Headquarters in San Agustín, and indeed, except for a sickly few, every missionary came to the meeting.

Fray Esteban addressed them after they had all settled. "I seek wisdom and advice on the part of each of you," he began his remarks. "I know all of you have just witnessed a terrible tragedy and are still feeling the sadness and the pain. This is one of the perils we face in the work for the Lord we have chosen, and our faith must guide us in facing our present struggles. It must also help us plan for the future.

"Like yourselves, I have my beliefs as to the cause of the present uprising. Many of us had raised our fears before to the authorities. Many times we warned that this occurrence was imminent. We had voiced our concerns repeatedly about injustices to the Indians, with very little response. Now we have come to this sad state of affairs."

The Provincial proceeded to put forth a list of options for the Franciscans, including the possibility of totally abandoning their missionary enterprise in La Florida. To a man, the friars rejected that option.

The veteran missionary, Fray Alonso, who had experienced very little success in his mission, led off with an observation that reflected the sentiments of all the others. "If we fail to carry on our work here, the most important reason for the Spanish presence in this land will be undermined.

"Robenedo and the garrisons situated throughout La Florida will succeed in imposing military might and subjugating the masses of people to the power of our country. España will predominate in its military conquest and obtain some minimal provisions in the way of crops, timber, and minerals. But Mother Spain will have failed, failed because we will have lost the souls of the native people of this land. The Christian faith here will most likely die.

"What Robenedo has done will cripple our missionary efforts for years. We will able to start all over again.... But this time it will be much harder because the people will hate us all the more. I see no easy way to remedy the situation we are in now, but I, for one, do not want to leave my mission. With the Friar Provincial's permission, I will return there immediately."

The other friars expressed unanimous support for this position. They all wished to return to their missions and face whatever the future held in store for them.

"I have one concern in all of this," Fray Esteban interjected. "What of the policies of the present governor? His agenda seems to be on a collision course with our own. If nothing changes, I fear that very shortly we will be in this very same situation again."

The friar in charge of Mission Nombre de Dios in San Agustín suggested that the friars should make an appeal directly to the Crown. It would list the problems the friars were experiencing with the governor and seek the Crown's immediate intervention.

Fray Tomás, until now a silent observer during the deliberations, reacted quickly to this suggestion. He rose to his feet and volunteered to help draft this document. He also offered to accompany those who would deliver it to the King.

"My own work here is now very tenuous since Governor Robenedo has already threatened to bring proceedings of sedition against me. Supposedly, I hindered his efforts to place garrisons in the outlying areas. To him, that makes me a traitor. My only hope for survival is that the Crown or those above Robenedo see fit to send us a different governor. I would volunteer to be one of those who might present such a case to the Council of the Indies or even to the King himself."

Three other friars spoke in favor of such a prospect and offered themselves as candidates for this endeavor. The convocation of friars concluded with a unanimous decision, approved by the Friar Provincial, that Fray Tomás would lead a group of four in formulating grievances against the policies of the present administration. Then, as soon as possible, these representatives would bring these complaints to the King.

The four friars would include with the list of grievances a statement that Robenedo's harsh tactics and unjust policies led to the present rebellion. The document would explain in no uncertain terms that only the governor's removal could heal the bleak situation presently facing La Florida.

The more politically savvy Franciscans suggested that absolute confidentiality would be needed if this mission were to succeed. The other friars saw the wisdom of this and agreed. Fray Esteban made it understood that this group of four would attempt to conclude their present obligations at their respective missions and be ready to leave for España at the earliest possible time.

✳

On the far side of the ocean, Felipe-Toloca continued in his studies, unaware of the recent developments in his homeland. He now approached the time when he would be ordained to the Subdiaconate, the first major step to the priesthood. Already committed through vows of poverty, chastity, and obedience to the life of a Franciscan friar, he resolutely looked forward to the day when he would return to his people as a priest. After nearly a decade spent in work, study, reflection, and prayer, he was only a year away from his goal.

Looking back, he realized that the better part of his time in formation had been spent in failure and frustration. He was already three years behind the group that had begun the course of studies with him. On three separate occasions, the teachers asked him to repeat a year of studies due to language and culture barriers.

Twice he was held back from taking temporary vows as a Franciscan. There was no problem with his commitment to poverty, as he really had no worldly possessions of any consequence. He truly believed he had the moral fortitude to live the unmarried life of chastity required of a Franciscan friar. What concerned the teachers most was whether he could live in complete obedience to the authority of a Spanish friar as his superior.

Repeated rejection only made Felipe-Toloca all the more determined.

His loneliness in this foreign land, however, also caused him problems. Isolation was his constant companion. Though they occasionally tried, his classmates could never quite penetrate his Potano personality to pave the way for friendship. He seemed to prefer keeping aloof from them, never becoming too familiar with any of the boys, after his initial episode of being labeled a "half-breed." That experience had left a permanent scar.

The more obstacles Felipe-Toloca faced, however, the greater became his resolve. He believed a Potano could do anything a Spaniard could, and do it better. He was determined to prove that. His quest for the priesthood had become almost a contest between him and those who felt he could never make it. Now he had almost succeeded!

Felipe-Toloca's great sustaining support were the letters from home. How eagerly he awaited them! Each month they would arrive: one from his father, another one from Fray Tomás, and one from Catalina, with occasional others interspersed from other family members or friends. Some months the letters would all arrive at about the same time. Sometimes they would come separated a week or two apart. But always they came religiously, and the young man would watch for their delivery with the anticipation of a child looking for a new toy, or an adult awaiting a special gift from his best friend. The letters were his link with all he loved.

Felipe-Toloca knew something was wrong when a month had gone by with only one correspondence arriving. It was the letter from Catalina of 8 April 1656, describing her fears for their father and the mission. Catalina's alarm came to be more and more his alarm when no letters followed. Anxiety for his family built up with each passing day. He remembered his father talking about Ycho, and he could well imagine the harm this rogue warrior might do after having been banished for so many years.

Felipe-Toloca's worry began to consume him. He had to do something, but what? What could he do in the face of impending disaster? Catalina had suggested something that seemed beyond his ability—appealing personally for help to the King of España. Who was he but a lowly aspirant to the priesthood from a far-off land? Who was he to address the Great Cacique of the Spanish? But if this option was beyond him, he had to find something else, because he could no longer sit and do nothing.

No longer wearing the habit of a friar, and with a small bag of clothing slung over his shoulder, Felipe-Toloca courteously shook the hands of his seminary superior and the two classmates who had accompanied him to the port of Barcelona. At dockside he was making his final farewells before his departure to his homeland.

"I wish you would reconsider," Fray Reynaldo said, making one last attempt at persuading the unbending young man and reversing what he knew was irreversible. In conscience, the concerned friar felt he had to try one more time to talk his charge out of what he thought was an ill-conceived action. But all he managed to say was, "It is never wise to make so hasty a decision."

But Felipe-Toloca had made up his mind.

"Pray for me and my family, Fray Reynaldo. That is all I can say. That is all I can ask of you.... Thank you for all you have done for me or tried to do for me. I am grateful...for everything."

With that Felipe-Toloca turned and walked up the large wooden plank connecting shoreline to ship. He regretted the action he was taking, but saw no other alternative. Some of his classmates, and even some of his superiors, had offered to intercede for him and his family with the Council of the Indies and the King. But that offer was not enough to prevent his departure. His family was in peril. Of that he was certain. He must go to them and do whatever he could for the people he loved and left behind so long ago. He had to postpone his vocation to the priesthood until he could determine for himself that his family had made it through the crisis.

From the ship, he waved one final time to those who had seen him off, but then, as always, his thoughts returned on his family and their well-being. He prayed once again, with dogged intensity, for these people he loved whose fate and good fortune were now in jeopardy. He continued praying as the Spanish ship moved slowly from the harbor at Barcelona and began to drift gently through the murky Mediterranean waters on the first leg of its journey by way of Santiago de Cuba to the land of La Florida.

XXVIII

"¡Amigo, despiertate! Wake up!"

A familiar yet disrupting voice sounded in Fray Tomás' ear. That and a gentle nudging of his arm were enough to shake him out of his sleep.

Tomás opened his eyes to see Fray Esteban Hernandez. The superior pleaded with him to hurry and get up.

"The cargo ship *Felipe Arnaldo* is leaving for España in thirty minutes. A friend of mine, Enrique San Pablo, is the ship's steward, and he has four berths free for the passage of our friars. He has already taken aboard other passengers wanting to return to España. Your *confreres* are awake and getting ready for departure. I left you for the last, because you said you had all your possessions already, *sí*? But, Fray Tomás, you must hurry. This opportunity may not be with us again soon."

How apt were his words. Since the decision to send emissaries to España had been made, a period of four weeks had already elapsed. Clandestinely, the Franciscans sought ways for the four friars—Tomás, Juan Diego, Fernando, and Jorge—to depart for the mother country. But, until now, there had been no success.

Passage to the Old World from the New had always been a complicated affair for the friars, but never more so than now. The rebellion had made many of the Spanish settlers in San Agustín fearful of continued residence and desirous of returning home. People would make their applications through the governor's office for return passage to España, and a long list had already been compiled. The authorities gave clearance for departure in the order of when the requests were made.

To avoid providing any explanations, the friars did not go through the regular channels. Ships arrived and departed, but no fitting opportunity seemed to present itself until late one evening, Fray Esteban happened to meet Enrique, an old friend from the Spanish mainland. As Providence would have it, the sailor was singing loudly on the bay front opposite the *convento*. He had obviously been enjoying an evening of revelry with his shipmates. The music was loud enough to rouse Fray Esteban from his sleep. When the friar went to confront the boisterous man to upbraid him for his disruptive ways, he recognized the culprit as his long-time friend. Learning the departure time of Enrique's ship, Fray Esteban made the request, "Do you have room for four friars?"

Enrique's reply was, "No, but maybe I can make room."

Within a very short time the traveling friars, accompanied by Fray Esteban, were scurrying down to the bay front from the *convento* headquarters of the Province of Santa Elena. They were relieved to finally be on their way to accomplish this mission on which so much depended. They were hopeful they could convince the high command of the Council of the

Indies, if not the King himself, that new leadership and new directions were needed in this New World outpost of La Florida.

When the five friars began to approach the *Felipe Arnaldo*, Enrique greeted them and grabbed a couple bags from their hands. He then directed them toward the landing craft at the bayside.

"Thank you for doing this for me, Enrique," Fray Esteban said in his parting words. "You can't imagine how much this means to me and my friends. Please, take good care of them; as I mentioned earlier, do not advertise broadly that there are friars on your ship. They would prefer to remain as silent passengers, keeping to themselves as much as possible, spending their time in prayer. Whenever I can do something for you one day, I will be your humble servant."

"No need for explanations, Padre. I will do my best as a favor to you. As you can see, the *Felipe Arnaldo* is not the grandest of ships that sail under the flag of España. But she always gets us where we need to go."

"Enrique is not underestimating the prowess of this frigate," Juan Diego whispered in Tomás' ear. "I have floated more seaworthy skiffs in the wash basin of the *convento*!"

"Quiet, Juan Diego!" Fray Tomás said in rebuke. "Thank the good God we have finally found a way home. We are fortunate someone cared enough to take us at all."

"Thank you, Enrique, for doing this for us," Fray Tomás spoke aloud. "We promise you, we will be no trouble at all. In fact, unless you need us for any reason, we will be quiet as church mice."

The four friars embraced Fray Esteban and bid him a friendly farewell. Then, they boarded the small boat that would take them out to the Spanish frigate.

Within a short time, strident creaking sounds reached the shoreline and the ears of Fray Esteban as the *Felipe Arnaldo* drew up its four heavy anchors and raised its sails to catch the soft wind pressing from the northeast. Fray Esteban watched the ship depart, with the light of a nearly full moon guiding its exit under a cloudless sky.

Gladness filled him for the first time in days as one of his exploits finally succeeded after so many disastrous events of the previous month. He then caught a glimpse of one of the friars waving to him—it appeared to be Fray Tomás. Fray Esteban made a sweeping sign of the cross in a blessing over the ship. The gesture could not be missed. The friar he had seen on the ship departed from the deck, out of view, probably into the privacy of the sleeping quarters below. Fray Esteban walked slowly, prayerful-ly, back down the bay front to the *convento*. It was 12:30 in the morning, but he did not feel ready to fall asleep.

The *Felipe Arnaldo* hugged the coastline of La Florida for at least four hours before encountering winds and increasingly higher waves. Sailing past the last stretch of coastline, the captain directed his ship in a souther-ly direction, heading for the port of Santiago de Cuba, which was the first stop on the trip to España. The wind had brought rain and the rain turned to squalls, rocking the boat heavily from side to side. Coming from the northeast, the waves pressed hard against the ship, but a determined cap-tain did his best to keep his ship on course. It was too late to reverse direc-tion and return to the home port now. Besides, the ship could not easily move north against the northeast wind.

With each new onslaught of waves, the frigate rose and fell. One heavy wave would crest, lifting the ship over the horizon, then drop the boat down, it seemed, to the very ocean depths. Then another wave did the same, more forcefully. It was followed by another and another.

A falling timber crashed down from the mast of the mainsail, and water began to flow hard into the open area below, where passengers were hud-dled together. Tomás and the others knew they were in trouble.

A cry went out for help from the workmen of the frigate from the deck above. The four friars scrambled up the stairway only to be greeted with a gigantic wave that washed them back down into the hold. The priests gasped for air, trying frantically to keep their heads above water.

The adults grabbed for the children; the young sought to aid the old. The friars began to seek out the most helpless in the group and place them in whatever secure position there was available. They could find none. As more water began to pour in, it quickly became apparent that none of their rescuing efforts was working.

The ship began to list in a starboard direction shortly after another mast came crashing to the deck. Very quickly, the water in the passenger quar-ters rose within an arm's length of the ceiling overhead.

"*Señor, ten piedad de nosotros,*" could be heard from various directions. However, these exclamations gave way to loud gasps for air that echoed off the top of the water between the last remaining space in the passengers' cabin area and the ceiling.

"*¡Señor, ten piedad de nosotros!*" Fray Tomás cried with the others as he, too, fought frantically for pockets of air in the dismal darkness surrounding him, which showed no signs of light and gradually fewer signs of life. "*¡Ten piedad de nosotros! ¡Ten piedad de nosotros, Señor!*"

※

Calm seas and a clear blue sky encompassed all that Felipe-Toloca could see. Eventually there appeared a tiny dot on the western horizon, with more tiny dots in sight. These soon became recognizable as clumps of trees that heralded larger islands. Soon, his ship sailed in sight of the first major port before it would make its way in a northerly direction for La Florida.

"Thank you, Lord," he prayed. "We are about there."

Santiago de Cuba was an important Spanish settlement that provided a haven and harbor for Spanish ships sailing west through the Caribbean and north to San Agustín. It was a stopover point that gave respite before and after the long ocean voyage.

It was after landing in Cuba that Felipe-Toloca learned of the devastating storm that had just passed by, having moved over the island of Cuba in a southwesterly direction. It destroyed ships in the harbor; and it was feared, ships at sea.

After a brief stop at the port of that city for the unloading of passengers and the loading of supplies, Felipe-Toloca's ship went on its way north to La Florida to the port of San Agustín. Far to the southwest, Felipe-Toloca spied the dark ominous clouds that signaled the last vestiges of the hurricane that he heard had wreaked vengeance on the waters they were crossing and the land they had just left. Other signs were soon visible of the havoc that the storm had played. Just hours from the island they had left, wreckage and debris from a ship could be seen floating all about them, but no signs of life.

The ship's captain sent out two small boats to check for any human survivors in the wreckage strewn around them. The rescue boats returned. Felipe-Toloca watched the men aboard shaking their heads, as the question rang out to them, "Are there any people amid all the debris?" A man aboard one of the rescue crafts lifted a piece of wood from the bottom of the boat and held it aloft. On the wood, something was printed that became more visible as the boat approached the large ship. Slightly battered, but clearly visible, were the words of a Spanish name. The ship's captain shook his head at what he read, showing signs of recognition. "*Felipe Arnaldo*," he said. "We'll never see that frigate fly the flag of España on these waters again. Never again. God rest the souls of all the good people buried with that ship in the waters of this sea. And thanks be to God that we were not where they were just a few hours ago!"

XXIX

There was a great stillness of land and sea and air, that eerie silence that often follows a storm. Eventually, a light breeze carried Felipe-Toloca's ship northward. For many hours, Felipe-Toloca rested his arms over a wooden railing on the port side of the Spanish ship, watching and wondering, as he eyed the coastline of La Florida intently, trying to detect any evidence of activity or motion. To his mind, nature seemed too much at rest, in an almost disharmonious way. The branches of pine and palm trees stood like silent sentinels, guarding their mysterious territories or holding a terrible secret. It was as though the signs without were confirming a warning he kept hearing within: "All is not well, Felipe-Toloca. All is not well."

He tried not to worry, telling himself to trust in God. Besides, he thought, worry was a waste of time. He would know the answers to his concerns within a matter of hours. But these thoughts did little to quiet the message addressed to him by the wilderness that he saw without as it spoke to the wilderness he felt within. It was a message that reflected those great fears he had back in España, which propelled him into leaving there in the first place.

Felipe-Toloca finally found a way to silence these fears by remembering the past. With his eyes fixed on the horizon, beyond which the sun had long since fallen, his thoughts drifted back to his youthful days at the village and mission. He remembered the beautiful land—the spring-fed rivers he and his family had traversed, canoeing in them, fishing in them, swimming in them. He saw in his mind's eye the neighboring forests where they had played and contemplated nature's wonders. He recalled hunting, and feeding off the land, and then building with what nature gave them.

His thoughts then turned to the time he spent with his father and mother, brothers and sisters who loved him dearly. He reminisced about the late nights he had spent teasing his little sisters and poking fun at his younger brothers. He remembered entertaining them with stories, until his father would come by to quiet them, and then he too would get swept into the conversation. His mother would finally come to correct them all, only to find herself becoming part of the revelry. How they laughed every time it happened! How close they were to one another!

Then, memories of Padre Tomás came flooding back to him as well. He remembered the stories of how the priest had saved his father's life and reared him in the faith. The priest had lovingly guided Felipe-Toloca in the same way.

How much they meant to each other! How devoted all these people were to him and he to them! His family, Fray Tomás included, mattered more to him than anything else in the world.

"How I miss you! How I love you!" The words formed on his lips as the deep emotions formed in his heart.

A sharp, bitter pain, almost indescribable—it hurt so much—wedged into his soul, leaving a void within him, deep as a bottomless pit and dark as the night that now descended upon him. Never in his life, even in those difficult days in España, had Felipe-Toloca ever felt so very much alone! Soon, he promised himself. Soon, he would be home and that loneliness would be at an end.

The ship proceeded up a waterway and then suddenly turned to port. An outline, glowing through the darkness, came into view. A wooden fort and the rooftops of a village could be seen in the light cast by the oil lamps on the streets and by torches on the bay front.

The ship had reached her destination—San Agustín.

As the vessel approached the harbor, the streets seemed empty, except for a few men at dockside waiting to greet the new arrivals. Apart from the two oarsmen of the landing boat, Felipe-Toloca was the last to come ashore. A short, broad-shouldered, middle-aged Spaniard helped him out of the boat.

"*Bienvenido, amigo*," were his words of greeting. He positioned the single bag of possessions handed to him and then pulled Felipe-Toloca onto the landing platform. He was surprised to notice that no one had come to greet the young man. "*A donde va, amigo?*" he asked, perceiving a somewhat bewildered look on the visitor's face.

Felipe-Toloca was not sure exactly how to answer him, as he really did not know what he was going to do or where he was going. "At this hour of the night, *señor*, I am not certain where I am heading. I had planned to go to my home, which is in the village and mission of Santa Fé."

"Ah, but *amigo*, certainly you have heard! Did not someone tell you when you left España?"

"I left España almost three weeks ago," Felipe-Toloca replied. "I have had no news before and no news since…" He caught his breath for a moment. Suddenly, he was afraid to ask what moments before he had so desperately wanted to know. Only reluctantly did he let the question fall from his lips, directing his gaze now to the ground. "If you would be so kind as to explain…what you mean.…"

"*Amigo*, there is no longer a Santa Fé Mission, nor any other missions surrounding it. They are now only in the pages of history.… Those missions were destroyed in recent rebellion in the western regions of the colony by the—the…what do you call them? Ah, Timucuans."

"But what of the people of Santa Fé? What happened to the cacique and his family? How are they?"

"*Mi amigo*, I do not know.… And even if I did, I would…" his voice trailed off as he began to take stock of the new arrival's reaction. "…I would probably not be the one to say."

In the flickering torchlight that fell on Felipe-Toloca, the dockworker suddenly noticed the young man's Indian features. Then he saw the painful expression etched on the traveler's face.

"My name is Pablo," the Spaniard continued. "My wife and I have a small house in the town. You can stay with us tonight if you wish. Tomorrow, the Governor's House will be open, and you can get more information there. I will be happy to go with you if you wish.….. I am sorry.….. I am very sorry." He regretted being the one to have to relay this sad news.

"Thank you, Pablo," Felipe-Toloca responded rather quickly. "But I will go to the Convento of Santa Elena. It is close by, and I am sure the friars will take me in for the night. In España, I was preparing to become a friar. They are my friends."

"As you wish…but remember, if you need me anytime, *amigo*.…"

"Felipe-Toloca is my name," said the Indian, "and yes, I need you right now…to pray for me. I believe I will need your prayers to get me through this night, and the day after, and the days after that.... And Pablo, thank you for being here to help me come ashore. I really did not want to leave that little boat that brought me here or that big one out in the bay either."

"Felipe-Toloca, a friend is one who helps you come ashore," said the middle-aged man. "In Pablo, you will always have a friend."

"Thank you, Pablo. I believe this is not the last time you will see me."

"*Buenas noches, amigo!* And yes, I will be praying for you! *Buenas noches!*"

The former Franciscan seminarian trudged down the darkened bay front road. He carried in his mind and heart the tragic news he had just heard. The burden felt unbearably heavy.

On arrival at the Franciscan headquarters of the Province of Santa Elena, Felipe-Toloca pulled on the bell of the *convento* entrance and silently awaited a response. The friar porter of the *convento*, appeared at the door and found there the dejected young man with tear-filled eyes and rugged Indian features, which provided him with the only introduction he needed. The priest immediately recognized Felipe-Toloca.

No words transpired between the two men in the next few minutes. They just looked at one another. Finally, the friar porter, one Fray Angelo, pulled Felipe-Toloca into his arms, in a Spanish-style *abrazo* and began to offer him silent consolation. That continued until he had the courage to look the young man in the eye.

XXX

To Felipe-Toloca life seemed to have ended. Anger, hostility, and rage competed with other emotions like grief, loneliness, and despair, leaving the young son of a fallen cacique confused and bewildered. He now had no family. He had no home. He had no people. And for the first time in his life, Felipe-Toloca felt he had no God.

"Why...why...why?" he asked as he kneeled before the hastily constructed burial site of his mother, brothers, sisters, and Tofuconatchu.

Why had the God of the Spanish people allowed this to happen? Why had that good and kind God he had heard about from Padre Tomás taken his family members from him in such a terrible way? The "good" God had even taken Padre Tomás, burying him in the vast, fathomless sea! It all seemed so preposterous!

Felipe-Toloca walked the now devastated mission grounds, but his eyes saw little as his mind wandered in thought. As if to match his mood, clouds moving from the east and the west of the Florida peninsula met almost directly overhead and billowed high above, casting dark shadows on the land below. A late afternoon rain threatened, signaling an end to the drought that had stricken the area the past several years. Felipe-Toloca, however, saw no end to the drought in his heart.

Returning to the burial site, he threw up his hands and uttered words in the Potano dialect. To the Franciscan friar following him, the cry sounded scarcely intelligible. Young Fray Antonio had accompanied Felipe-Toloca to the Mission since the young Indian had left San Agustín. The friar had been close to Fray Tomás and he was a constant admirer and trusted friend of the late great missionary. The latter had found Fray Antonio intrepid, imaginative, courageous, generous, and quite as resourceful as the older, more experienced priest. A somber look spread across his otherwise handsome Spanish face, casting a shadow over his dark olive complexion and deep-set, piercing brown eyes.

Antonio searched his mind for a consoling thought to offer, but he could find none. He was still trying to piece together the details Felipe-Toloca had shared with him and the other friars of the *convento* the previous night. He told them about the driftwood from the Spanish ship *Felipe Arnaldo* being spotted by his shipmates on their journey northward from Cuba to La Florida. The Franciscans were forced to come to the conclusion that their emissaries were probably dead.

The shock of this further loss had devastated the rest of the priests of the *convento*. Four stalwart brethren had gone down at sea. Their mission to unseat the merciless Governor Robenedo was doomed. The return of Felipe-Toloca, a grieving former Franciscan seminarian, provided the final symbol of all the failed accomplishments of their fifty-year missionary outreach to the native people.

What future was left for them? Should they have even come to La Florida in the first place?

"What were you saying to me, Felipe-Toloca? You must speak more slowly when you use your native language," the friar said, breaking the brief reflective silence that had fallen between the two of them.

Using the Spanish language again, the young Indian spoke softly and slowly. "My people have said that my father does not lie here with the rest of my family, but no one knows where Ycho had buried him. I must find him so I can give my father a proper burial. He cannot rest in peace, and I cannot rest until Ycho rests in his own grave. Ycho must die for what he did to my family!"

Felipe-Toloca kept talking in a rambling, confused fashion. Then, one by one, villagers began to drift into the area and move slowly in his direction, keeping a respectful silence and a respectful distance. From afar, they could see the great burden that weighed on the newly returned sole survivor. His sorrow and distress were so intense as to be almost tangible.

"Why did Ycho do this? They meant him no wrong. My father spoke only of peace. He tried to love everyone—his own people, the Spanish, everyone! He was only trying to do what he thought right! Why did you not defend my family?" he shouted to the Potano people lingering shamefacedly at a distance. "They would have died for you. Why did you not save them?"

He looked to the sky, "My father, I will avenge your death. Ycho, I will find you and kill you and any person who helped you with this crime!"

"Felipe-Toloca, Felipe-Toloca," the young priest repeated distinctly the strange sounding name that bespoke the two different cultural roots of the man's heritage. "You are right. Your people have betrayed you. My people have betrayed you also. But I knew Padre Tomás, and I knew a little about your father. The work they did—both of them—was great, very great, far greater than any cacique or any friar in La Florida. You and I must not betray them and all the good they have done. It is not lost.... The village and the mission are not finished or destroyed forever, that is, if we are willing to begin again. But that work will take both you and I and all these people here." He made a sweeping gesture in the direction of the growing crowd of Potanos.

"Let us try," the young friar continued. "We know what your father and Padre Tomás wanted for this people. The good God will help us, as He helped them. The people will help us, too. If you agree to help me, I will return to San Agustín and ask to be assigned to this mission.

"And I will ask of the Spanish authorities another favor, Felipe-Toloca, if I may.... The fallen cacique was your father. Your father's cousin, the son of your grandmother's sister, was the rightful heir to the caciquedom."

"Ynaja? Yes. But he was another traitor," Felipe-Toloca responded.

"And as such he has been executed by Robenedo's soldiers. I am sure there will be reluctance by the Spanish to accept another of your father's cousins as cacique, fearing, as they may, another rebellion. Felipe-Toloca, I will ask Robenedo to make you the new cacique of this tribe and village! Together we will rebuild what has been destroyed! Together we will try to carry on the work of your father and Padre Tomás."

At first, the suggestion shocked Felipe-Toloca into silence. Then he savagely shook his head. "They will never let us do it, Padre Antonio! Robenedo, I have heard, disliked both Padre Tomás *and* my father. He may respect you, but he will never respect me. It will never happen. Padre, you are a good man. I respect you, but I have seen too much already, too many failed dreams, too many failed hopes, from my childhood to this day. I do not want to be part of any other failure! Put away your ambitious plans. They will only bring us more grief."

"Will you give me the chance to hope, Felipe-Toloca? Will you give me the chance to try?" the friar asked.

"Hope!" he said and gave a sharp bitter laugh. "Anyone can hope. Anyone can try; but do not be surprised when they tell you 'No!' Do not be upset if they accuse you and I of being part of the rebellion and arrest the two of us for something we have not done. Remember, Robenedo has his spies. And they may now be asking why four priests from the *convento* went down with a ship destined for España, four priests who were not listed on any departure schedule. Robenedo may have all of you friars and myself, as a former friar-seminarian, thrown into the prison at the *castillo* before the night is over!"

Fray Antonio opened his mouth to deny what Felipe-Toloca was saying, to tell him that he was being unreasonably pessimistic and overly dramatic, but he could not. Everything the Potano was saying could very well be true.

When the friar said nothing, Felipe-Toloca shook his head and continued. "Please, Padre Antonio, leave well enough alone! I can begin now to search for Ycho. You can spend your time with your family back in España. Our lives will be much simpler, and we will live much longer. Away with your dreams and plans that will never amount to anything! The greatest plans of great men like Padre Tomás and my father have crumbled and burned. Do you think that we simple men could hope to accomplish what they did not?"

"Felipe-Toloca, I do not know," came the response immediately, "but I do know that I would want to try. And…" The friar looked to the ground, then directly into Felipe-Toloca's eyes, "I would hope that you would want to try as well. I am sure that the people in these graves and your father, wherever he lies, would ask a little more of you than just to seek the life of their murderer. Would they not, Felipe-Toloca? Would they not?"

The young Indian offered no response to these questions. He merely got up from the spot where he had been sitting and began to snap a thin branch in two. He tied the pieces together with a large, narrow leaf from a palm frond, in the form of a cross. Then he placed the cross in front of the burial site of his family and stood for a moment looking at it.

He made the sign of the cross on himself with a broad sweeping gesture. He touched his hand to his forehead, chest, then left and right shoulders. His lips moved visibly as he began a silent prayer—for his family, for the deceased Padre Tomás, for Padre Antonio, and for himself.

Felipe-Toloca hid his face in his hands and wept. He no longer restrained the emotions that had been building up inside him since he had first learned of his family's death. Now his chest and shoulders shook uncontrollably. The tears poured out between his fingers and dropped to the earth, falling over the graves of his loved ones, uniting his spirit with the spirits of those who had left him behind and all alone.

The sky, as if to join in unison with the mourning below, shed raindrops. First in a casual, intermittent manner, then, as if in an outburst of emotive strength, water began to pour out of dark, dense clouds. Bolts of lightning lit the darkened sky and thunder joined the cadence of the storm increasing it to a deafening chorus. The Indian and the friar both raised their water-drenched faces and stared at one another. In their look was a mutual recognition of the blessing this sudden rainfall was bringing to the Potano land and people. It marked the end to the long-standing drought in the land of western Timucua.

Perhaps this weather was a sign of better days on the horizon. Felipe-Toloca could not imagine anything worse happening than the tragedies that had already occurred.

Several weeks after the arrival of Felipe-Toloca and Padre Antonio back at the Convento of Santa Elena in San Agustín, astounding news reached the friars of that mission. Governor Robenedo had been arrested. An official of the King, accompanied by several soldiers, had arrived in La Florida with orders to apprehend the politician. Robenedo was to be taken to España to be tried for excessive and repressive measures used against the Indians of La Florida during his tenure. The Crown believed these measures were the main cause of the recent rebellion.

How all this came about no one knew.

A new governor, Enrique Ruíz Mendoza, arrived in the same ship that had delivered the King's messenger and soldiers. Padre Antonio spared no time in seeking an audience with him at the Government House. The young priest had a special suggestion for the future of the village and mission of Sante Fe.

The governor received the friar cordially, listened carefully to his unique proposal, and responded that he would take the matter up immediately with his advisors. That he did; within a few days, he summoned both Fray Antonio and Felipe-Toloca to his office.

"This is an unusual request Padre Antonio has made of me, Felipe-Toloca," he began, "but under the circumstances I deem it a fair and reasonable one. If you are willing, young man, I am desirous of appointing you as Cacique of the Potano people living in the village of Santa Fé. Everyone I have spoken to about this situation says that the people would be well served by you as their leader, even though by bloodlines you would not rightfully accede to this position. The circumstances in the western areas of the Timucuan nation call for drastic measures, and I have decided as well to appoint new caciques in other areas of the recent rebellion, where possible.

"Will you consider what Fray Antonio has proposed to me? I have found it to be quite acceptable—in fact, even desirable—to have you as cacique to bring order and peace to the village of Santa Fé. I will also ask that remnants of the people of a neighboring tribe, the Utina people, I believe they are called, come together to live with your people. Many from their tribe died in the recent uprising. And finally, I would desire to place a garrison of select Spanish soldiers in the village of Santa Fé, but only such men who would be respected by your people. They would never act except with your approval and my own.

"I know that all of this is much for you to consider; and if you need more time before making a decision, I completely understand. Know that I would look forward to seeing you as the new cacique and working with you in that capacity."

Felipe-Toloca responded without hesitation. "Governor Ruíz Mendoza, I do not believe I need more time to think about your proposal. I will accept at once. I have never thought of myself in such a position as cacique, but I also never foresaw such a tragedy occurring as has happened with my family and my people. For the sake of my father, for the sake of my family, for the sake of my people, I will accept the invitation to be the leader of my people. With Padre Antonio, I will try to carry on what my father and Padre Tomás had always tried to do. May those good people help me now with their prayers!"

Night had begun to descend over the town of San Agustín as the padre and the new cacique left the Government House. But the deep, dark night within Felipe-Toloca's spirit began to lift. A light and a peace he had not known in months began to enter his heart.

Fray Antonio noticed a difference immediately in the way Felipe-Toloca walked, in the way he talked, and in the settled and increasingly serene look on his face. The priest sensed the change. He began to see life in the Potano's eyes that before, had reflected only death. He saw a new and radiant hope replace dark despair.

They left the meeting with the governor, and from a distance, one could easily have mistaken the identities of the two men walking to the *convento* that evening. One could have sworn he saw the Padre Tomás and his loyal friend, the former cacique, Felipe-Toloca's father.

Part Four

The Respite

XXXI
- 1674 -

"Accedant qui ordinandi sunt ad ordinem Presbyteratus."

The Latin words rang out with a unique Spanish flair, as the visiting bishop from Santiago de Cuba, Gabriel Díaz Vara Calderón, called forward seven candidates for ordination to the priesthood. These young men came from the best families of San Agustín, and their relatives sat proudly in attendance. Felipe-Toloca was also among the spectators.

The cacique of the village and mission of Sante Fé joined the Spanish governor and other Spanish dignitaries in the front of the assembly that poured out from the small church into the surrounding area. They had come to witness this historic celebration, a first for this new land; many people came from far and near for the event.

Felipe-Toloca wore a simple deerskin coat that reached to his waist and he had matching pants of the same material. He had tied his hair at the top of his head in the traditional style of Potano tribesmen. The top-knot along with his clothing made Felipe-Toloca stand in stark contrast to the many civil and military dignitaries around him, who were dressed in their Spanish finery. Proud of his Potano heritage and protective of its culture, the cacique of almost twenty years would take advantage of every opportunity to represent his people when the occasion warranted it. He wore his native dress like a badge of honor and cut a striking figure with his simple garb and handsome features that reflected his Spanish and Indian ancestry.

The special ceremony he witnessed began to trigger thoughts about himself and his people. He pondered their struggles and their triumphs since their return after the rebellion of 1656, and their reunion with the neighboring people of the Utina tribe.

He recalled that they had reconstructed the mission chapel almost immediately. Ycho had wantonly destroyed it along with everything else. Then they rebuilt the large *buhio* for the council meeting house and then went on to fix the smaller thatched huts of the families. One by one, the dilapidated structures had been resurrected, with everyone— men, women, and children—working together. How good the Great Spirit had been to His people this year!

With the physical rebirth that took place, gradually there came a deep-

215

er spiritual rebuilding. A people that had been displaced and destroyed had become a tribe and a community once again. In tragedy and pain, they had forged a new identity.

Felipe-Toloca's own positive outlook had been renewed and strengthened by his ever-present adviser and guide, Fray Antonio. Fray Antonio had spoken truly when, long ago, he suggested that this amazing feat could happen. He had been the one to sketch out the way for all of this to become a reality. How much he owed this friar, for laying the groundwork, for his own emergence as cacique, and then for continuing on as his mentor and friend. No one, in his mind, could ever replace Fray Tomás, but Fray Antonio was a wonderful successor to that great friar.

"Kyrie eleison, Christe eleison, Kyrie eleison…Christe, audi nos, Christi, exaudi nos …Pater de coelis Deus, miserere nobis."

The Franciscan choir sang in a steady, even tone the opening words of the Litany of Saints. The cacique nodded approvingly to his friend, Fray

Antonio, who sat among the choristers. As the chants began, the seven men being ordained dropped to their knees in unison and then lay prostrate on the floor of the village church, as the bishop, priests, parishioners, and visitors sought the intercession of the saints on their behalf.

"Sancta Maria, ora pro nobis. Sancta Dei Genetrix, ora pro nobis. Sancta Virgo Virginum, ora pro nobis."

The words of the litany sought the intercession of Mary, the Mother of God. How many times had Felipe-Toloca sought her intercession as well for light and guidance in his own life? Would his life be far different now if he had not agreed to become the cacique of his people, he thought to himself? Should he be on the floor with these seven men today? Was not his heart still in that direction? Did he sense a bit of envy now as he cast his eyes upon the candidates?

"Sancte Petre, ora pro nobis. Sancte Paule, ora pro nobis. Sancte Andree, ora pro nobis."

As the intercession of the holy Apostles was being sought in prayer and song, the thoughts continued—the wishful thinking, the regrets, and the questions. It had all seemed too providential. Here he was, Spanish-trained, a son of two cultures, a man of even broader training than his own father. He had to do what he had done. He could not step aside and let someone else lead his people, even if it meant relinquishing his goal of becoming a priest. Surely he had done what was right!

"Sancte Dominico, ora pro nobis. Sancte Francisco, ora pro nobis."

With the invocation of the saintly founder of the Franciscan community, Felipe-Toloca was led to prayer. "St. Francis, what would you have me do? Am I, as cacique, where I should be? I am happy. I am respected by my people. I am even loved by them. I certainly could never abandon them. Besides, it was a Franciscan priest, Fray Antonio, who wanted me to do this in the first place."

"Ab insidiis diaboli, ora pro nobis. Ab ira et odio et omni malo voluntato, ora pro nobis."

"And yes," he prayed, "there is the reality of my own struggles with temptation, with sinfulness. I still cannot get rid of the lingering hate that clouds my heart ... for Ycho, especially, for his taking my family from me! I still hold him accountable, and I cannot shake that deep desire to find him and, with my own hands, to kill him on the very spot where he killed my father, wherever that may be! No, I am not worthy to bear the mantle of the priest. Holy Francis, help me come to grips with my anger and hatred. It is still there. I cannot rid myself of it."

"Peccatores, Te rogamus, audi nos. Ut nobis parcas, Te rogamus audi nos. Ut nobis indulgeas, Te rogamus, audi nos. Ut veram poenitentiarn nos perducere digneris."

"Forgive me, Great Spirit, for thinking the way I think and feeling the way I feel," Felipe-Toloca finished. Occasionally, he heard a decipherable Latin word or verse and the chant led him deeper into thought and farther away from the people and the ceremony around him.

His mind brought him back to his village, where he imagined himself far in the past, enjoying an early evening sunset on the Rio Santa Fé. He was there alone, thinking and praying, watching the autumn leaves, with their distinct shapes and myriad colors, drop one by one upon the river. Mentally, he would place a prayer to God with each leaf that fell below and floated by. "With that one I pray for father, and that one for mother, and that one for Catalina."

As each of leaf floated by and out of sight, to be swept into the eternal embrace of the river, an image of each of his family members drifted before his mind in sharp clarity. He imagined them being swept into the arms of the Great Spirit. "You seem to have left me, my dear ones, but I know you really have not," he said to them as though they were really present. "I hope you know that whatever I have been doing as cacique, I have been doing for you. Thank you for helping me carry on each day, for it has not been easy."

"Kyri eleison. Christe eleison. Kyrie eleison."

The chanting was coming to an end. The seven candidates arose and individually approached the bishop. In silence he imposed hands upon them, and a great stillness pervaded the assembly of people as well. It was as if one could hear the heavens open and the Great Spirit come down to take possession of His chosen ones.

Felipe-Toloca felt an inner peace about his not being numbered among them. A priest he was not destined to be. Indeed, he was precisely where he belonged! The Great Spirit had led him here, just as He had led these candidates to the altar, each in his own way. They would serve God as priests. Felipe-Toloca would serve God in his own way as Cacique of the village and Mission of Santa Fé. His task was no less important or holy, because he had responded to the true calling God had given him. Felipe-Toloca could not explain his feelings now. He felt at peace, and he also felt a great sense of pride about himself.

Then a sudden commotion stirred the people, as two little doves fluttered through an open window and encircled the congregation of slightly amused or agitated onlookers. A few daring individuals surreptitiously tried their best to capture the birds, but the winged interlopers always eluded them. The catchers finally realized the futility of their venture and decided to let the little creatures have their day.

"Accipe potestatem offerre sacrificium Deo, Missasque celebrare, tam pro vivis, quam pro defunctis. In nomine Domini."

The ordination prayers were drawing to a close, and the offertory of the Mass was about to commence, when those same two little doves suddenly alighted on the shoulders of Felipe-Toloca. There they stayed unperturbed and immobile.

Quite in harmony with the break between the rites and the flow of the liturgy, Felipe-Toloca rose very slowly and walked with his two friends to

the door of the church. Once outside, he received the birds from his shoulders onto the fingertips. Then, he noticed that each dove had black spots on its wings.

The cacique immediately remembered his words he had spoken many years before to his sister Catalina, about setting free the people and things we love. Perhaps Catalina, through these doves, was helping him set free some of the preoccupations of his life. He realized that worries about his vocation and his family had long held him bound. Now was his chance. He gently released the doves into the air. As they lifted from the ground, a burden lifted off the cacique's heart and true happiness, for the first time in years, filled him instead.

Following the ceremony, Bishop Calderón quickly slipped away from the newly ordained young men and their families. He pursued and then caught his quarry. Felipe-Toloca had just begun walking rapidly in a westerly direction toward his village, when someone grabbed him by the arm.

"You have quite a way with the birds of the air, my friend," the bishop quipped. "Thank you for giving my congregation a little respite by your obviously superior ability to relate to the animal kingdom. Oh yes, and I wanted to tell you, Cacique Felipe-Toloca, that I look forward to joining you and your people during my visit to the western missions of the Timucuan people. I have been summoned to administer the Sacrament of Confirmation. I have heard of the good you have been doing in your village. The Santa Fé mission is among the most prominent of all our outreaches in La Florida. And as the priests at the Convento of Santa Elena tell me, I may attribute that to your great leadership. We hope and pray that you will be there for many more years to come. You are very special among all the caciques of this region!"

"Thank you, my Lordship," Felipe-Toloca replied in very good Spanish, bowing low before the bishop in a genuine expression of respect. "Nothing would give me greater pleasure than to have you visit my people and celebrate the great mysteries of our holy faith with them. I shall be pleased to be among those who will welcome you there. Many years ago the cacique of our people, my father's uncle, Toloca, after whom I am named, welcomed a very special priest to our village, Fray Tomás Sanchez. My people have never forgotten that priest. As he was treated with great honor and respect, we will welcome you with the same!"

Indeed, the cacique proved most faithful to his promise. Never had the people of the village and mission of Santa Fé celebrated any event with greater splendor or festivity than the ceremony of Confirmation of the Christian adults and youth of the village. Long did they tell of the visit of the Spanish bishop from Cuba. They saw the great pride of their cacique that day as he accompanied his guest everywhere and introduced him personally to every single member of the village.

XXXII
- 1680 -

Every day Cacique Felipe-Toloca gathered the children of the village to his council *buhio* to teach them lessons or to tell them stories. None of the people of his village had the opportunities of education that he had received, so he felt a responsibility not only to lead and guide his young people as cacique, but to teach them as well. How else could they understand the great heritage that was theirs? In what other way would they understand the culture they sometimes felt the people of España were imposing on them?

Usually, he taught them about the customs and traditions of the Potano people. But sometimes the lessons he gave were about the customs of the people of España, which he thought his people also should know. Often he retold stories from the Bible in an engaging way, having the children act out the stories themselves, taking the parts of the Bible figures. On occasion he would personally teach the children the ways of the martial arts skills of defense that his own father and Tofu had introduced into the village many years before.

On a sunny day in early February, he gave them a break from their usual lessons. It was unusually warm for the time of the year, and so instead of keeping them inside the hot *buhio*, he took them on a special outing to see his new pet, an eagle. He had been nursing the bird back to health. It had been injured during a severe thunderstorm when a bolt of lightning struck the tree in which it had perched. The cacique had rescued the animal and called his new friend "Fallen Eagle."

Now, Fallen Eagle had fully recovered. Thanks to Felipe-Toloca's skilled treatment and tender care, the eagle could return to the wilderness once again. The cacique planned to set him free, allowing the bird to claim his usual domain—the limitless sky and the vast, broad land of the Florida peninsula.

When the children saw the majestic animal in his wooden cage, many felt captivated by the eagle.

"He seems so much at home with us right here," a young Potano lad spoke out. "Let us keep him! We will take good care of him!"

"My little one," the cacique interjected, "you have your home and your family. So also does Fallen Eagle. If we keep him, we imprison him in our world—a world that is strange to him. If we keep him, we take from him the earth and the sky. If we let him go, then we will always be a friend to him.

"The eagle is the greatest of the birds of the sky. In the sky, he can live most freely. In the sky, he will be most happy. In the sky, he can best sing praise to the Great Spirit."

The eagle fixed a proud eye on the cacique and flexed his wings slightly as if in agreement with the chieftain. The bird then bent low to look through the wooden pegs of his cage, peering in all directions at the children. Its ruffled, white feathers cresting the brown ones just below the neckline revealed the bold, forceful, resolute features of its prominent head.

"He wants to say 'good-bye' to us," another young Potano exclaimed.

Taking the magnificent creature from its cage, the cacique held it aloft for all to see.

"Show them what it means to be free," he said, "with the wind beneath your wings and all that is above you and below you within your grasp.... Take back your rightful dwelling place in the sky!"

He then released Fallen Eagle at shoulder level. The children watched fascinated as the bird began to flap its spacious wings. It pounded the air to gain further height, but suddenly, the bird began to struggle briefly and lose altitude. Then, the eagle caught its normal rhythm of movement with its mighty wings and climbed higher and higher into the sky. It soared above the village, circling it repeatedly and rising higher each time.

Felipe-Toloca broke into song spontaneously with a chant familiar to all the children, who quickly began to join him. It was a song taught him by his father many years before. As they sang, they watched in awe as Fallen Eagle displayed before their very eyes the wondrous flight described in the chant.

Soar, soar like the eagle, / Mighty lord of earth and sky.
Climb high above the highest cloud / Where none can ever die.

Spread wide your wings of glory. / Envelop all below.
Rising o'er the tallest oaks / To regions few will know.

You'll see with vision clear and bright. / You'll hear the furthest sound.
You'll overpower the strongest prey. / All creatures you'll confound.

In courage none will be your match, / In wisdom none your peer.
With speed so swift and flight so sure, / No foes you'll hold in fear.

Such grace of movement to behold! / Such beauty you display!
So great a spirit you possess! / All honor you this day!

"When you return to earth again, / Encourage us to fly.
And take us with you from this land / To heights beyond the sky.

And we shall also
Soar, soar like the eagle, / Mighty lord of earth and sky.
With him climb o'er the highest cloud / Where we shall never die."

"Fallen Eagle has much to teach us," Felipe-Toloca observed. "Only a short time ago, he was close to death. He had little strength. His right wing was injured. He had lost many feathers off his body. He looked terrible!

"But now he is very much alive.... He never gave up! He always had courage! How much we can learn from Fallen Eagle. No hardship, no disaster, no problem should ever take our spirit from us! With the help of the Great Spirit, all of us can surpass any problem we face. We too can learn to fly again!"

By the time the cacique had finished talking, Fallen Eagle was barely a speck in the sky. The children kept pointing out to one another what they thought was the final vestige of the great bird of the sky they had set free that day.

A great commotion arose in the north end of the village, interrupting the cacique's afternoon session with the children. The noise and shouting continued to grow, as did the crowd of people. They began moving in the direction of Cacique Felipe-Toloca. One word, a name, could be heard above the din. It was a name that the cacique had not heard spoken in many years.

Felipe-Toloca appeared very distraught at what he saw: an aged man with Potano features, his hands tied behind his back, being forcibly prodded toward the cacique by Potano tribesmen. Though the individual's face was not easily recognizable, the name of the man was.

"Ycho!" Felipe-Toloca said to himself, in a subdued, barely audible fashion. He wondered at first if his eyes played tricks on him. Then he accepted the truth as he stood face-to-face with the man who killed his father!

The children who had been with the cacique were quietly and quickly ushered away to their dwellings by family members or friends. Alone, the cacique confronted the man who had been his father's rival and a traitor to his father's people. This man had taken from Felipe-Toloca all that he held dear to him.

The closer Ycho came to him, the more Felipe-Toloca felt that longstanding hostility he possessed rising up from deep within him. Finally, the two men stood opposite one another at a safe distance. They silently eyed each other, waiting for the other's animosity to break forth in words.

It was the cacique who spoke first.

"I am Felipe-Toloca, the Cacique of the village of Sante Fé. My father was Cacique Tomás, whom you murdered some time ago, along with my family members. It is good that you have finally been captured and brought to accept responsibility for the crimes you have committed against your people." To the men guarding Ycho, Felipe-Toloca turned and asked, "Was he spying on our village and people when you captured him?"

"Most honored cacique," the intruder interjected, "I was not found spying. I have returned here freely from the exile your father imposed upon me many years ago. I have chosen to return to die in the only land that I could rightfully call my home. All these many years, I have been forced to wander, lost without my family and my people. Your father had forced this isolation upon me when he banished me. Every day I was alone, hated by my people, hated by many others. I was punished only because I did not agree with your father, punished because I could not accept your father's friendship with the people of España.

"Now, I have returned freely. Your tribesmen did not capture me. I gave myself freely over to their hands. Do with me as you will. I only ask that you do me the honor of allowing me to present my defense to you in a fuller way!"

"Is what he says true?" Felipe-Toloca asked the guards. "Did he surrender freely?"

When the braves confirmed Ycho's account, Tomás said, "Take him to the council *buhio*. Watch over him carefully. I will summon our council members and then meet you shortly!"

Quickly, the guards pulled, almost dragged, Ycho to the center of the village where the council *buhio* stood. The advisors of the cacique, mostly aged and respected members of the Potano village, hastily gathered with Felipe-Toloca and the infamous prisoner. He was regarded by all of them as an outsider, a foreigner, and an enemy. Why had he come, they all wondered? What new danger would he bring to their village?

"Proceed," the cacique began, as soon as all the council was seated.

Ycho stood in their midst under constant scrutiny. They kept him still in restraints, and on either flank stood the same two guardsmen who had brought him into the village.

"Proceed with your story," Felipe-Toloca commanded.

Ycho was a man of aged but rugged features, unmistakably of Potano lineage. He had to be of nearly the identical age his father would have been, had he lived, Felipe-Toloca thought. The eyes, the eyes—he noticed how tired-looking and sad they appeared. The cacique was affected by the man's sorry plight, but not quite to the level of compassion. Lingering still was that ever-present feeling of hatred that had plagued him since his family's death.

"You know you have committed many wrongs and caused much pain to me and all these people, Ycho. I find none of the words you have already spoken in your defense sufficient to excuse you. What else might you have to say to explain the terrible crimes of your past life?"

Ycho paused, lowering his eyes. Then standing very erect, he looked directly at Felipe-Toloca and began to speak. "I am sorry for what I have done to you and to your family, truly sorry. You must believe me.... But, honored Cacique Felipe-Toloca, I knew of no other way to redress the wrongs done to me by your father or the wrongs I felt your father was doing to our people by befriending the people of España.... I have never agreed with him—never!" The last words were spoken slowly and very emphatically.

"I still hold firmly to my position. I have not changed in any way from what I believed when I was forced to leave my family and my people, whom I, like you, truly love. You lost your family, and for that I am responsible.

But I lost everything, because I believed that my people were becoming slaves to a foreign nation, a foreign way of life. I lost everything because I wanted my people to remain as Potano. For many years, I became an outcast because I chose to stand for my people and to oppose all attempts to make them bow to the enemy caciques. For all of this I was made to pay a great price.

"What has happened since then? It is as I have spoken. The foreign cacique has taken from us our pride, our power, our land, our hunting-grounds. Now they have everything! We have nothing! Also, I have come to give you this information as well. Even now, as we speak, the English people are gathering members of enemy tribes to the north to attack and destroy the people of our nation. Our people will be caught between the warring nations of the peoples of the land of Europe. Once again, our people will die because of our loyalty to the people of España.

"Can you not see what fools we have become—not only your father, but all his advisors and friends—all of us. We have lost everything! Our people have died of diseases we never knew before the people of España arrived in our land. We were made slaves of this power we did not accept. We who possessed much before, now have nothing left. Each year our numbers become less and less. Why do we continue in this pathway of death?

"And what crime have I committed when you see that all that I have predicted has come true? All I sought to do was to rid my people of these vermin—the foreign nations of pale faces. Whether the people are of the land of España or of England, all, all have come to take our land and destroy our people!

"That is my story, most honored cacique! That has always been my story. I have nothing further to say, other than to bring to you a warning of the presence of the English invaders to the north, who come to do you harm. Act now! Rid yourselves of all of them! You have so little time left! My age and my health do not permit me to lead another foray to protect my people. You are the ones who must act now or perish.

"I no longer have any concern for myself. My only wish is to die here with my people! Do with me now...as you wish!"

A voice arose quickly from among the advisors. "He must die!" Another voice made a similar plea. Then another. Finally, all were chanting the verdict in unison.

Felipe-Toloca attempted to bring silence to the council chamber.

"Ycho," he said, after peace was restored, "I have long sought to find the resting-place of my father. You alone know where that place would be. Where, Ycho, did you bury my father? I must know!"

Ycho responded, "But I must know first, what is your decision about me, honorable cacique. Am I free to live or must I die?"

"My decision, Ycho, is…" Felipe-Toloca paused, then quickly added, "my decision is that today I will make no decision. Tomorrow morning, as the sun begins to rise, you will appear here before me. Until then, let us return to the peace of our homes…. Our council meeting is now ended.

In his mind and heart, Felipe-Toloca already held his verdict. He was simply delaying the timing of it, to give Ycho a few hours to prepare for the end of his life. His intention was to first visit Ycho and coax out of him the burial site of his father. Then, he would pray for Ycho's soul.

As the night pressed on, sleep began more and more to elude the cacique. A restlessness far greater than any in the recent past continued to harass him. All the years of turmoil and torment following his family's death had come to a head with Ycho's return. Now, these feelings descended upon him. Every emotion he had felt the past twenty years flooded back to him now.

"Father," he cried out, "now I will avenge your death. After all these years, I will finally be at peace, because your murderer will receive justice for his deed. Help me to learn first from him the place of your burial. I must know that if my heart is ever to be at rest!"

Tossing the coverlet from his bed, he lit the lamp he kept nearby and then began to dress. Shortly thereafter, he headed toward Ycho's prison cell.

The night felt clear and crisp; the stars glowed in a cloudless sky. Moving hurriedly to his destination, Felipe-Toloca was startled by a strange sound, and he stopped in his tracks. He heard a word being repeated. He looked around to discover the origin of the sound. And then he realized. The sound was not coming from without. It was coming from within. It was in a voice he knew well—the voice of his father, Cacique Tomás.

And what he heard echoing from the inner chambers of his soul was the command "Forgive!"

Immediately, words of Jesus from Luke's Gospel began to surface in his mind. "Father, forgive them, for they know not what they do." This prayer of Jesus on the cross began to bring a great feeling of peace to Felipe-Toloca…. Christ's plea both echoed and magnified the clear and distinct word coming to him in his father's voice. It repeated over and over again, "Forgive, forgive, forgive...."

In the darkness, in a clearing, Felipe-Toloca fell on his knees to ask of the Great Spirit and of his father forgiveness. And he felt the need, the command, to go even further than asking. Just as he knew that he was being forgiven for his hatred and hostility of these many years, so must he, in turn, forgive and let go.

"Ycho, Ycho, it is I, Felipe-Toloca." The voice of the cacique caught Ycho by surprise. The captive had been sitting silently, but awake, in a corner of his cell.

The chieftain continued, "Ycho, I have come to tell you that in my prayers this evening, I have begun to understand better your misguided ways. I cannot accept what you have done to my father, to my family, to my people, and to myself. But, Ycho, I can begin—I hope— to...forgive you.

"Nothing in this world can bring my family back to me. You can do nothing to right this wrong, Ycho. And I can do nothing that will right it either. Not even your death can undo what has been done.

"But, Ycho...I–I can change it. I can heal the wound by forgiving you. And it is only now, in these very moments as I speak these words that I am beginning to understand why I have not been at peace.

"Ycho, I forgive you for what you did.... Tomorrow, Ycho, you will go free. Tomorrow, I will let you go to find the peace you have sought with your Potano people."

The two men standing guard looked at each other in astonishment at what they had heard.

Ycho stood up, and through the slats of his prison cell, he attempted to grasp Felipe-Toloca's hand in his own. "Thank you, thank you, Cacique Felipe-Toloca. I cannot believe the words I hear. I promise loyalty to you as my cacique all the days of my life," he responded enthusiastically. "Tomorrow, before I leave, I will take you to the site where your father is buried."

Felipe-Toloca smiled at the man who had brought such hostility to his heart. He bade farewell to his old enemy with whom he was now joined, through forgiveness, in the bond of friendship.

✳

"Wake up, Cacique Felipe-Toloca, wake up!" the shout of alarm came to the cacique's ears.

Felipe-Toloca struggled awake to find his personal bodyguard calling to him.

"You must come quickly," the warrior added, helping him from his bed and into his clothes.

It was still dark, though the break of dawn was not far off. At the entrance to his dwelling, Felipe-Toloca immediately saw the two guardsmen he had assigned to keep watch over Ycho.

"Holata Felipe-Toloca, we regret to say that both of us had fallen asleep at our posts," one of them began to explain. "We were very wrong to do that."

"Somehow, Ycho must have noticed our carelessness and quietly forced open his cell door," the other guard added. "As he darted off, he made enough sound to waken us. He was too far away for us to catch him by hand, so I used the only other way I had to stop him. You know I am a very good marksman with my weapons. With one arrow I brought him down. Cacique Felipe-Toloca, I hope I did no wrong, but Ycho…is dead.

"He was an evil man," the guard continued in a rush. "He could not be trusted! It is better that he is dead!"

"You did wrong!" the cacique interrupted. "You did wrong! I had forgiven the man. Did you not hear me last night? I had forgiven him. He was to lead me to my father's burial site today!

"You should have let him go free. My father would not be pleased. And you have saddened my heart, too. I cannot believe you have done this!"

Immediately, the cacique proceeded to the spot where Ycho had been slain. Extracting the arrow carefully from his back, he lifted him on his shoulders, insisting that he carry him alone back to the cell area. After placing him on a cot in the cell, he began to examine carefully the entire room. It soon became clear to him that there were no indications of a forced escape by Ycho.

The guardsmen themselves had forced the prisoner to leave!

Summoning the two guardsmen, he had them apprehended and placed inside the very cell they had attended. If only they had realized the mistake they had made!

Sunlight crept into the eastern sky, illuminating faintly the large oaks and pines. They stood silhouetted against the backdrop of the reddish-hued glow of morning. A silent sentinel appeared, hovering high above the treetops. Seeing the sentinel, Felipe-Toloca thought of higher hopes and aspirations and better days, of dreams of future good and of possibilities still not exhausted, of a Presence that was divine that made all things still worth living for, still worth dying for.

Felipe-Toloca knew that, although he was lonely, he was not alone. Fallen Eagle, the sentinel, soared once again to the heights. The bird reminded the cacique that the Great Spirit hovered over him, embracing him in His protective care.

XXXIII
- 1690 -

Ycho had been right about impending raids by the English and their Creek and Yamassee Indian allies. Cacique Felipe-Toloca realized the danger to his own village when an excursion of Yamassee tribesmen crossed into Timucuan territory and attacked the mission of Santa Catalina to the north. The invaders burned the *pueblo*,[11] murdered many of the inhabitants, and captured others to use as slaves. They even took sacred vessels and vestments as booty.

In addition, a series of raids swiftly followed in the missions around Zapala to the northeast. The northern defense began to retreat south, and the missioners quickly joined them, abandoning the mission sites. This enemy force that increasingly threatened the Spaniards consisted of pagan Indians, English sympathizers in the Carolinas, and paid enlistees. Also numbered among those making forays into Spanish territory were Indians formerly Christianized by the Spanish.

One afternoon, Felipe-Toloca came upon Fray Antonio seated on a stump from a cut oak tree, and the cacique immediately noticed the friar looking very despondent.

"What weighs heavy on the good padre's mind today that makes him look so distressed?" Felipe-Toloca asked. The chieftain, however, suspected he might already know what troubled the friar.

---

[11] a small village

"Like you, Cacique Felipe-Toloca, I am concerned about our village and our people," the friar responded. "I am fearful for our beautiful mission chapel. But most of all I am surprised and disappointed by the departure of so many Christian people of Timucua who are leaving behind their allegiance to the Church and to España to join the pagan Indians of the north and serve the cause of the English. Why? And this, after all the many years our friars have worked for them—have all our efforts had no good effect? What do the English offer them that we do not?"

"Those are not easy questions to answer," the cacique replied. "Like yourself, I can only speculate. But let us consider, for example, the fact that the English provide certain material supports to the people of our nation that the Spanish withhold from them. The English provide them with horses, which the Spanish prefer to reserve for themselves. They provide them with firearms for hunting and for defense. The Spanish give them only to their own militia. And the English assure the Timucua of safety. Now what would you do if offered those kinds of benefits?"

"But what about their faith, my friend?" Fray Antonio quickly interjected. "Why are they so quick to return to their former ways? Do they not value their immortal souls, which can be lost when they leave behind their practice of the faith to join the enemy?"

"Fray Antonio, many people of our nation do not come from missions such as ours, blessed by good and devoted men like yourself and Fray Tomás. I have heard some complain that they were mistreated by the friars of their *doctrinas* or missions. Some say that they were punished severely when they disobeyed orders or that they were forced to perform hard and heavy tasks. Whether their charges are true, I do not know. But these might be among the reasons given for their departures from the holy faith brought us by the Spanish."

"I do not know, Cacique Felipe-Toloca, how much truth there is in these reports of abuses. Yes, there have been some irresponsible friars who have acted impatiently and at times unmercifully. But we, their brother friars, will report such abuses to our friar provincial when we know of them, just as we react to protect the people when members of the Spanish militia do harm to them. How tragic it would be if any friar was the cause of the apostasy of these people! Let us pray that such is not the case!"

After his conversation with Fray Antonio, the cacique went to the headquarters of the Spanish militia. This small, adobe building sat within the walled enclosure of the military compound. The presence of the Spanish garrison at the village of Santa Fé had been a mixed blessing since its inception at about the time when Felipe-Toloca assumed his role as cacique. The garrison provided a greater sense of security to both peoples. The Potano felt less threatened by hostile raids from without and the Spanish felt more protected from the threat of hostile uprisings from among the native peoples within. Unfortunately, mutual trust could not completely dispel mutual suspicion, and mutual respect existed alongside mutual fear. In general, both cultures lived with an acceptance of a reality that had to be. Though the Spanish military presence was a threat to his own leadership and the hegemony of his people, Felipe-Toloca had conditioned himself to live with the situation.

What he did not like was his having to adjust to the changing perspectives and shifting moods of the different men in command of the garrison. A succession of Spanish captains acted over the years as adjutant deputies of the governor to protect the village and oversee Spanish interests in the area. The current adjutant deputy was Captain José Ruíz de Benivares, a short, dark-skinned man in his late forties with protruding eyes, thin lips, and small ears. Felipe-Toloca did not know what to make of him, but he generally approached him with caution, when he approached him at all. Today, the cacique hoped to offer some suggestions regarding the defense of the village in the face of enemy attack.

The captain sat in conference with one of his soldiers, Lorenzo Guerrero. He immediately rose from his desk to welcome the cacique as soon as he saw the chieftain enter his office. The greetings on the part of both were cordial. The soldier, sensing his own presence an intrusion, began to leave, but Cacique Felipe-Toloca waved his hand to suggest instead that he remain.

"I will only take a moment of your time. I merely come to ask of you, Captain, a favor. My braves have been trained for years in many defensive skills. But they lack any training in the use of firearms. What will happen if an enemy bearing firearms ever attacks our village? We would be unable to assist you. Our men and women and children could very easily perish. We need to train them. We need to act now!

"Also the enemy comes to our neighboring villages on horseback. Even I, the cacique, do not ride a horse well. How would I, or my people, fare in combat with such an enemy? I fear we would have to rely only on you and your troops. This, Captain, is not a wise situation to be in, especially if the war party outnumbers your troops. Could you not consider some kind of training for me and my people?"

"My dear friend, Cacique Felipe-Toloca," the adjutant deputy began, drawing himself up to the full size of his rather diminutive stature, "you need not fear. Our garrison here is sufficiently large and trained well enough to protect all in the village of Santa Fé from any outside intruders. You will be well served by all of us should any unforeseen event occur. Please tell your people they have no need for any alarm. I promise you, we will defend you well if any English soldiers or their allies come anywhere near here. I promise you!"

"But, Captain, my own people would want to assist in any defense of their village," the cacique quickly retorted. "We have great confidence in your soldiers, indeed, but—"

The captain sharply interrupted the cacique. "There is no need for any further discussion, my friend. We will protect you, I promise. And we will do so well."

Felipe-Toloca bowed, somewhat in shame, first to the captain, then to the soldier. He then turned and left, not surprised, but disappointed by what he had heard.

Fray Antonio was leaving the mission church as the cacique exited the military compound's fortified front gate. The priest spied the Indian leader before the cacique had seen him.

"Now I believe it is you rather than I who is looking dejected. Why the sad and sullen face?"

"I do not think it is wise for our people to be unprepared for an attack by the enemy," Felipe-Toloca began. "What happened at the Mission of Santa Catalina could happen to us. Our people cannot defend themselves against firearms with the weapons we now have. Nor can we move into combat without horses. If we are attacked, we wish to help in the defense of our village and mission. But the captain did not wish to hear me. He says his men are able to ward off any possible threat to our people!"

Just as Felipe-Toloca finished his lament, the young soldier, Lorenzo Guerrero, walked out of the military compound through the front gate and made his way toward the cacique and the friar. He walked rapidly, and they could see at his approach that he had something he wanted to say to them.

"*Buenos dias, padre.* Greetings again to you, Cacique Felipe-Toloca. Inside, we were not able to speak, but I wanted to tell you that, like your-self, I did not agree with what I heard the captain say. I…I apologize to you for the way my people conduct themselves with your people on occasions like this. I wish there was a way I could help you, but…"

"But maybe there is," the friar suggested, as an idea suddenly entered his mind. "Why don't we carry this conversation on in private? Please, come with me to the sacristy of our mission chapel. What I want to discuss would be best said behind closed doors!"

"Better still," the soldier responded, "let me invite the two of you to my home this evening. My wife and children live in the village with the other military families. We would be honored to have you join us for dinner."

"Agreed?" the cacique asked of the friar.

"Agreed!" Padre Antonio answered, with a smile of approval.

They chose a suitable time, and the three men parted in preparation for their evening encounter.

Lorenzo Guerrero, his wife Margarita, and their three children were excellent hosts. The cacique and the friar did not remember when they had spent a better or more enjoyable evening with anyone. Marcos, Andrés, and little Angelita became fast and permanent friends with their guests, knowing nothing of society's bigotry and barriers. Padre Antonio and Cacique Felipe-Toloca became such an intimate part of the family interaction that evening that they almost forgot what had occasioned their meeting.

After the visit had lasted well into the evening, Lorenzo told the children that it was bedtime. Reluctant to retire for the evening but obedient to their father, the children made the rounds of parents and guests to give a fond and prolonged *abrazo* to each. Margarita excused herself to clear

the table and wash the dishes in her *cocina*.

"Now, Fray Antonio," Lorenzo remarked, "it is time for us to hear what special inspiration you received when I spoke with you last. I regret that our discussion only begins now at this late our."

"Lorenzo," Padre Antonio hastened to comment, "I know I speak for our cacique in saying that we have no regrets. We have thoroughly enjoyed our time with you and your family. You have become dear friends to us this evening. I only wish we did not have to change our conversation to discuss such weighty matters.

"Necessity, however, dictates otherwise. Now, you had indicated that you heard the concern expressed by Cacique Felipe-Toloca to the captain. May I now take the liberty of expressing to you my concerns as well.... "

Long into the night, the friar, the cacique, and the soldier engaged in animated, yet subdued conversation, making certain that they would not be overheard by anyone. Only after a long period of discussion did they finally reach agreement on the matters before them. Finally, the three men decided to retire for the night. There would be many more meetings to follow up on the important concerns they had addressed. Most importantly, they knew when they parted that a lasting bond of friendship had been forged among the three of them.

Walking back alone to the broad thatched hut that was his home, Felipe-Toloca seemed to hear deep within his heart a sound of voices chanting a war song, and in his mind's eye, he could see Indians from other nations as well as his own dancing the war dance. Though the sights and sounds were faint, they seemed all too real. The harder he tried to rid himself of them, the more vivid they became. He finally accepted the grim truth that trying to obliterate them was like trying to wish away the inevitable.

Part Five

The End

THE BATTLE MAP of CACIQUE

Positions of the Potano tribe, Spanish forces, and Carolinian militia in the final battles of Cacique.

 Spanish

 Potano

 English

Santa Fé de Toloca

Santa Ana de Potano

San Miguel de Potano

San Francisco de Potano

Santa Fé R.

San Martín de Ayacuto

Suwanee River

XXXIV
Friday, 19 May, 1702

For twelve years following the clandestine meeting between the cacique, Fray Antonio, and the militiaman Lorenzo Guerrero, the mission Santa Fé never came under surprise attack. Lorenzo always managed to relay advance warning to Captain Ruíz de Benivares whenever an enemy threatened a foray into the village. There were many such enemy reconnaissance patrols and raiding parties, but always the Spanish militia knew them well beforehand, and with proper preparation, repulsed these threats.

Somehow, Lorenzo could tell whenever danger was imminent, and his warnings always proved reliable. The captain and the other soldiers of the garrison were baffled as to his sources, but they came to rely on them for security after Lorenzo's first several warnings were confirmed by the enemy's presence.

And Lorenzo chose never to reveal the nature of the espionage network that he had planned along with the cacique and the friar that one evening many years ago. That night the three men decided upon an intrigue that involved a Potano array of sentinels, spaced at various distances, up to a radius of eight leagues from the village of Santa Fé.

The cacique regretted that the only service his people could provide the Spanish was this advance warning system, but Captain Ruíz would not relent on his insistence that the Spanish, "and the Spanish alone," would defend the village.

"Give them guns! Give them horses!" Lorenzo would repeatedly request of the captain.

The answer was always the same.

"Give them guns, give them horses, and the Indian people will one day use them against us! The policy of España is clear on this matter. It is not up to us to change it, but to enact it and enforce it!"

And always Lorenzo would remind the captain, "Our failure to train and arm these people in our defense could result in our being overtaken by a bigger and stronger enemy."

The captain would not listen. He remained unshakable in his certainty that his militia could handle any threat; if a bigger enemy came, he could get reinforcements from the militia in San Agustín.

So far the captain had been right.

Despite the threat of hostile invaders, mission life flourished. A mature-looking Fray Antonio, now in his early seventies, looked with satisfaction on the progress made since the virtual destruction of the mission in 1656. He found ready encouragement in the equally aged, yet ever-energetic cacique, Felipe-Toloca. With the cacique's support and the help of sympathetic villagers, Fray Antonio had not only personally overseen the rebuilding of the mission chapel and adjoining buildings, but had also helped the cacique in rebuilding the shattered spirit of the entire village. The success of the reconstruction promoted a good working relationship between the remaining Potano and Utina tribesmen and women who had come to live with them after the rebellion.

Everyone who remembered the days when Fray Tomás had directed the mission remarked how that same spirit pervaded the Santa Fé Mission once again. Repeatedly, the cacique would commend his friar comrade for being the true force behind this rebirth. Felipe-Toloca could not but acknowledge that from the very beginning, whenever the people's spirits were low, Fray Antonio had a way to make them soar. Fray Antonio had believed in the Potano people from the outset, even when many did not believe in themselves. The people had Fray Antonio to thank for defending their rights whenever his fellow Spaniards tried to tread on them. The cacique looked upon the friar not only as his priest and mentor, but as his very good friend. This man had truly been good to his people.

He said as much to the priest late one evening when the friar caught up with him during his sentry duty. The friar had found him at his post at the outermost periphery from the village.

"Fray Antonio, what are you doing in this wilderness at this late hour?" the cacique asked, as he batted away the mosquitoes swarming around the friar's face. "This is no place for a man of the cloth, and I know whereof I speak, having lived the genteel ways of a prospective friar in España. Mission life has brought you a long way from the comforts of your homeland, hasn't it?"

"How well you speak the truth, my friend! Never in my wildest dreams did I imagine what I was getting into," the friar replied. "But never would I change this life for any other!"

The cacique shook his head, then smiled approvingly. "I had all but given up hope, Fray Antonio, that our village would be built again. I thought we were a people lost, without a home. But you managed to help us find ourselves; we are a people once more. Our fallen spirits and shattered hopes were restored by you, Fray Antonio; I will never forget what you have done for my people."

"Nor will I forget what you and your people have done for me, Cacique Felipe-Toloca," the friar added. "Everything I have heard about your father has been reflected in you, his first-born son. I know how proud he must be of you, for carrying on his great care for his beloved Potano people. The good God has been with you! You have led your people very well!"

The conversation continued on into the early morning hours, as they reminisced about struggles shared and thankless burdens borne together. It was a moment forged from deep friendship and mutual admiration, honestly expressed and openly acknowledged. They had captured this opportunity so patently justified, yet it could have been easily lost in the frenzied pace of life, had not the friar taken the time to check on the well-being of his dear friend, the cacique.

Then, it all came to a sudden halt when the sound of a snapping twig interrupted them. Something or someone of sizable weight had broken through the nearby brush. Long adept at recognizing unwelcome intruders, the cacique instantly placed a finger over his lips, cautioning silence to the friar.

A nearly full moon blessed the two sentries with enough light to enable them to make out in the distance shapes moving in their direction from the northwest—hostile territory. They saw first one, then several half-clad Indian bodies, covered with war paint. Soldiers in red coats followed quickly behind them. Both Indians and soldiers carried rifles.

Then from the northeast, the cacique and the friar saw another contingent moving stealthily towards them. Deep to the west and further east, other parties could faintly be seen, slowly moving forward. These raiders rode on horses.

The cacique signaled the friar to move with him carefully, quietly, and quickly. Never once did they communicate by speech. Everything depended on their escaping undetected. The slightest noise or false step could mean quick capture or death. The friar tried as best he could to imitate the Indian's light and swift, soundless movement through brambles and bushes. It was an art, he long ago realized, he could not master. Pressed by the force of circumstances, he did as best he could, while praying for the help of every saint and angel he knew.

The cacique had already mapped out a quick escape route, precisely to make possible a hasty departure in the face of movement by the enemy.

Thanks to Lorenzo Guerrero, a single horse had secretly been made available, just for the cacique. It had been hidden away for Felipe-Toloca—just in case—whenever he went on sentry duty.

When the cacique and the friar reached the animal, Felipe-Toloca motioned for the friar to mount. "This is how Lorenzo has risked his life for me. Now his sacrifice could save us all," the cacique whispered to the friar, as he helped him onto the animal.

The cacique first led the horse a short distance; then he carefully mounted behind the friar and headed down the path that would take him to the next sentry, who would in turn pass the word to all the other posts.

"Alert the others; there is a major assault by the enemy," he quickly called out to the first Indian they encountered, "one we will not repulse easily. The enemy appears to surround us and comes in much greater numbers and with much greater force than in the past. We must use our special tactics to delay them so the Spanish militia will not be overcome."

The cacique and the friar saw clearly that special protective measures had to be put in place quickly to prevent the village from being taken. The chieftain and the priest raced quickly into the village. The friar's presence on the horse had prevented any questions being asked by the Spanish military guard posted at the gate. He had been disturbed and bewildered, seeing an Indian on the horse with the friar; but as Fray Antonio shouted at him the emergency of their mission, he had hastily ushered them into the area occupied by the military garrison.

Felipe-Toloca drew up their horse immediately in front of the residence of Lorenzo Guerrero. Half-asleep and disheveled, Lorenzo peered through the opening of his door, then welcomed the two wayfarers. They quickly told him their alarming news.

"A vast array of Creeks and English are moving in on us. We must act quickly. This time your militia will not withstand what is coming, I fear," the cacique warned.

Lorenzo immediately began to pull on his military pants and put on his boots.

Fray Antonio said, "The cacique promised you his help in such a situation. You will definitely need them now, I assure you. Just give the cacique several more horses, and he can put into place the defenses his people have rehearsed."

"Tell your troops not to fire on the first several horsemen riding toward the village," the cacique interjected, "or they will deliver me and a few of my braves to our eternal resting place."

"And they will deliver me to the same, because I will be riding with the cacique," Fray Antonio proclaimed, not allowing any rebuttals.

"Then I will go to the captain immediately," Lorenzo began, as he slipped into his coat, "and I will tell him about the contingency plans we made long ago to protect the village, with your help. I only hope that he will listen to me. All the past warnings I have given him have proven true, thanks to the information you have brought me. I hope that will be proof enough."

"We must move as we speak," the cacique cautioned. "There is little time!"

As the three men proceeded by foot toward the captain's quarters, they went over their strategy. "You know that, as in the past, you will not be given any guns or horses by the captain to help in the defense. I will get you several horses for the special purpose of your mission," Lorenzo said, "but please tell no one where they came from."

"I will tell the captain it was Fray Antonio who planned all of this. We will let him face the captain's anger afterwards for all of us," the cacique quipped.

Fray Antonio simply smiled, feeling no shame at his involvement in the intrigue.

"I will do my best to keep our militia from firing on the first few horsemen coming in the direction of the village, presuming that will be yourselves. The rest of the plan we have arranged I will reveal to the captain and the militia so they will not be in the dark," Lorenzo concluded as they came close to the captain's residence. Then, he bid farewell to his friends.

As he began to leave, Felipe-Toloca stopped him. The cacique placed his hand firmly on the shoulder of Lorenzo and gazed intently at the man for a moment. "You are my friend. You are the friend of my people always, Lorenzo. My people are your people. Thank you for what you do for us in giving to us our pride.

"On my part I assure you, no weapons will be used by my people in the battle that will ensue—no *macana,* no guns, no bows. We will use only the techniques taught by my father and our people from the days of Fray Tomás and the great warrior Tofucanatchu."

"And I know," the friar added, "that your father, Cacique Tomás, will be honored that you use the methods of combat that he taught you so well;

he will be praying that they prove sufficient to the task at hand. May the Great Spirit be with us and His angels guard us," the friar prayed; the two others echoed his prayer.

They embraced one another and parted for their destinies.

XXXV
Saturday, 20 May, 1702

Nations expand their boundaries
And consume the earth.
What the reason, why the effort?
What the price, what the worth?

The cacique set out on horseback with the friar, and two other Potano followed swiftly behind. But as he raced to the battle lines, thoughts that had occurred to Felipe-Toloca a thousand times before darted through his mind once again. What was it that they were defending? What were they protecting?

The homes of his people, certainly. This village had become the pride of his tribe—so recently rebuilt with the work of their own hands. Also, they fought for the land that had belonged to the Potano for so many generations. The hills, the trees, the Rio Santa Fé. For a moment his mind wandered in the beauty of these woodlands and the wonder of the animals that dwelt in them. With gratitude he thought of *la chuas,* the sinkholes, that provided an endless supply of water that came from deep within the earth and had saved his people in times of drought. These had created the waterways where he learned to fish and swim and ride his own hand-hewn canoe.

These memories led him to dwell on the traditions his people held dear. Tonight, the survival of their culture could be at stake. And this culture now included the *doctrina,* the mission Santa Fé, and all that these things had become in the life of his people. They were both a strange imposition from without and a special gift from within. To the Franciscan friars of the mission, his people owed the great legacy of being brought into a loving relationship with the Great Spirit who had seemed to them before an adversary, never a father and not even a friend.

This formed the new heritage of his people. Now the cacique rode out to defend and preserve it with the meager resources the Spanish had given him. He would also use whatever means were afforded him by his native talents and tribal teachings. He hoped it would be enough.

"Yes! Yes!" the cacique said to himself, and he spurred his horse on to greater speed, waving the others to follow closely behind him. "We must reach the enemy before they reach us, or we will be taken," the cacique warned his three companions.

The cacique directed his lead horse in a westerly direction toward the territory from which he and Fray Antonio had first come. They soon arrived at the land bridge, an area where the Rio Santa Fé went underground. The enemy would most likely attack here. Since the village and mission of Santa Fé were bounded to the north and east by the Rio Santa Fé, the river itself served as the principal bastion of defense. Where the river stopped, defense problems began.

When the four riders came to the land bridge where the river temporarily retreated underground just west of the village, they alerted their Potano comrades to prepare for a fight with the Northern invaders. Then the riders passed to the north and east, giving further signals to Potano sentries in areas not yet reached by the people of English heritage from the north and their allies. Riding directly north of the village on the far side of the river, the four began to circle wide in an attempt to get behind the approaching forces. After moving slowly for about ten minutes, the cacique pulled his horse up short and signaled for silence.

"There!" Felipe-Toloca whispered, indicating with a sweeping gesture to a clearing further ahead.

Before them hundreds of figures advanced across a small area. The invaders moved cautiously by foot and on horseback in a southerly direction toward the river and village.

"There are not only Creeks with the English," the cacique pointed out. "There are Apalachicolas as well. We are in for quite a battle, my friends. It is time!"

Harking to the cacique's words, the other riders began to move slowly apart, keeping well hidden behind trees and large shrubs. The chieftain waited until each was posted some distance from each other. Suddenly,

Felipe-Toloca sounded forth a loud war cry, which was echoed quickly and repeatedly by the others.

The enemy heard the sounds, which sent them into disarray. Fearing they were surrounded, the enemy became divided, though the majority of the raiders headed directly forward, toward the south, in the direction of the river. The English soldiers turned and fired behind themselves, in the direction of the sounds that came from the invisible quartet. Bullets ricocheted randomly in the night; but the four decoys kept moving clandestinely and hastily, never ceasing their high-pitched shrieking and whooping. Bullets flew and rebounded everywhere, narrowly missing the elusive phantom riders.

The rear division of the raiders' cavalry, afraid of being caught in the open, rode to the woods for protection. Little did they expect the surprises the defenders had waiting for them there. The first Potano welcoming party they encountered seemingly fell from the sky. An agile group of young braves dropped on the enemy riders from out of the darkness of the overhanging tree limbs. Then, they quickly incapacitated the invaders, knocked them from their mounts, and rode away with their horses. The enemy suddenly found themselves defenseless on foot. Stunned by the first engagement, they barely had time to recover before a second group of Potano sprang out from behind the surrounding trees. They wrestled the raiders to the ground, bound them with hemp ropes, and then relieved them of their weaponry.

Meanwhile, Felipe-Toloca, Fray Antonio, and the two Potano riders galloped from their places of concealment into the open field. In an attempt to divert the already confused remaining enemy cavalry, they separated in two directions, with the friar and the cacique heading for the area where the river descended into the ground, while the other two raced into the open land adjoining the river.

Their ploy worked. Against the protests of their suspicious Indian allies, the enemy horsemen that were left divided their forces in two and pursued the four riders. Then, quite randomly and quite mysteriously, many a horse and rider began to drop off the face of the earth. Only too late did the cavalry realize they had ridden into deadly terrain dotted with hidden, branch-covered holes that had been carefully constructed beforehand by the Potano.

Almost immediately, Potano warriors burst from cover, swinging down from undetected perches or rushing out from behind the shrubs and palmettos. They wrested more guns from their hapless victims, leaving them captive in the deep chasms, kept company by their now disabled horses and a bothersome community of roaches and rodents.

The Potano employed every manner and method conceivable to confuse the enemy and render them defenseless. In each trick or strategy, however, the Potano used only carefully devised hindrance tactics and their martial-arts skills. By these means, the cacique and friar managed to lure many unsuspecting English soldiers into traps and snares. Through wit and wisdom, the defenders were quickly demoralizing the opposing forces.

The four decoy riders successfully rendezvoused at a prearranged destination, from which point they began to alert the Spanish militia of the advance of the enemy toward the village. As they rode through the mission and village toward the military barracks, they discovered that all the women and children had been brought inside the walls of the military enclosure, where the final lines of defense were drawn by the adjutant deputy, Captain Ruíz de Benivares.

Lorenzo was instrumental in holding back the Spanish militia from firing against the four approaching horsemen, and he arranged to have the gate to the barracks unbarred so that he could personally welcome the friar and the cacique and their two comrades. Lorenzo's offer to help the aged Fray Antonio from his horse was met with a quick rebuff from the priest.

"I have just emerged from a barrage of enemy fire unscathed, and now you are considering me too feeble to get off a horse, *amigo!*"

"You have never appeared younger to me than today, Fray Antonio," Lorenzo quickly responded. "By such antics as these you have made yourself ageless, or shall I say—immortal!"

The friar and cacique embraced Lorenzo and told him of the large numbers of Apalachicolas and Creeks who had been approaching with the Carolinian regiment. They went on to proudly detail how the enemy had stumbled into the Potano's successful delaying tactics. Then, they spied the adjutant deputy, who did not look happy.

"Lorenzo prevailed upon me to join in your—your escapade," said Captain Ruíz. In his own mind he was thinking that a more appropriate term would be "fiasco," but pride held him in check. If he admitted that he was part of a fiasco, he would look like an idiot, and he was not the idiot here.

"I am certain that my militia could have handled this situation by itself, with no problems. As it is, we have been forced into a defensive posture that appears to me childish.Now that it is too late to do otherwise, I will try to do honor to the mockery you have made of warfare. And after this episode has ended, I will see to it that Lorenzo is relieved of further military responsibilities."

"But Captain," the friar quickly replied, speaking in a tone that verged on anger, "the enemy's advance has been delayed. His movement is greatly hindered. His troops are in disarray. And you, Captain, have the upper hand—all because of Lorenzo. Had it not been for Lorenzo, the enemy would be at your door this very moment."

The captain winced at his words, then looked upward, as firebrands, lobbed from without, began to drop within a few feet of the friar and the captain.

"The enemy is at our door," the captain bellowed. "We will pursue this matter later! Get to your battle stations!" he called to the militiamen.

The friar, cacique, and Potano riders headed toward the Potano women and children and herded them to a protected area of the barracks. Lorenzo then took up a position with other soldiers at a sentry post on the upper level of the barracks' walled enclosure. From his perch, he could survey the entire battle situation and take note of the advancing enemy. There were skirmishes going on all about them, and the invaders were firing upon the barracks as well. To Lorenzo's satisfaction, the numbers of the enemy that had penetrated their lines did not seem large.

Lorenzo felt a sense of pride over what he had helped set in motion. He was proud of Fray Antonio and the cacique and the Potano, who were admirably and honorably defending their village and mission.

Indeed, the English and their Indian allies were hardly making any progress in their attempt to advance on the barracks. The outer perimeter of Spanish military defenders held the invaders back with deadly resolve and lethal effectiveness, aided by the skillful Potano defenders.

There was only a handful of Indians slipping through the lines to torch the village and mission. Flaming brands were being put to the huts of the village, to the mission chapel, and to the friars' quarters, but with each effort a Potano would intervene. The defender would wrestle the hostile Indian or English soldier to the ground and subdue him.

The enemy advance was being hindered successfully. The Spanish militia at the river's edge, as well as the militia on the western front, kept the enemy troops from Carolina at bay.

Lorenzo looked around for the friar and the cacique, but saw only the friar protectively guarding some of the women and children. He then spied the cacique and his two Potano comrades cautiously scaling the barrack wall and lowering themselves by rope on the far side, scurrying off into the wilderness, into the fight.

Lorenzo understood. Aging, but agile, the cacique had to face the danger alongside his braves. He could not wait behind the walls in safety.

Captain Ruíz de Benivares suddenly appeared next to Lorenzo. Exhibiting an air of pride and self-assurance, he announced, "It is time to rout the enemy and give them a good thrashing, now that we have made spittle of them."

Then, bearing down for a short time on Lorenzo, he spoke in a coarse, commanding tone.

"You will accompany me, Lorenzo, and put the final touch of victory on this engagement. Let us act now, before it is too late. Get some of your Potano friends, and we will finish off this rabble!"

Lorenzo did not hesitate in responding to the captain's orders.

"At your service, Captain!" he replied, as he hurried to assemble a handful of Spanish militiamen. Once outside of the gate, he gathered a further fifteen Potano who held posts in the area. Lorenzo was happy to see the adjutant deputy reverse his earlier policy and provide horses to the Indians accompanying them.

Off they rode, laying waste to whatever enemy stragglers they found and routing the invading Indians whom had advanced too close to the village. To Lorenzo's amazement, the enemy swiftly fell back in retreat. Despite the meager size of his band, the captain decided to press on to debilitate and obliterate whatever forces were left in the area.

It was shortly after dawn, and all the area surrounding the village and mission rested in a deathly silence, the kind that exists in the aftermath of storms, in graveyards, and on the fields of war. The injured were being assisted by the able; the dead, both friend and foe, were being prepared for their final resting place. Fray Antonio ventured out of the barracks to inspect his mission and to assess the ravages of the early morning battle.

Smoke still rose from the charred embers where the village and mission had been put to the torch. Blessedly, most of the buildings had survived the attack. Fray Antonio shook his head and said a prayer of thanks that the damage had not been any worse. He then cringed as he looked toward the friars' convento and mission chapel. Both were seriously damaged by fire.

He spent the better part of the day rummaging through the wreckage, retrieving what he could of salvageable religious artifacts, many of which, he discovered, were destroyed or missing. Toward sunset an aged Potano crept toward him. The man wore a mysterious smile on his face. He proceeded to lead the priest to a location inside the surrounding woods. Still smiling, he proudly unveiled the tabernacle, candles, crucifix, statues, and images of the *Via Crucis* which, he wanted the padre to understand, he himself had rescued from the chapel at great peril.

Fray Antonio wept in gratitude, as he placed his arms around this man whom had put his life at risk for the sacred treasures of the faith. That cheery expression of joy and gratitude, however, quickly shifted to one of alarm, when the friar saw the stately cacique approach astride his horse. Other Potano horsemen followed solemnly behind him.

Lying stretched facedown upon Felipe-Toloca's horse lay a body. Fray Antonio noticed it was a Spanish militiaman, vaguely discernable in the moonlight by the colors of his uniform. He was one of several Spaniards being carried into the village, along with the bodies of Potano Indians. The cacique spoke no words as he descended from the horse and lifted the lifeless victim into his arms, cradling him affectionately. Tears crept down the cheeks of Felipe-Toloca, as he attempted to describe the events of the day.

"It happened about six leagues from here. Successfully taking hostages and forcing the enemy to retreat, the captain and our people went in pursuit of the raiders. They came upon a clearing and suddenly found themselves surrounded. Our people had walked into a trap. The invaders had regrouped into in a crescent formation and when our men rode inside it, the enemy closed in upon them, catching many of them in the center, with no way to escape. Only a few of our people were able to get away, and they brought news to us of this tragedy.

"This man did not escape. He is now in the eternal embrace of the Great Spirit."

The cacique wiped back the matted strands of hair from the victim's forehead and the clots of blood that clung to the man's nose and mouth. He then turned the body face-up in the direction of Fray Antonio.

The friar immediately recognized the face of one of his dearest friends and had to turn away. Slowly, he forced himself to overcome the temptation to deny the tragedy he was witnessing. He proceeded to make a sweeping gesture of the sign of the cross over the lifeless body before him, the body of Lorenzo Guerrero.

XXXVI
1703-1704

The military skills and bravery of Lorenzo Guerrero did not go unnoticed by the Spanish authorities. At the request of the current governor, Don Joseph de Zunega y la Cerda, the King acknowledged in a Royal *Cedula* Lorenzo's forty years of service to the crown and his valiant action that led to the repulse of the enemy by utilizing the skilled support of Potano warriors. To his wife Margarita and their three children, the Crown bequeathed an annual allotment to sustain them in the years ahead.

Cacique Felipe-Toloca, Fray Antonio, and a representative group of Potano were on hand in San Agustín with the family of Lorenzo to hear the governor's proclamation of the Royal *Cedula*.

"And as for that which touches upon the wife and children of Lorenzo Guerrero," the governor quoted the words of His Majesty, The King of España, "I approve doing them the favors, which you will see from the dispatch bearing the same date as this." The governor referred to the date of the document, September 4, 1703, and the royal seal. He rolled up the decree, and presented an accompanying document outlining the favors to Señora Guerrero.

"You will be properly provided for," the governor promised. "It is all there. If you wish to remain here in San Agustín, then know you have a home with us," he added.

"I believe she prefers to remain at the Santa Fé garrison for the time being, then to set sail for España," Fray Antonio commented, "to be with family. We will continue to look after her well, your Excellency, in the weeks ahead. Thank you for all you have done."

"Captain Ruíz de Benivares is now gone along with Lorenzo," the governor pointed out, "but his family is on the far side of the ocean and also will be duly aided by the Crown. What will become of the Santa Fé Military Garrison, I will determine today, my friends."

"The Adjutant Deputy, Captain Ruíz, raced forth in this foray with little prudence and few men, to pursue the enemy," the cacique pointed out to the governor. "His haste brought the death of my friend Lorenzo and some of my men. We will accept the captain's mistakes," the cacique added. "We can even accept the departure of the military garrison, if that is necessary, but I can assure you that neither I nor my people will abandon the village and mission of Santa Fé—never!"

"Your Excellency," the cacique continued with his eyes fixed intently on the governor, "my people would be well-served by being permitted weaponry for our defense, and horses. The English heavily armed the Apalachicolas against us. We can withhold their attacks by ourselves in the future, if we are provided guns and horses."

"Most honored cacique, Felipe-Toloca," the governor spoke, then halted momentarily, pondering carefully his next words, "we will continue to labor together, as in the past. I will send a new adjutant deputy and additional militia. I am sure we will together continue to prevent the enemy's advances."

"Excellency, we have lost Lorenzo Guerrero as a military friend to collaborate with the Potano people," Fray Antonio interjected. "Whom do these people have if they wish to relay their concerns?"

"They have you, Fray Antonio," the governor quickly replied, "and through you, their concerns will be met. I will see to that!"

"So then Governor Zunega, what about the cacique's request for guns and horses? Is that not a fitting one, given the circumstances?" Fray Antonio did not allow the governor any respite.

"What would your holy Father Francis say about your peacekeeping efforts, Fray Antonio?" the governor retorted.

"What would he say about yours, Excellency?"

The friar realized immediately he had let the words slip out too quickly. Aware that he had pushed the conversation as far as he could, he motioned to the cacique and the family of Lorenzo. After a gracious bow to the new governor, he sought a hasty retreat.

A new adjutant deputy, Captain Juan Diego Alvarez, was assigned to Santa Fé almost immediately, and the status quo resumed to the satisfaction of neither the Potano people nor the Spanish military garrison. The only positive result was that, at the direction of the governor, the new deputy formally presented Cacique Felipe-Toloca with a fine, Spanish-bred stallion. It was meant to be a permanent gift.

The need was as great as ever. Very little time passed before the Carolinian troops, under the command of Governor Moore, made sweeping advances again into Spanish territories to the northwest and northeast. Cacique Felipe-Toloca immediately resurrected the advance warning network that had served his people well in the past. One by one stories were being related to the cacique and friar, who continued to rendezvous regularly at the outermost perimeter of the defense.

In January of 1704, a Potano courier bore some disturbing news to the cacique and friar at their sentry post. He reported that the English, accompanied by their Indian allies, had recently attacked the village of Ayubale in the Province of Apalachee. According to the courier, the village had fallen, and he gave a vivid description of other hostilities in the area as well.

"After a valiant defense by the Indians and their missionary, Fray Angel de Miranda, from the morning hours until mid-afternoon, that village fell once ammunition was depleted.

Captain Juan Ruíz Mexia, adjutant deputy of Apalachee, went in pursuit with about thirty Spanish soldiers and settlers and two hundred Indians. Upon encountering the enemy, who were about 1,500 strong, many were killed; once ammunition was exhausted, the rest were routed, with the adjutant deputy being wounded and eventually captured.

"Fray Juan de Parga, the missionary of the village, had accompanied his Christianized Indians into battle. He had been discouraged from doing so by the adjutant deputy, but he went anyway. He, too, was captured...and beheaded.

"Another priest, Padre Marcos Delgado was also killed. About forty of the captured Christian Indians were tied to stakes and burned. To one Indian, Antonio Enixa from San Luís, a fire was applied slowly from morning until near sunset, when he finally died. He told his captors that as a Christian he would go to enjoy God, while they would go to hell, and that the Most Holy Virgin appeared near to him and was helping him endure his torture.

"The body of another man from San Luís, Luís Domingo, was slashed with knives. Into his wounds were inserted burning splinters. This cruel torment, however, did not prevent him from preaching to his captors until his death.

"I have heard," the courier continued, "that one of the captured missionaries, Fray Angel de Miranda, asked Governor Moore how he could permit such savage mistreatment of prisoners, since this was not a proper method of war. Such torturing of even criminals was unknown.

"Moore's response was that he only had eighty English in his band and one thousand five hundred Indians. He was not able to prevent this manner of brutality that is customary among the Indians from occurring.

Some time elapsed and another Potano scout brought word to Felipe-

Toloca of further atrocities. "On the Feast of St. John, during a raid by a small band of English and Indians," he began, "the holy and charitable Fray Manual de Mendoza was among those who lost his life. His *convento* was burned completely. The metal from the crucifix he wore around his neck was found half-melted around his body, though much of his remains had been reduced to ashes. When the search party went to carry him off, he fell to powder.

"In the early part of July, Adjutant Deputy Manual Solana set out in Patale with soldiers and Indians, and many died in battle or were captured." The courier caught his breath, and continued.

"Don Pedro Marmolejo, a soldier of the garrison of Apalachee, was burned at the foot of the cross. Another soldier, Baltasar Francisco, was also captured. The Indian captors cut out his tongue and eyes; they cut off his ears and scalped him, putting a crown made of *tascayas* on his mutilated head. His humiliation did not end there. They also bound him to a cross, slashed him all about his body, and put burning splinters in his wounds. They—they mocked and insulted him as he called on the Virgin Mary to help him and carry him to God. When the enemy departed, a witness to these events went with other soldiers to recover the bodies of those who had fallen."

The courier believed that in recent months the English and their allies destroyed at least four major villages. The villages' inhabitants had been killed, captured, or were in flight, and their animals and possessions had been taken as booty. Heeding the warning, Cacique Felipe-Toloca put his village on alert and continued his round-the-clock watches with the help of his Potano tribesmen and the faithful friar.

In August of 1704, the King invited his Viceroy of New España and the Governor of Havana to furnish whatever they could to relieve the plight of the *presidio* in San Agustín. He asked them to bring relief to the soldiers and Indians in the area under siege, and he implored them to help the children of those who perished in battle. He also sent encouragement to those who suffered despair from all that had transpired. That, unfortunately, included everyone in the missions and villages of La Florida.

On a regular basis, Fray Antonio spent his evenings with his friend, the cacique, watching for any sign of the enemy's approach. The two realized that Governor Moore's allies now knew the territory and would one day make their way back. It was only a matter of time.

A signal from a Potano sentry to the east warned that that time had finally arrived. On that fateful night, Fray Antonio and Felipe-Toloca were once again stationed at their common post. There was little time, and the friar and the cacique made a hasty retreat to where two horses awaited them.

On the way to their mounts, they rushed by foot through their usual escape route, but Fray Antonio, a little more aged and a little less adept at movements through the woods, could not keep pace with the cacique. As the cacique glanced to his rear, he noticed the friar veering off the path to an area he knew posed a threat. "Be careful, Fray Antonio," he began to say in a barely audible whisper. But before he got the words out, the padre slipped out of sight. Fray Antonio had fallen headlong into one of the pits, hidden by brush, that had been laid for the enemy pursuers.

Felipe-Toloca now feared the worst. The enemy was close behind. How could he rescue the trapped, and probably disabled, friar and get him back to safe quarters?

The cacique rushed to the pit looked down and saw no movement. He then lowered himself down into the hole, to find to his utter amazement and sorrow that Fray Antonio was more than unconscious. There was no heartbeat. Fray Antonio was dead!

He grabbed the friar and tried to revive him with every method he knew.

"You must live, Fray Antonio. You must live," he said. "For me, for my people. Please do not depart from me now. Please, Fray Antonio! We need you. I need you."

Blood flowed profusely from the nose and ears of the friar onto the hands of the cacique. Felipe-Toloca began wiping the friar's face with his own shirt. He tore the garment off himself and futilely tried to staunch his friend's blood loss.

"You must not die, Fray Antonio. You cannot die. Great Spirit, do not let his spirit go from us."

In the near distance, the sound of leaves crushed by human weight descended on Felipe-Toloca's ears and filled his spirit with alarm. The sound was but a short distance away. Someone was moving slowly, cautiously in his direction. *Probably tracing my footprints or the friar's, the* cacique thought. Someone was close to discovering him and the friar. What could he do to avoid capture and the inevitable torture?

He knew he now could no longer escape. His only alternative was some hasty subterfuge. "Forgive me, Fray Antonio," he spoke, under his breath.

Whether minutes or moments had passed since he had first heard the snapping brush, Felipe-Toloca could not tell, but soon, silhouetted figures peered over the side of the pit. They saw at the base of the trap the cacique and the now lifeless friar.

Words were exchanged above. Felipe-Toloca heard English and an Indian dialect unknown to him. The English he recognized and somewhat understood, having learned some of it from a number of British traders who had ventured into Timucan territory before English and Spanish relations became openly hostile.

"How many are they?" were English words the cacique understood.

"Raise your hands in the air and stand up!" more English words, and they were followed by more Indian dialect.

The cacique remained still, like the lifeless body beside him.

Shortly, he felt two men descend upon him, as hard-heeled boots stepped on his legs and back.

"Are they alive?" another British soldier asked from above. He felt a hand on his neck. Opening his eyes just a slit, he noticed the second invader feeling the body of the friar the same way.

"Bring them to the surface," came a command from above, "and take the scalps of both!"

"One's lifeless," spoke one of the Englishmen in the pit to the soldier looking down from the rim. "He's partially clad. The other is dressed as one o' them friars. He's soaked in blood. I think these two here must have fell into their own trap. Must 'a been set for us. Serves 'em right. Should we leave 'em or bring 'em up, what say ya?"

"Raise the friar. Lash him to a tree for now, and we will retrieve him later. We can decide his fate on our return, if some party behind us does not decide sooner."

They raised the friar to the surface and his hands were tied crudely behind him. He slumped forward without any semblance of being alive much less alert. The enemy quickly moved on toward the mission and left him tied to a small pine tree. Perhaps because of the dark or the impending battle, the invaders never noticed the fact that the captive lacked the friar's tonsure.

The man tied to the tree was none other than the cacique! Before his discovery, he had covered himself in the robes of Fray Antonio and placed his Indian clothes on the friar. The enemy had not suspected he was conscious. All they noticed was the heavy amounts of blood splattered across the friar's robe. His quick thinking had succeeded. His life was spared momentarily. Now all Felipe-Toloca simply had to contend with were his bonds. But the small tree to which the soldiers had tied him offered little resistance to his strength and ingenuity.

He soon freed himself from his modest shackling and descended to the bottom of the pit. Lifting the body of the friar on his shoulders, the cacique scurried off to an area he felt would be safe to make a temporary grave for the fallen friar. The devastation in his heart at the loss of his friend did not deflect him from continuing with the desperate duty he owed to his people. He must move fast now to help prevent the slaughter of Santa Fé by the enemy forces that soon would be at its gates.

With the enemy now both ahead of him and behind him, the cacique saw no alternative but to pass quickly through the woods and swim across the river. At the water's edge, he began to discard the friar's robe. Then, he decided instead to carry the friar's presence close to his skin, and continued to wear the garment of Fray Antonio. Felipe-Toloca felt as if the friar had actually rescued him, and wearing the robe made him feel as if the presence of his friend was still with him.

He pulled the robe back down over his body, slipped quietly into the water and swam for the village. His spirit and his energy seemed to grow with each passing moment, with each movement of his arms below the surface of the water. It was as if Fray Antonio were encouraging him along.

"Do not lose hope. You have a mission. We are still working together. You must save your people. Do not tarry. Time is so short," the friar seemed to say to the cacique.

When the cacique reached the other shore, he crept slowly out of the water and up the steep bank, where he came face to face with a Potano scout. The sentry failed to recognize him and tried to wrestle him to the ground.

"Stop, Tobatu. It is I, Felipe-Toloca," he whispered, "your cacique.... The clothes I wear helped me to escape. They are the robes of our friend, Fray Antonio. He is dead. But I know also he is alive in the spirit. We must hurry. The enemy is at our door."

The startled Tobatu, for a moment frozen by shock, looked at the face of the cacique, and then began to scurry after his leader, who had wasted no time in heading for the village.

The battle, however, had already begun. Shots rang out to the west and north. The Spanish militia was now being overrun from all directions. The Potano posted on the outer perimeters were being taken hostage or killed.

Felipe-Toloca knew the final battle was at hand. All that his people had lived and died for depended of the next hour's defense. He hoped and prayed the Spanish militia would be able to stand fast.

The cacique's primary goal was to rescue the women and children from disaster. He began to move from dwelling to dwelling, grabbing as many villagers as he could and calling for them to run to the east. They knew the safest escape routes to San Agustín. He would set them now on those diverse pathways.

"You must flee immediately. Take nothing with you. Even the fort is no longer a refuge for our people. May the Great Spirit guide you on your way," he would tell them.

"Where is Fray Antonio?" they would ask. "Why are you wearing his robes?"

"He is with us! He is with us! Only in a different way. We must believe that." Felipe-Toloca not only spoke the words, but deep within his spirit he felt them to be true. "We are not alone. We are not alone," he would say.

After the aged, the women, and children were roused and on their way, Felipe-Toloca gathered any remaining tribesmen not already at the fort and moved them next to the Spanish militia. When a Spaniard fell, a Potano grabbed a rifle and fired.

It was as if two warriors rose to fight for every one that had fallen.

With bullets flying in every direction, the robed cacique moved from one pocket of fighting to another. Felipe-Toloca himself moved without weapons. The only weapon he felt he needed was the friar's cloak. It was the only shield he wanted. He felt as if he moved with another spirit linked to his.

Mortar fire penetrated the village and mission behind them. Buildings went up in flame. But the final line of defense began to hold! On both the western and northern perimeters, the remaining Spanish militia and Potano tribesmen dug in and let very few of the enemy through their lines.

Even when the fort itself was ablaze, casting a mighty column of fire into the sky, the cacique did not lose hope. "We can see more clearly now the enemy when they approach," he would tell his people. "Hold your position! Do not weaken. We will withstand them."

Even the adjutant deputy, Captain Alvarez, began to take hope. Many times through the night, he blessed himself and began to prepare to meet his Maker. Then, almost miraculously, the tide of battle would turn.

On the field of war, Captain Alvarez watched the cacique engender spirit in his people, and suddenly, he found himself doing the same. He felt he was not fighting only for the Spanish Empire. He was fighting for the survival of a people and the survival of their mission.

The combat lasted long into the night.

The strength of the enemy was not powerful enough to overcome the heroism of those defending the village and mission of Santa Fé. Before sunrise, the enemy forces hastily retreated, surprised at the ferocity and courage of the force they encountered. They never knew that the defenders that repulsed their attack numbered only half the size of their war party.

Though the invaders fled, they left the mark of their coming in the carnage that remained behind. When daylight shone on the village, only a hollow shell remained of the habitats and structures that the tribe had so recently rebuilt. Charred embers and wisps of smoke were all that remained of many buildings. The fading flames sent smoke signals into the air:

"Destruction lies here."

A voice broke the silence. The Potano tribesmen, mud-caked and bloodied like the surviving Spaniards, gazed in the direction of the cacique. Felipe-Toloca had knelt in prayer, bent forward to the ground.

"Thank you, Great Spirit, for defending my people," they could hear him say. "Thank you, Fray Antonio. Thank you my father, Cacique Tomás, for being with me and praying for me. I know you were with your people last night. I know you have never left us."

Still clad in the friar's robe, stained in blood and dirt, the cacique rose from his posture of prayer. In his heart, the feeling of gratitude to the Great Spirit was mixed with a feeling of pain over the loss of Fray Antonio. The chieftain quickly sought out two tribesmen to help him recover the body of his friar-friend, so it could be given proper burial near the mission the priest had worked and fought so hard to maintain.

XXXVII
- 1704 -

Hollow in the heart is
  the feeling of farewell.
A lonesome memory of people
  one called family and friends.
How hard, to say goodbye
  to yesterday.
A relief to know it is
  only for a while,
And then, forever,
  to be as one again.

Almost immediately Cacique Felipe-Toloca called his faithful council members together. While his men had not routed the enemy, they had not allowed the enemy to overtake them. Even though devastation surrounded them, a moral victory had been won. He did not wish to lose the momentum of the spirited defense his men had presented against the invading forces.

"We will rebuild! We will start over again!" the cacique proclaimed forcefully. He no longer donned the bloodied friar's robe he had worn during the heat of the battle, but he exuded the same positive spirit that had been engendered by the spirit of Fray Antonio. "We must plan for our future defense. The Spanish military garrison will help us, as we have helped them," he added.

One by one, council members spoke, some in favor, most expressing skepticism.

"How would our aged, yet respected cacique resurrect a twice-destroyed village and mission? Yes, there is the Spanish military force. But a great number died in the last battle."

"Many of the young men among our Potano and Utina tribesmen have been taken captive or killed, such that of those that remain most are much older."

"The women and children have already fled or been sent to the fort in

San Agustín for a safe haven. It would not be wise for them to return to the village and mission of Santa Fé."

Such concerns were on the lips of more than one council member.

In the midst of a heated discussion, one of the senior councilors much respected for his wisdom stood to address the cacique and the council. His name was Onahu. "Worthy cacique and council leaders of our village," he began, "I understand the deep concerns you hold, and I share them. But I, for one, am in accord with the vision put forth by our most honored cacique. Like him, I do not wish to abandon what has been the home of our people for so many generations.

"This land, with its springs of life, has provided us with bounteous supplies of water, and our woodlands and fields have given us a steady supply of food for our families. This land has been our life and our destiny. Can we leave behind to the enemy what has nourished and sustained us? Can we give to others what is so dear to ourselves?

"As long as we remain here, the Spanish military will be here to support us. If we leave, they will leave. Let us stay!"

The majority were swayed by Onahu's words and cast their vote with the cacique.

But not all.

The cacique, not wanting his people divided, offered the following resolution. "I thank my friend Onahu for his words and for the courage that has always been reflected in his life. I admire him, as I admire my own father. These are days of special trial for us. Many see defeat on the horizon. All about us is devastation and destruction.

"I cannot fault my brothers who want to proclaim that the end is near. I hear their anguish when they ask, 'What have we achieved in all our days of struggle? What have we left to call our own? What have we left to hope for?'

"To them I say, you have fought well. You have labored hard. You have stayed with me. And if you decide to go to San Agustín to be with your families, then you may go with my blessing and favor. They need you, and you need them!

"But like my friend Onahu, I cannot depart. My home is here. Here I will die!"

The cacique stood and motioned to his council members. "Tell the villagers who remain what I have said, and then choose your own destinies. Thank you for all you have been through with me!"

Various council members came to personally express their thanks to the cacique and tell him how much they esteemed him. Then, the councilors made their way through the village to share the cacique's words with the remaining Potano and Utina villagers.

The cacique parted company with the tribal leaders and strayed off to sit in silence at the graveside of his friend, Fray Antonio. How grateful he was to the Franciscan Provincial for allowing Fray Antonio's body to be buried at the mission site where he had labored so long!

The Friar Provincial, ever supportive of Cacique Felipe-Toloca, also wasted no time in sending another missionary to be of spiritual encouragement to the villagers who remained. Fray Reynaldo quickly assumed his responsibilities with the same enthusiasm he found evident in the people he was called to serve.

Very shortly he wrote back to the provincial these words:

"If only all Christian people had the faith of the remaining people of the mission of Santa Fé. How easy would our ministry be!

"Maybe the best flock of Christ's people is the remnant flock, left after years of devastation, toil, and defeat! I believe these would be precisely the kind of people that would be ready for the final days, for the coming of the Messiah at the end of time. I think I am with just such a people now!"

The priest wrote his words without hyperbole. The collective group of people surrounding the cacique was the best, most cooperative gathering of human beings the friar had ever seen. They would exceed each other in acts of selflessness. They were a long way from reconstructing what had been destroyed, but each person helped in rebuilding the thatched hut of another. When sickness would strike, it was like a family coming to the rescue of a sibling in need. Whatever food was forthcoming for the benefit of one was offered for the benefit of all. Fray Reynaldo was astounded at the charity of this people that formed his little remnant flock! It was not long, however, before the remnant began to be less of a people and more of a remnant. An outbreak of disease swept the village and carried away some of the older members. One of those who had fallen prey to sickness and subsequently died was the cacique's devoted supporter Onahu.

At the funeral rite of Onahu, Fray Reynaldo spoke glowingly of the final days of the distinguished council leader. "I have known him for such a short time, but in him I have found a true friend. And in him I have found the Gospel of Jesus truly lived. In other places I have heard the Gospel preached. Here in this village, among people like Onahu I have found it in action.

"With few possessions, Onahu was always happy. Deprived of life's pleasures, deprived of life's successes, he was never defeated by life's hardships. He was always victorious. He was truly a faithful son of the Great Spirit and brother of Christ."

After the service, as Fray Reynaldo walked with the cacique from Onahu's burial site, he felt propelled to ask Felipe-Toloca how he felt about losing one of his most trusted allies. "Losing Onahu must almost be like losing your father, or Fray Antonio. He was always so faithful and so supportive of all that you have been doing. And with his death and the death of the others, we are so few who remain here."

"Fray Reynaldo," the cacique responded, with words reflecting thoughts that were, as usual, very carefully measured, "everything in life that happens to us is a blessing from the Great Spirit. Everything—good and bad. That is why we must always give thanks.

"Some of what happens is meant to support us…some to comfort us …some to sustain us…some to stretch us…some to purify us…some to test us. But all are blessings of the Great Spirit that are sent or permitted by His great love for us, for which we must always give thanks.

"In times when I have felt a great loss, such as this, in life—and there have been many—I try to remember:

"The Great Spirit does not want my self-pity. He wants my courage.

"He does not want my service. He wants my patience.

"He does not want my activity. He wants my stillness.

"He does not want my words. He wants my silence.

"He does not want my great works. He wants my loving heart.

"He does not want me to bring Him so much my successes as my crosses and failures."

The cacique paused for a moment to further collect his thoughts, and then proceeded.

"There is a kingdom of darkness out there, Fray Reynaldo. Always it is there to test me, to disturb me. It is seeking to eventually destroy me. That kingdom is overcome every time I am able to see my loss as my gain, my defeat as my victory, my cross as my crown. This I have learned by many encounters with the kingdom of darkness, and God has always given me help: my father, Cacique Tomás, and the great Friars Tomás, Buenaventura, and Antonio, and now you, Fray Reynaldo."

The friar looked at Cacique Felipe-Toloca and saw a great man, a man weathered by life's endless struggles, tutored by life's enduring lessons, and emboldened by life's failures. An old man, yet he appeared to the friar ever youthful, a man for all ages.

He saw weariness in the cacique's eyes, but he also saw courage bordering on valor. He saw in Felipe-Toloca's erect stature the determination that kept the cacique from bending to the forces of destruction. The friar ventured to tell the cacique of his great admiration for the endurance that the chieftain had displayed in the face of such constant struggle, but the cacique would hear none of it.

"I have not faced yet the final contest. My people have a saying 'One only knows a warrior by how he falls in battle.' I have yet to face the final test."

XXXVIII
- 1706 -

The cacique's words to Fray Reynaldo were not exactly prophetic, but very nearly so, if one were to judge by the contents of a letter delivered barely two years later on an overcast fall day. A courier delivered the post from the Spanish civil and military headquarters in San Agustín.

The cacique, the friar, and villagers joined in with all the members of the military garrison to listen attentively as the military officer proceeded to read what sounded to them as nothing less than the death knell of their mission.

From Don Francisco de Córcoles y Martínez
Governor of Florida for His Majesty the King —

To all military, religious, and civilian residents of the Mission of Santa Fé:

No longer can we bear responsibility for the lives of the inhabitants of your mission. You are to depart immediately for San Agustín. Your efforts to serve God and

His Majesty the King have been laudable. Your mission and that of your predecessors, to bring the Gospel to this region, has been a noble one. Success, however, is in God's hands, not in ours. Return at once! Francisco de Córcoles y Martínez

The military courier continued speaking.

Bearing the seal and signature of the Governor, Don Francisco de Córcoles y Martínez, and dated September 8, 1706, the Feast of the Nativity of Mary.

The courier then handed the document directly to Fray Reynaldo, and a copy of it to the adjutant deputy, Captain Juan Diego Alvarez, who was the presiding military officer of the garrison.

Though not the direct recipient of the governor's letter, Cacique Felipe-Toloca was the one who had to bear the brunt of the letter's contents.

Like a lost child in search of his home, the cacique cast confused and questioning glances at the friar and the adjutant deputy. He did not speak. He could not speak. The reality of the words of the governor settled on the cacique's heart as if they were a sentence of death.

Always, always before, there was a glimmer of light, a glimmer of hope. The mission, the village of Santa Fé was his life. It was his hope. Now it was neither.

Where would he go? What would he do?

A cacique without a people. A father without a family.

Captain Alvarez put into words what everyone seemed to be thinking, as he placed his hand on the cacique's arm.

"It is over, Cacique Felipe-Toloca! I must leave, my men must depart, and so also must your people and their cacique.

"The English are at our door. The territory is about to be theirs. All of us will be either killed or captured shortly. You know this, and I know this."

Fray Reynaldo hid his sorrow, furtively glancing at the cacique to see whether he could detect in his eyes some of the valor he had always found there before.

The cacique answered the friar's implicit query and that of his people in just a few words. "You are to leave immediately for San Agustín! All of you. You must waste no time! The governor is right! We have done all we could. Success is in the hands of the Great Spirit, not in ours!"

"And you, Cacique Felipe-Toloca, what about you?" Fray Reynaldo asked.

"This is my home, Fray Reynaldo," the cacique spoke dejectedly. He then paused and looked with loving eyes over the village and mission that was the only real home he had ever known. Gazing about him, in every direction, the cacique took in the sights and sounds so familiar to him for these many years, and he relished the memories of all the events that had transpired in this beloved land he had called "home."

"Here I will die, near the place where my family rests, near the resting place of Fray Antonio, near the burial site of my father, wherever that may be. But go, the rest of you, now! Hurry, before it is too late! My prayers, my love, will be with you always!"

Reluctantly, the villagers dispersed to their thatched dwellings to gather their few belongings. In a more hurried fashion, the militia began to pack up their possessions and military supplies.

The friar watched the others go about their business. Then, he slowly made his way to the mission chapel to pray, for his friend the cacique, for the cacique's father and family, for his own two predecessors, and for all the people who had helped the Mission Santa Fé in its century of service to the native people.

The cacique was lost in his thoughts and in his pain. Feeling alone, he sought out the friar. He found Fray Reynaldo in the chapel. The priest had his head buried in his hands. Sliding next to him, the cacique joined him on his knees.

"This is sacred ground and always will be," the friar whispered.

"The faith of many has made it so," the cacique responded. "We are but the last of a long line. What I have done, I did for them. I wish I could have done more."

"So, also, do I," the friar added, then made the sign of the cross.

The cacique slowly began to imitate the friar's gesture. He then drew his stately form up to its full stature. He made a profound genuflection in the direction of the chapel altar, turned, and walked out the chapel door. The friar's eyes followed his every move. More noble a human being the friar had never seen before.

✳

What once was a settlement of sizable proportions, Santa Fé de Toloca was now but a shell of human habitation. The raids of Carolina Governor James Moore with his parties of Indians hostile to the Spaniards had almost obliterated the Franciscan Friars' hundred-year-old outreach effort to the native Potano people of this region.

A cross still stood erect over a dilapidated Spanish-style chapel, now vacant of the reverential celebrations that were centered within its walls. A clapboard shutter banged rhythmically with the wind against the wall of the military barracks that once quartered a Spanish garrison. The bare structure was all that remained of a meeting hall that once housed the civic and social events of the mission, and was now quiet except for the sound of roaches and rats scurrying for leftover food.

The final phase of de-settlement had occurred, and the last day of occupation had seen a soldier and a friar make the final rounds of inspection as the remaining residents trailed off into the horizon. The soldier and the friar were symbols of the fortunes and failures of the mission from its earliest days. It was fitting that they were the last to go.

Mounted on his horse, an Indian cacique watched it all silently from a distance. His bearing was dignified. Though his bronze skin showed the wear of his years, his pleasant features were now overshadowed by a somber spirit. No one was near enough to him anymore to see the tear in his eye or to understand the memories of his mind and heart. He preferred to bear his sorrow alone.

Epilogue

After the entourage had passed beyond eyesight, the cacique turned his horse to make a final circle of the mission grounds. Up to now, the cacique had given no serious consideration to what he would do with his life, other than to remain close to the burial site of his family and ancestors. Long he had been the one who led. Now, it seemed that he would leave the leading to the Great Spirit and Him alone.

As that thought passed his mind, he happened to spy directly in front of him two small white doves, each with spotted wings, one in pursuit of the other. They were flying smoothly, with carefree abandon, and they quickly brought back to him the memory of the two little doves that were the playful pets of his little sister, Catalina. His mind went back to the many years before when they had given the birds to their friend, Fray Buenaventura.

He remembered his words to Catalina when she was feeling the weight of the death of Fray Buenaventura and didn't want to set those two little doves free from their cage where they had been imprisoned too long. Those words he had repeated many times to himself since then, whenever he faced hardship or grief.

"If you let them go free, they will be happy. And Catalina, what is more …you too will be happy."

Those words came back to him with full force. He had much to let go of in his life, just as Catalina had many years before. Could he follow his own advice to Catalina? Oh, how hard it was to say good-bye to everything one knew, everything one possessed in life, everything one was!

How very hard it was to say good-bye to yesterday!

Then, the two little doves descended from the sky and alighted together on a small stump just inside a clearing of the forest. The cacique got off his horse some distance away and began to move slowly toward the birds to get a closer glimpse of them. He moved ever so slowly, closer and closer, not wishing to disturb them as they began to preen each other.

The names of the little doves of long ago came to his mind. He whispered those names to them. "Juan…Juanita," he called out; as if in recognition, they turned their beaks in his direction and cocked their eyes upward and downward, then slightly sideways, as if taking a careful look at this intruder. They did not move until he got close enough to them to put out his finger as a resting-place for one of them.

The little bird did not oblige. Instead, both doves hopped off the trunk and proceeded bobbing on foot further into the woods.

Then, the two birds stopped to rest on an upturned stone. Once again the cacique put out his finger. As he moved toward the doves and the stone, the two birds suddenly whisked off into the sky, as if frightened by his approach.

"Oh, my friends, why did you leave me so soon?" the cacique spoke as much to himself as to his now-departed guests. "You were once a great healing to my sadness and loneliness, and my memory as well. Please come back!"

Felipe-Toloca turned to look at the spot where the birds had been and he noticed something shiny, barely visible in the dirt. He reached down to uncover the object and discovered a tarnished Christian medal of some holy person, but the image was too caked with dirt to be distinguishable. Felipe-Toloca tried to retrieve the medal and found it attached to a chain, and drawing the chain up, he found that it was attached to something else that would not give way.

To his awe and shock, the object holding the chain was none other than the remains of a human skeleton! Felipe-Toloca's heart began to pound. Perspiration beaded on his forehead, as he dug furiously with both hands. Slowly but relentlessly he cleared the dirt and dust from around the figure that had lain captive in the soil for what must have been many years.

Though the body was long decomposed, the bits of clothing, though worm-eaten and worn by decay, were still decipherable. To the cacique, they even began to seem recognizable.

"Could it be? It is impossible! This close to the mission and we never knew! The medal," he thought. "The medal will tell me!"

He then rubbed hard on both sides of the tarnished little medal. He put saliva to his fingers and applied it in an effort to clear away more dirt.

On the front side, he detected a figure of the Madonna, Our Lady of Loreto. He turned the medal over and began to rub hard. There was an etching on the top, with initials. One by one, he began to uncover the letters. First an F. Then a T. Then an H. Then an M.

He knew their meaning. "F.T.H.M."

"Felipe Toloca Hijo Mio."

"Felipe-Toloca, My Son."

Felipe-Toloca had discovered the remains of his father, the great Cacique Tomás!

"Father, Father, Father!" Felipe-Toloca bent down in reverence and kissed the medal that had long hung around the skeleton of the brutally murdered man who had faithfully led his people.

"I have found you! I have found you! My friends, my family, I have found my father! I have found my father," he shouted to the four corners of the earth. "I have found my father!"

Cacique Felipe-Toloca exulted in the joy of discovery and cried with the pain of loss. He felt the surge of defeat and accomplishment, failure and victory, of departure and of arrival. So many emotions! It was like leaving home and coming back again, like saying farewell and returning to a welcoming embrace.

But in the midst of it all, there was a sense of reconciliation with the past, present, and future. Felipe-Toloca was at peace. The one special quest of his life, the only one left that mattered, had been achieved. Felipe-Toloca had found the burial site of his father!

In the aftermath of the prayers and tears, of the laughter and of the pain, Felipe-Toloca slipped the chain with the medal on it off the human remains of his father and put it around his own neck. He then placed the dirt and debris back over the burial site, making sure the place would be detectable by no one but himself. He then drew the sign of the cross in the dirt over the grave and marked his own forehead in the form of a cross with the dirt on his fingers.

Rising to his feet, he silently offered a prayer for his father and his family. He then ran hurriedly to the open field, where his horse had remained grazing happily in its freedom.

"Let us go, my friend," he called out. "We have a mission somewhere else. Our mission is no longer here. Let us go where the Great Spirit is leading us!" And the cacique of many years turned his horse in the direction of San Agustín, hoping to be able to catch up with the remnant of his tribe, the former people of the village and mission of Santa Fé.

A little way above and beyond him, heading in the same direction, were two white doves, barely discernible in the sky. Occasionally, they would circle back and hover overhead.

They pressed on, as if they were guiding him to some unknown destination. Before long the cacique began to see the faint outlines of human figures far in the distance. He knew he was closing in on his friends from the Mission Santa Fé. He looked up to the sky as if to say thanks to his faithful guardians, but he did not see them. To the east and north and south he looked. He turned back to the west to see if they were perhaps returning to the mission area. But they were gone.

The doves had departed, never to be seen again. For Felipe-Toloca, they forever remained as a happy memory, a solace in distress, a sign that the Great Spirit was ever near. But just as powerful a sign of God's love remained with him in the form of the family and friends who had once called the Mission Santa Fé their home.

Afterword

Cacique combines fact with fiction in an effort to promote appreciation for Florida's Spanish mission story. Unlike the missions of California and Texas, Florida's mission artifacts have lain buried beneath the ground. Santa Fé de Toloca (or Teleco), one of the earliest and longest standing of the seventeenth century Spanish missions in northern Florida, remained buried and lost for over two hundred years. Thanks to research conducted since 1986 by University of Florida archaeologists under the direction of Jerald T. Milanich, the Santa Fé de Toloca site has been discovered and verified in the area of Bland, near High Springs, Florida. It is hoped that through this discovery and through the words of *Cacique,* the Florida Franciscan mission story will gain the wider audience that it deserves.

Franciscan missionaries first came to the area of St. Augustine in 1577, twelve years after its founding by **Pedro Menéndez de Avilés.** Throughout the remainder of the sixteenth century, the number of friars and of their converts increased; among those priests we find **Father Francisco Pareja,** known for compiling a complete account of the missionary activities among the Timucua people and for preparing a native language catechism. Father Pareja's books are the first Indian language books in United States history.

The missionary work of the novel's Fray Tomás Sanchez is based upon that of **Father Martín Prieto,** a seventeenth century Franciscan missionary to the Potano people. Just as Fray Tomás labored alone when his companion Buenaventura withdrew temporarily from the mission field, so too did Fray Prieto. He became acutely aware of the obstacles to evangelization and peace presented by the ongoing warfare between the Apalachees and Timucuans, and set out to negotiate a treaty:

"Fray Prieto dispatched two Apalachee prisoners held by the Timucua…to Apalachee ahead of him to inform its people that he was coming on a mission of peace. He followed them to Ivitachuco…accompanied by the head chief of Utina, the chiefs

of the Timucua villages in the vicinity of Apalachee, and 150 warriors from Potano and Utina. He found the entire population of the province led by some seventy chiefs assembled there to greet him and estimated the crowd at over 36,000.... Fray Prieto then presided over a meeting of the chiefs of the two peoples, all of whom agreed on peace."[12]

In 1674, **Bishop Gabriel Díaz Vara Calderón**, the Bishop of Santiago de Cuba, traveled for eight months throughout the Floridian areas of his diocese. He ordained to the diaconate seven young men and confirmed 13,152 Indians.

The accounts of the martyrdom of Franciscans **Pedro de Corpa, Blas Rodríguez, and Miguel de Auñon** occurred as described in Chapter III. Father de Corpa had preached against polygamy and was subsequently slain. Father Rodríguez asked that his attackers allow him to complete his celebration of the Mass; they agreed, killing him at the conclusion. Father de Auñon was slain along with a lay brother, **Antonio**, during what came to be known as the Guale revolt.

Beginning in May 1702 and continuing until 1705, the missions of northern Florida were overrun by order of Carolinian **Governor James Moore.** Moore supplied munitions and directed the raids that resulted in the deaths of hundreds of people, both missionaries and native Americans. Over 1400 Christian Indians were sold as slaves in the Carolinas or were handed over to other native villages for torture and enslavement.

The Christianized Indians who escaped the raids either escaped to St. Augustine or headed to areas as far west as Mobile. Others may have fled in terror into the woods or settled in villages among the Yamasee Indians. Some descendants of the native people of the Santa Fé Mission may have found their way to Cuba with the Spaniards who left Florida when the lands were ceded to the English in 1763.

Florida historian Michael V. Gannon has written that as a result of the destruction of the Franciscan missions **"a great civilizing work of the human spirit was wrecked."**

---

[12] From "The Famed Land of Apalachee" in *Apalachee: the Land between the Rivers,* John H. Hann, p.10-11.

Acknowledgments

My personal appreciation is offered to those who provided guidance in the preparation of this novel, none of whom, of course, is responsible for the use I have made of the archaeological or historical data supplied. Among these people are: the late John W. Griffin, Jerald T. Milanich, Michael V. Gannon, Kenneth W. Johnson, John H. Hann, Eugene Lyon, Kathleen Deagan, Jose Francisco Avila Marques, Jane Quinn, Charles Coomes, John Worth, Frank Ducey, John A. Armstrong, Monsignor Francis J. Weber, Father Matthew J. Connolly, Father Raymond C. Kammerer, Frances Alligood, Father Brian Gogan, C.S. Sp., and Sister Mary Albert Lussier, S.S.J.

I also express sincere appreciation to my original editor and typist, Betsy Coxe, who had seen me through four years of typing and revising, without whose patience and kindness the original serialized version of *Cacique* would not have appeared in print. I am also grateful to Sally Wooten, Kay Phillip, Monsignor Joseph Roth, Father Gregory Wilson, and Eileen McGuinness for continued encouragement on this project. I would like to thank Natalie and Tommy Lucas and Tony Sands for helping the final version of this story to see the light of day.

Father Dan Mahan and Jean Zander of Saint Catherine of Siena Press were gracious guides in making this project a reality; without their wisdom and expertise as skilled publisher and editor, mentors and managers, a professional rendering of *Cacique* would have been impossible. To them I express my personal praise and heartfelt gratitude, and good wishes for continued success in all of their publishing ventures.

+Most Reverend Robert J. Baker, STD
Bishop of Charleston

FOR MORE INFORMATION
ABOUT THE MISSIONS OF FLORIDA

The Cross in the Sand: The Early Catholic Church in Florida, 1513-1870 by Michael Gannon, Ph.D., University Press of Florida, Gainesville; Second Edition, 1983.

The Florida Catholic Heritage Trail edited by Michael V. Gannon, Ph.D., University Press of Florida, Gainesville; reprint edition, 1997.

Apalachee: Land Between the Rivers, by John H. Hann, Ph.D., University Press of Florida, Gainesville, 1988.

The Apalachee Indians and Mission San Luis by John H. Hann, Ph.D., and Bonnie G. McEwan, Ph.D., University Press of Florida, Gainesville, 1998.

Laboring in the Fields of the Lord: Spanish Missions and Southeastern Indians by Jerald T. Milanich, Ph.D., Smithsonian Institution Press, 1999.

The Spanish Missions of La Florida, edited by Bonnie G. McEwan, Ph.D., University Press of Florida, Gainesville, 1993.

*Faith in the Wilderness: The Story of the Catholic Indian Mission*s by Margaret and Stephen Bunson, Our Sunday Visitor, Inc., Huntington, IN, 2000.

Suggested internet sites:

The Diocese of St. Augustine:
        www.dosafl.com

Florida Museum of Natural History:
        www.flmnh.ufl.edu/staugustine

Florida Historical Marker Program:
        www.dhr.dos.state.fl.us/services/sites/markers

About the authors...

Bishop Robert Baker, a native of Ohio, was ordained to the priesthood in 1970 following studies at the Pontifical College Josephinum in his home state. Subsequently, he served as a parish priest and high school teacher in the Diocese of St. Augustine, Florida. In 1977, having received his Doctorate in Sacred Theology from the Gregorian University in Rome, he returned to Florida where he served as a pastor and member of the seminary faculty. He was ordained the twelfth Bishop of Charleston in 1999.

Tony Sands graduated from the School of Cinema/ Television at the University of Southern California. He has spent the last ten years working in the entertainment industry in Hollywood, most recently as the Director for TV and the Production Coordinator for Radio at Family Theater Productions, Inc. Tony made the acquaintance of Bishop Baker while on pilgrimage with him in Mexico, and subsequently collaborated with him on the writing of *Cacique*. He resides in Los Angeles, California.

Saint Catherine of Siena Press ...

...*is an Indianapolis-based publisher of inspirational and catechetical materials. You can learn more about this and other publications at:*

www.saintcatherineofsienapress.com

888-232-1492